SCOT
LANDER

ALSO BY SHEILA McCLURE

The Break-Up Agency

SCOT LANDER

SHEILA McCLURE

LAKE UNION
PUBLISHING

Published by Lake Union Publishing, Seattle

www.apub.com

Amazon, the Amazon logo, and Lake Union Publishing are trademarks of Amazon.com, Inc., or its affiliates.

ISBN-13: 9781662505324
eISBN: 9781662505317

Cover design by The Brewster Project

Cover image: © StudioThreeDots / Getty Images; © Cosmic_Design © Valentina Vectors © M_Videous © stas11 © arigato © smym © Millena © NGvozdeva / Shutterstock

Printed in the United States of America

To my own Scotlander: For the record?
I would walk five hundred miles.

Chapter One

'Here she is! LA's very own Miss Reliable!'

Willa smiled at the ultra-petite publicist doing jazz hands, then glanced over her shoulder to see who had entered the Paramount Pictures's hospitality suite behind her.

The doorway was empty.

Her shoulders slumped a fraction. Was it finally the time to give up hope that she'd ever be the fun one?

In fairness, she wasn't exactly exuding Girl Who Sets a Room on Fire vibes.

She was wearing her least wrinkled dress and sporting hair in what could, by the longest of stretches, be called an up-do (read: neon pink scrunchie savagely wrapped around her bum-length hair to an entirely accidental messy bun effect). She wasn't wearing make-up and had probably forgotten to sweep what little sleep she had from her eyes. She was also (Gasp! Shock! Horror!) flagrantly committing the cardinal sin of wearing open-toed sandals when she hadn't had a mani-pedi since that bright, sunny day seven long weeks ago when she'd dressed up to the nines for her best friend's funeral.

A pitter-pat of fingertips on a press packet pulled her attention back to the publicist. She looked young. Super young. Barely old enough to be trusted to babysit tiny humans let alone the roomful of entertainment reporters draped on the various couches and armchairs dappled around the corner suite as they awaited their five-to-ten minutes of sharing the spotlight with Hollywood's greatest.

Just as Willa was about to ask her if this was Bring Your Daughter To Work Day, the publicist launched into what sounded like a prepared speech. 'On behalf of the entire publicity team, we just wanted to say that, like, we're so glad you could make it. *As Fast As You Can* is *such* an important film.' She crossed both sets of fingers. 'We're hoping for Oscars! And after we heard about . . .' She made a quick scan of the room as she hiss-whispered, '*Aubrey's accident* . . . we were worried it wouldn't get that initial punch of publicity that is *so* important to a film which, I'm not ashamed to admit it, made me cry all my waterproof mascara off. I mean, Ben's performance alone delivers such a powerful emotive punch to the nation's psyche, and don't even get me *started* on Rachel!'

Ermm . . . This was a futuristic film about a beautiful vegetable gardener forced to rely on the kindness of a bereaved dot-com billionaire to plant the world's remaining packet of heritage tomato seeds.

'Yes.' Willa dutifully nodded. 'I'm so happy to be a part of the campaign.'

For a nano-second this caught Baby Publicist off guard. Willa knew what she was thinking. *Oh, you're not actually* part *of it. But we let you think you are.* And then, as if the moment had been entirely a figment of Willa's imagination, Baby Publicist brightly continued. 'Can you even believe how insane traffic was this morning? We *literally* had to chopper the talent in from the hotel in Santa Monica.' She cupped her cupid lips between her palms and whispered, 'Rachel won't stay here. Says they don't use enough environmentally friendly products. Anyhoodle! Sharon's running late but is promising to be here and to see *everyone*. You're a genuine hero for getting here, Willa. Heroine,' she deftly corrected. 'It's all about the lay-deeez in LA, am I right?'

No. She wasn't. But the poor thing had shadows under her eyes and was clearly operating courtesy of a caffeine overload, so Willa made an *umhmm* noise that she hoped sounded companionable.

It worked.

Baby Publicist put out a fist to bump. 'Us worker bees have to stick together, yeah?'

Coming from actual worker bee stock, Willa still found these moments awkward. Even though it was Sunday morning, and this was technically work, they were on the upper floors of one of LA's lushest hotels, surrounded by chef-made delectables and being handed amazing swag bags with fleets of make-up artists hovering on standby as, at this very moment, film stars were being shuttled into their nearby suites (with fancier snacks and bigger swag bags and personal make-up artists).

There were discreet waitstaff to hand. Long-term employees who not only knew the names of all the on-air reporters, but those of the segment producers, like Willa, who did off-camera interviews when their 'talent' was indisposed after an 'accident'. More importantly, the staff here at the Four Seasons knew what all of them liked to eat. If they were pescatarian, vegetarian, vegan, a carbovore. They knew who wanted their cafe lattes with hazelnut milk, who only drank sparkling water with a wedge of grapefruit in it, and who took their iced tea sweet like the southern belle she was rather than straight up, California style. If you had to run off and interview someone before you could finish any of the above, it would be magicked away so that when you returned, often minutes later, you could start afresh.

As Willa met Baby Publicist's knuckles and forced her face into a what-can-you-do-about-Sunday-morning-traffic face, she was shocked to catch herself thinking . . . *this is bullshit.*

At her father's auto repair shop, if you wanted coffee? You'd pour it yourself. Albeit reluctantly. That pot had burnt so many gallons of coffee in its time there was a crust. If you wanted a clean mug? You settled for 'clean enough' and used a bit of grease-free shirt sleeve to swipe the edge because the blue paper towel had run out earlier in the week. Bliss compared to the middle school where her mother, in between corralling underprivileged children into her Family and Consumer Sciences classes, taught the *under*-underprivileged kids some basic survival skills, like how to stay clean when Mom forgot to pay the utilities bill.

Her parents were the most practical and altruistic humans she knew. Which meant, of course, that they thought Willa's entire career trajectory was not only foolish for its absence of do-goodery (all that time wasted watching television? *No,* thank you), but unsustainable (*dreams are called dreams for a reason, Willy*).

Baby Publicist pressed two tiny palms to her elfin A-cup chest, her eyes full of Disney sorrow as she stage-whispered, 'Back to Aubrey? Is it, like, serious?'

Not if you used something other than Willa's best friend dying of breast cancer at thirty-one and leaving a bereaved husband and two toddlers in her wake as a comparison.

But this was Hollywood. A place where people didn't like *actual* pain, so she supposed Aubrey's 'accident' ranked up there. She briefly considered explaining how the cherished anchor of *Topline in Tinseltown* (aka TiTs) drank half her size-zero body weight in vodka at a *Friends Reunited Again* after party only to have an epic marble-floor face plant as she showed off her pole dancing skills on her new film director boyfriend's four-poster bed. Alas, before Willa could spill the beans, a woman from a Boston affiliate strode into the suite – '*Oh my gawd! If it isn't Miss Fun!*' – and Willa was rendered invisible.

Heigh-ho.

As she turned away from the desk, another publicist raced into the room, clipboard in hand. Priya Semple. Of all the publicists she'd worked with over the years, Priya was her favourite. If she hadn't been happily ensconced at the Paramount lot for so long, she could have easily set up a positivity cult. She exuded sunbeams. Over the years, they'd organised countless interviews and set visits together, so it didn't surprise her when Priya scurried up to the check-in desk then did a double take in Willa's direction.

'Babes! Hyieee! I barely recognised you.'

Again, Willa did a *who me?* glance over her shoulder. Instead of another reporter, she caught a glimpse of Ben Affleck being escorted by a team of purposeful vice-presidents of publicity to his suite. Their eyes caught and a glint of recognition stopped him in his tracks. 'Hey, Canada!' he called out with a wink and a double blast of finger pistols. 'How's tricks?'

She gave him a thumbs-up because she'd long ago given up explaining to the man she'd interviewed dozens of times over the past eight years that she was still, and always would be, from Oregon. Pendleton, if he was asking. Which, of course, he wasn't because he was already gone.

Instinctively, she stuffed her hand in her tote to text Valentina. This kind of thing literally made her weep with laughter. As she wiped away her tears, she would also ask Willa for the thousandth time when she was going to get a job that brought her actual, bona fide joy.

The first thing Willa's hand came into contact with was the embossed envelope from the lawyer's office. She ran a finger along it only to receive a paper cut in return. A stinging reminder that the one person in LA who'd been genuinely interested in where she was from wasn't here any more.

As she stuck her finger in her mouth to suck away the blood, she saw that Priya was giving her a knowing grin. 'You and Ben, huh? Buds forever?'

In lieu of waiting for an answer, Priya gave Willa a proper once over, sucked in a double lungful of air, then heaved it all out with a weighted, 'God, you're looking good. Stick thin, you lucky thing! That dress is hanging super sweet. Who is it? Vera? Rosa?' She scrunched her features into an adorable dare-I-say-it-out-loud face. 'It isn't from Goop, is it?'

Willa looked down at the dress she'd bought at Target three years ago. A basic, flowery midi she'd definitely strained the seams of a few months back. She was generally a size ten in a size-zero town, so this should feel like a compliment. For some reason it jarred.

Priya did a happy, wiggly dance. 'Seriously gorge. Look at your collarbones. They're popping.' She leant in and asked, sotto voce, 'Have you been on the mushroom smoothies?' then did a double take at Willa's bewildered expression. 'Oh god. Sorry. You're not . . . *sick* . . . are you?'

There were a number of things she could say here.

No.

That her heart was broken and she had no idea how to put it back together again.

Or, perhaps the most relevant: now that Valentina was gone, she was beginning to wonder if her life here in Tinseltown was as soulless and unfulfilling as the rest of her family made it out to be.

All of the above were true. But the only words threatening to tumble out of her mouth were, *I'm so sad. So unbelievably, bone-achingly sad.*

She didn't give in to the urge. Being honest meant she'd start to cry, never stop, cause a scene and get fired. With everything she'd lost recently, she at least had the wherewithal to know her job couldn't be next, so instead she put on her best you'll-never-believe-it face and said, 'Mushroom smoothies are so amazing.'

'Really?' Priya stepped in a bit closer, her voice turning confessional. 'I was tempted, but I always thought they sounded kind of gross.'

Oh thank god.

Willa wiped some invisible sweat off her forehead, stupidly grateful for the rare moment of honesty. 'I lied. Never had one. Never plan to.'

Then Priya looked at her. Really looked at her. 'You know? I've seen you at, like, a million of these things and we never get to chat. Would you like to grab a smoothie sometime? A good one? And not to talk business, just to – you know – start an anti-mushroom smoothie campaign or something.'

The invitation landed like a salve she hadn't known she'd needed. 'Yeah. I'd really like that.'

'You've got my numbers, right?'

Willa patted her pocket, the international sign for *got them on my phone*. 'I'll text you.'

And then, before either of them could find a way to extract themselves from something that felt very much like the beginnings of an actual conversation, another publicist flew to the door and called Willa's name.

Chapter Two

'Look at your shaggy little bedhead.' Charlie Foster, a long-term producer from an ABC affiliate, plopped a plate piled high with bacon and two suspiciously vodka-scented celery sticks on to the table, then folded himself into one of his long-limbed origami poses on the chair next to Willa's. 'You're so lucky you're not on camera.' He air-patted his own heavily done-up face, then washed the air in front of hers. 'It must be so nice not having to worry about your looks.'

Willa smiled but they both knew it wasn't a compliment. They'd started on the junket circuit about the same time, eight years ago. Despite his periodic on-air appearances when their own 'talent' was unavailable, Charlie had always had his eye on a job at TiTs. Specifically, Willa's job. As such, their relationship was that type of saccharine sweet I'm-being-nice-but-underneath-you-know-that-I-know-you-stole-the-life-I-was-meant-to-be-living.

'Sooooo . . . ?' Charlie poked at his bacon with his index finger. He looked disturbingly close to an immaculately dressed, oversized kitten batting a ball of string. 'How was Bennnnn?'

She flipped her hand in a so-so gesture then made a sad-clown face.

Ben had actually poured his guts out about his former marriage, his current marriage, lessons in humility he'd learnt as a parent and, more recently, as an advocate for Paralysed Veterans of America. Then, wiping actual tears from his eyes, told her she was like a maple-syrup-scented truth serum and invited her to help next time he hosted a soup kitchen for another one of his charities. But the interview was embargoed until tomorrow night so she couldn't say anything.

Which was hard considering her opening question – *Hey, Ben. Which side are your eggs flipped on today?* – had elicited such an outpouring of emotion.

Not that this was the first time something like this had happened. It was known as The Willa Effect at TiTs. An ability to ask an entirely bland question only to have a celebrity respond like a person in desperate need of a confessional. Aubrey said it was because stars felt 'deeply unintimidated' by Willa's 'mid-Western presence'.

Geography was not Aubrey's strongpoint. Nor was tact.

'No, seriously,' Charlie persisted. 'What did he say?'

'The usual.'

Charlie tsked her answer away. 'Willa Jenkins! Do not withhold crucial pre-interview information from me. I heard he was hugging it out with some Canadian reporter when he was on the way to his room and my boss wants soundbites on . . .' He held out a hand and started ticking off fingers. '. . . both of the Jens, the kids, the charity stuff, and something about mocktails at an after-party on a yacht fuelled by French fry grease. We're doing a segment on Sober-Eco-Friendly Celebs.' He shuddered at the last bit, then, giving his bacon a glance, curled his lips and said to the room, 'Could someone get this away from me, please?'

Willa gave him her best side-eye.

'Seriously, Willa.' He leant in and spoke in a hushed tone. 'Give me dirt. If TMZ gazumps me one more time this pretty face might not be hitting HD screens in an-y-bod-y's home ever again.'

She looked at the bacon, the approaching waiter and then at Charlie.

For the first time in what felt like forever, she was ravenous. And angry. Did he not understand what an amazing job he had? Rocking up to five-star hotels, 'kept waiting' in a room filled to the brim with Michelin-level snacks so he could interview celebrities the so-called average person only dreamt of meeting?

She held out a hand and stopped the waiter. To Charlie she said, 'Are you actually going to waste all of that bacon?'

'It's ick.'

'It isn't ick. It's quality food.'

He snorted. 'Willa, stop being weird. I like it when you're nice.' He stage-whispered, 'Are you *on* right now?'

Oh, she was on alright. 'Eat it.'

'What? No!'

'Eat it.' Her voice was level. Completely calm. 'Otherwise it will go to waste. You took it. Now eat it.'

Charlie looked over both of his shoulders in abject horror. 'Are you *shaming* me?'

She supposed she was. Him. Everyone around him who'd done something similar. Herself for not appreciating how fucking lucky she was to be alive and eating rare breed, applewood-smoked bacon as she waited for Sharon Stone to arrive for a five-minute interview about a two-minute cameo. (She was excellent, so . . . worth it.)

'Jeeee-ZUS! Take it if you want it so much.' Charlie shoved the plate in her direction, lurching a couple of pieces on to the white tablecloth.

A hush filled the room.

Willa took it and, to the surprise of everyone around her, she looked Charlie straight in the eye and began to eat one piece, then another, and another. Then she poured some maple syrup over the rest of the pieces and ate them too. Before the hospitality service manager could stage an intervention, she began grabbing other half-eaten or abandoned plates and eating them as well. Hash browns. Grilled asparagus with lemon zest shavings and curls of parmesan. A half-eaten triangle of brioche French toast with super fruit compote.

'She's *on*,' she could hear Charlie saying to the woman next to him. 'She just said. And I think Ben wasn't very nice to her. Did you know he thinks she's from Arkansas?'

'Willa Jenkins?' A publicist who looked like Zac Efron appeared in the doorway. 'Rachel's ready for you.'

Without so much as a backward glance she rose, followed the Zac lookalike down the hall, was introduced to Rachel, exchanged hellos with the crew, the agents, got mic'ed up, and waited patiently as Rachel received a touch-up of her powder and then, when everyone had stepped into place and the room co-ordinator swept her index finger into the we're-rolling spin, Willa opened her mouth and threw up.

◆ ◆ ◆

'Is there anyone you want us to call?' Priya asked, handing Willa a washcloth soaked in cold water.

Yes. But she couldn't pick up the phone any more.

She spat out the mouthwash one of the make-up artists had pressed into her hand with a whispered, 'I've always wanted to see someone projectile vomit on a celebrity. Thank you for that.'

'I'm alright, thanks,' Willa assured her. 'I'll just head home.'

'We'll courier your tapes over, and Charlie's volunteered to do your Rachel interview.'

Even in this state, Willa had to laugh. Of course he had. She got fifteen minutes to his five.

Priya dipped down to try to catch her eye. 'Is that okay? I can get someone else to do it if you want.'

'No, that's fine.' Maybe then her bosses would begin to see that she really did deserve that raise and promotion they hadn't given her for the past three years.

Down at the valet desk, she tugged a couple of dollars out of her coin purse. It wasn't much compared to the bills the actual clientele of the hotel stuffed into the palms of the valet staff, but she knew they appreciated the gesture.

When Jason, a forty-something surfer dude, pulled up and dropped the keys of her beloved Prius into her hand, he unexpectedly pulled her into a hug with a 'Heard about the Barf Monster incident. Make a grilled cheese sandwich and drink a root beer. Works for me every time.'

She patted him on the shoulder in thanks, then flopped into the driver's seat, turned left on Doheny, left on Third and headed home for another round of reading the lawyer's letter.

Garrish, Gottlieb and Greenweed
Family, Divorce and Probate Law
10879 Hooker Avenue
West Covina, CA 91791

Willaford Genevieve Jenkins
328 1/2 Loma Linda Drive
Los Angeles, CA 90023

Dear Miss Jenkins,

Allow me to offer my condolences for your recent loss. My name is Elijah Gottlieb, a probate lawyer based in West Covina. I had the pleasure of meeting your friend Valentina Ortiz before her unfortunate and, may I say, tragically early, passing.

She made it very clear that you would be immensely annoyed if I chose the more conventional method of informing you of her Wishes Letter (sending you a copy) and has asked, instead, that you come to our offices for a formal reading of said missive.

Her immediate family, as you know, have already relocated to Austin, Texas so will not be at the reading.

She also requested that I inform you that this is not a joke and that our business address is (quote) 'definitely not a clue to go to Hooters and order the bacon-wrapped wings and fish tacos (it totally is) and that when you go, please dress up, double down on the order and invite that cute bartender who is always flirting with you to join even though you think he isn't into you. He is. Make sure you raise a glass of that crappy lite beer you drink to me and cheer for the right team (Texas Stars Forever!!!!). Still bossy in heaven! Love ya, *chica*. Remember: carbs are your friend' (end quote).

I have scheduled you in at 9.30 a. m. on Monday morning so you are going against traffic, but please do ring if you need a different time as Valentina also expressed concern that you would have to work for those '*estúpidos idiotas que no reconocerían a un genio si ella caminara y se sentara en su cara*' (sic).

Warm regards,

Elijah Gottlieb

Elijah Gottlieb
Probate and Family Law
Twitter: @Lawfulfalafels
Podcast: Yenta Knows Best
Instagram: @Lawfulfalafels

Chapter Three

The first time Willa drove past the lawyer's office she missed it. She'd been expecting something akin to the towering glass and chrome structures in Century City. Hushed corridors where LA's most expensive lawyers battled out the likes of Kim and Kanye's squillions or which studio stole whose reworked idea first. She definitely hadn't banked on this.

Like most 1970s Southern Californian strip malls, there was a doughnut shop, a mani-pedi salon, a laundromat, a vitamin store, a pop-up bubble tea store and a restaurant. In this case, one called Lawful Falafels.

The number on the door matched the one on the law firm, so, half laughing that her bestie had still retained her sense of humour even while she was dying, and half terrified that this was some sort of cruel joke, Willa sat, staring at the storefront, knowing that the one thing she most wanted to find behind the door was Valentina.

Her phone rang. She briefly considered not answering it, but dutiful employee that she was, picked it up when she saw the TiTs exec producer's name flashing on her screen.

Putting on a scratchy voice, she answered, 'Hey, Martina. Everything okay?'

'Wonderful. Tip top. Listen, sugar. I heard about your little upchuck incident over the weekend and wanted to say thank you for not bringing whatever contagion it is you're carrying into the fold.'

I hope you're feeling better, Willa. Please accept my deepest sympathies that you're not feeling well. A florist is on the way.

'Always happy to take one for the team.'

'Good girl. Now, just as an FYI, the Four Seasons are doing a deep clean on the kitchen and are hoping that'll do as regards any food poisoning lawsuits? They've got five junkets on this week, so staying schtum sounds a good course of action, yeah?' No pause for a response. 'Anyway, while I've got you, I thought I'd run through a little bit of business to keep the wheels turning before you jump back in the saddle.'

Willa pulled the phone from her ear and stared at it. Seriously? Martina wanted her to work on her sick day? Then again, not a huge surprise. Everyone was replaceable in this town and most employers relied on that exact fear factor to keep staff in line. To be fair, she wasn't actually unwell. She'd overeaten, barfed on a major celebrity and was pulling a sickie to go to the will reading of a (non-celebrity) friend who, to Willa's knowledge, had nothing to bequeath. As Martina was already working her way through her bullet points, she quickly pressed the phone back to her ear and began taking her usual fastidious notes.

By the time she'd hung up, she had a full day's work ahead of her. Just the spur she needed to get out of the car and find out what her bossy bestie had been up to when she hadn't been looking.

From the second the restaurant door whooshed open, Willa was cocooned in aromatic wafts of lemon, parsley, onions, mint, cumin and . . . maybe coriander?

Inside was a bright, welcoming, trendy fast food falafel bar. It was not a lawyer's office. Behind the counter stood a portly red-headed man wearing a 'Body by Babka' apron and a jaunty green beret. He looked like a cross between a leprechaun and Santa.

'Ah!' he exclaimed, eyes twinkling with delight, as if he'd been waiting for her with great anticipation for many, many years. 'I'm guessing you're Willaford Jenkins. Fool?'

Ermm . . . She didn't really know where to go with this. 'Are we role-playing A-Team characters?'

He laughed as if she'd just said the most hilarious thing in the world, introduced himself as Elijah Gottlieb, then grabbed a spoon, took a huge dollop of a hummus-like dip from one of several beautiful ceramic bowls and lavished it on to a piece of flatbread. He sprinkled on some herbs, some crumbly feta and a smattering of chopped tomatoes, then deftly folded everything into an envelope shape, wrapped it in some brown paper and handed it to her. 'Sustenance,' he said gently. 'Just like my *Bubbie* used to make. I always find fava beans make these things easier. We'll have falafel after,' he added, as if they were heading off to play a couple rounds of miniature golf rather than hear her best friend's last wishes.

She held out her hands for the proffered gift and, so as not to be rude, took a bite. 'Ohmygod.' She beamed across at him. It was like an entire Middle Eastern spice market was having a party in her mouth. 'This is amazing!'

Elijah beamed. 'It took years of practice to get the recipe just right. I did all of this research' – he patted his belly – 'for you.' He pointed at her like a cheesy car salesman about to offer her the deal of a lifetime.

'Didn't you just say your grand—' she began as he stepped to a fluttery flyscreen door panel and asked, 'Shall we head back?'

He swept aside the multi-coloured tassels and beckoned for her to follow him.

After walking down a short corridor lined with personalised food hygiene signs ('Keep Your Matzo Offa My Meatballs'), they walked through another flyscreen panel, beaded this time, and entered what felt like an alternate universe. One Brad Pitt might have designed in between filming blockbusters and building houses for the poor.

Here there *was* an abundance of glass and beams, but there was also warmly polished reclaimed redwood, a sprawl of beautiful handwoven carpets, and an opulence of cushy leather chairs and lovingly worn-in sofas that looked so inviting they had to have cost a fortune. An actual, enormous eucalyptus tree grew right in the centre of the office and was surrounded by a circular bench upon which two fifty-something hipsters sporting yarmulkes sat drinking espresso. They leapt up upon Willa's approach.

'*Shalom aleichem!* Welcome,' said the beardy one. 'I'm Marty Garrish.' He pressed a hand to his chest. 'My condolences for your loss, Willaford.' He stretched out the same hand for her to shake.

She winced at the use of her full name, then, realising there was tahini sauce dripping down her wrist, morphed her expression into an I'm-too-gross-to-shake-hands apology face.

He laughed and introduced the other man, Leo Greenwood, after which, in unison, the three men chimed, 'And we're Lawful Falafels!' They chortled, gave happy sighs, and patted one another on the back as Willa tried to figure out how on earth Valentina had found these guys. They were strangely and wonderfully comforting. And making a really, really emotional situation much easier to handle. Then finally, it clicked. 'Is your phone number 1-800-LAWYER?'

They all brightened, and Elijah said, 'Yes! How did you know?'

Her voice cracked as she squeaked, 'Lucky guess.'

When she'd moved to LA, she'd known nothing and no one apart from the phone number of a casting agent her high school drama teacher had given to her. She'd scraped together her entire new adult existence with the help of Craigslist and hopeful guesses in the 1-800 number department. She'd needed a bed so had dialled 1-800-MATTRESS and *voila*! A blue mattress with fluffy clouds printed on it appeared the next day. She'd needed a job (the casting agent thing hadn't panned out) so called 1-800-GET-A-JOB and reached a temp agency that got her a two-week post as an assistant to a vice-president of marketing's assistant which had, after a very long eighteen months of waking at dawn and driving the length and breadth of LA to photocopy or type or anything else that would get her closer to her goal of being an entertainment reporter, finally led her to her first job at TiTs, which came with health and dental insurance. She hadn't had her teeth cleaned in two years and needed a dentist. So she'd dialled 1-800-DENTIST and had met the woman who would become the sister she'd never had. Valentina Ortiz.

Tears threatened as more memories poured in. The 'guac and talk' nights they'd started having every other Tuesday. The shared passion for kitsch and Disney and dressing up her husband Diego's scrappy rescue dog in their little girls' hand-me-downs. The competitive cartwheel contests that always landed them both dizzy and weeping with laughter on the tiny patch of lawn where they'd had countless barbecues. Knowing she was loved no matter what. Her body strained against the scratchy feeling at the back of her throat. She'd not cried once since Valentina had died. Sworn to herself she wouldn't. Vowed to be strong for Diego and the children who had, equally desperately, tried to cling to their old routine until the memories had proved too powerful. In what felt like the blink of an eye, Diego packed up the house and took the kids back to the families he and Val had left behind 'to see what adventures they'd find outside of the Ortiz Orbit'.

One tear fell. And then another. She held out her wrap and sobbed, 'What did you put in this thing?'

Rather than ignore the show of emotion or try to happy talk her tears away, the three men fell into a practised calm, dug in their pockets for fresh handkerchiefs, led her into an office off the foyer and gave her the room she needed to cry.

◆ ◆ ◆

What felt like twenty hours of gale-force tears later, Willa made herself drop her balled-up fists into her lap and take in the room. It had the aesthetic of a five-star treehouse rather than an office (the mini-mall was positioned on the edge of a ravine). She mopped her face clean and blew her nose (once she'd been gifted the soft cloth handkerchief speckled with floating loaves of bread and the logo 'Happy Challadays'). As Elijah slid a mug of fresh mint tea in front of her, she gave him a watery smile of gratitude and pronounced herself ready.

'Best way to start a meeting,' he said in an enthusiastic way that implied he regularly handed people a snack, brought them into the welcoming cocoon of his workplace, and offered so much kindness and warmth that the only possible reaction was to weep. He sat down at his desk, tapped a couple of papers into order, then gave her a bright smile. 'Right! We'll just wait for the other party to appear and then we'll get this show on the road.'

'Umm . . . We're what-ing for who?'

There was no *other* party. She'd been Valentina's best friend. Sure, Val had known people. The ones at work, the ones at the school gates. The ones at the gym where she taught Zumba on a Saturday (aka the Cheesy Burrito Bootie Burn). But none of them had been there when Valentina had needed someone to hold the barf buckets or try on unicorn-coloured wigs or—

A knock sounded on the doorframe and a rich, shiver-my-timbers baritone asked, 'Apologies. Erm . . . Is this the right office to find Mr Gottlieb?'

Elijah bounded out from behind his desk and began shaking hands with – *ooohhhhh, heavens* – the most beautiful man Willa had ever seen. And that was saying something because she had interviewed practically *everyone* from the Marvel franchise.

If perfectly beautiful men were her thing, she'd be melting into a puddle of drool and oestrogen, leaving her poor neglected ovaries to dance the tarantella in an attempt to win his heart. But perfectly beautiful men scared her a little. And by 'a little', she meant a lot.

'You must be Gabriel,' Elijah said, ushering the six-foot-something wall of hunk-a-liciousness to the chair next to Willa's.

Willa snapped to attention.

Gabriel Martinez?

Oh, now this was unexpected.

And also take-your-breath-away amazing. Whether or not he was who Willa thought he was, this Gabriel chap was the most exquisitely sculpted human being she'd ever seen. If ever there was a call for pirate/businessman chic, this Latino mass of muscles and style mavenry was calling for it. Midnight blue-black hair. Eyes as mesmerising as tiger's. And as watchful. And a face . . . *ohhh, mercy* . . . a face that looked as if it had been hewn from an exquisite slab of precious stone chink by exacting chink.

Elijah introduced Gabriel to Willa, then bustled back behind his desk.

It was true. She was sitting next to Valentina's long-lost brother.

Shell-shocked, Willa stared at Gabriel.

Gabriel, in turn, barely acknowledged her presence.

Valentina had rarely spoken about her estranged brother. Like, pretty much never. He was the 'We Don't Talk About Bruno' of the Martinez family. Once, in a chemotherapy haze, Val had muttered something about hoping with all of her soul that he was living his best life.

Taking gross advantage of the drugs Val was on, Willa learnt Gabriel was her second-to-oldest brother. He'd left home in the middle of Val's *quinceañera* before *abuela*'s flan had been served (an unforgivable sin, apparently). He'd never returned. And, according to family legend, was never mentioned again. But Val missed him. Desperately. For her twenty-third birthday, Diego had hired a private detective and discovered Gabriel lived in Palm Springs, where he'd transformed from an angry teen to the ironically private, super-successful branding and social media strategist behind Transparency – the go-to social media machine for celebs who needed an image makeover. Despite being sent invitations, he'd not come to Valentina's wedding, funeral or the Life After Death party (she'd refused to have a plain old wake. *Too creepy,* mamacita!). Willa had tried a bit of cyber-stalking a while back, but it had turned up nothing. No photos. No Insta feed. No heartfelt testimonials on Yelp. But he was here now.

How?

Was there a 1-800-LOST-BRO?

'Hi,' she said, her voice still sounding embarrassingly snuffly. 'I'm Willa.'

She waited to see if there was any hit of recognition. But no. He did the guy chin lift thing, then turned his tiger-eyed intensity back on Elijah. *Lordy.* He even moved like a jungle cat.

'Right!' Elijah held up two pieces of paper, then slid them in a synchronised move across the desk towards each of them. 'Wills. One each.'

'I don't want anything,' Gabriel said while Willa flinched back from the piece of paper as if it might bite her.

'Not to worry,' Elijah said first to Gabriel then to Willa. 'There's nothing here for either of you.' He tapped a third piece of paper, clearly a copy, then put it to the side only to bring another set of papers to the centre of his desk. 'These, however, *are* for you.' He put an envelope under each set of fingers, then paused. 'To read later,' he addended, then pushed the letters across.

Gabriel reached forward for his and slipped it into the dark leather manbag he'd propped against his chair.

Willa went to do the same but then, remembering that she'd also just stuffed a flatbread oozing with Middle Eastern delights into her bag, placed the envelope on top of the will.

'Now then,' Elijah said, his smile brightening further. 'I suppose you're both wondering why I've called you here today.'

Chapter Four

The waitress – Brandi, according to her name tag – aimed her pen in Willa's direction. 'So, that's two orders of Hooter's special wings, two fish tacos, two Slippery Nipples, one lite beer aaaaand' – she swivelled her pen so that it was aimed at Gabriel – 'a water. Want me to hold the ice?' She held her serious expression for a beat and then laughed to show him she was joking. Obvs.

Gabriel arched an eyebrow. 'Ice is fine,' he said. And then, to Willa's surprise added, 'In fact, hit me hard with it.'

Brandi laughed and pushed his (immovable rock of a) shoulder in a you-funny-josher kind of way, even though it was pretty clear neither she nor Willa knew if he was being serious. When he offered nothing by way of a response, she skipped away.

Willa watched until she got to the bar to put in their orders, then turned around to find Gabriel's opalescent tiger eyes boring into hers.

'So,' he said, pulling a paper napkin out of the dispenser with ninja-like precision. 'What do you think?'

Well, now. Wasn't that a loaded question?

What did she think about him appearing out of nowhere at a will reading for his estranged sister when he hadn't bothered coming to her funeral? Or perhaps, what did she think of Valentina's Wishes Letter? Or was it, what did she think of the fact that the two of them were sitting in a Hooters in West Covina at 11 a.m. on a Monday morning, one of them on a water fast and the other about to get jacked?

'I'm down with it.'

He snorted, using his fingernail to craft a meticulous crease into the napkin. Willa shivered as if he'd run it down her spine.

'Are you being serious?'

Her eyes snapped to his. His tone suggested she'd just said murdering someone wasn't *that* bad a crime. 'My sister has just gifted us – total strangers – a two-week' – he lifted his pianist's fingers into air quotes here – '"Totally Immersive *Outlander* Experience" . . . in Scotland . . . in October . . . led by someone who doesn't have a website to info-grab or, more importantly, on which to cancel. All of which is four days away. And you're *down with it?*'

'It was Valentina's favourite show,' she riposted. Lamely.

He gave her an *and* look.

'What?' She tried her best to sound both sanguine and feisty. 'Does there need to be some deep meaning beyond her wanting us to enjoy something she loved?'

'No.' (Still cranky.) 'I'm just trying to wrap my head around why my sister wanted the two of us in particular to do this thing.'

She was trying to wrap her head around it too. Going on a superfan experience based on a show she'd never watched with a man she didn't know – especially one who looked like Gabriel – was just . . . well . . . even for Valentina it was out there. And Willa was no stranger to weird. She had, among other things, waited in the same room as Snoop Dogg while he fought with his wife about firing the nanny and decided to improve his mood by coming up with the name of his next album: Snoopersonic (totally a bestseller and, no, she didn't get a thank you at the Grammys). She'd watched (and applauded on command) when Mickey Rourke used a chainsaw to make a startlingly accurate ice statue of himself. She'd also borne witness to Jason Momoa playing patty-cake with Liza Minelli to the tune of 'Send in the Clowns'. So the fact she couldn't figure out what the heck was behind this was saying something.

Brandi swished up to their table and expertly slid two huge water glasses on to coasters in front of them. She gave Willa a wink and a what's-with-that-guy look. 'Your drinks'll be up in a minute, hon.'

She picked up her glass of water and drank. Gabriel, she was a tiny bit pleased to see, had received a huge glass of crushed ice with just the tiniest bit of water at the bottom.

Oblivious, Gabriel continued, 'I suppose you two spent endless nights watching the Scottish totty together in your onesies?'

The words landed like scalding hot blades in her heart.

'Yeah, while we combed each other's hair and braided it,' Willa snarked before her internal truth serum gave her brain another injection forcing her to admit, 'But not *Outlander*.'

'Why not?' he demanded.

'It wasn't my jam, okay?' she snapped back. 'We watched all sorts of things together, but not that!'

'Why? Time-travelling nurses and sexy men in kilts too low brow for you?'

'Ooo!' she sing-songed like a kid in a playground. 'Looks like someone's awfully *au fait* with it.'

Instead of acknowledging the comment, he did the chin lift thing again. 'What was it you did for work? Interview celebs?' His upper lip did a weird twitch as if even saying it gave him hives.

Willa bridled. 'Are you suggesting that what I do is less respectable than giving a spit and shine to celebs who've wriggled out of drunk driving charges?'

He winced.

She tried to hold his steely gaze, but her insides were crumpling. It was never wise to let a man you were about to go on vacation with know that you've not only cyberstalked his company, but were also pooping on his profession. Because, obviously, interviewing movie stars was so much better.

Gabriel's eyes flared. He looked like a sexy demon.

She grabbed her water, taking gulp after gulp in a desperate bid to brain freeze the fallen-angel erotica away.

When she slammed the empty glass down, they stared at one another, chests lifting and falling in tight concentrated breaths until, unexpectedly, Gabriel tipped his head into his hands and began to shake.

Shame flooded out the rage. Judgemental jerk or not, Gabriel's sister was dead and all of that stiff-lipped, hypercritical fact-finding was probably how he kept his shit together. And, even though she wouldn't admit it, she silently acknowledged that his question had reopened a barely healed wound. Explaining why she didn't watch *Outlander* to this information-seeking heat missile was something she didn't have the emotional bandwidth for right now and, seeing as they would be together twenty-four-seven by the end of the week, she was hoping their immersive experience in the wilds of Scotland could, at the very least, be pleasant.

Before she could say anything, he dropped his hands. His eyes were covered in a sheen of emotion, but his remarkably lovely lips were, for the very first time, curved into a smile. 'This is exactly the kind of fight I would've had with Concha back in the day.'

'Who?'

'Valentina.'

The way his front teeth latched on to his lower lip after saying his sister's name squeezed her heart tight. Estranged or not, he'd lost someone too. 'Is that what you used to call her?'

'*Sí*,' he said in another nod to his Latin heritage, and then, 'You know her middle name was Concepción, right?'

'Yee-esss.' Despite the vice-grip on her chest, her voice actively conveyed a prickly *What part of 'we were best friends so I know everything there was to know about her' are you not understanding?*

'Concha is a nickname for it. It means seashell.'

Despite the weight of emotion in it, his voice was so soft her defensiveness dropped away.

Willa turned the unfamiliar name over in her mind a couple of times trying to marry it up with Valentina's multiple other nicknames (*guapita, mamiiiii*, Val, Queen Vee, Tenacious V, Nurse Ratched). She smiled. 'Suits her.'

After a couple more folds, Gabriel put the napkin, now transformed into an origami frog, on the table. 'I'm sorry. I'm being a dick.' He lifted his gaze to meet hers and offered her an apologetic smile that finally spoke to the warm, generous gene pool her bestie had come from. 'Can we start over?' He reached forward and used the pad of his index finger to make the frog jump.

She snorted and, ice sort of broken, reached out and shook his proffered hand.

'Willa Jenkins.'

He arched an eyebrow. 'I thought it was Willaf—'

She waved her hands, 'No-no-no. I mean. Yes. It is. But no one gets to call me that except Valentina.'

They both went awkwardly blinky-eyed, visibly grateful to focus on Brandi who was now sliding double portions of everything in front of Willa and very pointedly sloshing a fresh glass of water, with no ice, in front of Gabriel. 'Can I get you anything?'

she asked, grabbing his cup of ice and leaving before he could answer.

'Want some?' Willa offered when she'd left.

Gabriel eyed her impressive spread. 'Thanks, but no.' He tipped his head in the general direction of Lawful Falafels and said, 'I've had my carbs today.'

Willa could've made a point of reminding him that the woman they were here to discuss had specifically asked for this very detailed Hooters' menu extravaganza . . . as a dying wish . . . but resisted.

Instead she smiled and tucked a couple of napkins into her shirt collar and began to eat.

After two tacos, a few sinus-clearing bites of wings and an over-zesty 'Bottoms up!' with one of the shots, she tried to jumpstart the conversation again. 'Sounds like being an *Outlander* fan runs in the family.'

He gave a vague nod. 'I don't really understand this, though. The trip. Was she a superfan or something?'

'No. Well. Sort of?' She'd loved the show. A lot. Went to conventions, had an autographed picture of the show's star taped to her refrigerator who she regularly (teasingly) threatened to leave Diego for, but Willa was sure there was something more to loving the show beyond the eye candy and sexy accents. Whatever it was, she wanted Willa and Gabriel to experience it too.

'But why the "immersive experience"? It seems excessive.'

'Anyone who knew Val knew she always did things for a reason,' Willa said, a bit too defensively judging by the micro-wince it elicited in Gabriel. 'She said, didn't she?' Willa gently prompted, pulling her copy of the Wishes Letter and the accompanying brochure out of her bag and wiping away a tiny smear of fava bean mush.

She began to read, trying to convince herself as much as Gabriel that it made perfect sense. '"I want you two precious people to share something together. I am so excited to look down on the two of you (the Pearly Gates have got amazing views, homies!) while you enjoy something I loved so much. (Stop rolling your eyes, Gabriel!)"'

Willa looked across at him and, sure enough, he was mid-eyeroll. They both gave a nervous laugh and glanced up at the ceiling before Willa continued, "'You both work too much and aim so hard to please, it's time you took some time for yourselves. When you're done being cranky with me for throwing a grenade into your well-laid-out lives, remember . . . sometimes you need to step away from the person you think you are, to become the person you want to be.'"

She put the letter down and gave it a pat, as if that answered everything, knowing that all it did was elicit a deluge of questions.

'And this guy is going to help you do that?' Gabe stabbed his index finger at the kilted man on the side of the brochure Willa had not yet examined.

She flipped it over.

Oh, hel-*lo*.

Catalogue Kilt Man was most likely Photoshopped on to the outdoorsy background, but studio shoot or no, he was suhh-mokin'.

There was a crumbling stone something or other in the background, a carpet of purple plants – heather, maybe? – some rolling snow-capped hills off in the middle distance. But none of that was what captivated her. It was him. Catalogue Kilt Man. He was tall, like Gabe, but more solid versus the feline leanness of Gabe's musculature. He was wearing a kilt (obvs) and knee-high socks and a little black jacket with shiny buttons, but his face! His *face*.

She was no dreamer. Quite the opposite. But looking into Catalogue Kilt Man's blue-grey eyes elicited something so primal within her she wished with all of her heart she'd never seen this. Because catalogue men weren't real. They were air-brushed stock photos of men who were monetarily remunerated for making everyone believe they too could have a catalogue man in their lives if only they bought the right clothes, perfume, watch, face cream or any of an endless array of goods that would, in the end, only turn out to be non-refundable when they failed to make your dreams come true.

And this most definitely applied to Immersive *Outlander* Experience Catalogue Kilt Men with faces that told a thousand stories, legs for days and big ol' man hands that she could already imagine resting just so on her hips.

She'd learnt this lesson early on in her time in Hollywood. Not necessarily the hard way, because it wasn't exactly a hardship to meet deeply attractive movie stars. But there was always something that detracted from the dream that they were absolutely perfect.

Namely: a deal-breaker flaw. Sometimes you had to look a bit harder than with others, but it was always there, just waiting to be found. Sometimes it was physical – their voice, their laugh, the way they ate with their mouth open. But mostly it was *them*. The real-life aura they exuded as opposed to the onscreen one. A lot of them weren't very nice. Quite a few of them thought they were the shiznit. Some of them refused to wear deodorant and didn't have anyone in their inner circle who would guide them away from this poor olfactory decision.

What all of her up close and personal contact had taught her was that sometimes people really *are* good actors.

Beyond that, the simple truth was, movie stars didn't fall in love with entertainment producers from backwoods Oregon.

Ever the practical puss, she rolled her eyes at the brochure's exquisite example of A Rugged Highland Male and huffed out a very worldly, 'Yeah. As if.'

She tapped the Wishes Letter and said to Gabriel, yet another perfect male specimen who would come with a catch, 'Please feel free to take this opportunity to share anything that isn't allowing you to live your "hashtag" best life.'

Gabriel looked at her, the will, the drinks in front of her, then took the spare shot and threw it down his throat.

Chapter Five

'Alright, you two rascals.' Brandi, now on a first-name basis with them and well assured of an abscholutellllyyyEeeeNORMousTip, was waving them to the door. 'Your car is here. *Fancy*,' she added as she helped Willa hitch her tote more securely on to her shoulder. Then, with a wink, sing-songed, 'Make sure you do everything *I* would do!'

Willa rolled her eyes. As if she'd try to do anything sexy with the drop dead gorgeous, deliciously tipsy Gabriel with whom she was going to be spending the next two weeks.

And that's when it hit her.

This was a set-up.

This was Valentina matchmaking from heaven.

She tried to summon up a moment when Val may have been drugged up enough to think Willa and Gabe would be a good match, and lucid enough to Google an immersive Scottish holiday for two.

Nope! Nothing doing.

Which meant Valentina must've genuinely intended for them to go on vacation together. For what purpose? Was it really romance?

A ratty text from her boss asking Willa where her planning notes were hadn't sobered her up, but this did.

Willa and Gabe? (He was Gabe now. Anyone who'd shared not one, but two rounds of Rocky Mountain Bear Fuckers with her required a monosyllabic name.)

Gabe and Willa?

'You okay?' Gabe's voice rippled down her spine like warm butterscotch.

'Ummm.' Not any more! 'I just need to go to the Ladies.' She crossed her legs and made a pained expression because obviously the edible adult male across from her would have no clue as to why a woman who'd just had multiple highly alcoholic shots needed to go to the bathroom.

He nodded and slid on to a barstool to wait.

Like an idiot, she waved goodbye and tried her best to walk in a sophisticated catwalk style that probably made it look a lot more like she was desperately trying to hold it in.

Once in the stall, she propped her elbows on her knees and had a think.

Was this actually, genuinely one of Val's very unsubtle set-ups?

Despite having shared loads of childhood stories over the past few hours (Val's homemade piñatas, her childhood dream of becoming a mermaid, her first attempt at making *abuela*'s flan), she still knew very little about Gabe himself and, more importantly, whether or not he was single. If this was a set-up, it would be good to know if his slate was clean.

Unsurprisingly, Willa's was an immaculate whiteboard of possibility.

Especially now that she didn't have Val to mark her dates out of ten. In her usual forthright way, Valentina macheted her way through the chaff when examining Willa's online prospects. (*He gives me the shivers,* mija. *I bet he has a ventriloquist dummy,* for example.) Over the years, Val had abandoned subtlety and taken to planting options in front of their backyard barbecue alongside Diego as 'preferable alternatives to career-track guy/beardy-weirdy guy/waaaay-too-into-learning Klingon guy' etc, etc. To which Willa had said, 'Not everyone can be a Diego, Val,' to which she had said, 'True, *mija*. But they should at least be *trying*.'

The thing was, deciding she was fine with being single meant not having to go through the time suck that was online dating, and, more importantly, she didn't have to endlessly apologise about the fact that her life was *busy*. Between her bestie dying, the gym, some sporadic volunteer work she did at a local dog shelter, near mandatory mani-pedis, remembering which day to move her car out of the way of the street cleaner, remembering which day to put the garbage bins out, which exercise trends to sweat through, bucket list moments with Val (Dollywood, riding an elephant, eating all thirty-two flavours at Baskin Robbins), and, of course, her actual job, her days were *full*. Cramming a boyfriend and the ancillary things that went along with it – waxing, sexy lingerie, updated blow-job techniques, pretending to know the rules of ice hockey, pretending to *care* about ice hockey, and all of the other latest dating requirements – were nigh on impossible and most of the time she felt, and very likely looked, utterly frazzled. So at this point? Her one nod to a relationship involved rechargeable double As.

Gabe, on the other hand, looked as though he could handle anything and anyone and demanded as much from his partners in return. She had no doubt he would be as comfortable with a multi-lingual *Sports Illustrated* swimsuit model as a shockingly beautiful UN ambassador for children. Most likely on his terms, but, saying that, he exuded an aura of calm (control?) that she bet drew people to him.

Having been the recipient of his full attention for over three hours, she completely understood why celebrities came to him for 'reinvention' in the way they'd once flocked to gurus for inner peace. A few years older than her, and clearly miles ahead in the career-development trajectory, his energy was both charged and mesmerising.

Once he loosened up, he was funny, engaging, told great stories about 'the set' out in Palm Springs – including one about how he'd once had to coax one of the Kardashians (he refused to say which one) not to run down Main Street wearing nothing but an inflatable flamingo.

She suddenly remembered that she was supposed to be peeing and grabbed a handful of toilet paper squares.

What really made the whole was-this-a-set-up thing click into a genuine possibility was the conversation they'd had about favourite films and television shows. Now, of all the things Willa loved in the world, film and television were at the top of the list. The number of days she'd had screaming matches with her mom about how vitally important it was to watch *Buffy the Vampire Slayer* even though it was a sunny day knew no bounds. Gabe had given her a meaningful high five for that one. Her grin had grown ever wider as her *No way! Me too!*s finally peaked at a dog-whistle-pitched 'I'm so in love with you right now!' after they admitted to a shared love of inspirational sports dramas. Their eyes had caught and cinched in a way that lit a flame of possibility. One that sang to a future where they could be trapped on a desert island with their favourite boxsets and a truckload of moisturiser, and live happily ever after.

And then Gabe had asked, 'But no *Outlander*?'

Willa's smile dropped away at the memory. If there was one thing she could change about the past it was this. Had she known how sick Valentina really was, she would've dived into the entire *Outlander* universe like a giddy porpoise. All of those extra hours they could've shared together, lost on a principle.

'I'm just . . . I'm not really a superfan kind of person,' she'd said, making a hashtag symbol with her fingers and pulling a face. 'TotesEmbarassing, am I right?'

He responded with a neutral shrug. 'Sometimes being a super-fan allows people to think their lives could be better.'

Her heart had crumpled in on itself. Of course it could. The insight, so crystal clear now that he'd said it, had sent Willa into a tailspin.

'Obviously, yeah,' she'd stumbled over herself to fix the gaffe. 'I mean, I'm not judging. Loving a show and giving it your time and energy and sometimes all of your hard-earned vacation time is not something I dismiss lightly. After all, if there weren't superfans, I probably wouldn't have a job.'

Until that moment, she'd never connected Val's love of *Outlander* to a means of escaping her life. Which, of course, was completely idiotic of Willa. Val had been a young mum in an eye-wateringly beautiful marriage, dying of cancer. Of course she wouldn't have been happy about her reality. She gave Gabe a look that must've read something along the lines of *Well, I'm A Complete Fucking Idiot* chased up by an imploring *Am I The World's Worst Best Friend?*

'Hey.' Gabe reached across to give her hand a squeeze and, as if he'd read her mind, said, 'Don't think you let her down because you didn't love all of the same things. Valentina wasn't like that.'

'I know,' she whispered, wishing like hell she believed it. 'But why do you think she's doing this? What's going to be in Scotland that isn't here?'

They sought answers in one another's eyes for what felt like forever. And then, somehow, the energy shifted to something edged with . . . frisson? She was a bit rusty in that department and her natural I-can-read-you-like-a-book radars were drunk, so, on the off chance she was right, she'd decided to lean in and test the waters.

Like a humiliation saviour, Brandi skipped up to their table, cut the move short, and asked if they wanted another round of Woo Woos. She and Gabe had grinned at one another – relieved? – and given Brandi the thumbs-up.

It was Gabe's car service that had finally cleaved them from their booth.

Wondering why Gabriel hadn't emerged from the Hooters after three hours when he'd been assured it would be a quick fifteen minutes max, his driver had rung the restaurant and asked after him only to overhear his boss demanding that the bartender change channels from ESPN to Amazon Prime using his account so he and Willa could do a boxset binge of *Outlander* whilst playing a drinking game he'd just made up involving use of the phrase, 'Ya ken noo, Sassenach.'

Gabe knocked on the bathroom door, forcing her back into the here and now. A quick wipe, flush and hand wash later, she was outside blinking in the afternoon sun.

Slipping into the town car's lush interior had a semi-sobering effect on the pair of them – as if it was too adult an environment to behave like the giggling idiots they'd been in Hooters.

After they'd both chugged down some of the water from the central armrest's mini fridge (!!!), Gabe pulled the latest iPad out of his manbag. 'Right. Agenda time. Who do we need to hit to get you ready for wheels up on Friday?'

'Erm . . . no one?' She elbowed him in the side causing him to sloosh a bit of water down his shirt. 'I'm a lover not a fighter.'

'Willa,' Gabe dead-panned, pulling out a cloth handkerchief to dab at his shirt (and nipple), 'it's a turn of phrase. If you are completely serious about fulfilling my sister's very weird last requests, you've got' – he snapped his wrist out of his jacket sleeve – 'approximately seventy-two hours to do it.'

As it happened, a tight deadline and a seemingly impossible To-Do List were among Willa's favourite things. They quickly made a list on Gabe's iPad.

1) Tell Martina she was going to take some of her nine weeks accrued vacation time.

2) Deal with fall out of Step One by doing two weeks' work over the next three days.

3) Ask her neighbour to water her (mostly dead) plants.

And that was about it.

Gabriel looked at her through narrowed eyes, his long black lashes almost begging for her to reach out and touch them. He'd be perfect in a daytime soap. Or a night-time soap. Or being sudsed up with a bar of soap. Before her thoughts could take her anywhere closer to undressing him, he began to batter her with questions. 'You don't have family to tell? Friends to alert? Personal appointments to reschedule?'

She goldfished.

He frowned. 'Willa? Where's the life in your life?'

Uhhh . . .

'*Rude!*' She wagged a finger at him with what she hoped was a mischievous could-do-better-in-the-manners-department smile. She held up her hand and ticked off her fingers. 'My family live in Oregon. Valentina was— Well. You know. And I pretty much work all of the time, so there's not much room for extras.' She crushed the rest of her fingers down to show how much of a time suck TiTs was.

'And by extras you mean . . . a boyfriend?'

She gave an airy little *Perhaps* to disguise any excitement she felt that he wanted to know whether or not she was single.

Instead of pressing, he began addressing the practical elements of their situation. He asked where her work was, her apartment, whether or not she could go back out to Covina and get her car tomorrow or if he should send one of 'his people'.

She responded with the same rat-a-tat-tat style. Burbank. Angelinos Heights. One of 'his people' would be amazing but not necessary, oh okay, go on, then.

'Can we go to your apartment?' he asked next. 'Take a shower?'

She blushed again and began to stammer something about taking things one step at a time before he cut in with a very dry, 'Separately. Take showers separately.'

She filled the car with screeches of awkward laughter. 'I know. Hahahaha. Psych! Your face!' *Ohmigawd, kill me now.*

He waved a hand between them and said, 'If our next stop is TiTs, we're going to have to arrive smelling of roses, not whiskey and butterscotch schnapps. I'm happy to go to my club downtown if you prefer, but this way would be faster.'

'Wait. You're coming to my office with me?' That was weird. And also completely unnecessary. This was the modern era. She didn't need a man to swoop in and explain to her bosses that she needed to fly to Scotland this Friday even though— Ohhhh, *fiddlesticks.*

The week after next was Sweeps Week. The hallowed week during which the national ratings services measured the size of TV audiences in order to figure out advertising rates. For the next two weeks, the network owned her down to her cell structure. There was no way on god's green earth she could go on Val's non-refundable, once in a lifetime, will-fulfilling *Outlander* experience.

'I can't go.' She told him why.

'Yes. You can.'

'Yeah, right. You haven't met my boss.'

'Yes, I have.'

She gave him a side-eye. 'Do you do all of your stealth work from some sort of secret bunker hidden in the subterranean depths of the Disney Studios?'

'No. Palm Springs.'

Where living in a secret underground bunker made sense. But – she didn't know why this hadn't occurred to her earlier, but – what was he doing living a two-hour drive away from his dying sister and not visiting? She'd definitely invited him to her wake, so he knew.

Before her hackles could fly up, he tapped the side of his nose. 'People owe me favours and my sister has charged me with seeing that you fulfil her wishes, so it is my chivalrous duty to accompany you into the lion's den.'

'Even though it's a lioness's den?'

'Where you go . . . I shall follow.' His full lips quirked into a gorgeous Latino-Dread-Pirate-Roberts-type smile. He may as well have been tumbling down a hill calling out, 'Aaaaas youuuuuuu wiiiiiiiiiiish!' If she hadn't been sitting down, she would've swooned. But also . . . wasn't it interesting that he saw it as his mission to help her fulfil the Wishes Letter? Did that mean she was on duty to ensure he fulfilled his? She filed that little nugget away for later. Their long-haul flight was going to be one long Q&A session.

Two showers, four cups of coffee and one trip into the valley later, you could've coloured Willa Extremely Impressed.

'You're good,' she said, as she and Gabe left the studio's administrative offices weighed down by a pair of freshly delivered 'bereavement baskets' filled with soothing eye gels, a microwaveable body wrap, and an astonishing array of calming essential oil candles.

'I know,' he said without an ounce of braggadocio.

Frankly, she was a little shell-shocked. 'You told them the truth.'

'Which' – he gave her a bemused look – 'you see as a bad thing?'

She was about to launch into a little speech about how no one had known about the situation with Valentina because no one really cared about Willa's personal life when his eyes began to twinkle. 'When you went out to explain to the new intern about how to put show segment entries into the system, I promised your boss an exclusive with Britney and another with Rita Ora and Zendaya taking a barre class together.'

'Sweet cheeses!' she shouted. 'How did you manage that?'

He gave her a look.

Ohhhhh.

'Zendaya?' she prompted. The star was scandal free as far as she knew.

'Non-disclosure agreement,' he retorted, sealing those lovely lips of his with a finger zip.

A tiny sliver of annoyance slid under her skin. She was the problem solver around TiTs. But before it could fester, Valentina's words slipped back into a loop in her head: *Sometimes you have to step away from who you think you are . . .*

'So!' She scored off number one on their list. 'Let's do something on your list.'

Not that he'd said he had one, but surely he wasn't like James Bond, able to jump on a plane for two weeks without doing anything to prep?

She'd known Gabe a sum total of seven hours now, and still knew very few personal facts about him other than a familiarity with his gene pool. On the plus side, he was much easier to be with than her first impression had led her to believe. He was kind, charming, took shots of tabasco-laden rum like he'd been born to it and, yes, he made her tummy flutter.

Gabe blinked at her a moment or two and then said, 'It's going to be freezing in Scotland.'

She snorted. 'In October? It's, like, a hundred degrees here.'

Without a hint of a smile he said, 'Things are a little chillier in Scotland.'

He held up the very scant brochure and wiggled it between them. Her eyes snagged on Catalogue Kilt Man and her heartbeat did a little Highland Fling.

'Earth to Willa?' Gabe was waving his hand in front of her eyes. 'Are you equipped for this?'

She took the brochure and, after another quick glance at Catalogue Kilt Man flipped it over to the printed side and read out loud: '"Welcome to the world's first and only Authentic Fully Immersive Jacobite *Outlander* Experience."' She raised her eyebrows and threw Gabe a sheepish look. 'I'm not entirely sure I know what a Jacobite is.'

He shrugged as if that was perfectly normal and said it had to do with a rebellion against the English and Bonnie Prince Charlie, a royal from the House of Stuart.

'So, we're not going to be running into Mel Gibson and a bunch of guys wearing blue on their faces?'

He shook his head and gave his chin a comedic scholarly stroke. 'I think we are past the blue-war-paint era of Scottish history.'

'I'm going to have to trust you on that one.'

'There is always Google.' He pointed at her phone.

'What? And ruin the surprise?'

He gave her a look that read, *I'm all for ruining the surprise if it means being prepared.*

'No.' She wagged her finger at him. 'Valentina loved surprises. She'll want us to go in blind. Well, mostly blind.' She tapped the paper. 'Here're the activities we have in store. Cloth dyeing—'

'What? Like batik?'

Now it was her turn to give him an *I don't think so* look. 'I'm pretty sure the olden days Scots weren't known for tie-dye.' She read again. 'Knitting lessons, tea-leaf readings, sword fighting—' She lifted her eyebrows. 'I hope we don't have to fight each other.'

He flashed her a film-star grin and in an accent she was guessing was meant to be Scottish said, 'Never, lassie. I'll no' see you murdhered by my own fair hand.'

'Why, thank you,' she chirped. 'Otherwise Valentina will have to kill you with a lightning spear.' They both laughed, then frowned and, to ward off another rush of emotion, she wiggled the paper. 'There isn't much more information. Just lots of "authentic" this and olde worlde that. I'm guessing it means we'll be eating hunks of meat with our hands and sleeping in luxurious four-poster beds with quilts stitched by spinster aunties. That's how it works in castles, right?'

'My experience in the world of castles is relatively limited, but . . .' He trailed off, looking out into the middle distance as if trying to gather together all his castle experience so he could impart great wisdom. He turned to her eventually and said, 'I'm going back to my original point. It's going to be freezing. Do you fancy a bit of shopping?'

Chapter Six

Shopping with Gabriel Martinez was like being Queer Eyed by a straight guy. Deep immersion in awesome sauce.

Flinging back the curtain to her changing room, she pranced out and did a twirl in front of him and laughed an unfamiliar tinkly laugh of joy when he gave her fifth and final ensemble – a puffa jacket that was, effectively a sleeping bag – the thumbs-up. She struck a pose. 'I can't decide if I feel like Adventure Barbie or a Bear Grylls version of *Pretty Woman.*'

He gave her an assessing frown. 'I'm thinking more . . . North Pole Gal Godot.'

She grinned at him and gave her hair a saucy flick. 'I'll take that.' She paraded around in a circle and flicked some invisible reins for a fleet of invisible reindeer. 'To the Highlands, Rudolph!'

He grinned back. 'You look good, *guapita.*'

Their eyes caught and a ridiculous thrill swept through her. Who even was she right now? Someone confident? Someone pretty? Someone happy enough in her skin to actually let herself become attracted to this guy? He was ambrosia to the eyeballs, so, her body was all in. But her brain kept raising its hand to timorously ask if things weren't a bit more complicated. The fact he was a connection to Valentina meant he could be a mullet-wearing hotdog-eating champion and she'd still want to spent time with him. Besties like Val were unicorns. What they'd had was rare and so, so painful to lose. Valentina, in her wisdom, had known Willa would be lost without her and had handed her a lifeline. But was it meant to be a lifeline complete with tingles in her lady fandango? Or one where Friend Zone lines were very clearly drawn in the sand?

She pretended to gaze at her reflection, surreptitiously glancing at Gabe, who was inspecting his own pile of manly outdoor wear. Everything he'd tried on had fitted him immaculately. As if he'd Ashtanga-ed himself into whatever size models wore in order for everything he put on to look custom made. Now that she thought about it, he might be too perfect to actually be mortal. Maybe he was a figment of her imagination.

She turned round, reached out and poked him in the chest.

'Hey! What was that for?'

'Just checking you were real. That I wasn't hallucinating this whole thing.'

'Nope.' He gave himself a loud thump on the chest. 'Genuine flesh and blood.'

'Hunh.' She plopped down on the bench beside him. A small yawn escaped before she could pop her hand over her mouth. 'Sorry.'

'Don't be. It's been a weirdly long day.' He flopped a companionable arm over her shoulders which was quite the sea change from the Mr Frosty of this morning.

'Yes, it has,' she agreed, checking her phone for the time. 'Five thirty. We're a couple of powerhouses, you and I.' She held her hand up for a high five and received one in return. He let his hand rest against hers for more than the traditional nanosecond, as if he wanted to convey something deep and meaningful.

'*Dios*, I'm tired,' he said. Then with a stretch of his arms and legs, he pressed himself up to standing. 'C'mon. We better get used to making the most of our daylight hours.'

'Why?'

'The "true *Outlander* experience"? I'm no history expert, but I'm pretty sure they didn't have mobile phones or electricity.'

She gave a sniff. 'Perfect. I have it on excellent authority I look better by candlelight.'

He laughed. 'Oh, really? And how do you think you'll feel about candlelight when it's pouring rain outside and your stone garret is completely freezing cold?'

She pulled a face. 'Less desirable, but also grateful because I won't be able to use my straighteners.' She gave a little shrug that barely registered from the depths of her coat. 'I'm hopeful climate change will be on our side with this one.'

He gave her a side-eye.

She leant in to give him a little shoulder bump. 'Don't worry. I recycle *and* I drive a Prius.'

He gave a short laugh. 'Well done, Greta.'

When they got to the register, Gabe elbowed her out of the way and said to the earthy-looking checkout guy, 'No matter what this woman says, don't take her card.'

'Hey!' She grabbed his wrist. 'You already helped with work. I'm going to pay my own way.'

'No, you're not. This is my treat.'

'For what? Making you drink shots at Hooters?'

The checkout guy kept his eyes down and began fastidiously zapping barcodes.

'No. For convincing me I should do this hare-brained thing.'

'Erm . . . I didn't really do much convincing.'

'You did,' he said.

'How?'

He gave a heavy sigh, peeled her fingers off his wrist and, with surrender hands raised, asked, 'Can you please just let me pay?'

'No, thank you, Richard Gere.'

Gabe shot a *get lost for a minute, could you?* glance at checkout guy, who instantly developed an urgent need to get some more paper bags from another till. He lowered his voice and said, 'I missed a lot of Concha's big moments, okay? Meeting you, her best friend, reminded me of just how much I've missed. And I have to live with that. For ever.'

So he *had* been paying attention when she'd drunkenly run him through just about every picture she'd ever taken of Val and her family.

She nodded for him to continue.

'So . . . since I can't be a big brother to her any more . . . you're just going to have to let me do it for you.'

She was on the brink of snapping back that she already had two big brothers, thank you very much, when a) she remembered she still had two brothers to whine about and b) this was the first time he was openly acknowledging his absence in Valentina's life.

She asked the one question she'd been avoiding all day. 'What made you show up today?'

He laughed and swept a hand through his inky hair. 'The letter from the lawyer said I was being sued by her estate.'

'For what?'

'Breach of contract.' He looked down at his hands then back up at her. 'She included a crayon drawing I'd done for her when we were kids that said "Best Buds Forever".'

Willa cackled. That was definitely a Valentina move. Go big or go home. 'Suing you was the only way she thought you'd show up?'

'Pretty much! Trust my kid sister to be both a hoarder and to know which buttons to press twenty-odd years after we'd last spoken.'

She winced. 'Was it really that long?'

He nodded, his voice choked with regret as he said, 'And I will never, ever forgive myself for it, so let me do this. It's a pathetically small gesture, twenty-two years too late.' He pulled out a black AmEx card and in a completely non-showy way said, 'I think you've figured out I can afford it.'

True. And she would be paying it off in twenty-five-dollar instalments for the next two years, so . . . she offered him her hand to shake and, solely in the spirit of clearing up the whole boundaries/set-up/not a set-up thing asked, 'Does this make me your honorary kid sister?'

Expression implacable, those tiger eyes of his gave her a once over. 'Something like that.'

A swirl of something distinctly unsisterly left a trail of sparkles drifting around her belly.

◆　◆　◆

Courtesy of the forest fires blazing away in Malibu, the sunset down at Venice Beach was breathtakingly beautiful.

'Nice to see you again,' Ancient Chinese Man said, gently shifting his deck of tarot cards towards her on his little portable table. 'I was just about to head home.'

Willa gave him a shy grin. His name wasn't really Ancient Chinese Man. It was Pete Young. But when Valentina and she had first gone to him after the first of many bottomless brunches some seven years ago, he was rocking a Fu Manchu beard and looked like a dried apple. Willa had hooked him up with some sunblock, suggested he shave the few wisps of chin hair, and, since then, The Very Best Card Reader In The Whole of Venice (according to his sign) was looking a very youthful eighty-seven. She'd put money on him dating the patchouli vendor a few stalls down.

'You sure you're okay to stay for one more reading?'

'One?' He looked around, presumably searching for her usual tarot-cards-in-arms friend. When he didn't find her, he closed his eyes in acknowledgement that Val wouldn't be coming any more. When he opened them, she saw compassion, but not pity. Which was nice. Because she'd been throwing herself a big enough pity party these past couple of months to cover the both of them.

'Three card draw?'

'Three cards is good.'

Mind, body, spirit.

He gave her a hard look. 'Is this a new style?'

She looked down at the outfit that had arrived yesterday in a couple of taped-up Porridge Oats boxes from Scotland along with a letter on yellowed paper with swirly text explaining that 'it was kindly requested' for all participants to arrive 'in authentic garments to ensure THE EXPERIENCE was wholly immersive right from the start'.

It was a bit weird that they wanted her to fly in it, but there'd been so much upheaval in her life these past few days, what were a few extra side-eyes going to do her?

The bodicey bit was nice. It was beautifully embroidered and featured a deep red silk that added warmth to her light sepia-coloured skin tone. Courtesy of the dress, she had some serious boobage on display. To the point she wondered if they'd sent the wrong under-blouse with which to offer her some 'maiden modesty'. To be fair, she kind of liked how the outfit accentuated her curves in all the right places. Arrowing in on her waist, then blooming out into a huge, petticoat-accented skirt that, with the chunky heels she'd chosen, made her legs looks super long even though they weren't. It also had a name tag sewn into the waistband that said 'Moira for Pirates' in purple Sharpie which had made her wonder if there was an immersive pirate experience too.

'Cut the deck,' Pete instructed.

She did as she was bid.

He flipped the first card.

They both sucked in a breath.

He flipped the second.

A nervous giggle squawked out of her.

The third nearly undid her.

'Seriously?' she demanded of the cards. 'This is what you're giving me for body, spirit, soul?'

Pete looked at her. 'I thought we were doing past, present, future.'

She looked back down at the cards and wailed, 'It's not great either way, really, is it?'

Pete gave her his usual, Yoda-esque nod that said a thousand things in one. Life works in mysterious ways. What is written is written. Destiny can be a bitch. 'Let's take a look,' he said.

Pointing to the first card, the Three of Swords, he said, 'This can indicate rejection, sadness, loneliness, heartbreak, betrayal, separation and grief.'

'All of them at once?' she asked.

'Yes and no.' Pete gave her hand a pat. 'Ultimately? They point to a loss.' He let her sit with that a moment. 'And then, if you are open to it, a period of renewal.'

'What?' she scoffed. 'Like an ashes to ashes sort of thing?'

'Flowers grow from poop,' Pete said, the waves susurrating along the shore as if in agreement. 'The card can indicate a period of deep understanding. A gaining of knowledge that empowers you to go forward instead of staying mired in the past.'

'Yeah, but . . .' She tapped the next card which showed a turret in flames being blasted by the heavens with lightning as the body of a woman hurtled, headfirst, to the jagged cliffs below.

The Tower.

Her stomach churned. This was bad. Really, really epically bad.

Pete swallowed, thought a moment, then said, 'When someone experiences a loss, it is often the case that they withdraw not only from their regular day-to-day activities, but from themselves. They feel lost. Alone. Leaving that solitary place can be frightening.'

Tell her about it. She was dressed like a yesteryear serving wench and about to board a 777. If that didn't scream Things Willa Would Never Do In A Million Years, she didn't know what did.

'But,' Pete continued, 'as you know from the Death card' – he pointed to her third card – 'Death does not always mean death.'

She dropped her head into her hands. What on earth had possessed her to redirect her Uber driver to Venice? It was a rhetorical question, of course. She knew exactly why she'd come here. It was nothing on earth. It was someone up in heaven. This was a comfort thing she and Val used to do whenever they were dithering about something. They'd come down to the beach. Have brunch by the sea. Sometimes a bit of retro roller skating. Then they'd visit Pete, who always had some wise counsel to offer. Then, bellies full, skin salty from the sea breeze, they'd get in the car and talk and talk and talk on the long drive back inland and, almost always, feel better for it. (The post-cancer diagnosis two years ago had been the toughest one.)

Only this time she wouldn't be driving back home with Valentina. She'd be getting on a plane to Scotland with Val's sexy, estranged brother and a pamphlet with Catalogue Kilt Man.

She looked out to the ocean. The sunset which, moments ago, had seemed so romantic and beautiful now looked like a portal to purgatory. Flames surging up from beneath the horizon to remind all the wretched mortals yet to shuffle off their mortal coils who was really boss here.

'Thanks, Pete.' She gave him a twenty, pulled the handle of her wheelie bag round and aimed it towards Main Street. She shouldered her tote, then gave him what she hoped looked like a brave smile.

'Wait!' he called as she turned. 'Touch the deck. Let's do one more journey card.'

She gave him a doubtful look.

'I'm retiring,' he said. 'I probably won't be here when you get back.'

The news made her instantly and stupidly sad. Could *nothing* stay the same?

Fighting the sting of tears, she put her hand on the proffered deck. He looked into her eyes then flipped the card. He gazed at it awhile, his face unreadable. Then he turned it around with a slow, mischievous smile and said, 'Buckle up.'

Chapter Seven

By the time they'd got through security and into the lounge, Willa was fuming. This, despite the fact Gabe's four gazillion points had got them upgraded to first class.

Not even a glass of champagne delivered with a cheek kiss made her feel less of an idiot than she did now.

'The Princess Leia look suits you,' he said, settling into the armchair across from her.

Instinctively, her hand rose to touch one of her fastidiously whorled braids. They'd taken ages to get just right. She stopped her fingers from tracing the tingly bit of skin his lips had brushed and curled her hands into little balls in her petticoat-augmented skirt.

This was not going to plan.

Instead of enjoying being in first class with a finger-lickingly delicious Gabe (read: her body was lit up like the long-time, unlaid, horn dog), Willa was crackling with annoyance that he hadn't shown up in full regalia.

Why risk her professional welfare at TiTs to honour her best friend's memory if Valentina's *own brother* wasn't going to do the same?

'You read the notes, right?' Willa snipped, giving him a superior look over the rim of her champagne glass as she took a sip, then promptly choked when the champagne bubbles went up her nose. (Class in a glass.)

Gabe bit back a smile.

A low growl surged up her throat.

Just because he looked like a *GQ* model and she looked like something out of Historical-Re-enactments-R-Us was no reason to laugh.

She scraped her teeth along her lips. Hard.

Gabe's long legs were bossing some cranberry-coloured cargo pants no one had any business looking good in. His immaculate white T-shirt was spread across his chest like butter on warm toast and, over that, a half-buttoned green corduroy shirt made those amber eyes of his pop even more brightly than they had the day they'd first met. To cap it all off (ha ha) he was wearing a slouchy beanie hat that should have made him look like an idiot poser, but actually made her want to tease her fingers underneath it for the express purpose of running her hands through his oil-slick-coloured hair and say something ludicrous like, *Take me, tiger. Show me what a beast you really can be,* even though she already knew from one humiliating phone sex experience that erotic bantz was not in her toolbox.

'Gabriel?' she asked, as if he were a naughty schoolboy who'd shown up for soccer practice wearing non-regulation kicks. 'Why are you not in a flowy white top and a kilt?'

He smiled at her and gave his carry-on bag a friendly pat. 'It said we were "kindly requested to be in costume in the arrivals hall . . ."' He paused for dramatic effect. 'In Scotland.'

Oh.

Had it?

Her cheeks burnt with embarrassment.

Maybe it had. She'd been running round like a headless chicken at TiTs and hadn't had brain space for much else.

Without Gabe – her smooth-talking, favours-owing wunder-kind by her side – Willa had been piled high with four billion 'tiny little jobs' before she'd left including (deep breaths moment) . . . *including* bringing newly minted *junior* producer, Bryony Stokes, up to speed.

It hadn't just been a cringe moment. It had been soul crushing.

Not only was Bryony a willowy twenty-something whose studio exec father had landed her the post, she was also a shark. Ambitious, over-confident and prone to say things like, 'Yeah, babes. I'm all over that like gloss on a pucker.'

She was the girl Willa had always wanted to be. The one who knew exactly who she was, what she wanted and how she was going to get it.

'That's us.' Gabe pointed at the ceiling where a soft spa-like voice was gently suggesting people flying to the UK might want to consider making their way to the plane.

Did she want Gabe?

Val seemed to want her to.

But if he was flirting with her? It was so subtle her Spidey-senses weren't picking up on it.

'Can you even believe we're doing this?' she asked, gathering the endless yards of fabric in her skirt before she stood.

'Now that I've met you?' He extended a hand to help her up from her seat. 'I can.'

Wow. Thanks, bud. 'Which means . . . what exactly?'

He smiled a soft, closed-lipped smile. '*Tranquillo, chica.* It means I can see why my sister was friends with you. Good friends are hard to come by in a place like LA. Val always was up for an adventure and I'm glad she had someone to have them with.'

'I'm glad I—' Willa's voice cracked as the sting of tears scraped the back of her throat. This was an adventure they should've shared.

Gabe gave her one of his more penetrating looks then, with a low baritone 'C'mere, you,' pulled her into his arms for a hug.

He smelled delicious. Male and citrussy fresh. Strong and comforting in equal measures.

Once settled in the plane (lavender-scented hand towels disposed of and fresh glasses of fizz in hand), she set about extracting information from him. She thought things were going well until she realised Gabe had deftly flipped the tables on her pretty early in the operation. She still knew next to nothing about him and he knew pretty much everything there was to know about her. Mom and Dad met when they were both in the Marines. After two tours in Iraq, her dad had retired and opened up an auto shop with his dad (Grease Monkey & Son) in Pendleton where her mom joined him after her tours in Iraq and a short stint in Walla Walla, Washington where she'd retrained as a schoolteacher. Two older brothers. Both married to their high-school sweethearts. Dean worked in the auto shop with her dad, and Rob was a probation officer at the local penitentiary. Her brothers also led a 4-H group with their mom.

'4-H?' Gabe asked, as if that was the one thing in her life history monologue that stood out.

'You know? Head, heart, hands, health?'

He shook his head.

'It's a mentoring programme for kids. They do old-fashioned stuff like grow vegetables and can peaches and make pies for the county fair. Farmer stuff mostly, out where I'm from.' She gave an eye-roll to show she might be *from* the country, but she wasn't actually country herself.

'Sounds like you've got a close-knit family,' Gabe said.

She snorted. 'Unless being with them makes you want nothing more than to leave town, sure.'

Gabe frowned.

Willa looked away and drained her champagne. It wasn't an entirely fair comment. Or considerate, seeing as he hadn't seen his own family in twenty-plus years. She may have nothing in common with her family, but when she'd left for the bright lights of LA, they had all gathered on the driveway to give her Tupperware containers of her favourite foods for the long trip, reminders of the best rest stops to use, and waved her off while pulling checked hankies out of their pockets to blow their noses and pretend they weren't crying. They'd been proud of her (and perplexed as to why she couldn't be happy in Pendleton but . . . proud). Gabe's departure, on the other hand, sounded as if it had happened under a searing cloud of white-hot fury.

According to Val, the extended Martinez family were woven too tightly together – there wasn't enough space to know who you actually were. It was why she and Diego decided to move to LA. To find out if they could survive on their own. Make their own mistakes, pick themselves up, learn from them and grow.

Gabe had obviously needed a lot more space. Twenty years' worth.

And she got it. Willa knew first-hand that sometimes the loneliest place in the world was at the dinner table with your own family.

'Do you want another one?' she asked Gabe as the flight attendant approached them.

He shook his head and pointed at a bottle of sparkling water he'd picked out of the bank of mini fridges when they'd first come in. 'I want to get some sleep.'

Oh.

That was disappointing.

Clearly sensing it wasn't the answer she'd been hoping for, Gabe put on an appalling Scottish accent, 'So I can be at my rugged best for you when we land, lassie.'

58

Then he put up the divider between them leaving her to her own devices.

She sat back and took a sip of her drink, the fizz barely landing in her stomach before she grew restless.

She unbuckled her seatbelt, pretending she needed to get something from the overhead locker so she could steal a fresh glimpse of him. With his eyes closed and a careful 'do not disturb' expression arranged on his features, he seemed just out of reach. It was difficult to imagine how he'd look in yesteryear gear. Even trickier to picture him all rough and tumble. She squinted, trying to add in some stubble along his clean-shaven jawline, picture a crooked tooth appearing when he smiled, replacing his aquiline nose with one that might've been broken while taming a fierce stallion or defending a maiden's honour against a marauding pirate. Something – anything, really – to make him just a bit more . . . mortal.

'He's a bit of alright, isn't he?' came a male whisper in her ear.

She turned and met the wolfish smile of a flight attendant.

'Is that one with you?'

'Ish?' She wasn't really sure. 'No. Yes?'

'Oooh,' meowed the flight attendant, taking away her glass and pointing to the 'fasten seatbelt' sign. 'I would.'

She flashed him a playful *who wouldn't?* smile, then buckled herself back in.

She would. Right?

Maybe the better question was, would he?

Even though he made her tummy flutter, she got the feeling the butterfly faeries weren't swirling round Gabe. Maybe once they were away from all of the hullabaloo of LA and their cell phones were out of signal and they were bathed in candlelight as they ate . . . erm . . . some haggis . . . they'd feel more comfortable.

It slaughtered her that she couldn't just pick up the phone and ask Val what she'd been thinking when she'd booked this trip.

She was pretty sure her bestie wouldn't have wanted her to have to squint at her intended to make him seem more like someone she'd actually date.

She almost felt the accompanying finger flick on her arm as Val's voice popped into her head.

Stop overthinking things, bendita. *Just be!*

It was a fair comment. But, also, at odds with real life.

She had imagined this – being on the plane with Gabe – down to the finest details. The mile-high cocktail buzz. The compartmentalised food. The cascades of giggles they'd have to suppress as they took turns popping peanuts into one another's mouths. She'd seen it perfectly. How they would settle back in their chairs (economy plus had been as far as her dream had extended) and spend the flight talking about their hopes and dreams. When they'd exhausted themselves from all of that soul-quenching bonding, he'd shyly, but organically, offer her his shoulder to sleep on and then when she woke up in his lap he would be stroking her hair and gazing into her eyes. She'd feel like a princess and he'd be her prince and they'd get married in a castle in Scotland just like Madonna and she wouldn't have to spend the rest of her life worrying about making the most of ten-to-fifteen minute interviews with celebrities who didn't give a flying monkey's about her.

Since that wasn't happening and they were in first class, she exploited every nugget of the high life she could.

Three face masks, one pedicure, a sinus-cleansing Bloody Mary and two cheeseboards later, she and her new bestie, Marcus the flight attendant, hugged it out before he excused himself to make last calls for the toilet before landing in Scotland.

Gabe disappeared without so much as a glance in her direction, but when he came back . . . his twirl and smile knocked her breathless.

Woweeeeeewowowowowowoowowoweeeeewow.

Gabe in a kilt was pulse-quickeningly gorgeous. And Willa was openly gawking. The ghillie top – a loose blousy thing with a wide V-neck – fitted his shoulders and physique as if he'd been born to it. The leather thong that criss-crossed the gap from his sternum up to his throat was hanging loose, all but begging her to yank it free to make it easier for her to rip the top in two so she could rub her hands all over his smooth, golden chest. The kilt itself, a green and dark blue number, hung on his hips as if an adoring seamstress had stitched it exactingly into place. Working their way down, her eyes hungrily latched on to a scrumptious bit of leg that kept appearing as he stretched and reached for their things. And then she worked her way back up again because it had been so pleasurable a journey.

'Nice handbag,' she said, fingers twitching to stroke the furry exterior of his . . . sporran, was it?

'You like?' He offered the sporran some slick hand manoeuvres, as if he was modelling a twenty-thousand-dollar watch and not a fake-fur covered man-pouch atop his actual man pouch.

'I like,' she managed, hoping she wasn't drooling, because it certainly felt like she was.

He winked at her, then, after they'd landed, busied himself with getting her tote down even though one of the flight attendants was standing right there, quite obviously enjoying the show as much as she was.

She shot a grin up to heaven and sent a mental text to Val. *You do know he's well out of my league, right?*

As if she had literally said it, she heard Val shoot back, *You do know you're an idiot for thinking anyone is out of your league, right? You're a* catch, *mija. The only one who can't see it is* you.

'You okay?' Gabe's forehead was creased with concern, clearly wondering why tears had suddenly bloomed in her eyes.

'Yup! Great.' She swiped at her face. 'I just misted.' She dug into her clear plastic bag of liquids, pulled out a mini face mister and gave her face a squirt. 'So good for the skin.' She popped on her best *let's get crackin'* face. 'C'mon. Time to meet our fellow outlanders.'

After passport control, baggage claim and customs had been cleared, Willa's nerves kicked in. Travelling thousands of miles to a foreign country to pretend to live in Jacobean times wasn't a skill base she had in her wheelhouse.

Again, she heard Val's voice sing out loud and clear: *It's no weirder than interviewing famous people for a handful of minutes and pretending it's made all of your dreams come true.*

Shut up! she play-shouted in her head, as she gave her bodice an aggressive tug to shift it back into place. Dead or alive, Val knew how to hit a nerve sometimes.

'Alright, my pretty,' Gabe said in combo pirate-Scottish voice. 'Are you prepared to bewitch the masses?'

She grinned up at him, relieved to feel that click of connection cinch back into place.

Val was right. This was a trip of firsts. Why not let herself simply enjoy the experience with an open heart and mind?

It was the first time she'd gone on a proper vacation with someone. A sexy someone, no less. To a castle. A castle she'd never seen for an immersive experience in a television show she'd proactively avoided, but . . . she was with Gabe. What could possibly go wrong?

Chapter Eight

When they hit the arrivals hall, Willa scanned the crowd, her eyes almost instantly lighting on a small group of women wearing similar style dresses and an Idris Elba lookalike in a red kilt, all standing by a coffee shop. One of the women saw her and Gabe and pointed. The group opened up, steering large wheelie bags out of the way until, in their midst, she saw another man holding a handwritten sign on a bit of cardboard that read 'Balcraigie Castle'.

Her heart flew into her throat then dropped back into her chest where it began whirling round like a Tasmanian devil in heat.

It was Catalogue Kilt Man.

And he was even better than she'd imagined.

Big, open, kind face and features. An instinctive smile. Freckles. One, two, three on her perfect man tick-list.

A buzzing in her ears drowned everything out but him as the rest of her body went into overdrive. Sweaty palms. Quickened breath. Goosepimples. The full gamut of ohmygawd-he's-so-hot-he's-giving-me-palpitations movie responses.

She'd kept Catalogue Kilt Man's picture on her bedside table for the last couple of nights to serve as a warm-up act while she got used to the idea of fantasising about Gabe. It had made sense on the premise that Catalogue Kilt Man did not actually exist.

Catalogue Kilt Man was tall and fit. Not so much tall and lean as broad and solid. Like a Nordic wood chopper. His expression was kind, if not slightly perplexed. He wasn't strictly Marvel-hero handsome but could believably be cast as one of Thor's cousins. Half-brother? He was hot. To her anyway. He was wearing worn blue cords and a greeny-brown sweater with a neckline that allowed for a peek at a checked shirt collar. His waxed jacket looked like it had been in a smackdown with a mountain goat. And somehow his flat cap made him look ravageable rather than a poser. His eyes, after a few blinks, were like a sunlit stormy ocean, which seemed strangely fitting because while he didn't look entirely happy, he did look relieved, as if, just maybe, she was a rainbow appearing through a dark gathering of clouds.

The waves of his caramel-coloured hair were suddenly and unexpectedly backlit by rays of late afternoon sunshine pouring through the high windows of the arrivals hall. If a choir of heavenly angels began to sing the Hallelujah Chorus, she would not have been surprised.

And then he smiled.

Willa's pounding heart skipped a beat. *Sweet cheeses and a fruit platter.* Catalogue Kilt Man had a gap between his front teeth. She didn't know why, but that particular dental flaw was one of the sexiest things she'd ever seen. She stared, mesmerised as his upper teeth pressed down on his full, lower lip and scraped along the length of it as if he too was wondering what she'd taste like if he licked her. Not that she was into licking, but if someone turned the man into a lollipop, she'd want to buy them in bulk.

All of which was completely at odds with the fact that her best friend had sent her here to get it on with Gabe. Right?

Even so, she was gripped by a desperate, urgent need to learn everything about Catalogue Kilt Man.

She wasn't the type of woman who dabbled in a pool of men, picking and choosing from them as if they were a bowl of Skittles. Her flirtation techniques were sketchy at best. And more to the point, men like these rarely chose women like her. This wasn't a case of divide and conquer. This was a throw-your-ovaries-into-one-basket scenario and pray like hell you'd made the right decision.

What was she meant to do? Stay true to what she thought her best friend wanted or go with what her gut was telling her in the here and now?

She was only a few feet away.

It was hardly the time to put up a finger and ask everyone for a few moments while she pawed through her luggage, read the letter, absorbed its contents, redid her makeup (because she'd definitely cry, even if it turned out to be a shopping list), and then gifted a smile to her preferred suitor.

What little she knew about Gabe she really, really liked. And not just because he came in above-par packaging. Beneath the coolly gruff exterior, he was kind. He knew her world and didn't judge her poorly for it. Most importantly, he was the only remaining link she had to Valentina.

On the flipside, Catalogue Kilt Man reminded her of home in a way that didn't make her want to run for the hills. He exuded gentleness and strength. Good humour and grace. As if he'd laugh at dad jokes – like he'd *make* dad jokes – but know the difference between teasing and hurting, advice and unwelcome counsel.

Who knew that perfect could come in two entirely different sets of packaging?

Her bosom strained against her corset to the point she now understood exactly why women passed out in costume dramas. Their clothes were holding their emotions hostage. And she was feeling all of the Technicolour feels right now.

Absurd angst that Gabe hadn't announced his intentions to fall deeply, irrevocably in love with her.

Extreme distress that Catalogue Kilt Man wasn't striding towards her, dropping to one knee and declaring himself.

Utter bewilderment that hormones were overruling her usual pragmatic approach to life. She was a girl who loved charts and lists and order.

Was this what Valentina had wanted for her? Emotions running amok like unicorns in a pastel field of clover? She often encouraged Willa to loosen up, but . . . had she meant for her to completely overhaul her concept of emotional safety?

She was about to find out.

'Hi,' she said to Catalogue Kilt Man in a wispy voice she didn't quite recognise. 'I'm Willa.'

'Finlay Jamieson,' he said, eyes still very much glued to hers. 'Umm . . . tiny bit awkward, but . . .' His eyes dipped swiftly down then up again, as if trying to communicate something urgent to her.

'Hmmm . . . ?' she said dreamily.

Finlay's stormy blue eyes bored into hers, pleading for her to understand something very, very important, and while there was definitely a part of her that wanted to believe he was trying to tell her that he had just fallen deeply and irrevocably in love with her . . . she had the very uncomfortable feeling it was something else altogether.

Which was precisely the moment she realised she was suffering from an epic costume failure.

Her boobs, much to her horror, had popped up and out of her bodice. Even more horrifying was the hot pink, erect state of her nipples. 'Oh, fuck no!' she screamed just as Finlay pressed a hand-kerchief to her boobs. She must've been twisting round and away from him at precisely the moment his hand made contact with her chest because now, to their mutual alarm, his hand was tangled in the front lacing of her bodice along with his handkerchief. Far too mortified to derive even a nanosecond's perverse pleasure at the contact, she pulled back and stumbled violently into the luggage trolley, which knocked over Gabe – who, despite some rather impressive flailing, collided with a clutch of hipster Japanese women's enormous wheelie bags before crashing to the ground with a sickening thunk.

Finlay was by Gabe's side in an instant, laying him out flat. 'The handkerchief.' He made a give it to me gesture with his hand as the Japanese women pulled out their phones and began snapping pictures.

While hoicking up her bodice to contain her D-cups, she handed him the handkerchief. Finlay pressed it to Gabe's hairline. It instantly turned scarlet.

Oh god. She'd killed Gabe. Sinking to her knees across from Finlay she whispered, 'Did I crack his head open?'

'It's just a cut,' Finlay said calmly but firmly. In a stupidly delicious accent. He pressed two fingers to the nook just below Gabe's marble-hewn jawline. 'His pulse is a bit thready, but he's probably just knocked himself out for a wee bit. We should get the first responders—'

'I'm calling 911,' said the Idris Elba lookalike, pulling an enormous phone out of his sporran. 'I'm Jeff, by the way.' He put out a hand for Finlay to shake and then, clocking that he was busy holding the handkerchief to Gabe's bleeding head, gave him a little salute instead.

'Anyone got smelling salts?' shouted another one of their group, in a loud Australian accent. 'Pretty sure they would've used those back in the day.'

'I think they're called spirits of ammonia,' said another woman, whose accent Willa couldn't place.

'It's 999 here,' said a blonde woman in an English accent she'd heard before when she'd binge-watched the British baking show. 'My daughter, Jules, is ringing them.'

'There'll be volunteer first responders here at the airport,' Finlay said. 'Perhaps one of you can find an emergency phone and ring them?'

Willa opened her mouth to panic scream that she didn't want volunteer first responders, she wanted a team of crack surgeons, when she remembered that her father and brother were both volunteer firemen and that, when it came to a crisis, you really didn't care who showed up, so long as someone did. Preferably in a uniform.

To be fair, she was feeling strangely safe and secure with Finlay in charge.

His eyes were even more amazing up close. A beautiful blue-grey that spoke to a depth of character she instantly wanted to explore. He'd *seen* things and *done* things and had learnt from them. Quite the contrast to her world of film stars who had called upon people like Gabe to sort out their mistakes, no matter how frequently they committed them.

He exuded calm, assured control. Exactly the way you'd want someone to be in a crisis. His voice alone felt like having warm caramel poured down her spine. A bit too arousing at a moment when she shouldn't be finding anything erotic apart from Gabe, who still managed to look breathtakingly beautiful even though he was bleeding and possibly never going to be able to use his brain again.

All of which sent her heart rate rocketing, as if she was a carnival goldfish accidentally dropped from its clear baggie on to the dusty ground, desperately trying to take deep, gulping breaths, none of them successfully filling her lungs with the requisite oxygen.

'Hey.' Finlay's voice broke through her panic. 'You're alright. Breathe steady now. C'mon. There you are. Look at me. Right into my eyes. We don't want the two of you in an ambulance now, do we? Steady now. That's it, lass. One . . . two . . . nice and slow . . . three . . . That's it . . . steady now.'

Finlay was putting her into a trance. A strong, capable man-in-a-crisis-rising-to-the-occasion trance. The emotional equivalent of a perfectly grilled cheese sandwich and steaming mug of tomato soup.

It was a brand new sensation to feel so . . . focused upon. As if he really cared whether or not she launched into a full-blown panic attack. Especially with Gabe breathing his last between them. She was usually the capable one. The type of girl who, at best, received a pat on the shoulder and a 'You're alright, aren't ya, Wills?'

If he was secretly hypnotising her to quack like a duck, she was strangely fine with that.

His eyes cut away from hers.

One of the Japanese tourists was waving to him to move out of the way so she could sit next to Gabe and have her picture taken. A near dead, very hot Latino in a kilt wasn't one of your everyday sights, but . . . really?

Finlay, still holding the compress, rose up to his knees, and with a fluid, authoritative air said to the gathering crowd, 'Alright, everyone, let's give the poor man some space.' To Willa, he said, 'Press down on this for me, would you?' His eyes sought hers. 'Do you think you can do that, Willa?'

Uhhh. Was he serious?

'You just hold it down, not too hard, alright?'

Clearly, he was.

And in the time it would take a normal person to say, 'Sure thing!', a red mist descended.

Sure. She may have been on the brink of a panic attack a moment ago, but of all the things Willa hated most in life, being patronised was top of the list. Not because she was paranoid about her intellect – she was fine with her level of brain power. But being spoken to as if she couldn't follow a set of simple instructions was an instant trigger, transporting her back to her childhood. A lifetime really, of her family speaking to her as if she was unable to differentiate between Real World Problems and Fictional Problems predicated on the basis that she liked television.

Now, she didn't have it on excellent authority that belittling her was Finn's main goal. (He seemed like a Finn now. If he could speak to her using toddler words, she could give him a nickname.) Maybe he thought she was overtired. Perhaps he could sense the headache creeping in courtesy of too many in-flight beverages. Or maybe, because it certainly had sounded that way, he did think she was stupid.

Whatever his motives they no longer factored. Shunting every single pleasant thing she'd thought about him did. And really, now that she thought about it? He reminded her just a little bit too much of home.

'Yeah,' she answered tersely. 'I think I can just about rustle up the ability to hold a cloth.'

He stared at her with an intensity she couldn't identify, then gave a particularly irritating fair-enough shrug, got up, ushered away the tourists and asked the rest of the group to form a protective luggage shield around Gabe. As they gathered round, the fifty-something blonde woman from their group approached and introduced herself as Jennifer. She untwisted her beautiful shawl-wrappy thing from her shoulders and tucked it over Willa's shoulders with a practised motherly pat. 'For your maiden modesty,' she whispered kindly.

Willa's cheeks turned scarlet. Her boobs had escaped again. And with fabulous timing. Right in the middle of her self-righteous snippery to Finn.

Awesome. Just what she wanted. An assured place in the Top Ten Idiot Americans list.

'Should we put honey or something on the wound?' asked the young woman sporting some amazing rainbow-coloured hair. 'I think that's what Claire would've done.'

'Claire?' Willa asked, rather than 'honey?' Which would have been the more pertinent question.

'You know. Claire of Jamie and Claire in *Outlander*?' prompted Jennifer.

She caught Finlay giving her another one of those, are-you-sure-there's-a-brain-in-your-head looks.

Asshole.

'I'm in training to become a white witch,' said rainbow-hair girl, then stuck out her hand. 'Jules.'

Willa, one hand very ably holding the blood-soaked handkerchief to Gabe's forehead, took her proffered hand and shook it. Were they really were going to take this particular moment to play What Would Claire Do? Before she could ask, Jules looked up and said, 'Oh cool! Paramedics.'

◆ ◆ ◆

By the time the ambulance crew left, the sun had set, Gabe had regained consciousness, the cut on his forehead had been stitched and they'd all been given a sombre lecture on how to identify signs of a concussion.

Willa had also had time for her blood to heat up to boiling point. How could she have missed Finn's very obvious *I'm better than you* aura? Jetlag. Clearly. Nothing to do with the fact he was so good-looking her entire reproductive system had been liquified into hot sauce.

Because she was obviously a deeply mature woman above engaging in petty squabbles, she used her lifelong love of *Grey's Anatomy* to ask the paramedics some additional, *I already know this but I'm asking for the benefit of the group* type questions about subdural haematomas so that Finn knew she was well aware of the gravity of the situation and also to make it clear her vocabulary was polysyllabic even under duress, thank you very much.

'Alright, everyone.' Finn made a follow-me gesture, meeting everyone's eyes apart from hers. 'Now that you've all enjoyed the delights of Glasgow International, let's get you up the road to Balcraigie, shall we?'

Exhaustion overtook her as the group trooped like jolly little ducklings behind Finlay's broad stretch of shoulders towards the car park. The only thing that kept her from turning round and running back to the terminal, demanding entry on to the plane she'd just disembarked, was her promise to her bestie.

That, and the lure of Balcraigie Castle. Which, Finn informed them, was pronounced Bal-creg-ie.

When they checked in, she was going to order room service, take an insanely long bubble bath with whatever lush amenities were there and try her best to wash Finn out of her hair. Since he was the driver, they'd most likely never see him again and that suited her to a tee. Then, with any luck, everyone would develop a full-blown case of amnesia, and she and Gabe could start tomorrow afresh. Including Jennifer, who gratefully accepted her shawl back after Willa unearthed her new coat from her suitcase. Gabe had been right. It was cold here.

After passing a number of executive-style minivans with blacked-out windows, Finn stopped in front of a very battered-looking, moss green Land Rover Discovery with . . . *oh dear god* . . . a canvas-covered back that was going to be no protection against the increasingly chilly weather.

He held his hand out. 'Here we are, then.'

Willa tugged her new winter coat round her and shivered.

It was the kind of vehicle that, had it been in better condition, would have been used to drive the queen around her Scottish estate when she went hunting. In its current state, she doubted a sheep would see it as a cosy alternative to standing, say, unprotected on a barren moor in the middle of a blizzard.

When he opened up the back, a tumble of orange twine, straw and other mystery items fell out. Suffice it to say, nothing about this vehicle screamed Property of the Laird. Then again, if they were being truly immersive, she supposed, Finn would've shown up on a horse.

To her surprise, everyone else in the group thought the vehicle was absolutely wonderful.

Beneath the cheery cries of 'So *authentic*,' and 'I feel like I'm in another country,' and a giggled, 'You *are* in another country,' Finn got to work.

'Right!' he said, his tongue sexily running over his Rs and landing on his Ts like they were popping candy. 'If you hand me your luggage, I'll just pop everyone's bags on to the roof rack, okay?'

His eyes skidded across the group, giving everyone an encouraging smile until they landed on Willa, at which point his rather beautiful mouth turned in on itself and he looked away.

McBastard.

'Wow!' said Jeff, still glowing from his extensive photoshoot with the Japanese tourists who, it turned out, were also booked on an *Outlander* tour. 'This old jalopy looks like she's been through a few generations.'

Willa caught a look of surprise in Finlay's eyes and a softening in his voice as he ran his hand along the side of it with a soft, 'Yes. Well. A couple. It was my father's.'

The group *ooo*-ed and *ahhh*-ed and, using Finlay's big hand as a ballast, climbed into the back. Finlay said nothing more about it, but Willa was certain she'd heard what no one else had. He didn't have his father any more and more than anything, he desperately wished he did.

She closed the fissure of warmth trying to creep through her Ice Queen act. The last thing she wanted was a legitimate reason to empathise with Mr McTall Dark and Handsome.

◆ ◆ ◆

Three hours into the drive, Willa learnt that the six strangers she was jammed together with made up the entire group. She also learnt more about them than she knew about people she had worked with for years (excluding Finn, who was silently and fastidiously focusing on his driving. Gabe, also in the front, was oblivious to it all. He was sleeping like a baby beneath a tartan picnic blanket with Jeff's neck pillow as buffering against any further bumps to his head).

Snippets of their conversation hung in the air like wish lists.

Men in kilts who did housekeeping.

Men in kilts who were strippers.

Men in kilts who would defend your honour no matter how vile the enemy.

There were many fantasies about men in kilts.

One of whom was sitting among them. Baltimore Jeff, who gave a detailed explanation about his kilt's warrior tartan (of the McSnood clan), was married to Arizona Rosa. They were late forty-somethings who lived in Tucson, which, they announced with pride, had an excellent selection of burrito bars and about a dozen of Rosa's nieces and nephews. At the apex of his career as a structural engineer ('Jeff can put his hands to anything and come up with magic!') and hers as a glassblower, they devoted their out-of-work hours to their passions in the following order:

1) Their shared tantric sex needs
2) Renaissance faires
3) *Outlander*

They'd married late, 'missed the children boat', but had found one another. Soulmates brought together at the Sherwood Forest Faire in Texas. Rosa had been fleeing a group of masked bandits when Jeff had scooped her up on to the back of his horse as if she'd been made of air 'and that was that'. He was, to this day, her knight in shining armour.

Jennifer and Jules Brookland were a mother-daughter pair from the south coast of England. Jennifer looked, in her own words, 'completely mumsy despite Jules's many attempts to do something hip' with her but was hoping this trip would give her some inspiration. Jules had a unicorn-coloured mane of hair, was a loud and proud lesbian but open to pansexuality, and had studied medieval history at Bristol. They were the best of friends, superfans of both the *Outlander* books and the show, and had been saving all year for this – Jennifer from her job at a local Tesco and Jules from her job as an assistant outreach officer at a bakery founded and run by women who'd been through the prison system (and, no, Jules had not been arrested unless you counted the numerous Extinction Rebellion marches when she'd been corralled into police vans to clear the streets). They both wrote fan fiction and were beside themselves with excitement.

Then there was Fenella O'Callahan and ChiChi Orakwe, friends from an online *Outlander* study group who'd met in real life for the first time at Glasgow airport.

ChiChi was originally from Nigeria but had relocated to England to study first at Oxford and then at Cambridge. She was in the throes of completing a PhD in astrophysics.

'What's your thesis?' asked Jeff, completely enthralled.

'Time travel?' Rosa asked, dropping a wink to the group.

'In a way,' ChiChi replied. 'I'm looking at supersymmetry and its relationship to observation. I've been focusing on the constraints imposed on dark matter and statistical issues.'

'I can help you make that short and sweet,' quipped Jules with a laugh.

'How do you mean?' ChiChi asked in her lovely lilting accent.

Jules clapped her hands together, then placed them on the tops of her thighs. 'Well, how about this?' She changed her voice to sound lofty. 'For centuries men have gathered the statistics and as such, they are men-centric. Ergo . . . skewed. Ergo? Wrong. The end.' She grinned at the group and they all, including ChiChi laughed, saying she'd save a fortune on printer ink if she chose that approach.

Fenella was Australian born and bred to 'an Aussie-Irish dad and Thai mum'. She'd grown up on her dad's family's cattle station 'back in the ass-end of nowhere'. She said her goal was to leave Balcraigie with a ring on her finger. 'I plan on taking advantage of Gretna Green's loose marital laws.'

'Outrageously exploitative laws, you mean,' said Jules with a huff. 'What sort of heathen country passes a law saying it's okay to marry twelve-year-old girls? Oh, wait – would that be a country with men in charge?'

ChiChi raised her hand. 'Actually, I think you'll find underage marriage is still prevalent in a number—' she began just as Jennifer launched into a detailed explanation about how the law in Scotland had changed some time ago and, if Fenella was serious, she'd have to register an intent to wed straight away because Scotland required fifteen days' notice. To which Jules, horrified, asked, 'Mum? Why would you know something like that?'

Jennifer said nothing more on the matter.

'And what about you, honey?' Rosa cut in before the awkward silence grew too long. She gave Willa a little pat on the knee. 'What brings you to Scotland?'

This was the part of these getting-to-know-you sessions that always sent Willa into a panic. She didn't like people to know things about her. Not because she had a collection of skeletons waiting to tumble out of the closet or anything, it was more . . . at twenty-nine years of age, she still wasn't a hundred per cent sure who she was. In LA no one cared, they just wanted to know what you did, so . . . up until now she was what she did: an entertainment news producer. But here, far away from the studios and junkets and floodlights criss-crossing the sky at yet another premiere, she found it impossible to describe herself.

One solitary word fell into her head with a thunk.

Lost.

It was a start. But how else to describe herself? Shameless? She'd already flashed this group her boobs, nearly killed her maybe/maybe not lawfully intended and acted like a show-off with her subdural haematomas after Finn had unwittingly flicked her please-don't-talk-down-to-me switches.

She definitely wasn't going to admit she was here because of her and Val's ongoing feud about whether or not being an *Outlander* superfan was a waste of valuable time. Now, more than ever, Willa wished she could pull the spent calendar pages out of the trash so they could boxset binge together. Something, anything, to get back those precious hours she should have spent with Val. She'd never get a do-over for that decision and, frankly, deserved the shame that came with it.

'Well . . . erm,' she stuttered, glancing up at the front of the vehicle where Gabe was still asleep. To her surprise, Finn's eyes were flicking up to the rear-view mirror as if he too wanted to hear why she was here.

She looked away and announced lightly, if not a tiny bit dishonestly, 'It was a gift.'

'From your boyfriend?' Jennifer gave her a saucy wink. Or it might've been a bit of straw caught in her eye. It was hard to tell because it was getting really dark in the back of the jeep.

'Are you going to have a shag fest under the Scottish stars like Jamie and Claire?' Fenella asked in a really loud stage whisper before Willa could explain that not only was Gabe not her boyfriend, but he was also unlikely to speak to her again now that she had scarred him for life. Sure, the chunk of thick, ebony hair they'd had to shave off would grow back, but if he ever went bald? There'd be a scar and she the reason for it.

Not that someone as beautiful as Gabe couldn't make a scar look sexy. But after the airport fiasco? Actual amnesia was their most likely path to true love.

The car began to slow down and, when it turned on to an earth track, conversation, mercifully, turned to what lay ahead.

Chapter Nine

Finn had turned into a bamstick. There was no other way to explain it. How else could he explain his involvement in this shambolic, cockamamie, class-A taking of the Michael?

Saying that, he had to hand it to Orla. Of all of the bonkers schemes she'd come up with through the years, this one definitely took the cake.

His dad would—

He cut the thought short. What his dad thought didn't matter any more.

The fact that Finn had come running when Orla had cried wolf for the umpteenth time did.

When would he learn? He'd walked away once, twice, then a half dozen other times, and every time he came back it made leaving again that much harder.

His eyes flicked up to the rear-view mirror and snagged with Willa's. Her dark eyes were catching the light of the moon, giving her an air of wisdom beyond her years. Her expression, however, was impossible to read. Evil, murderous, #MeToo thoughts no doubt.

She was probably composing a mental letter of complaint about him. Which was fair enough. He'd write it himself given half a chance. How the hell his hand had got stuck in her—

He scrubbed a hand over his face. Trust him to accidentally cop a feel of the first woman in he-didn't-know-how-long to catch his eye.

Anyway, whether or not he fancied her was a moot point. She was taken and lived in LA.

With any luck, when Orla heard about it, she'd send him back to Inverness and he could get on with his life, pretending this whole debacle had never happened.

He bumped through the first of many potholes begging to be tended to. Maybe one of them would jolt his brain back into proper functioning order. Then he could do what he'd intended to do in the first place: send all these good people home.

Chapter Ten

Willa forced herself to look away. Again. Staring into Finn's North Sea eyes kept making her forget how much she wanted to dislike him.

As steady and kind as he appeared, there was definitely something he was withholding from them. A wariness she couldn't put her finger on.

He was probably a serial killer. Only murderers pulled off busy roads and on to deserted creepy ones like this.

She thought of the lonely stretch of highway leading to the dirt track she'd grown up at the end of and dismissed the thought instantly. That was different. American serial killers were always missing a tooth or had a haunting minor-chord cackle or . . . uh oh . . . were desperately good-looking and liked to start cults.

'Ooof!' Rosa bounced off the bench seat as the Defender crashed through yet another puddle. 'Bumpy!'

'I'm sure potholes are just the start of the authentic experience,' laughed Jeff, protectively cupping one of his mammoth hands over his wife's head after his own head conked the metal roof frame for the third time.

'It certainly smells authentic,' Jennifer said, waving her hand in front of her nose. 'What is that?'

No one else knew.

Willa did.

It was freshly tilled soil after a light rain. It was pine needles and sap. And something else earthy and floral she couldn't quite identify. But she knew the source. It was exactly what Finlay smelt like. She'd breathed him in like oxygen when he'd talked her down from her out-of-character panic attack. Taken in each scent, breath by breath, as if she were inhaling an aura of peace and calm that she could carry round with her like a balm. And then she remembered he was a judgemental know-it-all who was plotting mass murder and just like that she was cured of finding his personal man scent to her liking.

An energetic hush fell over them as the headlights illuminated two large stone pillars, then the vehicle pulled to a stop in front of a handful of large rocks. When he switched the light off, there was complete darkness.

'Are these the standing stones?' Rosa clapped her hands in excitement.

'Looks more like where you're supposed to park.'

'Where's the castle?'

'Are we going to get candles?'

'Should we wake up Gabriel?'

'The paramedic said he should rest.'

'What if he misses out on something . . . like the redcoats attacking? It'd be a shame for him to die so quickly after arriving.'

'No one's going to attack us. This isn't Jacobite paintball.'

Comments and questions streamed from the guests as Willa watched Finlay climb out of the jeep and come round the back to open the door for them.

One by one he offered his hand to them until, at last, it was Willa's turn. She half expected him to about face and run away, but the opposite happened. His expression softened into a gentle smile. 'I hope that wasn't too bumpy a ride for you.'

'It was fine.' Her ass would be bruised for days. But she wasn't going to tell him that.

Just as she began to make a show of wanting to climb down without his help, a surreal squawking noise broke through the evening hush. She grabbed his shoulder. 'What was that?'

He grinned and put a finger to his lips. 'Just wait.'

She froze in place, unable (unwilling?) to release her grip on Finlay's rather impressive musculature, while she and the other guests tried to figure out what and where the sound came from. (Stockholm Syndrome, and so soon!)

And then, as if someone had retuned an enormous celestial radio, the moon appeared from behind the clouds and at last Willa identified the sound. It was bagpipes.

To her surprise, the music was beautiful. It was also loud. Physically saturating her nervous system. As she grew accustomed to the music and began to fall into the melody, she closed her eyes, allowing her cell structure to succumb to the tug of another time and place. A lifestyle that was simpler to navigate. One where life largely existed between the rising and setting of the sun. She felt stupidly drawn to it. Stupid because it was, effectively, the life she'd left behind in Oregon.

'You alright, there?'

She opened her eyes to see Finlay sending her a questioning look. For a minute she forgot she hated him and, releasing her vice grip on his shoulder, put her hand in his extended one. As their palms touched, pure, electric heat poured through her as he helped her down from the jeep. How could it not? Everything about this moment – the moonlight, the music, the giddy freedom of not having to come up with three segments on Top Celeb Crop Tops and, of course, the divinely gorgeous (murdery) Catalogue Kilt Man – was magical.

For the first time in forever she ached for this vacation to be what it was promising: a journey to somewhere she didn't have to check her socials every five seconds, her cell phone every three, or worry about her weight/hair/manicures, etc for the rest of the time.

With each step towards the earth, she felt closer to a place where she could simply be.

The air smelt of woodsmoke, herbs and rich, loamy earth. There was a spiky tang of mystery cloaked around them, and, despite the night sky, she could also hear the sound of birdsong echo through the air.

It really did remind her of home. But with bagpipes.

A wave of nostalgia for something she hadn't realised she'd missed crashed into her like a truck.

Her response must've been physical because she felt Finlay's hand tighten its grip on hers. Her eyes shot to his and he looked as if he was about to say something, but before he could, two large spotlights flared to life, illuminating a teenage girl playing the bagpipes. She was in full Scottish regalia. Kilt, knee-high socks, a black felt hat with a white feather standing proud, an array of brooches and criss-cross belts and an impressively furry sporran.

Willa watched the girl intently, rapt by her focus and very open pleasure at playing—

What *was* that song? She closed her eyes again. It was probably a hallucination, or an earthquake, but the music seemed to travel through the ground and vibrate through her feet, up her legs and into her spine, rising like mercury in a thermometer right up into her very jet-lagged brain until she knew exactly what the song was.

'Amazing Grace'.

And how sweet it sounded. She would've never taken herself for a bagpipe fan, but maybe it was one of those right-place-right-time things. Only when she realised some of her fellow travellers were whispering and pointing did she take in the bigger picture.

The piper was standing in front of a huge, vegetation rich, stone ruin. She'd seen it before. In a pencilled outline on the brochure. All of which meant . . . this was Balcraigie Castle.

Pieces of a puzzle she hadn't had time to put together over the past few days began to fall into place.

Catalogue Kilt Man was real. And Balcraigie Castle was real. But neither of them had materialised in the form she'd anticipated.

Finn had come in a better-than-she-imagined/serial killer package. Confusing, but, for aesthetics alone, three points to Val.

The castle?

Nil points.

From this angle, it wasn't so much a castle as a majestically formed pile of rocks. With windows.

She shot Finn an *is that it?* look.

His expression turned pained.

Before a dark, gnawing need to scream *Take me back to the airport now!* could set in, a delightfully plump, ruddy-cheeked woman in her mid-thirties appeared. She was hardy-looking in a way that suggested if someone asked her to make thirty blackbird pies by sunrise she'd smile and get on with it. She was wearing a dark blue version of the female guests' dresses and was wiping her hands on a huge food-stained pinafore, her features wreathed in an open, happy smile. She was alight with positive energy.

'Finlay! There you are! I'd thought for a wee while you'd absconded with our guests, you rascal!'

There was an edge to the comment. One usually reserved for family. (Or murderers.)

To her shock, Willa's heart fell in on itself. Catalogue Kilt Man was married. Not that she wanted him for herself, but she had

dreamt about him just enough to make letting go of her precon-
ceived notion of him akin to detaching dog fur from Velcro.

A thought occurred. Maybe the reason this jolly soul looked
like she could make pies was because she *did* make pies . . . out of
Outlander superfans.

Before Willa could ask Finn if his wife was a cannibal, Gabe
appeared, flopped an arm around her shoulders and murmured,
'There you are, my luvvvvverrrrrr.'

It was then Willa realised she and Finn were still hand in hand.
She'd been clinging to it as if her life had depended on it.

Crumb nuggets. Not only was she cheating on Gabe, she was
cheating with Sweeney Todd. Wonderful. At least now she knew
why he hadn't been put off by her curves. (Had the boob grope
been a tenderness test?)

She glanced across at Jeff to check whether or not he was wearing a dirk. They'd be able to defend themselves with Jeff on their
side, right?

'What'd I miss? Where are we?' asked Gabe.

She answered 'not much' and 'Balcraigie Castle' at which he
scanned the area, arched an *are you kidding me?* eyebrow at her and
then, most likely courtesy of the painkillers, began to laugh.

'Concha got us good, didn't she, *mija*?' He laughed and laughed
and tugged her in close and gave her a kiss on the forehead, then
pointed at the castle and laughed again. She supposed, if she let go
of the whole room-service-and-hot-bath idea, it was funny. And
to be fair, a more genuinely immersive lean into the olden days
experience than she'd given the brochure credit for. Thread counts
probably didn't factor into accommodation guidelines back then.
Or club sandwiches.

Shifting her weight so she could prop him up a bit better, she
pressed her index finger to her lips and pointed towards the cheery
woman.

'Thank you, Shona,' she was saying to the bagpiping teenager. 'That was lovely.' She clapped her hands to begin a well-deserved round of applause to which Jeff shouted, 'Encore!'

Cheery woman ignored him and, to Shona, continued, 'Dougie'll whizz you back to the village, okay?' She turned back to them, gave a surprisingly dainty demi-curtsey for a woman who was probably close to six feet tall, then beamed, 'Well, hello, my lovelies. My name is Orla MacKenzie. I am your hostess here at the family seat, Balcraigie Castle.' She shot a slightly crinkle-browed glance in Finn's direction before turning her sunlit smile back on them. 'May I be the first to welcome you to the Far-um.'

Far-um?

'I *thought* we were on a farm,' Jennifer whispered. 'There was no way that road was leading to a proper castle. It explains the horse-poop smell.'

'It's cow muck,' Fenella hissed back. 'Trust me. Perfume of my childhood.'

Confirming Fenella's claim, a cow mooed somewhere off in the darkness.

And then, as if to ensure Jennifer's spirits weren't dampened either, a horse whinnied.

They laughed and started an excited conversation about whether there was going to be horse riding or cattle rustling or both.

ChiChi hushed them both and tipped her head towards Orla who was glancing at her . . . was that a pocket watch? 'You're a wee bit later than we thought, but no bother. We'll sort out your accommodation and then get a hot meal into you before you see to your jetlag and whatnot. Tomorrow's going to be busy, so we need you well rested!'

Orla's pure Scottish accent was like listening to a clear mountain brook wash through a sunlit glade. It cut through the cold, damp air and, against the odds, made Willa feel welcome. There was accommodation. A hot meal. And they would be attending to whatnot. How quickly her dream of a long hot bath and room service had been replaced with hopes of a roof and something – anything – warm to eat. Unless it was meat pie.

'Finlay?' Orla's voice carried a note of apology in it. 'You wouldn't mind getting our guests' bags into their stalls— *rooms* . . . ah ha ha ha . . . their *rooms* . . . for this' – she threw her arms out wide again – 'the world's only truly immersive Jacobean experience.'

'Stalls?'

'Did she say stalls?'

'Aren't we staying in the castle?'

'Claire stayed in the castle.'

'Have you actually looked at that thing? There isn't a roof!'

'Jamie stayed with the horses. In a barn.'

'Neighhhhhhhh, lassie,' whinnied Jeff as he grabbed Rosa round the waist with a sexy grunt. 'He stayed with Claire. Wheresoever she lay.'

Willa had been about to throw Gabe a playful *would you get a load of the tantric sex couple?* look but panicked he'd think she wanted to lay with him wherever he lay. Not that it would be a hardship. Who wouldn't want to be bedded by a living, breathing, Latino version of the Vitruvian Man?

She could practically feel a version of herself raising her hand with a wince-smile and whispering, 'Me'.

An imagine of Bryony, her replacement at work, popped into her head. If Bryony had found herself in this situation? She would have pounced on Gabe without a second's thought.

She fancied Gabe, so . . . why the hesitation?

Again she pictured Bryony with her coltish long limbs and her pert, sassy confidence born of a life growing up in The Hills with a dad in The Biz and her plans to take over TiTs using the power of . . . erm . . . her tits. It was a perfectly believable scenario.

The fact Willa had opted to fantasise about someone she thought was fictional rather than the man she was pretty sure she was being set up with was telling.

Perfect wasn't for the Willas of the world. This wasn't her being all boo-hoo, poor me. This was fact. Perfect was for movie stars and prom queens and international human rights lawyers with glossy hair and enviable cheekbones.

A memory of Val gazing adoringly at her husband – a slightly chubby, balding, weirdy-beardy accountant with an obsession for barbecued pork – caught her up short. An acute reminder that perfect meant something different to everyone.

'If you think I'm sleeping with Mr Ed, you've got another think—' Rosa was saying.

'Hush, now. We're visitors from a far-off land, reliant on the kindness of strangers.' Jeff cleared his throat and offered a grandiose bow to Orla. 'Pray, dear hostess, are the mattresses stuffed with straw? Or is this a manger-type situation?'

Orla shot him a grateful smile. 'We would, of course, love for you to be staying in the castle.'

Everyone's eyes shot to the left where the pile of rocks formerly known as a castle stood proud of the landscape . . . the spotlights shining straight through the glassless windows and up to what would have been the roof, had there been one.

'But this,' announced Orla with a broad sweep of her arm towards another, lower stone building with a thatched roof, 'is where you'll be staying. The barn. Just like Jamie, but with a few more amenities than he was afforded.' She gave another little curtsey bob. 'We know many of you are obviously Claire fans, but as part of the experience, we thought it would be interesting to enjoy things from both their perspectives.'

Willa suppressed a snort. She'd worked in the world of showbiz long enough to know when a screw-up was being tactically repurposed as a triumph. And, for some reason, it made her warm to the experience. She looked round to see if she could get a reading on the situation from Finn, but he was nowhere to be seen.

Off sharpening the carving knives, no doubt.

Fenella sidled up to her and whispered, 'I would've rather experienced things from Claire's point of view after a thirty-hour trip. Wouldn't you?'

Willa made a vague noise. She didn't have a clue what Claire's experience had been, but something told her admitting as much to this crowd would be a mistake.

Chapter Eleven

'This way, please. Mind how you go.'

Using their phones to light the way, the group began trooping after Orla, who was brandishing a not entirely effective flame torch. She guided them through a passageway cut through the centre of the stone building. As a group, they fell quiet, less with giddy anticipation this time, and more with a shivery wariness. Were they being led to their doom?

When they got through to the other side, they let out collective sighs of relief. The stone barn was built around a huge central courtyard. In the centre was an impressive firepit. Enormous logs (trees, really) had been cleaved in half into the shape of massive timber sofas each of which was dappled with inviting piles of plaid woollen blankets and pillows with embroidered stag's heads stitched into them.

A tall man with a huge shock of red hair and a hipster beard came into view. He was wearing a well-worn green coverall like the ones Willa's dad wore at Grease Monkey's. He threw a thick hunk of wood on to the fire, eliciting a cloud of red sparks beneath a massive cast iron tripod holding up an equally huge cast iron pot. Wafts of beef and gravy and herbs drifted over. Her stomach growled.

'Alright, love?' the man called to Orla.

'They're here!' sing-songed Orla with a happy clap of her hands, then, in a lower voice asked, 'I thought you were away driving Shona to the village?' And then, more urgently, 'Is Dad with the children?'

'Aye, but I'd got them to their beds first. They'll be fine. And Finlay's whizzing Shona back.'

Willa's eyes zapped between the two of them. *The plot doth thicken*, she thought. Who is this interloper? A brother? An accomplice?

Orla frowned at beardy-man, then gave a decisive nod. 'Right you are. Thanks, darlin'. Everyone?' Orla turned to the group, her warm smile back in place. 'I'd like you to meet my "Jamie".' She flashed them all her wedding band. 'He goes by any number of names round here, but you can all call him Dougie.'

Ahhh . . . so Finn wasn't married to Orla, Dougie was. An annoying tickle of approbation fluttered in her chest.

Dougie was giving a little bow and a warm smile, saying his name was short for Douglas but that no one apart from Orla called him that and only when he was in trouble.

The group laughed and smiled as a chorus of 'Hi there, Dougie's criss-crossed the courtyard.

Orla whispered something into her husband's ear, then turned to the group.

'Right, then. Let's get you all sorted so we can sit down to a nice bowl of stew.' A look of panic crossed her face. 'We've not got any veggies, have we?'

Willa sucked in a sharp breath and waited. If this was Hollywood? *Everyone* would have some sort of dietary requirement.

After a bit of head shaking and 'No, not me's', Willa realised everyone was looking at Jules.

'Wow! Talk about stereotyping,' Jules laughed. 'I'm good.' She held up her hands. 'So long as it's lived a natural life and been free to moo or cluck and eat whatever it's actually meant to eat, I'm fine with anything.'

'Everything you eat will have been raised or grown on Balcraigie Castle Far-um,' Orla said with genuine pride. 'Except' – she held up a finger – 'the milk and cheese, which come from down the road from our friends, the Frasers. And the bread, which comes from down the village . . .' Her cheery expression began to falter.

Dougie clapped an arm round Orla's shoulder and said, 'Och away, love. It's all made or grown in Scotland. And that's what matters most, am I right?'

The group cheered and started saying 'och away' to one another as they all gratefully accepted steaming bowls of stew and, after Dougie fished them out of the coals, the best baked potato Willa had ever had.

Orla and Dougie disappeared while they ate, presumably lying in wait for Finn's return, when he would no doubt fill them in on their new clientele and the airport debacle. But! A bit later, Orla reappeared and handed out generous pieces of something magical called millionaire's shortbread. It was a delicious stack of short-bread, caramel and chocolate, and because she was eight thousand miles away from LA and all the fussy eaters, Willa devoured her slice as if it was manna from heaven.

Fenella yawned first. Then Stella, then ChiChi, until soon enough the entire group was succumbing to big *ooo boy it's time to turn in* yawns.

A rough-hewn wooden awning ran the length of the U-shaped building which, every three metres or so, featured a stable door with an upside-down horseshoe nailed above it and a name plaque to its side.

Orla grabbed a clipboard from the polka-dotted oil cloth draped over a pile of pallets that she'd been using as a sideboard, then bustled across to the far door and began calling out names. As each couple disappeared behind the thick stone walls, Willa could hear excited *ooos*.

Okay, she'd admit it now. She'd been expecting screams of terror. Having grown up in rural Oregon, if something smelt like a barn and looked like a barn . . . chances were high it was a barn.

And yet not one person had run from their new room, ashen faced, screaming, *Get me out of here*, so . . . maybe looks could be deceiving?

She glanced at Gabe and gave him an *are you okay?* thumbs-up but received nothing in return. A pensive expression had gripped his beautiful features as he stared at the ever-decreasing flames in the firepit. She was tempted to ask what had him so preoccupied but something about the way he was blinking just a little too rapidly to be divining the mysteries of the universe told her to leave him be.

Now that she thought about it, even before she'd knocked him out cold he had been really quiet since they'd arrived in Scotland. From the moment they'd got off the plane, he had gone into a sort of deep-thought mode. Which could explain why he hadn't noticed her windmilling backwards with Finn's hand stuck in her cleavage.

As if she'd conjured him with the power of thought alone, Finn appeared at the far end of the courtyard, bumping a few of the group's wheelie suitcases across the cobbles. He looked across, saw her, and did the guy chin-lift thing with his lips curving into something approaching a smile. Her heart did an involuntary set of cartwheels as she waved back like an idiot.

He frowned. She followed suit.

Proof, if she needed it, that they'd decided not to like one another. Something about the way he held her gaze rankled, but frankly she was too tired to engage in a staring contest, so looked away.

She scanned the courtyard and saw Orla leading the penultimate couple – Jeff and Rosa – to their room. With breathtaking speed, it suddenly clicked that everyone had been led to their rooms in pairs. Even ChiChi and Fenella. The possibility that she and Gabe might be sharing a room hadn't even occurred to her.

She started when Gabe leant in close, his lips brushing against her ear as he whispered, 'You don't snore, do you?'

She cackled like a maniacal witch. 'Delicate flowers like me don't snore!' *Cackle snaffle snort.*

Her heart began to race as she pictured Gabe whipping off his kilt, crooking a finger and beckoning her to join him in a super-king manger.

Her skin went clammy. This was Val's *brother*! She couldn't—

And then it struck her . . . Even if they could and he was willing . . . she genuinely wasn't sure she wanted to.

It was too much, too soon, too intimate, too . . . perfect.

And therein lay the problem. He was perfect and she was normal, and those two types of people didn't have sex together – wanton or otherwise. History was proof of that (briefly excepting the moment in time that was Marilyn Manson and Dita Von Teese and, well, Hugh Hefner's entire reign).

Even plain old sharing a room without sexy boom-boom would mean hiding in the bathroom every time she changed. And if, heaven forbid, this was one of those weird set-ups where the couple-sized bathtub was in the middle of the room (because, yes, some freakishly hopeful part of her was still convinced there was going to be swish amenities), she'd have to cut a hole in a sheet and stick it over her head and the bath so he couldn't see her body every time she wanted to clean herself. Gorgeous models of perfection didn't dig back fat, except in Botticellis and even then . . .

Orla emerged from the room where ChiChi and Fenella were staying and headed towards them with a jolly, 'Right, then!'

Willa held her breath as Orla looked down at her check list, then up at the pair of them, smiled and, to Willa said, 'Gabriella Martinez?'

Gabe stiffened.

Errrr. Willa pointed at Gabe. 'This is Gabriel Martinez.'

'Really?' Orla's eyebrows dove together as she ran her finger down her sheet. 'I'm sure the booking was made as Gabriella.'

Gabe cleared his throat with an accompanying eyeroll and said, 'That would be my sister's doing. She used to call me Gabriella.' And then, as if he'd been unceremoniously possessed by a teeny-bopper pop star, he started singing, 'She used to call me Gabriella. Gabriella. Caaaaall me Gabriella.'

Willa hard-stared at him. 'Gabe? Is this you exhibiting signs of a concussion?'

He shook his head, the energy vanishing as quickly as it arrived. 'No. Just tired.'

She narrowed her gaze. There was something else. Had his mysterious silence been the slow, belated creep of sadness over his sister's death? Perhaps it had finally been knocked loose in his fall. That, or he was suffering from a massive brain bleed. She held up a selection of fingers. 'How many?'

'Seven.'

She double-checked he was right. He was. She did a few more. Nailed it every time. Just as she was about to give him some long division problems she wouldn't know the answer to, Orla cut in with a gentle, 'Shall we call it a typo and go with Gabriel instead?'

'Probably a good idea,' Willa said as Gabe abruptly strode off to a fresh row of luggage that had appeared at the archway. She pointed at Orla's clipboard. 'Whatever else Val said, just keep it as it is. She would've wanted the trip to be exactly as she specified.'

Still looking perplexed, Orla nodded and then, as if she'd made an executive decision that the customer was always right, beamed her sunny smile and said, 'This will be Gabriel's room, then,' and pulled open the door next to her.

When Gabe returned with both of their bags, Willa waited for him to go in first and then followed. They shared a grin, delighted and surprised to see the small, but charmingly decorated room. The walls were whitewashed stone, glowing with the warm light from a small wood stove and a couple of tactically placed hurricane candles. A simple bed made out of pallets and a mattress was on one side of the room and – ha! – a tub stood on the other. It was one of those old-fashioned claw footed numbers that, judging by the odd rust spot poking through, was a relic from the past. Yeah. That never would've worked.

'The wee wee shoppe is through the back.' Orla pointed to a door at the far end of the room. 'Those are shared, but there are plenty.'

'Wee wee shops?'

'Where you spend a penny?' Orla prompted.

'Nope.' Willa shook her head. 'Still not with you.'

'The loo? The toilet?'

'Ah! The bathroom.'

Orla explained, 'Sometimes in the UK you have to pay to go to the public conveniences. It used to be a penny.'

Willa grinned as the 'penny' dropped. She loved that sort of yesteryear wordsmithery. She saluted Orla. 'Wee wee shoppe. Noted.'

'Bed,' said Gabe and promptly threw back the grandma-made-looking patchwork quilt, climbed on to the bed with a few creaks from the pallets, kicked off his shoes, then tugged the quilt back over him, kilt and all, laid back and closed his eyes.

Oh. Okay. 'Night, night then.'

She and Orla looked at one another and shrugged.

'Does he need to be watched or anything?' Orla asked. She pointed at her own head, then Gabe's.

'No. I mean, I could stay here and watch him if you think he's behaving unusually.'

'I think you'd be a better judge of that than me,' Orla said kindly.

Gabe began to fake snore. Loudly.

Alright, then. It looked like someone wanted his alone time.

'I guess we'll be going now,' Willa said pointedly.

With a shared smile, the two women left the room.

'Now, then.' Orla closed the door behind her and pointed to the end of the building. 'You're away up in the hayloft.'

Willa snorted. 'Is that like the barn equivalent of the dungeon?'

'More like the honeymoon suite.' Orla's smile broadened, then dropped at the sound of her name being called. 'Excuse me for a moment, darlin', would you?'

'Of course.'

She took out her phone and began rapid-fire answering all the emails Bryony and her boss had sent.

A few minutes later, Willa looked up from her phone at the sound of voices. Or, more accurately, voice.

It was Finn. He and Orla were huddled in the stable's archway having quite the intense conversation. Snatches of what they were saying were audible. But not much.

How could you—

Even legal?

You promised—

Insurance—

Already have public liability—

This is the last time—

And then, as if he hadn't just been immersed in an incredibly heated discussion, Finn appeared in the courtyard, his demeanour only slightly ruffled. He picked up Willa's completely oversized suitcase as if it weighed little more than a feather pillow, gave her phone a glance, then held out his hand. 'Would you like to follow me?'

Ermmm . . . not particularly. Orla was warm and friendly and awkwardly wonderful. The kind of girl Willa would've latched on to in high school to make surviving backwoods Oregon more bearable. Finn was . . . confusing to figure out. She knew the whole serial killer thing was a stretch (or was it?) but what did press against the realms of believability was that he'd have a barbed conversation with Orla, then, in the blink of an eye, decide to turn his hand to the hospitality industry. Unless he'd made her cry and this was his version of penance. Playing nicey-nicey to the klutz who couldn't control her boobs.

Without waiting for her answer he headed towards an outdoor stairwell that led up to a door on the side of the building.

Willa silently trooped after him, staring at his taut butt, wondering what on earth had possessed Val to book this madcap vacation. Why did 'stepping outside of herself' to take a look within entail cranky Scotsmen and barns? Surely a spa in Sedona would have done the same trick?

When Finn swung open the door and stood to the side so Willa could enter, she gasped with pleasure. The room was far bigger than Gabe's. And unexpectedly fancier. There were actual lightbulbs, for starters – old-fashioned filament bulbs that looked as if they'd been there from the days they'd been invented. There were strings of fairy lights woven around huge wooden ceiling beams which, at six-foot-something, were about the height of Finlay's head.

The decor sang true to the room's origins. In the centre was a massive bed which, judging by the epic headboard, was entirely made of straw bales apart from the crowning glory: a huge set of antlers.

'What's hanging from them?' She pointed at the clutches of dried plants hanging from the antlers.

Finlay leant in as if he hadn't seen it before. He sniffed. 'Heather.'

The way he said it made it sound like nectar of the gods. Who was she kidding? The way he said everything made her insides turn molten. Shame about the 'tude.

'I suppose your friend—' Finn began just as Willa started pointing at things and naming them as if she'd never seen furniture before.

'Sofa!' she cried as her eyes lit on a hay-bale sofa covered in a beautiful duck egg blue blanket. 'Stool!' She pointed and grinned at the hay-bale dressing table.

Finlay stood silent during her little vocabulary display. When she'd exhausted the number of inanimate objects she could name, he tugged off his flat cap, shoved his big, farmery hands through his hair, then began a fairly obvious health and safety speech.

Low beams. Watch her head. Uneven floorboards. 'There's no wood stove in here for obvious reasons, but the straw round the walls should act as insulation for you.' Finlay pointed to a big chest at the foot of the bed. 'Orla's charged the dower chest there with a few more blankets and quilts if you need them or I can up and away to the house for a hot water bottle if you like.'

As tempting as it was to make him run and fetch things for her, she declined the offer.

There was a bath in the corner of the room – one of those old tin ones that could double as a washing tub. And, she noted, a curtain to pull around it. Not far from it stood a big old Butler sink big enough to wash a toddler in and, to her surprise, behind a wooden door Finn was opening, her own wee wee shoppe.

'Yours is the only room with an actual loo.' Orla appeared at the door, her cheeks flushed and expression slightly strained. 'Has Finlay shown you the loo?'

'He sure has!' They both looked to Finn who did some lacklustre jazz hands.

With a flick of her head, Orla indicated Finlay could be done now. They traded micro-glares as they passed one another.

'Is there anything we can get you?' Orla's eyes darted round the room as if she'd lost something. 'A hot water bottle? A cup of tea? Och, my brain's not right.' She gave herself a little shake. 'See, there's a flask of hot water there if you—' At the sound of a door slamming, Orla went stock still, as if she'd just remembered something incredibly important and then, as if the moment hadn't happened at all, dropped one of those dainty curtseys of hers and said, 'I'll wish you a good night now, Willaford. Your new dress will be hanging on your door in the morning for the handfasting ceremony!'

Hand-fastening ceremony?

And then she was gone.

Chapter Twelve

A bell clanged once, twice, then several times in rapid, increasingly loud succession. Willa leapt out of bed fairly certain she'd only just got to sleep. Between panicking Gabe had fallen into some sort of after-accident coma and wondering what on earth a hand-fastening ceremony was, she was pretty sure she'd seen more of the night than slept through it. In the part when she *had* slept? She'd pretty much had the most erotic dream in the history of erotic dreams. There had been moaning and groaning and fingers digging into flesh in a way that had only made her hunger for more. There had been kissing and straddling and lots of urgent thrusting. There had even been spanking. And she'd *liked* it.

The bell sounded again.

Too groggy to think clearly, she tugged on a fitted, scoop-neck T-shirt over some yoga leggings, jammed her feet into her rattiest but most comfortable pair of Uggs, then put the bodice on over her T-shirt and climbed into her petticoats and overskirt, which she'd left in an ungainly pile on the floor last night. It wasn't a very comely olde worlde aesthetic, but it was warm and would have to do. There was no mirror to check herself in and, to be honest, she didn't want one. Her dress was wrinkled and her Princess Leia whorls had undone themselves. The best she could do was pray no one had brought a travel iron and whip her hair into a big, long plait with straw accents. And then her boobs began to escape the confines of her bodice.

As she tried to stuff them into some sort of submission, her hand grazed against her nipples, reminding her of the stubbly cheek shifting across them in her dream before a tongue swirled round each one, lazily bringing them to taut peaks. It had been such a heated sensation she'd grabbed whoever's head it had been and begged for more. Definitely not a move in her real-life repertoire. She was more of the completely-grateful-for-what-she-got-so-long-as-it-wasn't-painful camp versus the bring-it-here-big-boy school of sexy nights in.

A knock sounded on her door. '*Hola, bendita.* It's your Jamie here!' Gabe pronounced Jamie the Spanish way, giving it an extra sexy twist.

Willa flushed hard and stuffed her phone in the front of her bodice.

Did Gabe know she'd been having pornographic dreams about—

She stopped and thought a moment. Had it been him? She tried to remember the colour of the thick, wavy hair she'd grabbed.

He knocked again before she could nail anything down.

'Coming!' She pulled open the door and there he was, looking all sexy gorgeous in his kilt. His head was no longer wrapped in bandages, but still sported a solitary plaster over his cut. He had a big, warm smile on his lips and a huge swathe of beautiful fabric over one of his arms.

'I didn't kill you!' She flung her arms around him.

He gave her back a pat that felt a bit more like being burped rather than hugged, but, hey, it was friendly. She'd take it.

'I'm guessing this is for you?' He held up the swathes of fabric which turned out to be a gorgeous dress in a fawn-coloured plaid with burgundy stripes. 'Ready to get your Jacobite on?' he asked, handing it over.

'Am I ever!' She sagged under the weight of the dress, then high-fived him, not really having a clue what getting her Jacobite on would entail, but the first rule of taking risks was to say yes to the unknown, right? She was pretty sure Gwyneth had said that at some point. Gabe said he'd wait while she'd changed but another round of bell clanging suggested waiting until later to put the dress on was probably wise.

'Good morning, everyone. Time for your morning porridge!' Orla was at the firepit doling out huge dollops of oatmeal to the rest of the guests, all excitedly chatting away about what was yet to come. When Willa and Gabe approached, Orla gave them both a warm smile and, after a quick glance up to Gabe's head, asked, 'And are your accommodations to your liking?'

This would be interesting. There was absolutely no mistaking Balcraigie's stables for the 'rural chic' retreats she was pretty sure Gabe would be used to with his membership to Soho House.

'They're perfect.' He gave Orla's arm a squeeze and dropped one of his (trademark?) winks. 'It's exceeded my expectations.'

Charmer.

And also . . . what *had* he been expecting? A bit of bracken and a blanket under the stars? She'd been expecting ridiculous thread counts and butlers.

'And you, Willa?' Orla was asking, as she gave the huge pot of porridge a stir. 'How'd you fare?'

Memories of her triple-X dream sent a rush of red to her cheeks. 'Oh, fine. All good. Without incident.'

Orla looked up from the porridge pot. 'That's just grand. Oh! Are you not wearing your new frock?'

Willa looked down at her hastily tugged-on outfit. Compared to the other guests who were wearing more elaborate frocks than they'd worn yesterday, she was definitely looking like something that the cat dragged in.

'Messy eater,' she said, pointing at the bowl Orla was filling with a huge dollop of oatmeal. 'I wanted to make sure I didn't spill anything on it. It's so beautiful,' she added, meaning it. Dress-up or no, it was the prettiest dress she'd ever seen.

'Well, you'll have to hustle a wee bit after your breakfast, so here's your porridge. There are a few berries and things over on the tea table to pop on top if you like. We've a busy day ahead, so make sure you get enough to eat.'

Willa and Gabe headed over to the little table underneath the covered walkway where the rest of the group were loading their bowls of steaming porridge with dollops of homemade jam, fresh strawberries or raspberries and, in Jeff's case, whopping great spoonfuls of set honey.

'It's heather honey,' he said when he caught her looking. 'It's got a different taste from the stuff we get in the squeezy bear at home. It's more' – he rubbed his fingers together as if trying to divine just the right word – 'genuine.'

Willa dug her spoon into the honey pot (an actual honey pot!) and watched as the thick, crystallised dollop melted into a golden puddle atop her porridge. The heat released a sweet, herby scent that instantly transported her back to the first moment she'd leant in and smelt—

'Good morning, all.' A lilting baritone came from behind her. 'Did everyone sleep well?'

She whipped round, heart in her throat as her eyes connected with Finn's blue-grey ones. Here he was. The star of her sex dream.

Mortified, she turned away. She'd never had a good poker face and if a frozen smile could betray the fact that she'd pictured herself buck naked riding Finn like the winning horse at the Kentucky Derby, she was sure her face was doing it right now. She fastidiously focused on shovelling porridge into her mouth while everyone else told him how delighted they were with their rooms, the antler clothes hangers, the jam jars filled with colourful wildflower posies and all the other little touches Willa had somehow managed to miss because she'd been too busy alternating between worrying she'd killed Gabe and having pornographic dreams about a man who very clearly disliked her.

It was actually shocking that she hadn't put two and two together straight away. The rough straw-coloured stubble that, when it caught the sun, looked red gold. The large, capable, callused hands. The alpha-male strength combined with an unusually insightful level of tenderness. Here it all was, standing right beside her in living, breathing colour. A ripple of goose pimples ran the length of her spine then turned to lightning as they arrowed between her legs.

She made a silent note to herself to never, ever get horny over a catalogue model again. When dreams came true, it was far too easy for them to turn into nightmares.

'This is, hands down, the best oatmeal I have ever had,' Rosa gushed. 'Do you have this every morning?'

All eyes turned to Finn.

The corners of his mouth tipped down and, once again, Willa saw a micro-moment of absence shift through him. As if, for the blink of an eye, he literally disappeared somewhere far, far away. Where had he gone? And more to the point, why was a question about steel cut oats making him sad?

After a moment, he said, 'Oh, aye. It's famous round these parts. Orla's porridge.'

'What makes it so creamy?'

Finn's soft smile returned. 'Cream.'

Everyone swallowed and licked their lips.

Oh, this was too much. Turning a solitary, monosyllabic word into a delectable poem?

She shifted her stance. Just because he could roll his Rs and visit her nocturnally did not mean her lady garden should be at his mercy. And yet, here she was, wishing she could strip off the layers of petticoats hothousing a bajingo puddling like a pat of butter on a summer's day.

'She puts loads in.' Finlay made an *mmm* sound, then pointedly looked at Willa before adding, 'Delectable.'

Oh my god. He wasn't a murderer. He was a porn pimp! Had to be. There were probably hidden microphones or cameras or . . . oh, she got it now . . . there were subversive messages being fed in through the hay bales FORCING her to have filthy, wanton sex dreams. There was no other explanation for her having the only room with electricity. Pictures of her moaning and groaning as fantasy Finn went down on her had probably gone viral in some niche world of erotica. A get-yer-rocks-off-in-the-hayloft kind of thing.

Jules asked whether the cows were raised organically or biodynamically. A discussion on the merits of rewilding ensued while Willa remained caught in the questioning storm blue light of Finlay's eyes.

Why was she here they asked.

She thought of the letter burning a hole in her luggage (double Ziplocked to prevent damage). She could practically hear it calling out to her to please, please, tear it open and read it, but . . . something more powerful overrode it, insisting it wasn't time yet. She made a quick mental note to ask Gabe if he'd opened his yet.

'Butter!' Orla called out, joining the group. 'The salted kind. That and cream make porridge better than the usual claggy gloop that puts people off. Also I use a spurtle.'

'A what?' Jeff asked.

Orla sucked in a horrified breath. 'Have you not heard of the golden spurtle?'

'I'm not being funny,' Jules said, 'but it sounds like something you really hope a guy doesn't get on you when he . . . you know . . .'

Fenella made gagging sounds while Jennifer hiss-whispered that a bit of decorum might not go amiss.

Completely unflustered, Orla produced a small wooden paddle. 'This is a spurtle. Just a wooden rod used since the 1500s for the express purpose of porridge making.'

'Oh, gosh.' Rosa leant in to take a look. 'Is it that old?'

Orla's expression briefly shadowed and then she said, 'This one dates back all the way to 1987.' She let the laughter die down then said, 'It's also very important to—'

'I know!' Rosa raised her hand with pick-me enthusiasm. 'Stir the porridge clockwise with your right hand, otherwise the devil will come for the person doing the stirring!'

'That's right.' Orla grinned. 'You're also meant to eat it standing up with each spoonful dipped in a bowl of cream shared by the whole family, but as we've got so many of you today, I took the liberty of pouring the cream right in. I'm happy to hand out my "secret" recipe if you're interested.' Amidst a chorus of *yes, please*'s she gave her hands a clap and then rubbed them together as if she were holding great surprises in store. 'Alright, you lot. You've got ten more minutes before we ask you to bring your mobiles and other devices that connect you to the outside world down. We'll be collecting those when we gather here in the courtyard for the handfasting ceremony.'

Now, Willa was all for a bit of a social media detox, but hand over her phone? Not this week and also, as a general note, not a snowman's chance in—

'Here you go.' Gabe dug into the pocket of his evergreen-coloured wax jacket and handed over two mobiles and a mini iPad without so much as the bat of an inky eyelash.

Orla smiled her thanks, put the items into a wicker arm basket, then walked around the group collecting more. 'You'll be getting them back each evening, unless you'd prefer not to. We'll be keeping them in the gun safe in the house, so don't worry. We won't be hacking into anything or posting photos on your Instagram.'

Willa shot a glance at Finn, but he was scooping a bit of porridge into a bowl.

Fenella held her phone above the basket then retracted it. 'Don't you want us to be posting photos of our experience? For future guests?'

'Ah!' Orla's eyes darted towards Finn then back to the group. 'No, no. That would detract from the truly immersive feel, don't you think? This is your unique experience. Never to be repeated.'

Willa was no sleuth, but something about the way Orla's eyes shot back to Finn made her think that last line had been for his benefit.

A chorus of agreement was followed by a quick flurry of digging into sporrans and wicker baskets that produced another six. Orla turned to Willa. 'Is yours in your room, darlin'?'

It was not. It was in her bosom. And, as if to show everyone just how dedicated to communication with the outside world she was, it began to buzz.

'I'll just get changed, shall I?' she said, then turned and ran up to her room without looking back.

◆ ◆ ◆

Ten minutes later, she'd answered three INCREDIBLY URGENT texts from Bryony about whether or not she could charge her lunchtime juice bar purchases to TiTs, hammered out a few emails to publicists about interviews Bryony should have chased up but hadn't and then one to her boss reminding her that the interview questions for Britney were saved on her desktop.

When she scurried back downstairs, phone tucked in to her bodice, she gave everyone an apology smile, realising she alone was holding up the mysterious hand-fastening ceremony. *Nice one, Outlander,* she reprimanded herself as she found her place in line next to Gabe. Then, stupidly pleased that she'd made an *Outlander* reference without even trying, she grinned up at him. He grinned back with a *what did I do to earn that lovely smile?* and for a very peaceful moment, they just stood there smiling at one another.

'Right, then, laddies and laddettes.' Orla cupped her hands and made a trumpet sound as if heralding some great news. 'It's time for you to meet your Jamies and Claires.'

Willa and Gabe's foreheads furrowed in tandem.

If LARPing was on the agenda, surely they'd be one another's Jamie and Claire? Right?

Holding up a beautiful purple and sage knotted rope concoction, Orla called out, 'Behold! The handfasting cord.'

As Willa processed that it was a hand*fasting* cord and not a hand-fastening one, the rest of the group unleashed excited *ooo*s and *ahhs* as Jennifer announced, 'I've been so excited for this part I haven't been able to sleep for days!'

'Oh my days. *Mum!*' Jules heaved a melodramatic sigh. 'I've been telling her over and over that it's cosplay! She doesn't get to bring him home.' She slipped her arm round her mum's waist and squeezed. 'But you get to keep me!'

'That's right, love, I do. But don't rain on my parade with all of your Zoomer pragmatism.' Jennifer's expression turned dreamy. 'Two entire weeks of a man enjoying my company and *listening* to me when I speak . . . Best bit of escapism I will have ever paid for.'

'We do a handfasting every year!' Rosa beamed up at Jeff, then wrapped her arms around him as he pulled her feet right off the ground so that they could share a kiss. When he put her down again, her cheeks were flushed and she shot them all a happy smile. 'So lovely to have other people tie the knot with us. Even if it is pretend.'

Willa's stomach twisted with something new. Envy maybe? The energy zapping between Rosa and Jeff was . . . well . . . it was beautiful. It looked exactly like the kind of true love everyone wanted in real life. The kind Valentina and Diego had. The kind her own parents shared.

'We have worked hard to find the best Jamie . . . or Claire . . .' Orla said with a special look at Jules and a nervous one at Gabe, '. . . as per the instructions on your booking sheet.'

Again, Willa and Gabe exchanged a look. Booking sheets?

There definitely hadn't been anything like a booking sheet in their scant paperwork.

They'd had flight details, sealed letters from Val and the brochure featuring Finn, but that had been it.

'Rosa and Jeff,' Orla was saying, 'you two are, of course, being paired together as requested. Instead, you will have a "son" to help you out. Everyone else? Get ready. You're about to meet your shiny new Scottish spouse.'

Still staring at one another, Willa and Gabe's eyes widened as they began to understand. Not only were they not sharing a bedroom, but they were also going to be split up.

'Valentina?' Willa asked.

Gabe nodded. 'Valentina.'

There was no other explanation for it. This was Valentina rubbing her hands together with a gleeful *mwah ha ha* up in heaven. She loved playing Cupid and had clearly kept them in the dark on purpose.

But . . . hadn't she already played Cupid by putting Gabe and Willa together for the trip?

Okay, sure, it wasn't exactly as if they'd spent the entire flight under one of those first-class duvets making out or anything, but . . .

If Val hadn't yanked Willa away from TiTs during Sweeps Week to fall in love with her sexy estranged brother so that she could spend the rest of her life having him run his perfectly manicured nails through her hair as they watched boxsets and solved celebrity crises before making sweet, sensual, lit-by-moonlight love at night . . . why was she here?

Gabe's perplexed expression turned completely neutral. Precisely the way it had been when they were at the will reading. Not exactly icy, but it sure wasn't warm and cuddly.

Willa turned away, unable to hold his steady, unreadable gaze.

'You will be spending the next two weeks,' Orla continued, 'side by side with your Highland husband or wife as you immerse yourself in the eighteenth century.' She went on to talk about health and safety and how each of the 'specially chosen spouses' were all trained in first aid, crofting crafts (whatever those were) and making cups of oolong tea for when the weather turned inhospitable. 'And believe me, that could be on the hour, every hour, so I hope you all have strong bladders or a penchant for an outdoor wee!'

For some reason, having all of this new information announced in a no nonsense, but enchanting Scottish accent made being married off to someone she'd never met before, only to be put straight to work, seem perfectly reasonable. The same way a French person could make goat intestines stewed with wild garlic and a dollop of mustard sound like an aphrodisiac.

'And without further ado . . . here they are!'

Feeling as if she'd just been plunged into someone else's fan-fiction paradise, Willa watched as a set of jolly-looking thirty-something men and one young-ish woman – all in kilts – emerged from behind the stables and began to line up in front of them.

There was a collective farmer/hipster/outdoorsy vibe coming from them. Apart from the last guy who exuded more style than your average brawny, I'll-just-move-this-wee-boulder-out-of-your-way-lassie type.

All different shapes, sizes and skin tones, the spouses-to-be were wearing variations on what Willa could only describe as a 'working man's' kilt. Something Carhartt should capitalise on if they hadn't already. Too embarrassed to look at their faces, she focused on the rugged-looking twills, woven in patterns from camouflage through to style-maven guy's black kilt, which he'd matched to a pair of immaculately polished Doc Martens. She chanced a glance up at his face. He, too, looked very catalogue-man-ish. But for quite a different catalogue. Super Fit Urban Men In The Highlands?

Excepting him, they all wore wax jackets, like Gabe's, but theirs were decidedly more weather beaten, giving them an added level of ruggedness which, combined with the untamed, uncombed hair, the stubble in some cases, beards in others, was impressive. And then, to her surprise, one more person jogged into the line-up.

Finlay Jamieson.

Oh *hell* no.

As the guys threw their greetings his way, a deluge of emotions washed through her.

Desire. Fear. Panic. And the scariest of all . . . curiosity.

As her nerves threatened to set in, she reminded herself that this was all a fiction. It wasn't *Highlander Bachelor*, or *Married at First Kilt* or any other type of reality show where one lucky couple actually walked off into a tartan-carpeted happily ever after. This was cosplay, pure and simple. Allowing herself to think this was anything beyond Val playing one of her good old-fashioned tricks was incredibly unwise.

She doubled down on her mantra: *men who seem too good to be true always are.*

Fenella chose this moment to lean over to Willa and sexy growl, 'I wouldn't mind having a bit of rumpy pumpy with McSteamy Farmer Boy.' She tipped her head towards Finn and started doing bowm-chica-bowm-bowm swirls with her hips.

Willa's hackles instantly rose, primed for a fight. She might not want him herself, but, confusingly, she didn't want anyone else to have him either. Which, given that he was here in the Olde Worlde Hotties parade, was a problem.

She tried to imagine him paired with Fenella. Annoyingly, it worked. She was petite, gorgeous and feisty. She knew farming life like the back of her hand and had yet to pop out of her corset and make a complete fool of herself. They'd make a fine yesteryear couple. Or ChiChi. She was smart, beautiful and cocooned in a cloud of sensual intellectualism that meant she and Finn could outwit any trouble they might encounter whilst engaged in mesmerising swordplay. Or he could be Jennifer's toyboy for the week. Jules's experiment in pansexuality. Anyone apart from Willa, the one person whose eye contact he was fastidiously avoiding.

Having given everyone a chance to ogle the 'talent', Orla continued, 'Far-um work can be hard and dangerous and, as you can see from our assembled Highlanders, we will be pairing you with someone who is used to the rigours of survival.'

Survival?

They were getting married to a stranger and then having to fight for their survival? What was this? Corset-and-Kilt Hunger Games?

'This is so bloody brilliant!' Fenella did another happy dance.

ChiChi unleashed a throaty cackle laugh.

Jennifer was quietly scanning the men with a mix of nerves and hopefulness whilst Jules's cheeks turned a bright, happy pink.

Willa jabbed Gabe in the side with her elbow but he remained motionless, staring straight ahead at the line of future spouses.

And that's when she realised he wasn't staring at the group. He was staring at just one of them. Hipster guy. Who was staring right back at him. At the moment she clocked what was going on, Gabe turned on his heel and walked out of the courtyard.

Hipster guy took after him, the hidden pleats of his black kilt flashing out with each stride in bright, unmistakable, colours of the rainbow.

Chapter Thirteen

'Willa, wait! We've not done the handfasting!'

Among the many things Finn had expected to happen today, elbowing Dougie out of Orla's hare-brained scheme so he could fake bind himself to a woman who clearly disliked him was not one of them.

And yet, here he was, racing after her as if the actual love of his life had left him at the altar.

Though she'd had a head start, he easily caught up to her beneath the archway that led out to the main drive. The dress looked like it weighed a tonne. He lunged forward and grabbed her hand. She tried to tug it away. In yet another out-of-character move, he pulled her to him, holding her close. 'Leave him, lass. Let me look after you while they gather themselves.'

He winced. The line sounded like something straight out of a costume drama which, all things considered, wasn't entirely out of place.

'But—!' She looked up at him, her dark eyes flashing with irritation, short, sharp breaths turning into little clouds of cinnamon-scented air between them. 'Wait.' Her eyes narrowed. 'If I'm not being bound to Gabe . . .' Her brain wove together what he'd said as he'd been sprinting after her. 'Oh, you are kidding me, right? *You're* who I'm being bound to?'

'Why not say how you really feel?' he sniped back.

Her expression shifted. She was upset. Hadn't meant it as an actual slight. He shouldn't have snapped. 'Sorry, I just—' She hard-stared at him for a moment then said, 'I'm not being paired with Gabe.' It was more statement than question. As if she was rewriting a mental checklist.

He shook his head no. 'I'm afraid the powers that be stuck you with me.' If you looked at it from a certain squinty-eyed angle, this was completely true.

Her gaze flicked out to where Gabe and Lachlan had disappeared.

He let go of her arms. Holding her in a clutch better suited to the likes of Mr Darcy felt weird now.

Willa stepped back and rubbed her fingers against her temples as if trying to grind the new set of circumstances into her brain. 'Sorry to be a thicko. Let's blame jetlag. I need to get this straight. I'm not being bound to Gabe.'

'Not so far as I know.'

She sucked in a breath to ask another question, shook her head, looked over her shoulder at the space where Gabe had gone and then back at him. 'Is he being bound to Rainbow Kilt Man?' She tacked on a little laugh to indicate she knew it was a bonkers suggestion, but . . .

Finn knew the answer, but Willa didn't seem entirely ready for a solid 'yes' just yet. Finding out her boyfriend might not be that into her was something that needed to come from the source. He'd seen the yearning look she'd thrown at Gabe's door when he'd led her to her room last night. Clocked it right in his gut because for some stupid reason it had rankled. Now, though, he felt bad for her.

Coming all this way to have your world blown apart was something he wouldn't wish on anyone. 'I believe that was the plan.'

To be fair, he didn't definitively know whether or not Gabe was gay. Lachlan was. All he knew was what Orla had told him this morning: Lachlan and Gabe – who had been booked as Gabriella – had been a special request from the beginning. According to the booking forms, 'Gabriella' had had a lifelong dream of doing yoga by a loch with this particular teacher and was willing to pay extra to make it happen. It had taken Orla ages to book him, but she'd finally convinced him on the basis that some Americans were coming, and they'd heard about his wild yoga retreats and that maybe it would be a good opportunity to go international. Or maybe he'd needed the money. Who knew? Orla had so many plates spinning right now there was barely air between them. When she found out Gabriella was actually a Gabe . . . she'd been up half the night fretting about it, trying to ring the woman who'd booked the trip, getting a disconnected number. In the end, she'd decided to go with the-customer's-always-right mantra, even if the paying customer wasn't actually here. When Finn was told Dougie was the one who'd be paired with Willa, he'd volunteered to take his place. Dougie was many things, but Teflon-skinned was not one of them. Finn on the other hand? What did he care if an LA superfan hated his guts? Scots were meant to be roughtie-toughtie warrior-types, right? He could play strong and silent for a fortnight. Or however long it took Willa to pack her enormous bag and head back to the land of sunshine and Botox. 'His name's Lachlan,' Finn volunteered. 'He's not a local.'

Willa tilted her chin to the side and looked up at him. Her warm brown eyes were full of questions. 'That's weird, right?'

'What? Not being local?'

'No! Keep up, Sherlock. Not being paired with the person you came with. And also—' Her voice wavered. 'Being paired with a guy when you're not gay is a bit . . . it's a risk from your point of view, right?'

There were a few things he could say here – yes/maybe he's bi?/ are you blind, woman? – but a curious need to cushion whatever blow she was going to receive won out. 'Maybe it's a more authentic approach to marriage in the eighteenth century? A strategic alliance rather than a love match?'

She snorted. 'Oh, yeah. I hear the Jacobites were really progressive on the gay-marriage front.'

As tempting as it was to admit he was grasping at straws here, admitting he didn't have a clue what happened in the series would be bad. Willa and the other visitors had paid a lot of money to be here with the so-called Jacobean experts. Not to mention the fact that Orla had already spent money to earn money and refunds were out of the question.

'Aye,' he said vaguely and then, because he realised the answer actually mattered to her, added, 'It's a little-known fact.'

Willa gave him the side-eye, shook her head, then turned to head out towards the main entryway. 'I've got to find out what's going on. Gabe's my responsibility.'

Responsibility?

He reached out and grabbed her arm again. She stared at his hand on her arm, then up at him. 'Wow. You really like to man-handle your women, don't you?'

He instantly released her and held his hands up. 'Sorry. Sorry. I just . . . Orla said this was likely to happen.'

'Hang on.' Willa's features screwed up in confusion. 'You *knew* this was going to happen and did it anyway? You deliberately put someone in front of Gabe who'd make him run for the hills. In a foreign country. With a head wound. And you didn't think to warn either of us?'

He could point out that the head wound hadn't been a factor until she'd knocked him over with the luggage trolley but given that he was partly to blame for the incident, pointing out the particulars didn't seem the wisest path to pursue.

'Finn?' Orla beckoned to him to join her just outside the archway.

'What?' he asked, not moving. There was only so much covering for her he was willing to do.

Her features tightened in frustration before she popped on her friendly-Orla face and asked, 'Will you and your bride-to-be be joining us?'

'Yes,' he said at the exact same time as Willa said, 'Absolutely not.'

'Oh, dearie me.' Orla wiped her hands nervously on her skirt. 'Finn wasnae meant to be your laddie anyway. Never mind. I can rustle Dougie up from the fields if you just give me a few moments.'

Finn shot Orla a look.

'I'm sorry.' Willa's disdain was clear. 'You want me to borrow your husband so I don't feel left out?'

Finn bridled on Orla's behalf. Willa was obviously having a shit time, but Dougie was one of the nicest men on the planet.

'How about I have a go with *all* of the hand-me-downs?' Willa continued, clearly on a roll now. 'Better yet, is the scarecrow free? Or why not crown me the resident spinster right now to get it over with.'

'Well—' began Orla.

Finn shot her a what-the-fuck look. 'Hey.' He readjusted his stance so that the only person Willa could see was him. 'I asked to be your Jamie.'

She blinked at him in the way someone might start a slow hand clap.

Undeterred he continued. 'I volunteered to marry you because, believe it or not, I wanted to get to you know you.' In the way he might also be curious about a fire-eating dragon, but . . . every day was a school day.

She took the olive branch for what it really was, a challenge.

'Oh, I see,' she said, with a haughty lift of her right eyebrow. 'I've bewitched you with my superlative breast?'

His eyes involuntarily went there.

'Uh-uh.' She pointed her index finger upwards. 'Up here, sunshine.'

'Trevor, one of the other lads, was supposed to be your Jamie.' This was a total lie, but her arched eyebrows indicated she was prepared to listen. 'I elbowed him out of it. Told him he'd be better off with Fenella.'

'Why?' Willa demanded.

Because Trevor was a lad's lad and Fenella looked as though she could handle a bit of periodic ball-crushing. Willa? Not so much. 'I wanted a chance to make up for being such a numpty at the airport.'

Her eyes narrowed, clearly trying to figure out if he meant it. Or maybe she didn't know what a numpty was.

'If you like,' Finn continued, 'I'll step aside. Make the switch back to the original plan.'

Orla sucked in a breath, clearly about to launch into some other fixer-upper option, but before she could, Finn put up his hand. If she began speaking, he knew she was pretty much guaranteeing they'd be reported to the tourist board for fraud. Or mass bigamy. 'We need to let Willa decide. This is her journey. Her choice.'

Willa stared at him, her eyes occasionally flicking across to Orla, and then, with the aura of a princess who'd just been told she wouldn't be receiving her usual slippers this week owing to a mix-up at the silkworm factory but that she could have these scrubby, velour house shoes instead, gave him a quick up-and-down scan, then said, 'You'll do.'

Orla took a step towards them.

The moment was fragile. She wasn't reading it. Willa's phone buzzed and as she tugged it out of her bodice and began tapping away, Finn pulled Orla aside and asked, 'Can you give us ten minutes?'

She began panic-talking him through her extensive and exacting timeline for the day, her voice actually shaking as she admitted if everything didn't run precisely to plan, they would be ruined. They agreed to start the handfasting ceremonies with the guests they did have when Willa approached them with a terse, 'Hey. No more plotting behind my back.'

'Fair enough,' Finn said, then, before either woman could protest, he pointed Willa towards the main yard outside the barns. 'C'mon.'

'What?'

'We're going to find your mate.'

'I thought that was you.'

'The other one. Gabe.'

She scowled at him but started walking.

The best thing he could think to do to keep Orla's guests from demanding instant refunds was to get Willa and Gabe to talk. It was how he regularly dealt with any 'warring' teens over at the agricultural college. Usually whatever beef they were embroiled in had begun as a misunderstanding and the only path to resolution was speaking to one another.

As they left his stepsister in their wake, he lowered his voice and confided, 'I've not read the booking notes, but Orla said Lachlan knew Gabe already. That they'd met as teens. This was meant to be a reunion. Does his name ring any bells?'

'Lachlan? No.' Her brow furrowed as she hoicked up her skirts and powerwalked alongside him. 'How could he know Gabe if he's Scottish? Gabe's not been to—' She stopped abruptly and then, almost to herself said, 'What is going on, Val?'

Val? Who was Val?

Willa looked up at him, her Bambi brown eyes actively seeking something from him. Comfort? Reassurance? Unlikely. She'd made it clear she thought he was on a par with cow dung, but . . . something about the things she said and the way she behaved didn't match up. As if beneath all of the bluster was a genuinely kind soul who'd decided to put on a grouchy suit to hide how she really felt: scared, undesired and alone.

His fingers twitched with the urge to reach out and sweep some of that long dark hair of hers away from her face. But with their brief, tumultuous history, he guessed she'd probably slap his hand away and start screaming for help.

He focused on the task at hand. Finding Gabe and Lachlan. He pointed to their left. 'They've probably gone over to the castle. Unless you think he's heading out to the main road to try hitch-hiking or something?'

She shook her head. 'I honestly don't know. Gabe's more of a mystery than I had originally given him credit for.'

'What do you mean?'

She heaved a dramatic sigh and gave an unexpectedly comedic eyeroll. 'How much time have you got?'

'Well . . .' He looked at his bare wrist and pretended to read the time. 'We are meant to be fake married for the fortnight so . . .'

'Two weeks might not be long enough,' she quipped, a hint of humour still glinting in her eyes. 'Even if we're fastened at the hand.' She made a sucking noise and smashed the backs of her hands together.

'You know what one is, right?'

She bristled, then begrudgingly admitted she didn't.

'It's a traditional element of a Scots wedding ceremony from pagan times. It's tribal, really. Obviously, this one isn't legally binding. It's part of your "authentic experience", but that should've been made clear in the paperwork. I think Orla had it all detailed in your bookings?'

'Yeahhhh.' Willa let the word pour out of her long and slow as she ran her index finger along her full, lower lip. 'I think you're referring to the bookings neither Gabe nor I ever saw.'

'What?'

'We didn't sign up for this.' She huffed out another laugh. 'I wouldn't have even dreamt of booking a vacation like this in a million years.'

One second is all it takes to fall in love forever.

His father's oft-used phrase careened into Finn's mind so hard and fast he panicked he'd said it out loud. His dad had called it The Gut Factor. The feeling he'd had when he'd first laid eyes on Finn's mum. *I just knew, son. From the moment I saw her. I just knew.*

He glanced at Willa. She was actively scanning the fields beyond him, then, without any ceremony, lifted up her skirts and began purposefully striding towards the castle.

He met her pace easily, glancing over at her occasionally to check she was alright. Annoyingly, his eyes kept dipping downwards. He'd never considered himself a boobs man before now, but his body was telling him otherwise. And not just because of yesterday's epic costume malfunction and his role in it. The truth

124

was, ever since he'd laid eyes on Willa Jenkins, his body had been telling him lots of things he didn't know about himself.

He could still wake up with a raging erection for one.

That certainly hadn't happened for a while.

Not to mention still being here at Balcraigie. He'd meant to leave last night.

Was Willa why he'd stayed?

God, he hoped not. He couldn't think of a woman less likely to be his soulmate. Not to mention the fact she'd likely knee him in the balls if he tried it on with her.

But how else could he explain his well-laid plans being blasted to smithereens? He'd had it all planned out. Volunteer to do the airport run. Wait for Orla's mismatched group of *Outlander* enthusiasts to gather together. Tell them it had all been a big mistake so that he could send them on their merry way, call the estate agent and put the farm on the market the way they should have fifteen years back when every single hope and dream they'd had for Balcraigie had died along with his dad.

But then he'd seen Willa. Her big smile. Her happy wave. Her complete absence of self-awareness when her bodice ribbons had come untied . . .

'Hey. Second warning.' Willa was waving her hand in front of his face and pointing her fingers upwards. 'Eyes are still up here, bud.'

Finn winced and scrubbed a hand over his face. 'Sorry.'

She looked down at herself and then back up at him. 'Lordy. They really are out on display, aren't they?'

Wince still in place, Finn responded with care. 'I suppose if it's true to the era then . . .'

He didn't really know where he was going with the thought, so he let it peter out.

Willa stopped, balled her hands into fists and popped them on her hips as if she were ready to draw out a pair of pistols. 'If I tell you something in confidence, will you keep it to yourself?'

He made a my-lips-are-sealed gesture.

She looked around her, checking they were alone, then whispered, 'I haven't watched *Outlander*.'

She took a step back from him as if waiting for a huge physical reaction to the news. When there was none, she added, 'Or read the books.'

His entire bone structure heaved a sigh of relief. 'Me neither.'

'Seriously?' She did a double take. 'Then . . . why are you guys hosting *Outlander* experiences?'

'That's not exactly what we're—' He stopped himself mid-flow. What should he say? Admit that what they were doing here was fraud, pure and simple?

There was something about Willa that demanded honesty, but having seen the rest of the group's genuine excitement about being here in Scotland – arriving in the costumes Orla had magicked up from the local amateur dramatics society, cooing over beds made of old pallets, clapping their hands at a bowl of porridge – he felt he owed it to them to stay quiet. They believed in the holiday they'd been sold. Flown halfway across the world for, in some cases. Saved for a year. So much effort for something that had been scrabbled together out of sheer desperation.

When he'd left for the airport, the compost loos had only just arrived. A lorry with a crane had been guiding them over the stables' roof while the lads ran round like chickens with their heads cut off. Chainsaws bit into huge logs that had been sitting in the yard for years. Chests' worth of blankets and bedding dating back to his great-grandparents were hanging on the wooden fences so Orla's children could beat them with their cricket bats. It had been total chaos. His last glimpse of the place had been watching Dougie and a couple of the lads carrying his and Orla's mattress across the courtyard.

When he'd devised the plan to send everyone packing, he'd thought he'd be doing them a favour. The guests and Orla.

When he'd jacked in that plan and bundled everyone into the jeep and driven them here, he knew he was exercising one of the biggest leaps of faith he'd taken in years. Even now, he still wasn't a hundred per cent sure why he'd done it. There was so much at stake. And he wasn't even talking about the guests. Honestly? Being strung out by the tourist board was the least of their worries. He was thinking about Orla. Her family. Her dad. Everyone who worked at Balcraigie. His parents. Especially his parents.

And even though everything was, as predicted, already falling to bits, he knew in his heart Orla was right. Balcraigie Castle was meant to be more than a crumbling heap of neglected stone and ivy. It deserved life.

But he still wasn't convinced they were the ones to do it.

To Willa, he finally said, 'This is Orla's operation. I'm just one of the worker bees.'

Willa gave him a *right* nod that suggested she didn't entirely believe him, but he could feel the energy between them shift a little. Not exactly friendly, but the playing field had been evened.

They walked in silence towards the castle, each of them with an ear cocked for voices and, eventually, they heard them.

'I think they're away by the doocat.'

Willa shot him a questioning look.

'The dovecote.' He used the English pronunciation.

'Nope.' She shook her head. 'Still don't understand.'

He thought of how he'd explain it to his students, many of them lifelong city dwellers. 'It's like a hen house for pigeons and doves. Except . . . this one's not got a roof. Or pigeons and doves.'

Willa smirked at him as if he'd said something funny, then let her smile drop away. 'Will you come with me?'

'Of course.' He was surprised at the request, and even more surprised at his instinctive response. If she wanted him there, he'd be there. Even if it tore at the seams of painful memories he'd much rather keep shut tight.

Eyes focused on the pathways which were, unsurprisingly, covered in all sorts of bits and pieces, he guided her past the raised main doorway as the old ladder they'd once used to clamber up into the castle had long since rotted away. They picked their way round to the side where an open archway led through to what would have been the grand receiving room if it weren't covered in ivy and growing trees in the centre of it, then the dining room, the breakfast room and, with a quick right turn through a dodgy archway, a shortcut through a back passageway led to the massively overgrown walled garden where, up a twisted stone staircase, standing in the remaining arc of the doocat, stood Gabe and Lachlan.

Chapter Fourteen

It wasn't the view that took Willa's breath away. Although it should have. Up here, high above the stables where she could easily see up and beyond the castle walls, was an enormous inlet – a loch maybe? – that spread all the way to the horizon.

Surrounding it were vast, sprawling fields that stretched to the water's edge and up, deep into rugged hills that hinted at a dusting of snow. There were sheep in some, cows in others and arable crops – potatoes, maybe – covering acre upon acre of lush farmland. As the hills grew into mountains, they extended further and further north, gradually fading in detail like a Chinese ink painting. It was one of the most exquisite views she'd ever seen.

But the beauty didn't break through the shock of what was in front of the view.

There, at the far end of the dovecote, Gabe and Lachlan were in a fierce clench. Clinging to each other as if they were long lost . . . well . . . definitely not brothers.

Blood roared through her ears. Little bright specks of light forced her to open and close her eyes as if she was one of those dolls who was tipped awake then not awake. Which, not being funny, was how she felt. Was this even real? Heartbeats ricocheted round her chest like a pinball intent on a high score. Throat. Chest. Gut.

Each pulsing beat an assault on her ribcage. And yet . . . there was a part of her that wasn't surprised at all. If anything, she was grossly disappointed with herself for not seeing it in advance.

This hadn't been a set-up for her and Gabe. It had been a set-up for Gabe and Lachlan.

More than anything, Val had wanted Gabe to know he was, and always had been, loved. Val wasn't here to do it any more, so she'd found someone who could do the job for her.

Willa had been brought along for moral support. Her usual role. Good ol' reliable Wills. There with the box of tissues and comfort snacks when you needed her. She'd done it for Val countless times when work got too political (the world of dentistry was far more Machiavellian than one might think), or the strain of young motherhood took its toll or, on the very, *very* rare occasions when Diego did something to piss her off, Willa had, without fail, battled through traffic, pulled up at the house with pints of ice cream, drugstore facials and an endless stream of positive affirmations.

Her cheeks burnt with humiliation. How stupid to think this trip had been about her. It was akin to thinking a celeb's smile when she walked in the room was full of genuine delight that she – Willa Jenkins – had finally arrived.

She swiped at her nose, her eyes stinging with shame and, yeah, even though she hadn't been entirely sure what her feelings had been for Gabe, she'd admit it, betrayal.

She'd thought they were on this trip together. For one another. To bond over their mutual loss of her very best friend. But here she was, on her own again. It was the same old record, same old tune. Always the third wheel, never the bride.

Her chin began to wobble. She was a shitty country song.

How could Val have done this? *Why* had she done it? Willa had risked her *job* to come on this trip. Of all the things that had held her in LA when Val had died, her job had been it. It was all she'd had left. When she'd met Gabe and he'd been so warm and charming (eventually), then effortlessly swept away all of the obstacles between her and Scotland, she'd felt that zing of life again. That hint of possibility that there was something beyond the TiTs studio that could give her a sense of purpose. A reason to be happy.

Token spinster friend with a broken gaydar hadn't really been the end game she'd been aiming for.

She turned to go before they saw her only to come nose to chest with a big, check-shirted wall of heather-and-hay-scented Finlay Jamieson.

She looked up into those storm-blue eyes of his and silently pleaded with him to let her pass. She felt an ugly cry brewing and didn't have it in her to fight. When he didn't budge, she hissed, 'Move.'

'No.'

Her cheeks flared with heat. '*No* is not a two-syllable word,' she snipped, despite the fact every Scottish-soaked word that came out of Finn's mouth felt like getting a bumper crop at a candy dispenser. 'Shift yourself,' she growled.

Finn broadened his stance so that he completely blocked the narrow stone stairwell. 'Not until you have a wee natter with your pal, there.'

'Oh, is this how we're playing it?' She might not want to talk with Gabe, but maybe she *did* have it in her for a 'wee' bicker with Finn. She crossed her arms and shot him a cranky smirk. 'Me big Scottish McManly man pretending to understand what I'm feeling? Shall I run off and find a talking stick? Unpack all of my childhood issues while I'm at it? Is that what you want? Emotions here, emotions there, Willa's got feelings everywhere!'

Finn leant against the wall indicating he had all the time in the world. 'If you like.'

'Pah!'

A lock of his straw-coloured hair fluttered in her derisive gust.

Still, he stood, waiting like an irritatingly patient parent more than happy to watch their child scream themselves to silence in the cereal aisle.

In all honesty, she'd love to offload on someone she'd never see again. Val had been her go-to emotional laundry basket. A completely judgement-free friend who she could dump all her dirty problems into. After spinning them round a bit ('Do we really need to have the blue-versus-green-mascara-will-change-everything discussion again?'), Valentina always returned her more trying life issues clean, neatly pressed and stacked in an appealing colour-coordinated order.

Right now she was a tangle of inside-out leggings, scrunched-up socks and savaged sports bras, but she wasn't about to put on that particular light show in front of Finn Jamieson. Losing the plot would only confirm what he already thought about her: that she was a superficial, Californian hot mess.

She put her hands on his chest and tried to push past him. Not so much as a whisper of a teeter. Not that she had the brain-space for this sort of detail right now, but having actually touched it? She could silently admit that Finn's chest was really, really nice. It wasn't over-the-top gym buffed like a lot of the guys back home. It was more . . . organically strong. As if his day-to-day life had crafted the curve of his pecs and the – oh god! She was groping him. Not good. Definitely not good.

'You've got to talk with him, Willa.' His voice was low and rumbly and literally vibrated from her feet all the way up to her top of her head. Or maybe she was freezing to death. The wind was brisk up here and the stairwell had not come equipped with central heating.

'Don't want to,' she said sulkily, then sneezed.

'Are you feeling alright?' He frowned as he inspected her. 'You're looking a bit peely-wally.'

'That sounds like I have leprosy.'

'It means you're not looking a hundred per cent.' His frown deepened. 'Is that you shivering? Here. Take my coat. I'll not have you freezing your tits off— freezing to death,' he quickly corrected.

Despite herself Willa half-laughed. Her boobs should have come on this holiday by themselves.

Finn shrugged off his worn wax jacket and slipped it round her shoulders. The inside was quilted and she instantly felt the heat from his body transfer to her shoulders, cocooning her like a forcefield.

'You okay there, Willa?'

She tugged the two halves of the jacket close round her, then pursed her lips at him in a *happy now?* expression to hide her actual reaction. A swoon. The gesture was pure chivalry.

'C'mon, lass. Go and speak with him.' His smile was gentle, encouraging. 'You know I'm right.'

She did. But she wasn't quite ready to admit as much.

In all honesty, her choices were fairly limited right now.

She could scream until he moved, run back to the stables, crash through the handfasting ceremony, flounce up the stairs to her hay-loft, cram all her clothes back into her bag, then dramatically bump her wheelie bag down the stone steps, slip her stylishly oversized sunglasses on and demand someone call her an Uber.

A perfect plan if she were Elle Woods or Kim Kardashian. They, at least, had the guarantee of someone chasing after them to make sure they were okay, even if it was a camera crew. Something told her the chances of Gabe running after her to beg for forgiveness were slim to nil.

The thought pulled her up short.

Why did Gabe need forgiveness? All he'd done was hug a hipster in a rainbow kilt. This, after being an absolute gentleman from the moment she'd met him. Rescuing her car, buying her clothes, getting her upgraded for a long-haul flight and not mentioning once that she was personally responsible for scarring him for life because of her own epically stupid costume failure. From the moment he'd first clinked shot glasses with her, he'd been exactly what she'd needed. A friend.

She huffed out an aggrieved sigh. Was the universe really guiding her towards a moment of true grace or would she choose the easy route and destroy the first two weeks off she'd had in years by being in a huff? God, she wished it was LA time. Then she could excuse herself to answer the inevitable text flurry over who was or wasn't Ready to Rock This Year's Movember Moustaches.

'So . . . what?' she grudgingly asked Finn. 'You think I should just walk out there?'

'Unless you're planning on teleporting yourself, it sounds a pretty good way to me.' Again, his tone was kind, warmed with what she could now recognise as his gentle, trademark humour.

Asshole.

She wanted – no, she *needed* – someone to be cranky with, and Finlay Jamieson was in the unfortunate position of being perfect for the role.

She put on her best snarly voice, got right up in his face and said, 'And what makes you so wise and all-knowing Mr I'm-Just-A-Worker-Bee?'

Ha! She'd got him there. That'd make him budge.

She waited.

And waited.

Not so much as a flicker.

Cripes.

She was so close to him now she could feel his breath on her lips.

He moved in closer.

Man he smelt delicious. Buttery toast served on a hay bale.

She was desperate to lick her lips but as this was turning into a rather intimate smackdown, she ran the risk of licking his as well. Definitely not an option. So she bit down on her lower lip. Hard.

'I'm your husband,' Finn said, his lips almost grazing hers as he spoke. 'I know everything.'

Seriously? That's what he was going with? The husband-knows-best line?

'I'm sorry,' she said. 'I think you've confused me with someone who's just escaped from a break-off Mormon cult.'

She tipped her head to the side, which let just enough sunlight in to see that his cheeks were pinking.

Awwww.

He'd been kidding.

She felt the tight knot in her chest give a little.

'Talk to him,' Finlay said. 'You'll feel better. I promise.' He spoke with conviction. As if he completely believed in her ability to face this situation head on even if she didn't.

'But—'

'Talk to him.' He gently swept his work-worn hands along her shoulders down to her elbows and then, with an encouraging nod, turned her round.

She looked at Gabe, who was now standing apart from Lachlan, but still holding hands and still very much in his thrall.

He looked so beautiful. So perfect. And, for the first time since she'd met him, she felt as if she was finally seeing the real Gabriel Martinez.

She'd deeply wanted to believe that Valentina had set this whole elaborate adventure up so that, even though she was gone, Willa would always have a link to her through Gabe. But that had never been the plan. And with that realisation Willa felt a raw, savage pain rip through her as the tenuous link to Val was torn away.

She must've cried out, because Gabe turned in alarm.

'Willa.' He scrubbed his hands through his inky mop. '*Dios*, I'm so sorry. I shouldn't have— I need to— This is—' He held out his hand towards Lachlan and choked back a sob.

'I'm Lachlan.' Sexy Hipster Beardy Man stepped forward to shake Willa's hand. His hands, like Gabe's, were soft and supple city-man hands, but not without an undercurrent of strength. His aura was warm and open. Compassionate. As if he was filled with nothing but peace, vegan sausages and organic, virgin-harvested sage smoke.

He cupped her hand in both of his and just held it, gazing at her with a soft smile on his face, until he kind of blurred. The hot tears of embarrassment she'd been trying to keep at bay had finally begun to streak down her cheeks, plopping quite unceremoniously on to her boobs.

Fucking boobs!

She tugged her hand out of Lachlan's and pulled Finn's coat closer round her. Her gaze shifted to Gabe, hoping for some sort of explanation, but he said nothing.

'I'm Finn.' Finlay stood close behind her, as if sensing she needed the support, and stretched his hand out towards Lachlan.

She glanced up at him and smiled, grateful for the awkward-silence intervention and, curiously, for the physical reassurance of his presence.

Gabe nodded at Finn, then shifted his gaze back to Willa. 'Maybe we should talk alone?'

'Finn's about to be my husband,' she said slightly too defensively. 'We do everything together.'

She felt Finn's eyes land on her but wasn't going to risk catching the horror undoubtedly flaring in them. Two rounds of rejection today just might finish her.

'Okay. Good. Umm . . .' Gabe began, then faltered, scrubbing a hand across his face.

It was weird seeing him so unsettled. So . . . human.

A line from Val's final wishes came to her. *Sometimes you have to step outside of yourself to become the person you want to be.*

What wasn't mentioned, was that the process of shedding one skin would, in turn, expose a fresh, unweathered one. Soft and vulnerable in a world full of jagged edges.

'I'm guessing you and Lachlan are previously acquainted?' Willa prompted.

'Yes.' Gabe's eyes flooded with emotion. 'We, uhhh . . . Lachlan and I—'

'We met a long time ago,' Lachlan said, stepping back and sliding his arm around Gabe's shoulders in such a comfortable move it was as if he'd been doing it for years.

'How?' Willa asked.

'He was an exchange student,' Gabe said to Lachlan, whose eyes he couldn't seem to stop staring into. With a hand pressed to Lachlan's heart, he turned to Willa and, between them, they told her everything.

Lachlan was from Edinburgh. He'd always known he was gay and came from a family who had been incredibly supportive of him and his sexuality. When he'd been placed at Gabe's high school in Texas, his family had questioned whether or not he'd feel safe, but he'd said he didn't want to be frightened being who he was. And when he'd gone to his first class, the two had met and fallen instantly and completely in love. Their romance was strong, but they kept it out of the public eye. Everything had gone well until Gabe's father had found out. He'd been horrified and refused to believe he had a gay son. Things came to a head at Valentina's fifteenth birthday. The family was throwing a huge party. All the siblings were bringing their partners. Gabe wanted to bring Lachlan, who was days away from returning to Scotland. His father refused. Gabe gave him an ultimatum, accept us both, or he would walk away.

'I suppose you can figure out the rest,' he said with another scrub of his perfect jawline.

Yeah. She could. He ran away, made an incredible success of himself by helping people out who'd needed guidance after a fall from grace.

'Did you go with him?' she asked Lachlan.

He shook his head. 'To my shame, no. I returned home. But he's always lived here.' Lachlan placed his hand over Gabe's, which was still resting on his heart. 'And now, thanks to his sister, he's actually here. Two whole weeks to catch up.' Unexpectedly, he laughed. 'Who knows? We might not even like each other any more, but . . .'

In tandem the pair said, 'First impressions speak volumes.'

If ever there was a moment to throw up in her mouth a little, this was it. But, despite the blow to her ego, she could see that these two had needed to meet again, even if to close a door on a chapter written long ago.

'Did you . . .' she began tentatively, and then, in a rush asked, 'Did Valentina tell you this was going to happen?'

'Not specifically.'

'So . . . you read her letter.'

Gabe nodded.

She was desperate to ask him what was in it, but the distinctive screech of bagpipes cut through the air before she could.

She threw Finn a questioning look.

'That'll be our cue to head to the altar,' he said.

She looked over at Gabe and Lachlan only to find them caught in a dreamy-eyed staring contest.

Feeling desperately awkward in the glow of such intimacy, she cleared her throat, hooked her arm in Finn's and said, 'I guess we'd best get down to the stables and get ourselves hitched.'

Chapter Fifteen

As Shona and her bagpipes squawked out wedding marches with an almost imperceptible hint of Rihanna to them, the group gathered together inside the stone remains of the old chapel just beyond the stables. Finn took advantage of the fact it was too loud to talk and tried to gather his thoughts about Willa. Yes, they'd got off to a false start. She'd struck him as a flibbertigibbet. An ineffectual, too-woke-for-her-own-good, butter-wouldn't-melt, city slicker. A beautiful one. But someone he'd definitely swipe left if dating was on his agenda. Which it most definitely was not, especially with things at Balcraigie reaching boiling point. But now that he'd had a few glimpses at the real Willa, she was a welcome distraction from the avalanche of problems hanging above him.

Whatever she'd thought this holiday was going to be, finding out her boyfriend was gay obviously hadn't been on the agenda. Not that openly declaring her intent to fake marry a man who put her teeth on edge was the solution, but something beyond pity had compelled him to go along with it. There was more to her charged, emotional reaction to Gabe's news than met the eye and if working at the agricultural college with teenagers had taught him anything, he knew that waters didn't always have to be still to run deep. Even so, it was going to be a long couple of weeks.

As Orla directed everyone to their places, Willa leant in. 'This is completely surreal, right?'

'Och, away.' Finn swiped at the air. 'We're always doing this sort of thing up here in the Highlands. Perfectly normal.'

She snorted. 'Am I the only one to get a groom with six fingers?'

Finn shot her a look. 'You may laugh now, lass, but you'll soon find you've got the best of a questionable bunch of ruffians.' He broadened his brogue for effect. 'And be warned, I'll no have my bride keeking about for an alternative.'

She crooked her finger and jigged it a few times. 'Translation, please.'

'Keeking?' He turned his hands into a telescope. 'Looking. Snuffling about for someone who isn't me.'

'How very Cro-Magnon of you.'

He was about say something to ensure she knew that he knew they were both doing this under duress, but Willa suddenly stood stock still. He turned and saw Gabe and Lachlan appear in the chapel doorway hand in hand.

The smile dropped from her face.

Before he could ask if she was absolutely certain she wanted to go ahead, a friend of Orla's from the Balcraigie Players, clearly playing the role of minister, stepped into place with a dramatic, 'My flock! My ken. My dearly beloved. Who will be the first lucky couple to be joined as one for the rest of their living days? Or, in this case . . . two beautiful weeks in one of Scotland's finest estates?'

Orla pointed at Finn and Willa. They both recoiled in horror. Finn fought the urge to tell Orla he'd been right, this entire scheme was doomed, then remembered what was at stake and forced on a smile.

He led Willa up to the small pallet stage in front of the straw-bale altar, decked out with fistfuls of late season heather and thistles.

Orla's am-dram pal raised his hands to the heavens and cried, 'Are ye prepared to witness two hearts bound together as one?'

The group let out cheers and a couple of whoops. One of the lads from the farm shouted out, 'Get in there, Jamieson,' to which Finn shot back, 'That's my future wife you're talking about, mate. I'll have you showing her respect and nothing less.'

'Right you are, Finn. Now quit your faffing and get on with it!'

'Aye. That's what we're here for, that's what we'll do.'

His nerves knotted in his chest as the am-dram minister began unveiling a rather impressive Scottish-tinted *Princess Bride* impersonation, bleating on about harmony and bliss and obedience.

He had to admit, even though this entire thing was for show – a fiction – there was something about standing beneath a wedding bough in the remains of the old chapel with Willa's hands in his that gave him goosebumps. The sun made a rare appearance and filtered through the traditionally decorated tree branch dappling diamond-like speckles of sunlight throughout Willa's dark hair. Her espresso dark eyes were bright and her expression was a combination of nerves and something unexpected. Hope.

Struth. He hoped she was faking it.

He'd heard the other women in the group talking earlier this morning about how much they were looking forward to wedded life with a rugged, kilted Highland male. Not one of them mentioned hoping to work from dawn to dusk with a sweaty, smelly contractor. Nor had they expressed a desire to physically labour until their bones ached, falling into bed the minute after they'd shovelled down their tea, only to get up a handful of hours later and do it all over again.

Such was the life of a true Highlander.

These poor folk were in for a bit of a shock.

Or . . . said a quiet voice in his head, *maybe they're here for all the right reasons. Perhaps they will enjoy it.*

The thought caught him off guard.

Perhaps, continued the quiet voice, this was precisely the immersive experience *he* needed. A last-ditch chance to throw himself into life at Balcraigie and figure out what it was he did – or more likely didn't – want from the place. To sell or not to sell. That was the question.

Ranald, their pretend minister, took interwoven strands of green and purple cord and held them up for the 'congregation' to see. 'As I tie this knot, so too will your lives be bound!'

Finn's pulse accelerated. Stupid, considering he knew it was all fake, but Willa must've been feeling it too because her hands began to shake.

He ducked his head, trying to catch her gaze. They really didn't have to do this if she didn't want to. She shot him a look that said, *Please fuck off with your sympathy looks.*

He shot one back that said, *Fine. Happy wife, happy life.*

She grinned at him, clearly pleased that she'd 'won' that round.

Oblivious, Ranald took hold of his right hand, then Willa's left, and pressed them together. He asked them to hold their wrists just so, then began a rather impressive swirling motion that swiftly became several rounds of soft cord fastening their wrists together.

'This cord,' continued Ranald in his sonorous voice, 'holds not only the man-made fibres you see before you, but the fibres of hope and love. The fibres of *promise* for your new life together that these people, your friends and family, have brought here today, giving their gifts openly as they witness this, the joining of your two lives in marriage.'

Finn heard one of the women sniff and the tugging of tissues from a packet.

Willa glanced up at him, her lips pressed together as if she was stifling a giggle. They shared a look that, stupidly, made him feel closer to her. As if they were sharing a secret no one else knew.

'This cord now binds you to one another.' Ranald tied a single knot in the rope. 'Thus bound . . . may the knot remain untroubled for as long as your love shall last.'

Willa's hands were properly shaking now. She wasn't falling under the cosplay spell, was she?

'May it be granted,' Ranald crowed, 'that what's done in the presence of the heavens, may not be undone by man.'

Willa gave a nervous laugh. 'Sounds ominous.'

'Hold tight to one another,' Ranald shouted in response, 'in good times and in bad . . . and watch,' he lowered his voice for effect, 'as the thistle endures the seasons, so too will your love strengthen and grow.'

'Got it,' said Willa, her tone on a par with the spinning finger indicating it was time to move past the flowery stuff and skip to the end.

'Is this the kiss-the-bride part?' Finn asked when Ranald just stood there, staring at them.

Ranald's face lit up as if Finn had just reminded him of his forgotten cue. 'Indeed it is.'

He'd been kidding, but . . . oh god. Dilemma time. Should he actually kiss her?

Maybe a peck on the cheek would do.

Willa eyes shot to his lips.

Christ on a bike. Was he actually meant to kiss her? She was still stinging from a very public rejection. He didn't know the ins and outs of it, but he knew hurt when he saw it and he didn't want to add to her pain.

'Blood of thy blood, bone of thy bone.' Ranald shot a meaningful glance at Finn. 'You may now kiss the bride.'

Chapter Sixteen

'Why do they call this a wedding breakfast when it's actually a wedding lunch?'

'Is it traditional to have sausage rolls?'

'It is if you're taking it as a wink and a nudge for what's going to happen later, lassie!'

'Trevor! You big hunk of spunk! I thought this was strictly "look don't touch".'

'What's brown sauce? Is it like barbecue sauce?'

Willa half-listened as the new couples excitedly exchanged questions and answers, proposing toast after toast even though their pewter flagons were charged with tea or instant coffee. ChiChi was giggling like a madwoman as her new husband crooked his arm into a strongman flex, then asked her to hang from it. Which she did. Jules and her new wife were dissecting the wedding bough and having a very deep discussion about one of the plants which had bright red, fairy-tale coloured berries on it.

Jennifer was pawing through her wicker arm basket and unearthing a needle and thread, insisting her strapping young husband take off his jacket so she could stitch on a button that had gone flying when he'd scooped her up in his arms and carried her out of the chapel after they'd been pronounced man and wife.

Jeff and Rosa were staring dreamily into one another's eyes, as were Gabe and Lachlan. If you could catch diabetes from watching couples so sweet on one another they practically oozed sugar, now was her chance.

But Willa was too busy figuring out how to solve a teensy tiny problem.

Her lips were trapped back in time. About forty minutes ago, if anyone wanted to know when the clock stopped. She couldn't stop touching them, as if needing constant affirmation that they were still there.

The moment may have only been the blink of an eye. Possibly longer. She had no idea. All she knew was that from the moment Finn's lips had touched hers, she had been completely and utterly transported.

It was, hands down, the best kiss she'd ever experienced. So perfect, it had felt preordained. As if Finlay Jamieson had been put here on this earth, on this farm, in that kilt, for the express purpose of cupping her face in those incredible hands of his and showing her what a real kiss was meant to feel like.

From the moment their lips had touched, she'd known nothing and everything all at once. Fireworks, possession, protection and heat. Actual washes of the stuff, pouring like sexy lava through her nervous system. And they hadn't even tongued each other.

She'd genuinely thought she was levitating by the end of it.

'Here you are, lass.' A steaming mug of tea appeared before her. She followed the arm holding it out to her, up and along the increasingly familiar shoulder line, then up to her new fake husband's face. 'Get that down your gob.' He nodded at the mug. 'You'll need your strength for the day ahead.'

And just like that her picture-perfect Cinderella balloon popped.

146

'Is everything okay?' she asked, taking the tea. It was strong and milky and sweet all at once. The kind of thing you'd give someone after they'd had a shock.

'Aye. Fine.'

He didn't look fine.

He was scanning all the happy, giggling guests with an expression that suggested it was just as well they were enjoying themselves now because they wouldn't be for much longer.

Before she could ask him what was going on, the dinner bell in the stable yard rang. Finn beckoned for her to follow him to the yard. 'You'll have to change,' he said. 'Make sure you put proper work boots on. And wool socks.'

'What?'

He glanced back at her. 'You've packed some outdoor gear, right?'

Err . . . 'I've got a puffa jacket that could double as a sleeping bag and pants you can unzip at the knee.' She'd been assured they were very, very cool.

'No boots? Hiking? Walking? Something like that?'

She pulled a face. Nope. Nothing like that in her luggage. 'I did bring an excellent day cream with SPF.'

He shook his head and walked away.

She pulled up her skirt and glanced down at her old, comfortable Uggs, the stitching coming dangerously close to unravelling. They'd been a gift from Valentina years ago and she'd always equated the comfort they gave with their friendship. They were the only boot-type shoes she'd packed, and she wasn't prepared to sacrifice them.

Before Willa could decide whether her Converses or the running shoes she'd packed back when she thought there might be a gym here would work, Orla bustled into the centre of the stable yard and stood next to a table piled high with brown hessian cloth.

'Right you are, my lovelies.' She grinned, but not as brightly as she had earlier when she'd wished them well and sent them off to be married.

Finn reappeared at the edge of the courtyard. Something about his thin-set grimace told her he and Orla had had words.

Orla continued, 'Now that you've all got your Jamie . . . or Claire . . . it's time to truly immerse yourselves in Highland life.'

They all threw one another giddy looks. Jennifer let out a little whinny she was so excited.

Orla held up one of the brown pieces of fabric and snapped it out. It was a dung-coloured pinafore. She handed it to Jennifer. 'Here you are, lassie. Put that on over your travel dress and perhaps something else to keep you war-um. And make sure you wear your waterproof footwear.'

Willa shot a look in Gabe's direction. They really hadn't prepared for this during their *Pretty Woman* shopping trip. Before she looked away Gabe mouthed, *Can we talk later?*

There was a part of her that didn't want to, but the only thing that had really changed about Gabe was that he looked happier. As lonely as it made her feel, she knew taking things out on him would only make her feel worse.

She gave him a quick nod, then turned back as Jennifer accepted her smock with a curtsey before disappearing into her room to change.

Half an hour later, the group had all changed into the repurposed potato-sack outfits (complete with Balcraigie branding) and reassembled in a line. A ragtag group of wannabe Jacobites awaiting their call to battle.

'Well, don't you all look a picture?' Orla took up her clipboard and ran her finger down it. She looked up with a bright, openly anxious smile. 'Okay. Jules and Blair? You two are in the castle today.'

Jules's face brightened. 'Ace. What're we doing? Preparing the bed chambers in advance of our wedding nights?' She made as if to start chasing Blair round the yard.

Orla winced. 'Not exactly. You'll be clearing the old kitchen area in the castle.'

Jules threw out an exhilarated air punch and beamed at her new bride. 'You up for this, babes? I see a new bread oven in our future.'

Orla stepped forward, openly worried. 'I'll have to ask you to be very, very careful in there and remember that you have all signed health and safety waivers.'

Blair, Jules's new wife stepped forward. She was a taller, Xena Warrior McPrincess version of her bagpipe-playing sister. With a discreet *ahem*, she produced a glittery pink riding hat from behind her back and, with a bow, presented it to Jules. 'For the protection of your fair bonnet, m'lady.'

Jules ran a victory lap round the courtyard, demanding high fives as she swept the group with a sunlit can-you-believe-my-luck smile. 'Prepare yourselves for some of the best bread you've had in your lives, fellow outlanders!'

'Eh!' Jennifer's new husband, Errol, protested. 'Watch who you're calling an outlander. I'm full-blooded Scots, me. I've done ancestry dot-com and everything.'

Jules's smile remained undimmed. 'See you peeps later.' And with that, she took Blair's hand in hers and the pair headed off to the castle as Orla shouted after them, 'There are gloves and tools in the walled garden!'

When they'd gone, the rest of the group turned to Orla, expressions expectant. 'Righty-o. Here we go then.'

After a few minutes everyone had been assigned a job. Jennifer and Errol were off to check the state of the potato fields and then on to the hen house for egg collection. Jennifer threw them all a delighted look as she and Errol walked off with snatches of conversation about her 'to-die-for Spanish omelette' floating in her wake.

Fenella, Trevor and Trevor's border collie, Bess, were sent off to fix a stone wall in one of the fields.

ChiChi and Alastair were dispatched on a mysterious 'mechanical horse' errand.

Gabe and Lachlan were charged with unearthing the walled garden. ('As much as you can, lads. It's a mammoth task, we're no' expecting miracles.')

Willa wished them luck and made a we'll-talk-later gesture to Gabe.

Jeff and Rosa were dispatched with their 'son' Kirk, and Dougie on an unnamed task and then it was just Finn and Willa.

Orla looked down at her list and then at Finn. 'You're away to the barns then, are you?'

'Aye. So long as you're still happy with that.' Finn didn't sound like he was asking permission.

'Why wouldn't I be? They're your cows, aren't they?'

Finn sucked in a sharp breath but said nothing.

Willa's eyes pinged between them as an undercurrent of shared frustration hummed between them.

After a few moments of silent standoff Willa asked, 'Do you two need some alone time?'

'No,' they said together.

'Oooo-kay,' Willa breathed. 'Just askin'.'

Finn started to say something to Orla, reconsidered, then turned to Willa. 'Why don't you grab an extra jumper. It'll be turning colder later. We don't want you catching cold.'

It was the kind of thing her parents would say to her and her brothers before having an ultra-polite conversation about whether or not her dad's offer to take them all out for a spontaneous pizza dinner had been wise considering the state of the cheque book.

'Sure thing.' She smiled, throwing Orla a questioning look she hoped translated as *are we cool?*

Orla gave her hand a pat and said, 'If you've not got anything you're happy getting mucked up, I'm sure I could lend you something.'

She excused herself, but left the door to the hayloft ajar so she could earwig on the snippets of terse conversation floating up from the yard.

'. . . never get everything done this way.'

'If you have any better suggestions . . .'

'. . . not the herd. Not yet . . .'

'. . . then you're going to have to give this a go . . .'

'. . . *fifty acres?*'

'. . . not impossible . . .'

When Willa finally came back out, running shoes peeking out beneath her skirt and her new puffa jacket zipped up to her chin, Orla was nowhere to be seen. Finn's expression no longer bore the tension it had a few moments before, but storm clouds still hung over his head.

◆ ◆ ◆

'Ah!' Willa cried when they turned the corner and headed towards Finn's old Land Rover. 'The trusty Jacobean steed, groomed and waiting for the day's journey.'

Finn's mouth briefly twitched into a smile but he said nothing. Awesome. If this was a portent of things to come, she wasn't going to have to worry about oversharing.

After Willa remembered the passenger door was on the far side of the jeep, she climbed into the cab. Once he started the motor she brightly asked, 'Where are we going, O Ball and Chain of Mine?'

'Barns.'

'Wow. So this is the famed Scottish wit and repartee I've heard so much about then, is it?'

He shot her a glance. 'Aye.' And then, 'Sorry. Just a lot on my mind.' He lifted his index finger off the steering wheel and pointed towards a long dirt track. 'We're away down the new barns.'

The small gesture was a classic guy-in-a-truck manoeuvre. One she'd seen her dad and brothers perform a million times. Strangely, she found it comforting. As if he was a new flavour of ice cream with just enough sprinkles of the familiar to make her feel not entirely outside her orbit.

If this had been work and he a celeb, she'd instinctively have known whatever he was grumpy about had nothing to do with her. (Spanx too tight, a need to wee, an embarrassing photo about to hit the tabloids.) But since they had literally just promised to be one another's truly beloved, she felt she was allowed to press for more than the odd monosyllable.

Before she could think of the perfect question, a pebble-dash-covered two-storey house came into view.

'That doesn't look very Jacobean.' Willa pointed at the house. 'Who lives there?'

'Orla and Dougie,' Finn said. 'Their kids. Orla's dad.'

'Oh wow. Three generations in one house. That's cool. But . . .'

Anticipating her question, Finn said, 'Orla's father is my stepfather.'

'Soooo . . . sorry. I'm confused.'

'My mum married Orla's dad after my father died.' Finn shot her a quick look. 'Orla was Duncan's from his first marriage.'

Ah. That explained a lot. The wilful staring contests she'd seen between Orla and Finn were your normal mixed family drama. 'How old were you when all of that happened?'

'Nine,' he said, eyes still glued to the track ahead of him. 'Orla was seven.'

'Are either of your mothers still—'

'Around?' Finn finished for her. 'No. My mum died a couple of years back. Orla's mum is alive but lives abroad.'

Willa threw him a look.

Finn explained. 'She'd come up from Birmingham to work in a hotel during the summer season, met Duncan and stayed when she got pregnant. After a few years, she decided she didnae take to life in the Highlands and took off with a ski instructor from New Zealand. Duncan took up with my recently widowed mother and that was that.'

It twisted her heart to hear how bereft of emotion his voice was. As if a robot had crawled inside him and taken possession of his larynx. 'There's a lot to unpack there.'

He tipped his head as if to say, *depends upon what you compare it to.*

Failing to come up with something deep and meaningful to say, she held out her fist and he lightly bumped it with his own.

After a few moments' silence, he gave the steering wheel a squeeze and straightened his arms. 'Luckily for me, we don't unpack emotional baggage here in Scotland. We just stuff it in an attic somewhere and forget about it.' There wasn't an ounce of humour in his voice.

Her brain flashed back to the swish surrounds of the hospitality suite in the Four Seasons where she'd held up the trauma of Los Angeles traffic against Val's death. Even though the window dressings were worlds apart, they both came from places where people didn't talk about the hard stuff.

'Right!' Finn swung his truck to a practised stop in front of an enormous clapboard and rail ties barn. 'How are you around livestock?'

Chapter Seventeen

Finn knew he was being a git, but handovers with Duncan never brought out the best in him.

He didn't like owing the man and even though, on paper, Duncan was the one who owed him, it never felt that way. He was about to explain as much to Willa – forewarned was forearmed and all that – when Duncan jogged out of the barn and propped himself so close to the Land Rover that Finn was forced to roll down his window rather than open the door, step out and give each other some much needed personal space. As ever, it felt like a power play.

'Alright, lad?'

I'm thirty-three years old now, Dunc, but . . . whatever.

'Aye.'

The passenger door slammed. Finn watched, gobsmacked, as Willa skipped round the front of the Land Rover towards Duncan. She looked like a bouncy, ebony-haired unicorn.

When she got to Duncan she extended her hand, then, at the last minute, pulled it back, opting instead for a curtsey. 'Greetings, gentle sir. I'm known as Willa.'

Duncan smiled. A miracle.

'Alright there, lassie? I'm going to presume you're one of Orla's guests, then?' He shot a glance at Finn that was difficult to read. 'And Finn's.'

'Yessir.' Willa dropped the yesteryear demeanour and gave him an America-style salute. 'I'm Finn's fake bride. Mrs Willa Jamieson, at your service.'

She threw Finn a smile, her chin lingering on her shoulder for a moment as their eyes met. A hit of electricity crackled through him as powerfully as their kiss had. Then she looked away. Probably because he hadn't apologised or explained himself after the wedding. He wasn't sure what had possessed him to do it. Maybe there'd been a bit of *See . . . I can play along with your charade* when he'd first lowered his mouth to Willa's, but the moment their lips had connected? Fireworks. And now he was doing the classic guy thing of ignoring how vulnerable it had made him feel by being an arse. Orla's news hadn't helped. He thought of this morning's phone call with the bank manager. A sharp reminder of their collective reality. This marriage thing was pretend. And no amount of perfect kisses would change the fact that unless they took in this year's harvest, these next few weeks at Balcraigie would be their last.

While his brain churned through the uncomfortable reminders of just how knee deep in shit they all were, Willa was throwing sunshine-bright questions at Duncan. Why wasn't he being a Jamie? Was he into cosplay? Had he ever been to LA? To his surprise, his stepfather was answering them. In monosyllables, sure, but it was more than he usually got.

They were more of a storm-clouds-and-low-rolls-of-thunder kind of family. Willa, he suspected, came from a white-picket-fence-avocado-on-toast-no-toxic-feelings-allowed kind of family.

He watched as Duncan eventually ran out of steam in the face of Willa's machine-gun-question style. He didn't have much in his arsenal beyond a tight nod, so he tipped her one of those, then stuffed his hands in the pockets of his gilet and started giving Finn a quick run through. 'I left the girls out as you said, had a wee look round. No one looked ready apart from Jolene. She's not pushing yet, but she's standing away from the herd, so I reckon you'll have a wee one before long.'

'Thanks.' Finn reached for the door handle and gave the door between them a pointed look. Why did Duncan always have to get into his space?

Duncan took his cue and shuffled back a few steps. 'I'll shove off then, shall I?'

Willa's eyes shot to Finn.

'Thanks, Duncan. It was good of you to cover for me.' It was a begrudging thank you and they both know it.

'Nae bother, lad.' Duncan gave the Land Rover's bonnet a couple of claps with his hand. 'It's always a pleasure to spend some time with the girls. Especially now that—'

Finn shot him a look that dared him to say it. He knew he had to sell the girls, but goddammit, he was going to pick the moment when he hooked the livestock trailer up to the truck, not Orla. Not the bank. Not anyone.

Duncan didn't take the challenge, just turned and walked towards his own, weather-worn blue Land Rover with a hand raised in farewell.

'Wow,' Willa said when he'd driven off. 'That wasn't awkward at all.'

When he didn't answer, she persisted, 'Is this part of the whole *Outlander* thing? Playing out some centuries-old family feud?'

He shrugged.

'Oh my god,' Willa giggled. 'I forgot you hadn't watched it.' She cackled again.

'What?'

'We are going to be so busted if anyone finds out.' She pulled a fake grumpy face. 'You were supposed to be able to help me fake it!'

He held up his hands in surrender. 'Sorry. Do you want a divorce?'

She bent forward so abruptly he thought she was going to throw up. Just as he was stepping forward to check she was okay, she shot back, gales of laughter pouring out of her as her head slammed again his chin. 'Oh god!' she screamed. 'Are you okay?'

He rubbed at his jaw. It hurt, but, compared to everything else? He'd survive. 'I'm fine.'

'Are you sure?' She stepped forward and cupped his face with her hands, giving his cheeks soft little kitten pats. Too abruptly he took her hands in his and gave them back to her.

She curled them up into tiny fists and pressed them against her chest as her eyes blinked away whatever it was she was trying not to feel.

'I'm fine. Really.'

It wasn't much of an apology, but the tenderness of her touch had caught at the seams of something he hated admitting to himself. He was lonely. Coming back to Balcraigie always made him feel it more, as if his busy life in Inverness was just a disguise for the fact that no matter what he did, or where he lived, he was destined to be the cheese who stood alone. He knew it was partly his fault. He'd been the one to shove a wedge between himself and the villagers here at Balcraigie, but they hadn't exactly helped. It wasn't as if it was his father's fault he'd been born in England. Or that he'd scraped and saved to buy the farm when no one else nearby could.

It was interesting, he noted, how much help they were giving Orla, a born and bred local. If he'd asked to borrow costumes or asked for a volunteer to fake marry a bunch of superfans in the name of saving Balcraigie, he knew exactly the response he'd get. Cold shoulders.

He ignored the glaring omission that, in order to know there were costumes to borrow and actors to make use of one had to actually *be* part of the community. This was a place that looked after its own and somehow, through the years, Finn had felt squeezed out of it.

Willa waved her hand in front of his face. 'Hello? Are you sure I didn't give you a chin concussion? And if not, can you please McSplain to me what the fuck is going on?'

'What's McSplaining?'

'Mansplaining with a Scottish twist,' she said as if it was obvious. 'Look.' She shifted her fists to her hips. 'From what I've seen? An "immersive Jacobean experience" isn't all that's going down here at Balcraigie Castle, am I right? Or am I right?' She gave a little round the world hand snap.

Despite himself, he laughed. 'You've a magical way with words, m'lady. Perhaps you should pursue poetry while you're here?'

A flash of mischief lit up her eyes. 'I'd be good at it, huh? Stop your blether . . . I need some heather.'

He gave her a round of applause. 'Oh, aye. It's clearly your gift.'

Willa's smile softened. 'Look, I don't give a monkey's if you've seen the show or not. This whole thing is a level of weird I'm not used to, but seeing as we're outliers on the superfan front? We owe each other a pinky promise not to tell the others.'

'I'll shake on that.' They did and, once again, the moment of connection was more than skin against skin. It felt like a promise. A pact.

'Right, then.' Finn pointed towards the barn. 'Now that we're joined at the hip and know each other's deepest, darkest secret, how about you tell me why you're here if you're not slavering after the Scottish totty.'

She stopped and gave him a quick once over. 'A girl does not have to have seen *Outlander* to appreciate the merits of a man in a kilt.'

A hint of swagger entered his step. She thought he was a hottie, huh? Well, the feeling was mutual. To detract from his weird strutty walk, he spun the spotlight round to her. 'Los Angeles? That's where you're from, is it?'

Her expression briefly shadowed. 'Only about twelve people are actually *from* LA.'

So . . . 'Where *are* you from?'

'The land of dream crushing and aspiration hobbling.'

'Texas?' he guessed.

She laughed, her expression reading as if he had so very much to catch up on. Poor, simple Scottish totty that he was.

'I'm from a small town in the bumfuck middle of nowhere, Oregon.'

'Sounds lovely. You work for their tourist board, do you?'

She gave him a you-have-got-to-be-kidding look. 'Sorry to break it to you, bud, but the small-town American Dream done broke a long time ago. For me, anyway. I couldn't wait to get out of there.'

Finn winced. While farming in rural Scotland hadn't been his mother and father's inherited professions, it had been their most precious gift to Finn. From as long as he could remember, he felt predestined to be the caretaker of this land. He loved it. Absolutely, bloody loved it. The smell of the earth after it had been ploughed. The cows. The sheep. His awareness of the weather and how it affected everything. The bees, the hay crops, when the heather would come into bloom and so much more. It was as if the knowledge had come preloaded in him. Not being able to plan for a future here at Balcraigie was like looking at a set of Ikea instructions: painful before it had even begun. He cleared his throat and gave his neck a scratch. 'What does your family do?'

'Grease monkeys and do-gooders.'

'And you? Did the apple fall far from the tree?'

She flickered jazz hands on either side of her head. 'Entertainment news producer. And don't worry. It's far less glamorous than it sounds.' She gave him a quick explanation about the show she worked on, then pointed at the phone lodged in her cleavage. 'Who knew interviewing celebs would be as demanding as working at the Pentagon?'

'Wait a minute.' He stopped just short of the main gate to the barn. 'You're an entertainment reporter and you haven't seen *Outlander*?'

He practically saw her toes curling in her shoes. 'Aren't we supposed to be doing chores or something?'

Yeah. They were. Rather than push, he clapped his hands together, gave them a swift rub, then said, 'Absolutely right, m'lady. The cows aren't going to get themselves in on their own.' Finn walked them through the empty cattle barn to reach the rear gateway.

To be fair to Duncan, a man he was traditionally reluctant to credit with attention to detail, the barn looked exactly the way Finn would've sorted it had he been here this morning. There was a thick bed of fresh straw in the main pen. All the mother and calf 'nurseries' had been cleared out, standing ready for fresh occupants, as were tidy stacks of straw and hay, both of which were close to hand. The water troughs were scrubbed and refilled and, from the slight tang in the air, charged with a dollop of apple cider vinegar – one of the natural tonics Finn liked to give the cows for their wellbeing. The mineral licks were hanging from the gates where Finn liked them and the back scratchers had even been cleaned.

He silently acquiesced that, whatever he might think of Duncan as a stepfather, being idle wasn't a label that would ever stick.

Making a mental note to be less defensive next time they spoke, he pointed out to the twenty-acre field away up on the hilltop where the dozen expectant mums were soaking up some of the late morning sun. 'There they are. The ladies.'

'Oh my gosh!' Willa clapped her hands in delight. 'They're *stripey*! Are those Oreo cows?'

He snorted. 'They're Belted Galloways.'

'Is that what they're called here?'

'Well, I don't think they were named after the biscuits.'

Willa good-naturedly rolled her eyes. 'To-may-toe. To-mah-toe. You say Belted Galloway, I say Oreo.'

'Does that mean we're calling the whole thing off?'

She scoffed. 'Nice try, hubby. You're not getting rid of me that easily.'

For the first time since this whole thing had begun, he didn't want to. Were they complete opposites? Absolutely. But that kiss they'd shared – those few perfect moments that had sealed their pretend marriage – had felt like a real connection. Spoke to something humming beneath their stabs at witty bantz. Something better than lobbing one-liners at each other. It was like she got him without him having to go all touchy feely and explain why he was the way he was.

He nodded towards the hill speckled with black and white cows. 'Let's see if you can figure out how to get the ladies in.'

She pressed her lips forward, thinking, then asked, 'Our job is to get them from all the way over there to here where they will have baby cows?'

He put out a fist for her to bump. 'Well done. You're practically a farmer now.'

She stared at him for a minute then out at the cows again.

'Don't worry if you can't figure it out. My students never do.'

'Students?'

'I teach at a nearby agricultural college. Your equivalent of high school.'

From the look on her face, he may as well have told her he worked for the sewage department, and just like that he was back to disliking her. His work at the ag college meant the world to him. It had lifted him up and out of the emotional shitstorm he'd been battling after his mum had passed. Helping the scores of teenagers who came to the school full to the gunnels with attitude and shaping them into young adults capable of proper animal husbandry was rewarding.

When she asked what he taught he pointed at the cows. 'Livestock handling. Animal care.' What was it with this girl? One minute she seemed sharp as a tack, properly insightful, and the next she was like a bubble-brained Barbie.

'But . . .' Her gaze moved out to the sprawl of farm beyond the barns. 'If you work there, does that mean . . . ?'

He filled in the blanks for her. 'It means I don't work here. It's the school holidays, though, so, I'm not bunking off either.'

She pulled a face. 'I don't get it. If you don't like *Outlander* and you don't work here, what are you even doing here?'

It was a good question. One he asked himself regularly.

'Orla asked,' he said without elaborating. She didn't need to know he'd come to put a stop to all this nonsense. Having failed at the first hurdle, he was on a not-so-magical voyage of discovery, finding out just how many more problems Orla had kept from him. 'Right. Let's hear your grand plan about how to get the ladies in.'

Willa stared at him, then gave a girlie twist back and forth, curling a strand of hair round her finger. 'A glass of milk and some Oreo cookies?'

She was shitting him, right? 'Yes. That's it exactly,' he deadpanned.

'Raspberry jam?' she asked, as if she actually thought she was on the right track. 'That's Scottish, right? Who doesn't like raspberries?'

'I thought you Americans were more the grape-jelly type.'

'Yeah, but these are Scottish cows,' she parried.

Finn filled his lungs instead of answering. He really didn't think he had a fortnight's worth of patience for this type of nonsense.

'C'mon, then, lass.' He beckoned for her to join him at the gateway. 'It's time to learn from the master.'

'I'm not sure there's enough room for me.' She batted her eyes at him. 'What with your ego taking up all the space.'

Christ. An airhead ego-shaming him. Just what the doctor ordered.

And just like that she became a thing of motion. She grabbed a bucket off the wall, handed it to him, then pulled a twenty-five-kilo sack of mixed grain out of one of the feed bins. She plopped it on the ground, expertly undid the chain-stitched sack, poured some into the bucket, picked it up then began to shake it loudly, calling out, 'Cows! C'mon, cows. C'mon in, girls.' And, as if they'd known her all their lives, the girls pricked up their ears and began jogging down the hill towards the barn. When they charged towards her, she opened the gate, got them all in the main pen then pulled the gate shut behind her with a satisfying clang.

He looked at her, shocked. 'How did you know how to do that?'

She smirked at him. 'It's how all domesticated cattle are called in. Round-ups are for huge herds out on the range. And Oreos are for girls like me who don't know how to say no to trans-fats.'

He had to laugh. 'I'm guessing this is the sort of thing you got up to in the bumfuck middle of nowhere?'

163

'Yup.' She tipped an invisible cowgirl hat at him. 'And just so you're a bit more *au fait* with bumfuck lexicon – small towns are also called cow towns . . . for a reason.'

'I suppose now's the part where I should feel like an idiot for patronising you.'

'Pretty much!'

He looked down and made a connect he should've done an hour back. She was wearing trainers. She might be able to call the cows in like a pro, but if one of the girls stood on them? She'd be hobbling round with broken toes for weeks.

He took the bucket from her, flicked the grain into a nearby feeding trough, then deftly picked her up and flipped her so that she was hanging over his shoulder.

'Hey!' She pounded his back. 'What are you doing?'

'I thought I told you to put on appropriate footwear.'

'Excuse me, Mr Highland Health and Safety. No one mentioned we were going to be playing cowboy.'

'You really didn't plan for this at all, did you?'

'I didn't know what I was planning for,' she protested, her voice more heated than he would have expected from someone who'd bought and paid for a two-week holiday.

'Why? Didn't you read all of the bumph?'

'What's bumph?'

'The fine print. You know, the pamphlets and whatnot.'

'Whatnot?'

She was being obtuse now. 'The stuff that Orla sent out when you booked the holiday.' He set her down on a hay bale just outside the pen the girls were now inspecting with the glee of children set loose in a ball pit.

Willa put her hands on her hips and harrumphed. 'I told you. I didn't book it.'

'So who did?'

Chapter Eighteen

'It was her last gift to me.'

Finn took off his flat cap and scrubbed his fingers against his head as if he was trying to knead the new information into his brain. 'Gabe's sister gave you an immersive Jacobean experience but didn't tell you anything about it?'

'Yes. We were best friends. She gifted us this trip in her will.'

'Her will?'

'You know what a will is, don't you?'

Finn just stared at her.

She clapped her hands together. 'C'mon, Scottie.' Being a smart alec was the only way she could get through this topic without dissolving into tears. 'Catch-up time. She's dead. A will is how you give presents from the afterlife.'

Finn looked genuinely shocked. To the point she wished she hadn't said anything.

'What do you mean she's *dead*?' he asked.

She knew it was a reflexive question. A way of buying time to put together pieces of a very complex puzzle, but it rankled. He might have an accent that made listening to him akin to swimming in a sea of ambrosia, but this little display of intellect proved he was as incapable of thinking outside the box as everyone back home. If

Valentina's goal had been to find a place filled to the brim with all of the reasons she'd left Pendleton all those years ago, she'd done it. With bells on. Angel bells. But still. When she got to heaven? The two of them would be having words.

She glared at Finn, waiting for him to connect the dots. Less than an hour ago, he'd told her his own mother had passed away so he clearly understood the concept of death and loss.

'This is Gabe's sister we're talking about,' he finally said.

'Yes. Valentina. She was my best friend. I only met Gabe a few days ago.'

Instead of watching that bit of information settle, she climbed down from the huge rectangular hay bale, grabbed a pitchfork from the wall rack and began stabbing at it. 'Valentina got cancer. It was nasty. It took her from us and now, for some reason I am still trying to divine, she gave us this vacation. I get why she sent Gabe, but I am trying, for the life of me, to figure out why Val had me come along.' Lordy, she wished this day would end. It was way too full of the feels.

Her assault on the hay bale grew more pointed as she continued. 'She knew I hadn't watched *Outlander,* but she wasn't mean, so it isn't like she's trying to guilt revenge me from beyond the grave for not watching it with her, even though I guess she has every right to, because honestly? I should've got over myself and watched it. But I didn't. And she died. And when I got the call from the lawyers and went to the will reading, I guess I thought she was setting me up with Gabe so we could both have her in our lives through each other. Stupid, huh? Thinking someone like that would fall in love with someone like me.'

'Hey!' Finn's voice was sharp and commanded attention. He grabbed hold of the top of the pitchfork so she would stop stabbing at the bale. She looked up and latched on to his eyes and instantly wished she hadn't because they were so full of compassion all she wanted to do was throw herself into his arms and cry and cry and cry.

'What?' she spat instead.

They tussled over possession of the pitchfork until – surprise, surprise – the big, strong, muscly Scotsman with bulgy biceps won.

She scowled at him. 'What do you want from me?'

'It's our wedding day,' he growled back. 'I won't have my new fake wife talking about herself like this. You're a wonderful woman, Willa Jenkins.' He was shouting now.

'How do *you* know?' she shouted back. 'You don't know anything about me.'

She could see he thought she'd made a good point. And then he ignored it.

He held up his hand and started ticking things off. 'I know you're beautiful. I know you're kind. I know you miss your friend so much it hurts, but you've done what she asked of you despite the pain and confusion it's caused. I know you're forgiving, otherwise you wouldn't have been Gabe's flower girl. You looked really sweet by the way, with your wee posy.'

Her lower lip wobbled. He was extremely annoying when he was being nice. All her relationships in LA were about being nice, holding the seething broth of contempt beneath a bright smile and an acquiescent *sure, boss* nature. Being able to be openly shouty with someone was really, really fun. And now Finn was ruining it by being sensitive.

He softened his voice and stepped closer, reaching out to tuck some loose strands of hair behind her ear. Her stupid head leant into his touch. Then, to make things worse, he let the backs of his fingers brush along her cheek. She'd always wanted someone to do that. It felt every bit as comforting as she'd imagined.

'I know you're brave,' he continued, closing the space between them. 'I know you're stronger than you think you are.'

'Yeah, right,' she snuffled, using the sleeve of her puffa jacket as a tissue. 'Real brave.'

'Hey.' He tipped up her chin with a couple of his fingers, waiting until she met his steady, solid gaze. 'How many folk do you know would stand in front of a herd of pregnant cows intent on getting their Scooby snacks?'

She gave a little hiccoughy laugh. 'Admit it. You were hoping I'd get run over.'

He feigned horror. 'Aw, c'mon. I wanted you to gaze upon my Scottish McManly Muscles.' He struck a pose. 'Look at that, eh? I am made of Highland Man strength.' He started making even more ridiculous poses until she was giggling like a hyena.

'Stop!' she eventually insisted. 'You're gonna make me pee my pants.' She clapped her hands to her cheeks. They felt flushed, her hair was dishevelled, and no doubt her mascara was smeared everywhere, but for some reason none of it mattered.

'Thank you,' she said. 'You didn't have to say those things.'

'I did. They're facts, pure and simple.' He sat down on the remains of the bale and patted the space next to him. Once she'd joined him, their thighs lightly touching, he said, 'For what it's worth, I wouldn't have let you be trampled by the cows.'

She barked a laugh. 'That's mighty kind of you, McCowboy.'

They sat in silence for a few moments until Finn broke it. 'Whatever your friend's reasons were for bringing you here will become clear.'

Biting back the urge to bow and say, *yes, sensei,* she thought instead of the letter in her bag. She could read it now and figure everything out, but the simple truth was, she didn't want to. Reading it felt final. Too final. As if, once she undid the adhesive, pulled out the letter, unfolded it and let the inevitable flow of tears plop down on the ink, her friendship with Valentina would really be over. Like a lightbulb burning its last, final rays of light and then . . . darkness.

'C'mon.' He bumped his shoulder to hers. 'You look like you could do with some cow therapy.'

◆ ◆ ◆

'Cow cuddling is the new goat yoga!' Willa pronounced, draping herself over one of Finn's favourite girls, Heidi.

'If you say so, dear.'

'I do.' She gave him a superior smile.

He pulled off his flat cap and shifted it back into place. If he were a poker player, this would definitely be one of his tells. 'Your boots okay?'

'Fabulous.' Willa glanced down at the oversized, steel-toe-capped boots Finn had found for her up in the barn office. Orla's presumably. She attempted a jazzy soft shoe number and ended up stumbling over her own feet. 'I think the biggest hazard here is myself.'

He grinned at her, then wandered over to one of 'his girls'. He knew all of them by name. Their tag numbers. Their calving history. Their due dates. Nicknames. All the calves they'd had. Their calves' calves. 'Just a wee hobby.' Or so he claimed.

'So, to be clear, this is a wee hobby you have here at the farm where you don't live any more?' It was a pointed question, and she felt a bit intrusive asking it, but he'd discombobulated her by being nice, so she had to regroup. It felt much safer disliking Finn than accepting him as an actually ally.

Trusting someone meant relying on them and the past few months without Val had been terrifying. Showed her just how deep loss could cut.

The simple fact was, leaning into her friendship with Val had made one thing very clear: Willa had never laid a foundation of her own in LA. She'd just borrowed someone else's. And now that Val was gone, Willa was like the cartoon character stepping blindly off a cliff into—

'You alright, there, lass?'

She dug her fingers into Heidi's fluffy coat and began to scrub. 'Boy, oh boy! They do love a good scratch behind the shoulders, don't they?'

'If cows had knickers to get into, this would be the way to do it.'

Willa hooted. 'Is that how you get down with the ladies? Sidling up beside them and giving them a good ol' back scratch?'

'Aye,' he said drily. 'That's exactly how I do it.'

'Underneath all of your roughtie-toughtieness, you're a bit of a softie, aren't you?'

He barked out a laugh. 'Depends upon what you're using as a measure.'

'A sponge?'

He snorted. 'A chunk of granite, mebbe.'

It was her turn to snort. 'Even granite turns into soft, fluffy sand given the right conditions.'

'What? Being pulverised by my environment?'

'Well . . . You did marry me even though you obviously think all of this superfan stuff is nonsense.'

'Aye, well . . .' His eyes cinched with hers. There was something there she hadn't seen before. A vulnerability that suggested she was right. He had a big, kind heart and at least a little bit of it was looking out for her. The atmosphere between them switched from friendly banter to a warm, giddy feeling that seemed as if it had skipped right past flirting and straight to open desire. His teeth dragged along his lower lip. Her tongue swept along hers. He closed the space between them. She tilted her chin up to keep her eyes glued to his. And then her boobs buzzed.

Feeling twists of disappointment and relief, she answered the phone with her eyes still linked to Finn's. 'Bryony! What can I do for you this fine, sunny Los Angeles morning?'

Chapter Nineteen

Finn pulled up the zip on his wax jacket, grateful for its warmth. The sun had long since dipped below the horizon giving more room for the autumn chill to set in.

'So . . .' Orla drew out the word in a jolly sing-song as she took a big scoop of steaming cottage pie and charged Willa's plate. 'How was everyone's day?'

The response was muted at best, apart from Alastair who shouted, 'I'm pure done in, lass! Gie'us seconds on that grub, will ya?'

Orla tsked and told him he'd have to wait for all of the guests to be served so he turned his energies to translating what he'd just said to ChiChi.

If anyone had told Finn he'd be spending his October holidays participating in a handfasting ceremony with a lippy entertainment reporter from Los Angeles, he would've laughed until he wept.

And yet, here he was, among a crowd of folk in olden days gear, acting as if everything was perfectly normal. He still couldn't believe they hadn't figured out it was a set-up. Orla's 'genius' plan to keep the farm ticking over until they got the broken harvester fixed. He was amazed no one had baulked when they found out the castle was a ruin, that they'd be staying in repurposed horse stalls. Not to mention the fact they'd literally been doing farm chores today. Sure, there'd been the handfasting ceremony and Orla had pulled it out of the bag with the AmDram costumes, but when they figured out the reason they were here was because their 'Jacobean experience' was paying for replacement parts for a modern day tattie harvester? It wasn't worth thinking about.

He looked round the courtyard. A couple of folk were washing up at a small hand pump, others were queuing, tin plates in hand, waiting for steaming servings of cottage pie (Orla didn't do itty-bitty modern-cuisine-type servings), a few more were already parked on stumps pulled up close to the firepit, visibly mustering the energy to offer a few words of thanks before they fell to eating. Even Willa, who'd kept up an impressive stream of sarcastic comments throughout the day, was now silent. She was, he was pleased to see, sitting near Gabe and Lachlan.

He had to hand it to Orla: if this were a painting, it would sing of days gone by. And while they all looked tired, no one looked unhappy. The tableau of weary tourists reminded him of the terrible paintings his mum used to pick up in car boot sales to hang in the barns so 'the cows had something to look at through the winter'. Duncan had taken them all down when she'd passed. As if his mum's bin-end purchases had offended him all along.

Finn framed the real life 'painting' with his hands. If it had a name, it'd be called Exhausted Workers Returning From the Fields. He cleared his throat. Something like that, anyway.

When he caught Willa looking at him, he turned his hands round and pretended he'd been picking dirt out of his nails.

She gave him a little smile then went back to eating. His focus stayed on his hands. They were not city slicker's palms. They were work worn. Scarred in places, used to mucking in whenever and wherever they were required. Farming wasn't for the precious, and, fair play, these folk, they weren't complaining. Not one of them had asked to change out of their cumbersome, unfamiliar costumes. Or said they were too cold or that the work was too hard. Even Willa who, bless her, was in a permanent state of conflict with her bodice and who he knew for a fact had acquired some new blisters today.

As he ran his thumbs over the calluses on his palms, he caught himself smiling at a long-forgotten memory. He'd been ten, maybe. Eleven? His hands had been covered in blisters after a full day of mucking out the barn. He'd been all begritten, complaining loudly that he should be let off his evening chores because he was walking wounded. *Fair enough, son,* his dad had said. He'd turned to walk away as if the matter was settled, then turned back and asked him if he wanted happy cows. He'd said aye, 'course he did. The herd was brand new then. A 'starter pack' of three cows and calves bought down in Kirkcudbright, the 'birthplace of the Belted Galloway'.

Next, his dad asked him if he wanted a baked potato for his tea . . . straight from the bonfire he'd just been tasked with putting together. He'd said aye, 'course he did. They were his favourite. And then his father had asked him if he'd wanted to feel the pride of knowing he'd been the one to make all of those good things happen . . . with his hands. Even though they were tired, and sore and the plasters kept coming off.

He'd said nothing then, but had wrapped his hands up with tape, pulled on a pair of oversized gloves and got to work. That evening's baked potato still ranked up there as one of the best he'd ever had.

That night, as he, his mum and father were eating, his father renamed chores Farm Delights. He said if they were going to be doing something for the rest of their lives, knowing they'd never be able to cross off the final item on a to-do list because there would always be one more thing to do, he wanted it to sound fun.

In a weird way Willa reminded him of his dad. Always able to find the silver lining, even though this trip was clearly not what she'd thought it would be.

If he had the stomach for it, he'd ask her to put a spin on bringing his cattle to market.

Even thinking about loading up the girls knocked the oxygen out of him. Over twenty years of building the herd and in the time it took for a gavel to hit the auctioneer's desk – poof! – they'd be gone. Then the pigs. Then the sheep. Everything would have to go. Feed prices were through the roof. And the return they got at market wasn't worth it.

But if selling the animals meant they could get in the all-important harvest, it was a sacrifice he'd have to make.

Finn cleared his throat and, after a *want some?* glance from Orla, took a plate and joined the group by the fire.

'I don't think I've ever felt like such a weakling,' Jules said with a stretch and a yawn. 'And I haul twenty-five-kilo sacks of flour around all day.'

'Dinnae listen to her. She's absolutely brilliant.' Blair gave Jules a friendly elbow in the ribs. 'I've not seen someone tackle a bramble pile the size of a caravan with such ferocity before. Belongs on my rugby team, she does.'

They grinned at each other, then began showing off the various injuries they'd received courtesy of the brambles.

'What about you, ChiChi?' Rosa asked. 'How'd you and Alastair get on?'

'Well . . .' ChiChi threw her unlawfully wedded husband a playful grin. 'I think it would be fair to say that he is far better at dealing with dark matter than I am.'

After calls for an explanation, Alastair took over. 'We needed to change the oil in the tractor and ChiChi here thought it'd be a great idea to step in the grease pan after I was finished.' Amidst a chorus of Oh no!'s and Are you okay?'s Alastair continued, 'You cannae see it, but she's got an egg-sized lump on the back of her head.' He shook his head, pointed at Gabe with his fork, then Jules, and, in a perfectly amiable voice said, 'You lot are definitely injury prone.'

'Hey!' Lachlan protested. 'Gabe didn't knock himself—'

'I'm fine,' Gabe cut in.

Out of the corner of his eye, Finn caught Willa stiffen. She focused on her meal, missing Gabe putting his hand on Lachlan's knee and giving him a small it-wasn't-her-fault shake of the head.

Finn had actually seen him try to speak to Willa a couple of times today. Once over lunch and again when they'd got back from the barns, but Willa had come up with excuses both times. The fact she was sitting near them was a good sign, though.

'Will we be doing any scything?' Jeff asked.

Orla's near permanently cheerful smile faltered.

Before she could answer, Fenella laughed. 'That's *Poldark*, you dill!' She turned to Trevor, her fake spouse, and said, 'No offence, *mo luaidh*, but if Poldark walked right now? I'd dump you like a hot potato.'

'Eh, well, lassie.' Trevor thrust his chest out and gave it a thump with his fist. 'You havenae seen me throw a caber aboot, have ya?'

He jumped up and on to the stump he'd been sitting on, wobbled, then fell off, knocking Fenella off her stump in the process.

'Right, then, matey.' Fenella huffed her irritation as she reluctantly let Trevor pull her up. She swatted him away, batted some of the dust out of her skirt and scanned the group. 'Who's up for a husband swap?'

There was an unexpectedly weighty silence until ChiChi volunteered Alastair. Amidst his cries of protest she shouted, 'But I'd like him back for Wednesday. Wednesday night, anyway.'

Fenella and Jules crowed a pair of raunchy 'Ooooooo!'s.

Jennifer set her wicker basket on her lap, pulled out her ever-present knitting and innocently asked, 'Why? What's Wednesday?'

ChiChi threw Alastair a look.

'New moon,' Alastair said, a note of pride in his voice, as if he wasn't often in a position to impart facts to the group. 'There's a meteor shower too.'

'Orionids,' said ChiChi with an uncharacteristic giggle. 'I've not seen them before. There's so much light pollution down south.'

Alastair gave her cheek a tender little thumb and knuckle pinch. 'ChiChi says we'll be able to see things extra clearly up here in the Highlands. She brought her telescope and everything.'

The two shared a look that suggested their day together, despite the oil spill, had been a good one.

'Eh, Fenella! How 'bout I show you *my* telescope.' Trevor began to swagger around the firepit, hips thrust forward, completely unfazed by the chorus of groans and Fenella's screams of 'Oh god, no! We kill venomous snakes where I come from, matey!'

After the laughter had died down, Fenella turned to ChiChi. 'I'll take you up on that husband swap, thanks, doll. Maybe you can knock some sense into this hunk o' spunk's brain. You're alright with building stone walls, are you?'

'What about you, Willa?' Rosa asked with a knowing wink. 'We saw that you went down to the barns with your Jamie. Was it like in the books?'

Finn bit back a smile. This should be interesting.

Her eyes shot to him with a panicked, *what do I say?*

He shrugged. How would he know?

Willa lifted her shoulders and gave a nonchalant, 'Absolutely. Identical.'

Trevor grunted out a protest. 'Shaggin' in the barns on the first day, eh?'

Fenella glared at him. 'If I'd had Finn as my husband? I would.'

'I thought it was look don't touch!' Trevor scowled. He let his tin plate fall with a clatter on the washing up table. 'Trust Finn Jamieson to make his own set of rules yet again.'

He felt the group's eyes turn to him. Finn shook his head, irritated. Trevor McNulty had worn a chip on his shoulder ever since they'd met. Always picking and pushing and testing to see just how far he could push Finn until, one day – and it would happen – Finn threw the first of a long series of overdue punches.

'I obey the word of law according to Orla,' Finn said.

Orla, to his relief, didn't contest the declaration.

Gabe jumped in. 'Willa's very much in the don't-ask-don't-tell camp of keeping confidences, aren't you, *bonita*? A lot like Claire, you learnt many lessons about loyalty at the nunnery. Right?'

'Yes,' she said solemnly. 'When you came to pick me up from the nunnery I said as much, didn't I? What happens at the immersive Jacobean experience, stays at the immersive Jacobean experience. And that holds true for barns as well.'

The two shared a smile that, even from his spot outside the fire circle, warmed Finn's heart. They'd make their peace.

The conversation moved on to everyone's favourite episodes and Finn's gaze, once again drifted to Willa. A huge yawn and then another consumed her.

He slid on to the stump beside her. 'You should head off to your bed.' Finn nodded towards the stairwell leading up the hayloft. 'We've got another busy day in store tomorrow.'

She stared at him for a moment, then up at the stairs, her eyes glassing over in a way that suggested she was barely able to grasp that she would have to move all the way from here to there.

He knew he'd face ridicule for what his gut was telling him to do but fuck it. It was his first and only fake wedding night. Not to mention it would annoy Trevor, so . . .

He scooped her up in his arms and began to head towards the stairs.

Behind him there were catcalls and whistles from the lads and sighs and requests for the same from a few of the women, apart from Fenella who warned Trevor if he touched her, she'd slap him.

'They seem to be getting on well,' Finn said to Willa as she sleepily slid her arms round his neck, nestling into the nook between his shoulder and neck as if she'd done it countless times before.

When he reached the top of the stairs and got the door open, more wolf-whistles rang out. As he entered the hayloft, he was struck anew by what a good job Orla had done. It was pure rural chic versus the epically messy storage room it had been a week ago. She'd worked hard to put this lark together. And she already worked hard before that. Cleaning jobs down the village, anything Dougie needed, the kids, her dad and she still, somehow, made room for the Amateur Dramatic society. Which did beg the question: why was she so driven to stay at Balcraigie Castle Farm when selling the place meant she could put her feet up?

He shoved the thought aside. Thinking about it opened the door to too many other questions he'd long since decided weren't worth seeking answers for.

'Are you going to tell me a bedtime story?' Willa asked when he slipped her under the quilts, clothes and all, after he'd helped her tug her boots off.

'If you like.'

He sat down on a hay bale and looked at her.

She looked so . . . unguarded. Her features soft and vulnerable in their openness. She was trusting him to be with her in her private space. 'What would you like your story to be about?'

She snuggled deeper under the covers, eyes closed, forehead crinkling a bit as she thought and then, through a yawn said, 'You.'

He snorted. 'Oh, I'm sure there's something far better. A fairy tale, perhaps?'

'No.' She gave him a few sleepy blinks. 'Though it could be a fairy tale about you.'

He thought for a moment, aware there was a group of people no doubt timing his entrance and exit, then said, 'Once upon a time, there was a grumpy farmer called Finlay who'd packed his bags and left his home in Inverness during what should have been his tattie holidays.'

'What's a tattie holiday?' she asked through a yawn.

'It's the October school break.' He explained how, back in the day, they used to stop school for two weeks so thousands of children across Scotland could go out into the fields and collect the potato harvest. By the time he finished, about a minute all told, she'd fallen asleep.

He pulled the quilt up and over her shoulders and gave it a soft pat. 'Sleep well, *ma cridhe*,' he whispered, then turned out her fairy lights and silently walked away.

Chapter Twenty

Aubrey Washington: Hey Willz. 😄 😄 😄 Do you know where my red blouse with the tiny flowers on it is? I need it for the set visit this afternoon. Jason likes red and I like Jason, you hear me? 🐿 🌰 🍒 🐾 ☀

Bryony Stokes: Willa? Bryony here. Thanks for the reminder on how to write a segment intro. Do you know anything about a red top for Aubrey? She's convinced you know where it is, but it seems a bit below my pay grade to find it, so I'm thinking we just order some new ones in? Who authorizes budget for that sort of thing? #NoCashToSplash

Charlie Foster: Willa you sly dog. Taking a vacation in a Highlands spa are you? Is this because of the Bacon Incident? You definitely seemed a bit weird and don't worry – I've confirmed with Ben you're from Canada so there's that problem solved. Who's the new girl on the block? She seems verra verra shiny.

Bryony Stokes: Willa? What's a running order and why do they keep asking for one for a show two weeks ahead of now? Isn't news, like, new?

Aubrey Washington: Have replacement blouse, but cld you pls locate red top?

Bryony Stokes: I've used Dad's card to get some curated tops in from my mom's stylist. Aubrey's gushing over them, so can you tell me where petty cash is? I only need a couple of k.

Charlie Foster: This 'Bryony' creature has snaffled herself a date with one of the supporting actors from today's set visit. Watch your back, gurl! She's got talons. 💅💅💅

Priya Semple: Hey woman. Priya here. In a miraculous turn of events, I've got a window for lunch. Want to meet me at The Grove for some salad and goss? Also . . . who's Bryony? I'm guessing she's new at TiTs, but she doesn't really seem to understand BOUNDARIES. I keep getting a lot of very strange calls from her. Biyeeeeeee. Xoxoxo

Chapter Twenty-One

To say Willa's morning shower had been bracing would have been putting it mildly. *Cryogenic preservation* just might've about covered it. Reminding herself that the world's sexiest celebrities paid to be submerged in ice baths for the express purpose of getting their glow on, Willa forced a positive spin on the arctic rejuvenation after what had been a fitful night's sleep. Answering emails and texts from or about Bryony were not the tonic she'd hoped they would be.

The Zendaya body double hadn't been at TiTs forty-eight hours and was already personal shopping for Aubrey, dating off-limits celebs and – overnight news flash! – going on a week-long juicing break in Italy with the show's exec producer after sweeps. Charlie's warning about watching her back felt real. Too real.

Choosing not to acknowledge the muck and dirt on her dress (and now her sheets), she tugged on her outfit, petticoats and all, plotting how to talk things out with Gabe and then, with his blessing, get on the soonest flight back to LA. Finn wouldn't care. He'd probably be relieved. The man clearly had better things to do than hang out with *Outlander* buffs he had pre-ordained as idiots. The one thing that didn't sit right about leaving early was Val.

She had built up an image of Val in heaven. She could see her perfectly, lounging upon a lavender-coloured velvet sofa that was floating on a fluffy white cloud. There'd be a bowl of popcorn in her lap and a blissed out expression on her face as she enjoyed the show down on earth. Leaving now would mean failing Val, destroying the image and being crushed under a tsunami of guilt that would destroy the letter she'd written and leave Willa living in a purgatory of unanswered questions.

With this in mind, she went down to join everyone as the morning porridge bell sounded. She couldn't help but smile. It truly did look as if she'd stepped back in time. Her fellow guests were coming out of their rooms, stretching, yawning, tweaking one another's corset ties. Complaints of creaky bones and tight muscles were minimal compared to the excited chatter of how beautiful it was and how well everyone had slept. *Outlander* fan or not, this was kind of cool. And also? It felt *real*.

She scanned the area for Finn and then, when she couldn't find him, Gabe.

'Looking for your hubby?' Rosa appeared beside her, shawl wrapped round her shoulders against the morning chill.

'Gabe, actually.'

'He and Lachlan already ate,' Jules shouted over the noise of whacking her boots together before sitting down to tug them over her skull and crossbones stockings.

Jules caught her looking and threw her a wink. 'You like?'

Willa gave her a thumbs-up. 'Very chic.'

'How're you getting on with your kilt then, Jeff?' Orla, porridge pan on hip, appeared in the courtyard, warily eyeing the straining waist straps of Jeff's age-battered kilt. 'Will you be wanting a wee extension on those straps?'

Jeff patted his tummy. 'Probably shouldn't have had second helpings of the cottage pie last night, but you're one helluva cook!'

He gave a big, happy guffaw. 'Longer straps would be great.' He began unbuckling his kilt right there in the stable yard.

When Orla protested, he flicked up the edges of the kilt to show he was wearing a pair of hillbilly long johns. 'I'm comfortable enough with my masculinity to strut about in my turkey legs, so long as it offends no one's sensibilities.'

'The only offensive thing is that you don't know how to sew, laddie!' a newly arrived Alastair heckled good naturedly. He was, to be fair, literally darning a sock.

'No one wants to have Jeff sew anything,' Rosa said. 'Building infrastructure? He's your man. See to a bit of hemming? You'd be better off asking a porcupine to do the job for you.'

'We've not got porcupines round these parts, but we can probably rustle up a stag for you.' Trevor feigned getting some antlers up his jacksie.

Fenella thanked god ChiChi had switched grooms with her today. ChiChi looked scared.

In desperate need of some caffeine, Willa headed over to where Dougie was pouring steaming mugs of tea from the largest teapot she'd seen outside of the countless *Alice in Wonderland* remakes she'd covered. Amidst a speckling of blue stars, 'Balcraigie Castle' was painted in a lovely, hand-crafted yesteryear script.

'Fancy,' she said.

'A present,' Dougie winked, filling her mug with a flourish. 'We only use it for our extra special guests.'

Willa curtseyed her thanks. 'I am humbled, m'lord.'

Dougie let out a huge bark of laughter. 'Did you hear that, Orla? This one here just called me a lord! She clearly hasn't divined that the likes of me are common as muck.'

'What?' Willa protested. 'You own a farm with a castle on it.'

'Aye.' Dougie and Orla shared a look. 'Well.'

Feeling very much as if she'd put her foot in it, Willa thanked him for the strong, sweet tea, then went over to where Orla was folding Jeff's kilt into a large wicker basket.

Fatigue shadowed Orla's features until their eyes caught and her smile brightened. 'Good morning to you, Willa. Can I get you some porridge? We've got stewed apples to go alongside it today, if you like?'

'Definitely.' Willa patted her grumbling tummy. 'I never used to be an oatmeal kind of girl, but you've converted me.' She pointed at her filthy dress. 'I'm so sorry, but—'

Orla cut in. 'It's easy enough to get mucky out here on the farm.'

Willa apology-winced. 'Is there any chance I can get another one? It's just – I might have accidentally slept in it and now my bedding's a bit – bleurgh.'

Orla's eyes widened.

Oh crap. She'd over-asked. From childhood, Willa's parents had ingrained in her a deep horror of ever being 'that guest'. The one who passive-aggressively doubled their host's workload.

Willa began talking over Orla, speaking super quickly, as if log jamming all her words together made the situation better. 'I can sort out the bedding. Turn it inside out or something. In fact, forget I said anything at all. This is authentic, right? Totes Jacobean. Check me out. Down with the outlanders.' She struck a pose.

Orla stared at her for just a fraction too long before popping on her cheery smile with a bright, 'Honestly. It's no problem. Just get your dress to me whenever you're able.'

Willa knew the tone well. She used it regularly when Aubrey or one of the execs dumped a shit ton of extra jobs on to her extensive list of things to do with a 'you don't mind, do you?'

Though she never admitted it (#FearOfGettingFired), of course she minded. She worked her ass off and on bad days it seemed like she was the only one who actually worked for a living at TiTs. But the perks of the job – like, having one – put her on a par with mothers who spoke of the joy of a child versus the trauma of childbirth. No matter the pain, you just kept coming back for more.

This definitely wasn't one of those days for Orla. Besides, what did Willa think? That Orla was made of time and money, dispatching a servant to the Jacobean Dry Cleaners and another to the dressmakers to get her sorted? No. Anything anyone asked Orla was likely going to be done by Orla herself.

'I can wash it.' Willa batted at her skirts, hoping the feeble gesture proved she knew how to clean things. 'Honestly. I'm good.'

'No, no. I can get something else for you.' Orla stared at Willa's body clearly trying to divine what, if anything, in her arsenal of dresses would fit Willa.

'Seriously. I'm so happy wearing this. I actually feel closer to Mother Nature this way. It'd be wrong to be too clean, right?' She silently pleaded with Orla to please, please forget this had happened.

Orla's eyebrow furrow deepened. She looked genuinely worried. 'Are you sure wearing a smelly dress won't take away from the magic?'

Willa's throat seized. She couldn't admit to Orla that, apart from the food and beautiful setting, there was no magic for her. The only links she had to *Outlander* were regret and sorrow. 'I'll be fine,' she assured her.

'So long as you're positive,' Orla fretted, absently ladling a huge dollop of porridge and stewed apples into her bowl.

'Really. I'm happy.' Again, the rapid talking took over. 'It's amazing here. What you've done . . . I mean . . . I don't know what it looked like before, but now? It's like . . .' She pressed her fingers to her head and pretended to get an electric shock. 'Time travel.

Doctor Who mach ten thousand. You've transported me. Us.' She swept her arm out wide, narrowly avoiding slapping ChiChi in the face.

Orla's fragile smile gained a stronger footing when she looked round at the others who were chiming in with hearty 'Hear hear!'s.

'Thank you.' Orla pressed her hands to her heart, managing to upend a dollop of gooey porridge on to her pinafore. She looked down at it, sighed, then swept her finger through it and popped the porridge in her mouth.

Unexpectedly, Willa's eyes stung at the familiarity of the gesture. It was a mom move. One she'd seen her own mother and then Val perform countless times. What was a cum-coloured food splodge on their boobs when there was laundry to do, dishes to clean, and other people's wishes to fulfil?

An ache for that sort of closeness washed through her. She'd never felt the closeness her brothers shared with her parents. Val and her family had been the closest thing to a 'chosen family' that she'd had but even then . . . How did a twenty-nine-year-old woman find unconditional love?

She started when Rosa gave Willa's arm a gentle squeeze. 'That was nice, back there. You've obviously read the books.' She laughed softly and shook her head as if remembering an old friend. 'Claire's always talking about how smelly everyone was back then.'

'I know, right?' Willa agreed, possibly too enthusiastically for someone who didn't have a clue.

'Jennifer,' she whispered once she'd wedged herself between Jennifer and ChiChi's thick petticoats and overskirts at the long breakfast table. 'My pits stink! Maybe a bit too much.'

After a very brave sniff, Jennifer suggested soaking the armpits in a bit of white vinegar, some of which she just happened to have in a travel bottle if Willa needed any.

Of *course* she did. Jennifer was one of those people you wanted to be with when Armageddon came. Her wicker arm basket would be a survival kit. Travel sewing kits, astronaut food, the lot.

She was suddenly consumed by a powerful, urgent impulse to ask Jennifer to adopt her. Not be her actual mom, but . . . Without any offence to her own mother – who was great and who she knew, on an intellectual level, loved her – Willa had always hungered for someone like this: a woman who went on holidays with her lesbian superfan daughter, carried travel packs of vinegar, and sniffed a stranger's pits because it was the nice thing to do. A mum who supported her daughter no matter what her passion.

'Thank you, Jennifer.' She clutched the small bottle to her chest, then opened her arms. 'Can I have a hug?'

Jennifer very kindly agreed despite the fact that this was not a Super Soul team-building retreat.

'Are you okay, love?' Jennifer asked when Willa finally released her from the hug.

'Yes. Definitely. Why? Do I look weird?' She probably looked weird. She felt weird.

Jennifer took a quick look round, then lowered her voice, 'I thought you might be upset about Finn not making it today.'

Willa felt as if someone had just smashed a cast iron pan against her head. 'What?' Her stomach churned. 'Come again, please?'

'Oh goodness, I've put my foot in it, haven't I? Sorry, love. You'd best speak to Orla.'

'Finn's done a runner, has he?' asked Alastair, who apparently had bat ears.

'Finn's not coming?'

'What? The scoundrel!'

'Shall we hunt him down? Put him in the stocks?'

'I'd nail his ear to them. Orla! Have you got any stocks round here?'

Gabe chose this moment to appear. 'What's going on?'

'Bloody Finn's done a runner on poor Willa here,' Fenella said in a way that suggested she'd seen it coming all along.

Gabe's pressed a hand to his chest as if the news had physically hurt him.

Was she humiliated?

Damn straight she was.

But did she want Gabe to pity her?

'No! Please! I am not upset.' Willa cut through the cacophony of support. 'I'm kind of a lone wolf sort of gal at the best of times, so really – this is good. Better than good.'

'He didn't strike me as a hit-and-run kind of guy.' Jeff shook his head in disbelief. Before Willa could firmly deny any sort of hit-and-run action, Jeff threw a meaningful look at Rosa, then to Willa and said, 'You're welcome to join our fold, honey. I'd be proud to call you my daughter.'

Before any of this could fully register, Orla appeared with a huge tray of savoury buns she called McTattieWiches. 'Tattie scones with egg and sausage.'

Some very unJacobean machinery – a digger (driven by Trevor) and a tractor (driven by Errol) – ground to a halt outside the courtyard. Clearly lured by the scent of McTattieWiches, the men ran in, grabbed a couple each and began devouring them.

After he'd eaten two and grabbed a third, Trevor noticed no one was speaking. 'What's going on here? Has the cat died?'

Jules told him about Finn.

Trevor's pale, vitamin-D-hungry face instantly turned puce. 'The fooking bastard. He's always bailing—'

Orla cut him off with a short, sharp, 'Hey!'

To Willa she said, 'I'm ever so sorry, Willa. I was gonnae tell you after you'd had your breakfast. I'm afraid Finn's had to go elsewhere for the day.' She turned to Trevor. 'But he'll be back later. He promised.'

'Aye, right,' scowled Trevor, then stuffed the rest of his McTattieWich into his mouth before disappearing off again as Orla apologetically explained to Jennifer and Fenella that they would be on dry stone wall duty together but not with the lads.

'Why don't you come with us, Willa?' Fenella asked. 'We can show these bloody men what a hash they make of things, eh?'

Willa nodded. She'd like that. But first she needed to talk to Gabe.

Chapter Twenty-Two

Finn dropped his head into his hands. Things were worse than he'd thought. Much, much worse.

To his credit, the bank manager – a kindly man named Colin Robertson – waited until Finn's head had regrouped before clearing his throat and tapping the stack of papers on his desk. 'Making this decision could put you and your family – your stepfamily – in a good place, Finlay.'

He knew it would. And also that it wouldn't. 'There's no way Orla and Dougie could buy quality acreage in the volume they need around these parts.'

'Actually,' Colin began.

Finn's head started buzzing again as Colin pulled out a stack of possibilities fresh from the estate agents. All of which would meet Orla and Dougie's criteria. A modern home. A granny annexe for Duncan. Close to the same schools, the same shops, the same amateur dramatics society. 'Their lives would, essentially, remain unchanged. The only thing they wouldn't have, of course, is Balcraigie Castle Farm.'

'That's the rub, isn't it?'

'Aye,' agreed Colin. ''Tis.'

'What if we get the tattie crop in?'

'If – and I know you know it's a big if, Finlay – *if* you do . . .
you'll have bought yourself a reprieve until the next calamity.' He
tapped the sheaf of papers again. 'You can make this happen. Orla
can't. Ball's in your court, son.'

'Aye, right. Okay, then.' Finn pushed the chair back and rose,
gave Colin a brisk handshake. 'Thanks for that, Mr Robertson.'

'Colin, son. I've known you since you were a bairn. I think
we're free to be on a first-name basis now that you're carrying your
father's mantle.'

Finn shot him a sharp glance, trying to figure out if he'd meant
anything beyond the obvious.

No. It had just been a comment.

'Right you are. Thank you. I'll be in touch.'

'Don't leave it too long, Finlay.'

'No, no.' He was already at the doorway, lifting one hand in
farewell and pulling up the livestock auctioneer's phone number
with the other. 'We'll speak soon. Dinnae worry.'

Chapter Twenty-Three

Lachlan approached Gabe at exactly the same moment Willa did. *Oh boy.* Cock blocks at dawn, was it?

She turned to go.

'Willa, wait.' Gabe held up a hand, then asked, 'Lachlan, give us a few minutes, will you?'

Lachlan demurred with a hand on his chest and a half bow. Bloody zen-yoga-hipster-beardy type. Not that any of this was Lachlan's fault. Or Gabe's. It was entirely her fault that she'd decided the only reason Val had sent them on this trip was to fall deeply and irrevocably in love. Having Finn run for the hills had just been some extra delicious rejection icing on the cake.

'C'mere.' Gabe crooked his arm for Willa to take and then, to Lachlan, 'You wouldn't mind hunting down those tools we needed, would you, Lach? I'm just going to show Wills what we've been up to.'

'Good idea.' Lachlan smiled his benign, Dalai Lama smile and jogged off.

A part of her hoped he would trip, but her karma was already down the pooper, so she willed him a graceful journey to the tool shed. Why make things worse than they already were?

'You okay?' Gabe asked once they were out of the courtyard and heading towards the castle ruins.

'Yeah,' she lied. 'Why wouldn't I be?'

'Willa. It's me. You can admit to being upset.'

'I told you!' she screeched. 'Not upset! Finn's his own person. Who am I to try to tie a Highlander down? Besides' – this little speech of hers was quite freeing – 'he underestimated me, my intellect and my rather impressive farming skills on the basis that I interview celebrities for a living, so frankly, I was hoping he wouldn't turn up today. This is a win. One hundred per cent. I mean, the man thought *I* thought cows ate Oreos.' She fuzzed out a raspberry. 'McJackass.'

He gave her a look.

'Okay, fine. I'm a little bit narked.' She pinched the teensiest bit of air between her fingers.

'You really are handling it with grace.' Gabe feigned a look of admiration.

'Impressive, huh?' She gave a smug little shoulder shimmy and shot him a smile, hoping it communicated to him how grateful she felt for the space to hurtle from one end of the emotional spectrum to the other.

'Well, for what it's worth,' Gabe said, 'it's his loss, and although I know you've had other invitations, you are very welcome to join me and Lachlan.'

'Ohhhh, no. That's cool. You two have got your whole reunion thang going on.'

'Shall we walk for a bit?' Gabe suggested. 'Talk when we get there?'

'Good idea.'

Gabe set a good pace and by the time they reached the castle walls, Willa's heart was pounding hard enough to mostly drown out the screams of self-recrimination threatening to consume her.

A smile lit up Gabe's face as they hit the first arch. He stopped just short of where they could see in. 'Do you remember what it was like when you first came in here?'

'What? You mean yesterday morning? Yes, Gabe. I can remember yesterday morning.'

'Okay, *bonita*. Point made.' He laughed, completely unperturbed by her shirty response.

She looked at him, then. Really looked at him. Only twenty-four hours had passed between the moment he'd first seen Lachlan but it was like she was meeting a brand new person.

Gone was the cool, inaccessible, ultra-desirable Latino and in his place was a smiley, kilt-wearing, happy guy. One whose mood refused to be tamped. He was also a bit scruffy-looking. He had all sorts of funny little cuts on his forehead and cheeks and, in one case, a bruise.

She grimaced and pointed. 'Do I need to call a hotline for you? That looks like it hurts.' She did a dramatic little double take. 'Wait. Have you and Lachlan been playing kilted *Fight Club*?'

He huffed out a good-natured laugh. 'With the brambles, aye.'

She snorted. 'Okay, Madonna.'

'Hey! Not fair.' He shot her a cheeky side-eye. 'I've not married anyone and I am not speaking with a Scottish accent.'

'Oh, aye, right you are, laddie,' she tried to roll her Rs and failed. 'You ken y'are.'

She got a soft kick in the bum for her efforts. And then, with a courtly half bow, he stepped to the side so she could enter the castle gardens.

The expanse, which she was proudly informed was the equivalent of three acres, was almost entirely clear apart from a beautiful collection of ancient-looking trees in orchard formation. The stone walls had autumn-coloured ivy still clinging to them. There was a massive burn pile off to one side, but apart from that, they had single-handedly unearthed an utterly breathtaking walled garden.

'Oh my god, Gabe,' she managed. 'What are you? A new breed of Marvel gardening hero?'

'It's amazing, isn't it?' He explained how Duncan had appeared on the digger after they'd managed to clear about a metre's worth of brambles. Despite their protests that they were happy to do it by hand, he'd overruled them and systematically cleared the lot with Lachlan and Gabe acting as his skivvies. 'Duncan deserves a cape for this. He's like . . . a ballerina with his digger.'

'I'm sure he'd love to hear that,' Willa teased.

'Yeah. Maybe not,' Gabe said, eyes glued to the garden, an undimmable smile on his lips. 'What do you think?'

She pointed at her dropped jaw to show just how amazing she thought it was. She walked up to one of the trees. 'Oh my gawd. These have *apples* on them!' She was beaming now and so was he.

He put on a wicked witch voice and reached for one. 'Yes, my beautiful young maiden. Would you like to try one of my very special apples?'

She smirked at him. 'You could totally lure someone into your secret lair with your wicked witch act. It's very nuanced.'

His bright smile remained, then softened as the energy buzzing between them shifted into something demanding more than pithy one-liners.

'I'm sorry,' he said.

'For what?' She was playing stupid. She knew what. But he didn't actually owe her an apology. This was one of those scenarios that drove her nuts in romance novels. When a simple miscommunication between the couple (he's gay, she's not) keeps them at odds for tortuous ages when a simple straightforward question would have sorted things out in no time. It'd be a boring romance, and very short, but far less irritating. And yet, here she was, happily bearing the mantle of the one prolonging the misunderstanding.

'I had no idea Val had organised the whole Lachlan thing,' Gabe said. 'It's important to me that you and I stay friends. I don't think I would've come here without you cheering me on. Are you up for that? A friendship with . . . apples?'

He picked one off the tree and handed it to her.

She clutched it to her heart, hoping he couldn't see her hands trembling. He was bearing the brunt of the apology for her idiocy.

'Of course.' She opened her arms and they had a weird, awkward-angles hug. What was the most embarrassing aspect about all of this was that it hadn't even occurred to her that her relationship with Gabe didn't have to involve romance. She had no doubt he would be an amazing, loyal friend. Just like his sister had been.

She made herself say the words they both needed to hear to draw a line under any further misunderstandings. 'How could I be mad when the best friend a girl could have reunited her brother with his first love?'

'It was pretty badass.' He blew a kiss up to the crisp, blue sky above them. 'I miss you, Concha.'

She closed her eyes and, as clear as if it were real, saw Valentina blowing one back at the pair of them. *I miss you too, Val. Forever and a day I will miss you.*

'She's the gift that keeps on giving.' Willa tried to control the crack in her voice as she continued. 'And I'm happy for you. Lachlan seems really nice. And I fully expect to be your bridesmaid at the real handfasting ceremony. What is it?' She looked at her non-existent wrist watch. 'A year from now?'

Gabe smiled, tipped his head back and forth. 'Who knows what will happen? But it's nice. Having someone who knew me back then. And my family. It's kind of like completing myself, you know? Coming full circle, but better.'

She nodded a weird bobbly-headed nod because what he'd just said was something she was so hungry for it made her bones ache.

Gabe pointed back towards the barns. 'I told you I read my letter, right?'

She made a vague noise. She didn't want to talk about the letters.

'It was really useful.'

'Useful?'

He nodded. 'When I saw Lachlan, I – I was angry instead of happy and that felt wrong. He is the only man I've ever let myself fall completely head over heels for and then he disappeared. Well, I disappeared and then he disappeared, and I was angry, you know? I felt abandoned and pissed off that I hadn't handled it better.' He balled his hands into fists and fake-punched himself in the head. 'For years, I've been thinking of what I'd say to him if I ever saw him, and what do I do when I get the chance? I storm off. It's what I did back then, and I did it again yesterday and . . . I need to stop doing that. I need to face stuff head on. Whether or not it turns out well.'

She got that. Big time. Not watching *Outlander* was her form of protest that Valentina wasn't fighting harder to beat her cancer. It had been a completely unfair reaction to something Valentina had next to zero control over. You didn't fight cancer. You endured it. Did the best you could in the face of a malignant invasion. And when her best friend had reached out to her, literally asking her to be by her side as she came face to face with her mortality, what had Willa done? She'd said no. And she would have to carry that burden of guilt forever. There was no way she could make up for it with Val, but she could try here, now, with Gabe.

She ducked her head to catch his eye. 'You were a teenager when you met. Like . . . Romeo and Juliet's age. How on earth were you meant to handle something like that with the equilibrium of a seasoned therapist?'

Gabe scrubbed his fingertips through his oil-slick-coloured hair. 'I know, but being with Lachlan again – realising how much precious time we'd missed – it really brought home to me just how much I'd missed with Valentina.' His voice thickened as the grief took purchase. 'I never met her kids. Her husband. I don't know any of my other siblings' children. I don't even know if I'd recognise them if we passed one another on the street. I was their big brother and I walked away. Walked away and didn't look back.' His eyes were dark now – pure dilated pupil. 'I thought I was leaving behind all the pain I'd ever experience in the world, not even considering that what I'd actually done was create a huge black hole where all of that messy family stuff should have been.' He clawed his hands into his chest as if to prove the black hole's existence. As abruptly, he threw his hands up. 'So, my dad doesn't like that I'm gay. So what? I let my fear of that disapproval take twenty years of family time away from me.' He clawed at his chest again. 'I'm the one who did it to myself and I'm the one who's going to have to live with that.'

His raw, unfettered remorse crashed through her like an earth-quake. She still went home to see her family, sent birthday presents for her nieces and nephews, made pumpkin pie with a whipped cream smiley face at Thanksgiving. But she'd always had the sense that they all knew the reason she came back wasn't because being there, with them, was a choice. It was an obligation. And acknowl-edging that created the same, terrifying black hole Gabe spoke of.

Willa swirled her toe round in the dirt making one circle, another, and then a third connecting the first two. Was there a way to make her two worlds one?

She could be practical. She was sleeping on straw bales and called in cows and was about to go and build a stone wall. In petticoats and a corset, no less. A honking, stinking one. It was all stuff her family would've loved doing. Pragmatic. Down to earth. Real.

And yet . . . proving she could do farm chores wasn't the link she needed. She didn't want to be loved for the things she did. She just wanted to be loved.

She'd felt that type of bond with Val. The same one she saw between Jennifer and Jules. So why couldn't she feel it with her own family?

Maybe if she were to read Val's letter . . .

She swiped at a couple of tears and blurrily caught Gabe doing the same. 'Did your letter from Val . . . Was it like . . . Did it spell out . . .' Oh god. She wanted to know and also she really didn't.

She looked up at the sky and shouted, 'What the fuck, Val?'

Gabe laughed as if she had finally gone round the twist, then copied her.

As clearly as if Val had descended from heaven, she heard her friend's familiar laugh and a very dry, *You could just open the envelope, stupid.*

Yeah. She could. But then all of this would be over and she'd have to admit to herself that it was time to move on and that would mean deciding whether or not her life in LA had any actual content in it beyond regurgitating stories about celebrities with whom she'd spent five-to-ten minutes of not-very-private time and possibly moving back to Oregon because she couldn't really think of anything else she wanted to do in LA, but she definitely couldn't think of anything she wanted to do in Pendleton, all of which would mean she'd be stripped bare of the way she defined herself and would, at the ripe age of twenty-nine, be forced to start over.

Which clearly meant her best bet was to not read Val's letter.

Gabe reached across, took her hand and said, 'My letter basically said that the things that terrify us the most are the things that are the most worth doing.'

Willa smiled through another rush of tears. 'What else?'

'It wasn't long.' Gabe's voice went scratchy again as he recalled snippets of the letter. How Val had said that their dad had regretted his actions but was too proud and too old-fashioned to know how to start over. That they all loved him. That their lives were richer because of him. He had started out stoically, but both their faces were streaming with tears now. Each of them desperately missing that brave, beautiful, vivacious woman they'd been lucky enough to have in their lives. They hugged and sobbed and made ugly crying noises so awful that they ended up cackling too.

'Oh, there you are.'

They both looked across and saw Lachlan.

Instinctively, Willa pulled away from Gabe's embrace. 'Sorry, I—'

Lachlan shook his head in apology. 'No, lassie. The two of you are enjoying a well-deserved greet.'

'Uhhh . . .'

'A good cry,' Lachlan said, tugging tissues out of his sporran and handing them one each. 'Bamboo. Earth-friendly.' He plopped down on the ground beside them. 'Oh god, I love a good weepy session, don't you?'

Willa breathed out an emphatic, 'Yes,' then held out her hand for another tissue.

'Hallelujah,' Lachlan said companionably. 'Better out than in. Sometimes when I feel the need for a proper sob, but can't get it, you know, primed, I get in some chocolate, some ice cream, bring the duvet out to the sofa and pick out a fil-um that's guaranteed to make me cry.'

She and Lachlan looked at one another while Lachlan rubbed Gabe's back then, as one, they said, '*Romeo and Juliet* with Leo and Claire.' Then, 'Yeeaaas, Queen!' Then more tears. More tissues. More sharing of films that were sure to induce puffy eyes and a headache.

Gabe started laughing. 'I'm guessing I don't need to worry about the two of you hitting it off, then.'

'Och, away,' Lachlan said. 'If you love her, I love her.' His tone was so full of warmth she felt as if they'd been friends for a hundred years. No wonder Gabe had fallen for him. He was like a sexy, Scottish, kilted James Blunt. Full of warmth, kindness and humour that knew no boundaries.

After a few more minutes of chatting, talk turned to plans for the walled garden and orchard, which Willa took as her cue that it was, in fact, time to do some chores. She excused herself, saying she was off to find the girls.

As she left, Gabe jogged up behind her. She turned around and smiled at her new friend.

'I just wanted to make sure we're cool.'

'Yeah, of course.' They were. Definitely.

'You should read your letter,' he said.

She nodded. She knew she should.

He looked over his shoulder to where Lachlan was doing a sun salutation in the middle of the orchard. Shirtless.

'Go,' she said.

He leant in and gave her cheek a kiss.

'You'll be okay,' he said.

She had no idea why, but she believed him.

Chapter Twenty-Four

The next day, ignoring the catcalls, sotto voce *boo*s and Trevor's utterly charmless greeting (no one needed to bear witness to one of his crotch grabs), Finn marched through the courtyard looking for Willa.

She stood up from where she'd been peeling potatoes with a couple of the other guests and wiped her hands on her smock. It caught him by surprise how at home she looked in her Jacobean gear. Someone had sewn a 'maiden modesty' panel into her dress, and her long hair, loose today, was caught behind a kerchief.

She raised her eyebrows, justifiably waiting for a) an explanation and b) an apology for disappearing yesterday. When he'd returned late last night from the auctioneers in Inverness, Orla had still been up, folding laundry and pulling things out of the oven. She'd told him Willa had seemed okay with his not being there. That she'd joined Gabe for part of the day and Jennifer and Fenella for the rest of it.

He was glad to hear she and Gabe had made friends again but knew how his absence would've translated to her: an abandonment.

Tears had rolled down her cheeks when she'd told him that she didn't know why Valentina had sent her here. Now that Gabe knew why he was here, she'd admitted to feeling like a useless bystander.

He didn't think he meant anything to her, but he had a feeling his absence would've compounded that. Today he was making it his mission to ensure she knew there was someone apart from Gabe who had her back.

'Piglets,' he said, reaching out to take her hand.

She looked at it like he'd just offered her a handful of cow dung and stuffed her hands in her pinafore. Fair enough. She did, however, follow him as he headed out of the courtyard, no doubt mouthing something to the rest of the group on the lines of, 'Don't worry, I'm going to slip some arsenic into his tea.' Which, frankly, would solve a lot of problems. For Orla, anyway.

He pointed at the Land Rover, engine still running, then drove to the barns in silence. The impression he'd made on her (a bad one) was worsening by the minute, but he was full of feelings and his usual ability to go beyond your average stoic Scottish person's limited capacity for expressing them wasn't functioning. He knew he'd be pushing it, but he was hoping Willa and all her Hollywood-talking-stick energy would help him.

When they arrived, Willa didn't jump out of the jeep. 'What?' he asked.

'I should be asking you the same thing.'

'I told you.' He opened his car door. 'Piglets.'

'Yeah . . .' She spun her finger round. 'And . . .'

He shook his head. 'And . . . piglets.'

'If that's the way you want to play it, Braveheart.'

He slammed the door shut. It drove him nuts when people's history of Scotland was a foundation laid by Mel Gibson. He liked history. He liked Scottish history. It was complex and tribal and passionate. A people united by one thing – the love of the land they'd been born to. And, hundreds of years on – thousands, even – he was no different.

She followed him into the barn where, true to Duncan's text, their sow Isla had had a dozen little fat piglets.

An instant sense of calm washed through him. Being here, with the animals, inhaling the barn scents, hearing the gentle rustling of the cows beyond the rail-tie wall brought his hammering pulse down a few notches.

'Oh my god!' Willa, irritation forgotten, beamed at him. She had this amazing glow when she was overcome with pure happiness and, he had to admit, it was nice to bask in something positive for once.

She rushed into the pen, not waiting for him to run through a health-and-safety spiel and, having clearly done this before, plonked herself down in a corner where she could watch the little things, all dozen of whom were currently nestled on and around their mum after a good feed.

'You're a lot more cow town than you like to admit, aren't you?'

She gave a shrug, not meeting his gaze. The gesture was a kick in the gut. Yet again, he'd managed to unwittingly insult her.

'I meant it as a compliment.'

'It wasn't one.'

'Why? You're good with the animals. What's wrong with that?'

She whipped her head round and stared at him, mouth open but no words coming out. He got it. The answer should be obvious. But it wasn't. Not to him, anyway. Which wasn't a huge surprise seeing as he was making a hash of just about everything he put his hand to lately.

'Look, how about we do a do over?'

She gave a single shoulder shrug.

'I owe you an apology.'

'Oh, wow! How very Mr Manners of you.'

She caught his flinch and he saw the remorse he was feeling cross over to her. Not the plan at all when she was clearly the one who'd been treated poorly.

'I should've told you I was going to be away. I'm sorry for that.'

'Yeah, well . . . I know how to build a wall out of rocks now, so if you do it again I can pre-build your cairn.' She faked a couple of karate chops to show him she was kidding/not kidding/but actually kidding. Sort of.

And then what she'd just said registered. His mouth went dry. 'Did you— Were you up at the cairn?'

'Yeah. Trevor showed it to us.' She pointed out, up towards the hill where they'd buried his father. 'Really amazing stones. They stack well.'

A Highland cow slamming into him would've hurt less. 'You used the stones from the cairn to fix the wall?'

She bridled. 'We've been through this before, Finn.' She pointed her index fingers at herself. 'Just because I interview celebrities for a living does not mean I suffer from a microscopic IQ.'

He'd pissed her off. Royally. But how was he supposed to know what she did and didn't know. She was as easy to get close to as . . . Duncan. And that was saying something. 'I wasn't—' He stopped and tried to put himself in her shoes. She'd been doing what she'd been told and if anyone should pay for this, it was Trevor. He tried again. 'It wasn't an accusation, it's just . . . that's my dad's grave.'

'Oh god, Finn.' Her hands crossed over one another on her chest. 'I'm so sorry. I wouldn't have snapped at you like that. Of course we didn't. No. Trevor made a special point of saying what a cairn was and that we were, under no circumstances, to use any of the rocks in it for the wall. But he didn't say who was laid to rest there. I'm so sorry.'

The pressure released a bit. As did the flaming ball of wrath he'd been about to unleash on Trevor.

Willa wove her hands together in prayer position, her eyes seeking his for absolution.

He pulled off his cap and scrubbed his hand through his hair. 'No, I'm sorry. I jumped to a conclusion and shouldn't have.' He huffed out a short laugh. 'You really drew the short straw, didn't you? In the Jamie department.'

'Well . . . when you consider Trevor as an alternative . . .' she began, a soft smile tweaking at the edges of her lips.

The connection thawed something in him. Reminded him that he'd sought her out. Wanted Willa, of all the people in Scotland, to be the one who helped him figure out how he was going get through today, tomorrow, and with any luck the next fortnight without any of the guests knowing the farm was facing imminent foreclosure.

He crossed over to her and slid down the wall so that they were sitting side by side, watching the piglets. He'd seen this scores of times and still . . . they were the cutest little things. All snout and diddy little legs. Polka-dotted. What wasn't to love? An ache he rarely liked to acknowledge pressed against his chest.

'My dad used to bring me out here,' he said.

'When piglets were born?'

'No – well, that too, but . . .' C'mon, Finn. Wear your big boy pants. 'He used to bring me out here when he wanted to talk about difficult stuff.'

'Like?'

'The farm mostly. The responsibilities that came with it. The castle.'

'It's a good place to do that.'

'Aye.'

Willa turned to him after more than a few awkward seconds had ticked past. 'Finn, are you trying to tell me you need to have a difficult conversation with me? If yesterday was cold feet, or you've got better things to do elsewhere, or there's a jealous girlfriend who's going to come claw my eyes out, I'd be mighty grateful if you gave me a heads up. My ego can only take so much without immediate access to ice cream. Preferably rum raisin.'

He smiled. They barely knew one another, but he already felt familiar with her tendency to cosset her fears in humour. He owed it to her to be straight.

'There's no jealous girlfriend. No girlfriend at all. I didn't have cold feet. But I do have a lot to do. Crisis-management stuff.'

She made an I-need-more beckoning gesture.

'Where should I start?'

'The beginning is usually traditional, but I'll leave the structure up to you.'

He started at the beginning.

Chapter Twenty-Five

The trouble with trying to dislike a guy pouring out his life story in a delicious Scottish accent while holding a piglet in his lap is that it's pretty much impossible. Doubly so when that particular Scotsman was Finlay Jamieson, a man whose story – a proper heartbreaker – was bringing tears to her eyes.

She should be furious. Enraged that Finn and his family had been so duplicitous. They'd been brought here for the express purpose of getting money to fix a potato harvester?

The money Val had spent on this immersive experience could have gone to her kids, her husband, a cancer charity.

Then again . . . all the guests were having a ball. They were even having a competition over who was getting the most blisters. (ChiChi was winning.)

Confusion tore through her. Only someone who was desperate would have done this. Gone to this level of effort to make ends meet. And it wasn't like Orla was planning on lying around in a gold-plated bath full of ass's milk after this. She was going to pour what money was left over from hosting them into farm machinery. Nobody's coffers would be overflowing at the end of this.

Another set of questions pulled her up short. Should she tell Gabe? Would knowing this whole thing was a set-up change the reasons everyone had come?

A full-on existential crisis set in.

She scoured her brain for answers to questions only Val could answer. Why had she chosen this specific place to reintroduce Gabe to Lachlan? And why bring her along as a third wheel?

Sometimes you have to step away from the person you think you are, to become the one you want to be.

Maybe she'd got it wrong. Maybe Gabe was the one who'd been brought along to be her support system and Lachlan was the sugar pill, a gift from the past to keep him here.

She had to stay. Right? This was one of those quests where you didn't find the answer until the end. So that's what she'd do. She'd stay.

For herself. For Val. For all the guests who thought they were here on a legitimate holiday. After all, what they were doing probably wasn't that far off from what the real Jacobeans did. A stark reminder that farming life continued to be physically and emotionally draining several hundred years on. The fact Finn, a man who struggled to spend time with his family was here, trying to help them with this deceit, told her all she needed to know. These were desperate measures.

If this failed, they'd lose Balcraigie.

'I don't know how easy it's going to be to keep this quiet.'

Finn's expression twisted as if she'd shivved him. 'If I could give everyone their money back I would.' He gave the piglet a stroke. His hand was shaking.

She bit her lip. 'Look, it doesn't have to come to that. When they understand your life history—'

'History doesn't matter. The future does.'

Willa sucked in a breath. 'History does matter! It's part of who you are. Being twelve and watching your mum marry her dead husband's chief rival the year after he died is . . . is . . .'

How did you say *a real fucker of a start in life* but prettier?

'Movie stuff?' Finn volunteered.

'Yes,' she agreed. That was it, exactly. 'Actors would totally fight it out to play you.'

'Yeah? Well . . .' He shook his head and sighed a big, heavy sigh. 'If you could ask the scriptwriter how I can save the farm I'd owe you.'

'Well.' She grinned. 'Putting other people's real-life problems into film context is actually one of my superpowers.'

Finn raised a go-on eyebrow.

Willa instantly warmed to the task. 'We need to turn your life into the equivalent of an inspirational underdog story. One of those low-budget films no one thinks will do well but actually pulls in millions at the box office.'

'Comedy or tragedy?'

She gave him a come-on look. 'Inspirational with funny bits, but deep, inescapably gut-wrenching emotion at the heart of it.' She held up a hand so she could continue. 'I know being the dour Scot is kind of your thang, but hear me out. Everyone, and I mean everyone, loves a grump who is touched by the largesse of his community. Especially if he's a hottie.'

He shot her a look. She blushed. It was all very embarrassing.

'Okay, then.' He spread out his hands as if opening the floor to her. 'What do I do to avoid turning this into a tragedy?'

'You've got to ask the villagers for help.'

He lifted his eyebrows. 'Yer bum's oot the windae, lass.'

'Translation, please.'

'Not a chance. They hate me. Always have.'

'No,' she corrected. 'They hate who they think your father was and, by proxy, you – mostly because you've done nothing over the years to change the impression because, from your perspective, you were protecting your father's honour.' On a roll now, she shifted round so she was facing him, cross-legged. 'Look, I don't like to brag, but I am a bit of an expert on the inspirational film oeuvre, and this is one of those moments when you're going to have to dig deep, realise you're part of something bigger than yourself and reach out to the people you've never thought of as allies.'

'Now you're speaking in tongues.'

She thought for a moment then said, 'I'm going to do a shrink thing and repeat to you what I heard when you told me about your past and, more pressingly, your future.'

He made an oh-god groan.

She held up her hand. 'You want my help? We have to do a bit of touchy-feely stuff. I need to make sure we're on the same page.'

'Fair enough.' He leant back against the thick wooden ties and closed his eyes as she repeated his story to him.

His parents – Scottish mother and English father – had met at a pub in Edinburgh when his mum was finishing her university course. It had been a love-at-first-sight connection. His mum was from Balcraigie and had been having a long-distance relationship with a boy she'd known for ever and wrote to him the next morning to tell him it was off. It had been his father's idea to buy Balcraigie Castle. Finn's mum used to play in the derelict castle as a girl and had countless, unfulfillable dreams about living there one day. His dad wanted to make those dreams come true and poured every penny he'd earned, and some he'd inherited when his own parents passed, into buying it. There hadn't been a solitary room that was fit for purpose, but they hadn't cared. They had hopes and dreams enough to carry them through the renovations his architect father had for the castle. Finn had grown up living as wild and free as a boy in the Jacobean era might have. Roaming the hills. Fishing in the loch. Picking berries from the hedgerows in the summer and teaching himself to start fires with a pair of sticks in the winter. Money was tight. They lived in a double-wide caravan parked in the walled garden. When it began to look as if they might never be able to afford to do up even a handful of rooms, the council had come to them, asking if they would sell some perimeter land so that the village could build some more affordable housing. It would be enough to do up five rooms in the castle. His parents agreed. Finn's father volunteered to design the houses for free. He was, after all, an architect. The council said no but kept the decision quiet. Some pretty awful homes were built – shoddy workmanship, an eyesore – and the only one who looked as if they'd come out of the situation with anything positive was Finn's family who everyone knew were going to be living in a castle.

'It was at this point', Willa said, watching as Finn's shoulders began twitching and flexing as if reliving it all in a REM nightmare, 'when the usually friendly villagers turned.' Almost overnight, his father had gone from being a hero whose ownership of Balcraigie 'kept things local' to that 'bloody Englishman, storming in, taking over, lording it about everyone with his fancy this and fancy that' completely forgetting that Finn, his mother and father had lived in near poverty for years. Farming, it turned out, had not been his father's gift.

Willa swallowed before starting the next bit.

Tragedy struck. On a rare morning off from farm work, Finn's dad died. Their border collie had swum far out into the loch to try to 'round up' Finn and his dad who'd gone fishing. His dad dived in to get her when she began to struggle. When his dad didn't climb into the boat after he'd got the dog safely in, Finn, who'd been eight at the time, had thought that his dad was playing one of his practical jokes on him. Swimming under water all the way to the shore. But he had drowned.

They'd been utterly heartbroken. His father had been the centre of their universe. Their light. Their joy. And then, for reasons Finn still couldn't understand, his mother married her ex a year later. Duncan. Duncan used the money they'd earmarked for the castle to build the modern, pebble-dashed 'monstrosity' next to the stables and that had been that. Life went on as if his father had never existed. And Finn had spent the rest of his childhood in a not-so-silent rage.

His mum changed. Was prone to depression and days-long silences. Orla learnt how to cook out of necessity and, only later, when she'd met Dougie, out of joy.

Finn's childhood was defined by losing his dad and gaining a stepfather he couldn't – or maybe wouldn't – bond with. He'd endured a childhood of being picked on for being 'English muck' as his stepsister received the full glow of a community 'looking after its own'. There had been a complete wall of silence from Duncan and Finn's mum regarding any sort of future for the castle that, until now, had lain completely neglected.

When Finn had gone off to college and then university – more to get space than to study agriculture, which he'd been born to – he'd finally felt he had room to breathe. 'And that's when you decided to teach at the agricultural college instead of coming back to Balcraigie. Even though you inherited it when your mom passed, over the years you'd come to think of it as Orla's.' She had to tread carefully here. 'A penance, maybe – a peace offering for a complicated childhood. And even though Duncan and Dougie are good farmers, it's a tough market. Especially when you've double-downed on your potato crop to clear some bills, the potato harvester breaks and there's no money to fix it.'

'Eh, well.' He washed his hand over his face. 'It's a neat and tidy way of telling me I dropped the ball.'

'What? No,' Willa protested. 'I wasn't saying—'

He cut her off. 'I know you weren't. This is me giving myself lashings for something I should have done long ago.'

'Which was?'

'Move back here and help my family.' He gently lifted the piglet from his lap and laid it on top of the pile of polka-dotted porkers already sleeping in the crook of the sow's legs. He pressed his hands to the chest-height railings and looked out to the sprawling farmland beyond the barns. 'I know my stepfamily and I will never be close, not the way my mum, dad and I—' He stretched his jaw against a hit of emotion and began again. 'There's no sense in rehashing what's happened in the past. But if I'm going to help Orla and her lot, and prove that my dad had nothing but good intentions when he bought this place, what we need to focus on is the future.'

A flush of pride warmed her. Misplaced or not, she felt like he'd included her in the statement. Not just in a could-you-help-me-out-with-a-few-errands way, but in a bigger, broader sense. And it surprised her to realise she wanted to be a part of the solution.

'So how are we going to give you and Orla the happy ending the audience want?'

'Is this you trying to get me to do some positive imagery or something?' He flashed her an unexpectedly bright smile. Her heart flipped.

She gave a hapless little shrug. 'I can't help being a source of pure, motivational energy.'

He laughed, then let his smile fade. 'First and foremost? We can't let anyone know that Orla's set this whole thing up because the potato harvester is broken. If they knew she'd had them pay good money in exchange for their labour while she tried to get parts in?

We'd have to give all of that money back – and from what she told me last night, it's gone.'

'Okay. Noted.' Willa made blinker gestures with her hands. 'Eyes on the prize. Do not reveal deceptive holiday ruse to guests.' She hesitated. 'Gabe?'

'Not even Gabe.'

She looked up at 'heaven', asked Val for permission to keep Gabe in the dark and received it. 'Done. What next?'

'We make sure the guests have a bloody good time and pray the parts for the harvester come in.'

'Cool. How?'

Finn gave a self-effacing laugh. 'You and I head down to the village. Me with my tail between my legs, you with your sunshiny American charm, and we convince folk to help us. Otherwise this place is going to have a "For Sale" sign on it in three weeks' time.'

'Which we will not let happen,' she said definitively, before addressing the final and possibly stickiest problem. 'How do we give a fully immersive, once-in-a-lifetime experience to *Outlander* superfans?'

Finn's expression sobered and his voice grew thick with an unexpected charge of emotion. 'Research, lass. Prepare for battle, then head directly into the eye of the storm.'

'Awesome. I'm all in.' She stepped towards him and put up her hand for a high five.

Just as their hands connected, her phone began to buzz. They both started laughed. 'What are you?' she asked. 'A phone mast?'

'Yes. That's it exactly. All the texts in Scotland come through me.'

They stood there for a moment, smiling at one another, their hands still pressed together and then, when her phone buzzed again, Finn pulled back. 'Looks like your real life wants a word with you.'

'You know Hollywood!'

Finn frowned at her. No. He didn't. Whatever problems were buzzing away on her phone would no doubt pale in comparison to what Finn and his family were going through. And yet, as soon as she dived into her bosom, took the phone out and began thumbing through the texts, she could feel the closeness between them begin to diminish.

Chapter Twenty-Six

Aubrey Washington: Hey Willz. 😴 😴 😴 I can't find that list of questions you'd written up for the interview with Britney. Resend?

Bryony Stokes: Willa? Where are the questions for Britney? Also, I can't log into your account any more. 🔫 I might have accidentally changed the password and can't remember what it was. 🙈 Anyone in IT I need to sweet-talk for that? 🧁 🕯 🏮 And also, there might have been a teensy accident with a mushroom smoothie in your pen drawer. Soz! 🍄

Bryony Stokes: Never mind. 😇 😇 😇 I pulled out the charm and I'm back in. Might need to talk to someone about fluffing the petty cash supplies. BTW your filing system is certifiable.

Charlie Foster: Willa? I'm actually being serious here. Bryony's like IRL Lindsay Lohan on steroids. Before the fall. 🔪 🔫

Martina Glaubitz: When you come in for the morning meeting could you please bring all of the run sheets for the Zendaya/Rita Ora special? Having RuPaul do the interview should really pull in the numbers.

Bryony Stokes: Hey Willa. Weird question. Do you know how to get hold of RuPaul? I might have accidentally said you already booked her????? #BubbleBrain!

Mom: Hi there sweetie. Just wanted to let you know we're planning on making a bit of a splash for your dad's sixtieth. I know it's a few months off and not very 'Jenkins' of us, but if you could think about coming up for a couple of days one of your brothers will pick you up from the Portland airport so you don't have to worry about the puddle jumper over to Pendleton. Oh, and could you pick up some of those California almonds for your dad? He loves to snack on those. Says they remind him of you.

Chapter Twenty-Seven

Willa sent off her last email and popped her phone on top of the 'headboard' bales. There'd been so many messages and emails flooding in in the end, Finn had brought her back here to the hayloft and she'd been glued to her phone for most of the day. She'd answered as many questions as she could, but her father's oft repeated edict was gnawing at her brain like a primordial earworm. *Gotta be in the game to get the touchdowns, Willy.* The only question was: which game did she want to be in?

She'd been right about the texts. The 'crises' at TiTs paled in comparison to Finn's To Do list. Now that she knew what was going on behind the scenes at Balcraigie Castle she felt compelled to stay and help Finn. It's what she'd been raised to do. Help people who needed it. The fact she was beginning to like Finn a whole lot more than she originally had was a different story, but . . . Pushing all of that aside, she was fighting an increasingly panicked feeling that Bryony was trying to get her job.

If she lost it? She would be right royally screwed. Interviewing celebs about the rigours of fighting a pterodactyl on a green screen wasn't a highly transferable skill. If she returned home to find her security pass had been revoked? She would end up doing exactly what her mother had predicted the day she'd packed up her car to head south: turning back around and getting the only guaranteed job going in Pendleton.

Don't be too proud to take shifts at the Dairy Queen, honey. Scowling because you think you'll spend the rest of your life making M&M Blizzards won't change things. Remember, those cavity machines pay bills. Dreams don't.

She tried not to let the memory rile her. Saying stuff like that was her mother's way of being helpful. She was the grandchild of Latin American immigrants who'd earned their keep through physical labour. Her mom had been the first in her extended family to go to university and even that hadn't been easy. The only way she'd been able to pay for it was to serve in the military. During a war. She wasn't a cosy, cuddly, c'mere-let's-watch-*Gilmore-Girls*-and-eat-pints-of-ice-cream kind of mother. She was more of a do-something-productive-with-your-time – other-people-don't-have-half-the-time-you-do-moping-about-a-life-that's-pretty-great mother. It had taught her resilience. And not to rely on anyone. Which was why her friendship with Val had been such a comfort to her. They 'got' each other in a way she'd never felt understood by her own family. Val could read her moods and do just the right thing to make it better and with absolutely no judgement. Having that perfect a relationship taken away from her, and so cruelly, felt like walking around with only one lung.

A soft knock sounded on her door. 'Willa,' Finn whispered. 'It's me.'

A shiver swept down her spine.

Stupid, sexy Scottish accent. She'd have to become more immune to it.

She padded across the thick, worn-by-time planks as lightly as she could, aware Gabe was below her and that it would be very easy to misread Finn's pre-planned visit as a booty call.

Just because he was deeply attractive, and far more sensitive than he appeared, didn't mean there was any *depth* to her visceral response to him. It wasn't *genuine* attraction. This was, at most, a holiday crush. All she had to do was keep it at bay for the next ten days, then she could get on the plane, giggle with the flight attendant until they reached the big city with its superhighways and palm trees and pollution and juice cleanses, where she could get back to the business of doing what she loved.

She opened the door, sending covert looks left and right like a spy, but all she got was a face full of tweed jacket. She looked up.

Blue-grey eyes met hers. Straw-coloured waves of hair stuck out from under his flat cap, grazing the collar of a green and fawn checked shirt. His shoulders were filling out his tweed coat with Disney-hero panache and his thighs . . . Knee-weakening. She'd met Channing Tatum a number of times and had never bit down on her cheek as hard as she was now. Well-worn moleskin trousers were now ruined for her. The bastard.

She ushered him in, trying not to sniff him as he entered. He was so solidly Finn. A man. A farmer. A teacher. A brother trying to make amends. A Scotsman.

She felt flimsy in contrast. A shadow human. How could she not when her biggest form of personal identity was her job?

After she'd closed the door behind her, he took his hands out from behind his back with a flourish. In one hand he held a laptop. In the other, a steaming bag of microwave popcorn.

'Ooo!' She pounced on the popcorn. 'Gimme.'

He gave it to her and looked around the room. 'Where do you want to do this?'

An awkwardness descended. The most comfortable spot was on the bed. But . . . it was a bed. And, having given her Jacobean top a scrub in the bath, she was wearing a unicorn onesie with the word 'smitten' stitched into the front of it. She really should have pre-thought the impression she was giving.

She pointed at the foot of the bed. 'What if we make a little coffee table out of one of the bales and use the bed as a backrest?'

◆ ◆ ◆

Much further into the first series than either of them had anticipated, Willa was feeling decidedly torn. Jamie and Claire clearly had the horn for one another. She, Willa, was sitting next to someone who made her horny. She also had signed a waiver promising not to jump him like the sexy hot potato that he was. This, after having experienced that one – perfect – kiss. It was torture.

When they reached the point where (#SpoilerAlert) Jamie and Claire started undressing one another on their wedding night, she and Finn began fidgeting, clearing their throats, and basically acting like teenagers in Health class on How To Have Safe Sex day.

Willa broke first. 'Well, this isn't at all cringe.'

'Nope,' Finn agreed, using his forearm to open another bottle of alcoholic ginger beer he'd bolted down the stairs to find after the two of them had nearly died of mortification during the first of Claire's many sex scenes.

Not that Willa was counting, (she was totally counting) but Claire had had more sex with her English and Scottish husbands in the space of . . . what was it, a few weeks? . . . than Willa had had in the past five years. And boy howdy did she want to have sex right now.

To disguise her discomfort she began to do what she always did when she was nervous. Talked to excess. 'Their wedding was nice. Good percentage of candles. Our minister was better. And the sausage rolls. In fact, now that I think about it, from the angle they shot it? Their minister – vicar? Whatever – he looked like a satanist. But maybe he was trying not to stare at Claire's boobs. Do you think it was spring or summer? I mean, that was a fair amount of cleavage on display. Four out of five stars for the kiss, but I think ours was totes better.'

What. The. Actual. Fuck. Was. Pouring. Out. Of. Her. Mouth?

Finn's eyes shot to hers, then back to the screen.

Awesome. The old I'm-going-to-pretend-you-weren't-talking manoeuvre. Cool, cool. She was down with that. She was down with all of this. Just because she'd masturbated to a picture of this guy before she'd met him, then flashed him, then freaked out when he'd accidentally grabbed her boobs, freaked out *again* for patronising her when, really, she'd deserved it, because, you know, first impressions are a thing for a reason, only for him to kiss her at their wedding as if he had actually wanted to, not to mention all of the mega-bonding in the pig pen earlier with actual tears and hugs and plans to save his family home, there wasn't any reason to get bent out of shape. Who cared if he didn't want to talk about the tingling feeling in her lips every time she remembered that kiss?

She did.

So she changed the topic. 'On the flipside, maybe time-travelling women forced into a marriage of convenience with strapping young Highlanders deserve a bit of nooky.'

Finn gave her a wary side-eye, then, his attention caught by the absence of moaning, turned back to the screen. 'Oh. Would you look at that.' He was tipping his head as if the sight in front of him was something brand spanking new. 'They're talking. After sex.'

Willa made a vague noise. 'Well, you know what they say, a bit of a chit-chat after the consummation of a clan-arranged marriage that saved the bride from certain death comes highly recommended.'

'And you know this from personal experience?'

'Oh, personal. Obvs.'

'Shame.' Finn stuck out his lower lip. 'I was hoping I'd be your first.'

And then they both realised what he'd just said.

She said, 'Ha, ha,' and 'Nice one,' and 'Sorry, bud,' then really wanted to go and find a dark corner somewhere where she could curl up and die.

'You've led quite the life.' Finn grinned, then took a chug of his drink. Willa followed his Adam's apple bobbing up and down the length of his sun-gold throat stubble. She forced herself to drag her eyes up to his lips, then to his eyes just as an orgasmic groan of pleasure burst from the tinny speakers.

Finn closed the laptop. 'I think it's getting a bit late, don't you?'

'Definitely.' She faked a yawn. 'Very late.'

He held the laptop to his chest but made no move to leave.

Her heart made an erratic oh-my-god-he's-going-to-kiss-me beat. 'You okay?' she asked when he didn't move.

'Aye, I just—' His blue eyes flicked across to meet hers. 'Sorry about today. About including you in this mess. This is meant to be your holiday and I've pretty much ruined it.'

'Finn.' She was serious now. 'I'm happy to help. Particularly as the whole *Outlander* thing—' She pointed at the laptop, then flapped her hands at it while she tried to figure out exactly what to say, finally settling on, 'I don't really know why I'm here. Helping you makes me feel useful.'

As she spoke the words, the truth of them settled her. She was a producer. She made things happen. Correction. She made magic happen, never letting anyone know what was really occurring behind the scenes. Stroppy presenters. Truculent film stars. A real-life farmer fighting for the land that made him the man he was.

If she could do this – ensure the guests had the best immersive Jacobean experience possible – perhaps then the great, gaping hole that had nearly rent her in two when Val had died would begin to heal.

'Thanks,' Finn said, his voice rougher than it had been a moment earlier. 'Well, then.' He gave her a half bow. 'I wish you goodnight, m'lady.'

She held out the sides of her onesie and curtsied. 'M'lord.'

When she looked up at him, the intensity of his gaze seared through any protective layers she'd put in place. It was like wearing factor 10 sunblock in the desert.

She got the feeling that Finn, like her, was going through a personal metamorphosis. He thought he'd found his happy place at the Inverness agricultural college, but from what she'd seen? His happy place was here. And unless he did something, he would lose it.

It was a heck of a way to become a butterfly. To throw himself into saving the place that brought him equal mixes of pleasure and pain. The fact he wanted to save it, not just for himself, but for a stepfamily he'd never quite bonded with spoke volumes. He was an honourable, kind man who would put his pride to the side to tend to the greater good and she did not fancy him one tiny bit. Her erogenous zones always threw a glitter party when she wished a man goodnight. That's just how biology worked.

He touched his fingers to his cap. 'G'night, then, Claire.'

'Night, Jamie.'

When she closed the door and pressed her hands against the smooth, golden sheet of wood, something told her the absence of footsteps meant Finn was on the other side, doing exactly the same thing.

Chapter Twenty-Eight

Finn powered through his morning chores, eager to get into town before the Thursday market traffic set in.

As he popped his favourite wheelbarrow back against the wall, Orla came in with one of her small baskets. She held it out to him. 'Some food for you, in case you and Willa are out for a while.'

He took the basket and, after a knotty moment's silence, said, 'You're doing a brilliant job, you know. Folk seem to be loving it.'

She looked at him wide-eyed with disbelief. 'Finn! It's a shambles. I lied to these people. They're good, lovely folk who wanted a wee bit of a holiday and I've got them building stone dykes and clearing out brambles and clambering round a castle that is a health-and-safety disaster zone. I'm off my heid, is what I am.'

A hug would've been useful here. Some words of encouragement. Unfortunately, avoiding eye contact was what he and Orla were used to. They acknowledged one another, sure, but they didn't ever really look at one another.

He looked at his stepsister now. Really looked at her. A year younger than him, Orla should be glowing with youth. A thirty-two-year-old mum of two living on a beautiful farm on the edge of a breathtaking loch, surrounded by villagers she'd known since she was in nappies. She was in the heart of a community that had supported her from the very beginning. And she looked absolutely knackered.

'I'm sorry,' he said, feeling his chest release after years of waiting for just this moment.

'For what?'

'All of it. I—' He hesitated, unsure if he should say anything and then thought, *Screw it*. In for a penny and all that. 'I could've been a better brother to you and I – I just want you to know that I'm here now. For whatever you need.'

Orla's spine endured a short, sharp shudder. In its wake, she stood, rapid-blinking at the lunch basket, as if giving herself permission to believe him would be a step too far. Her response felt like a sucker punch. Not that he'd been expecting a warm hug and tears of gratitude. He hadn't earnt her trust. He couldn't expect it with a few muttered half sentences of apology.

'Aye,' she finally said. 'Right you are.'

'You know,' he pressed on. 'The bank manager said there are buyers if we want. Ones with deep pockets.'

She nodded, tears springing to her eyes. They weren't tears of relief.

He ducked his head until he was looking her squarely in the eye. 'We won't let them take it, Orla. The farm. The castle. Any of it. Okay?'

A round of rigorous nodding and lip biting ensued. When she'd gathered herself, she pointed at the basket. 'I put a cheese and pickle sandwich in there for you.'

He pressed his hand to his chest in thanks. This was Orla's love language. Knowing and making someone's favourite food.

'Thank you,' he said, meaning so much more than those two little words could offer. Thank you for not making him pay for being such a complicated stepbrother. For leaving her and her family to sort out the farm even though, in name, it was his.

Leaving had been his way of showing them that he thought of the place as theirs. The grand gesture had totally backfired. He'd failed to notice that they'd been keeping the place ready and waiting for him, just the way he liked it, for when, or if, he returned. An epic, sprawling gift of the Magi. They had loved him like family all along. Unconditionally.

If Willa were here, she would be stage-whispering instructions like, *Hug her* or *Say something nice about her cooking*. His lips twitched at the thought and Orla must've seen something in it because she smiled back at him.

After it all got a bit too much, standing there smiling at one another, Orla dug into her pinafore and pulled out a list. 'These folk might be useful to speak to, down the village. They know about' – she fanned her hand across her outfit and then out towards the castle – 'the situation.'

'Thanks.' He turned to go, digging into his pocket for his keys, then stopped. 'Orla?'

She turned round and smiled, the worry already eased from her eyes.

'If it doesn't work out, getting the money for the harvester, you and Dougie, your kids and your dad, I'll look after you, alright?'

'I know, Finn,' she said. 'You've always been there for us.'

Chapter Twenty-Nine

When Willa emerged from her hayloft, the first person her eyes lit on was Finn. He didn't say anything, but she could tell from the softening of his features that he liked what he saw. Though everyone was gathered in the courtyard, pouring teas and coffees for themselves, accepting bowls of porridge, and stretching out the kinks from the previous day's work, the moment felt strangely private. A Prince-Charming-sees-his-Cinderella-type moment.

Fenella's piercing wolf-whistle cut through it the way a heavy metal soundtrack broke into a costume drama. Discordantly.

'Cooooeeee! Someone's looking proper sick today.' It was difficult to tell if Fenella was pleased or angered by this.

Jennifer wondered aloud about bad things actually being good things.

Gabe raised his tin coffee mug and winked at her.

ChiChi sent a whorl of ululation her way and Trevor said, 'I'd do that' to which he received a punch in the arm from Jules and a noogie from Blair.

Willa flushed. She wasn't used to being the centre of attention. Not like this. But before the group allowed her to descend, they demanded she give them all a twirl. She had to admit, she loved the dress Orla had brought to her earlier this morning. It was a beautiful, deep forest green tartan with a little cape thing sewn down the back. A perfect match to the claret red triangle sweater wrap Jennifer had gifted her last night at the firepit.

As she stood there, all eyes shining up at her, she felt ridiculous and a little bit like a princess. She knew she wasn't revolting to look at, but years of knowing there was always someone thinner, prettier, or more famous than her had inured her to being skipped over. Left on the side lines while others basked in the limelight. Something that used to annoy Valentina no end. *You're freaking catnip*, mija. *The only one who doesn't know it is you.*

So, today, for her best friend and for herself, she enjoyed the attention. Basked in their praise, even letting some of it seep in. After giving everyone a regal wave, she slid down the banister to join them.

Once she'd got a mug of coffee (a new addition to breakfast, courtesy of Lachlan, who'd said he'd had enough of Gabe glowering like Black Jack Randall in the morning. *Still gorgeous*, he'd quipped, *but a right proper arsehole to garden with*), Willa settled herself and her preponderance of petticoats on to a stump beside Gabe. They clinked mugs.

'Howzit?' she asked.

'*Bueno.*' He yawned, then apologised. 'I had to do some work last night. Didn't get much sleep.' Then he said something in Spanish that sounded like a prayer of thanks to the coffee gods.

She clinked her mug to his again. 'Speaking of work . . .' Willa not-so-casually segued.

Gabe held up a hand, stopping her. 'This better not be you telling me you're bailing and heading back to LA.'

'No.' It hadn't been, but now that he mentioned it . . . maybe after today's errands with Finn . . .

Gabe's expression hardened. 'Willa?' He drew out her name in a dark, warning tone. 'What aren't you telling me?'

Rather a lot as it turned out. But she'd promised not to say anything.

She scrunched up her nose, then told him about Bryony's latest series of empire-building manoeuvres.

He fuzzed his lips. 'I know the type. Don't worry. She'll fuck up soon enough and they'll come running to you. Treat 'em mean, keep 'em keen. And when they come back? Pay rise and promotion. Those are your terms, okay, Willaford?'

Instinct tugged her spine upwards at the use of her full name. Val was the only person who got to call her that. She considered the alternative – never hearing it again – and decided to let the usual rebuke she would have unleashed go unsaid. Gabe could use her name. For now.

'Cool. Got it. Thanks, boss.' They sat in silence, drinking their coffee, the banter of the group around them now more familiar with the handful of days they'd spent together ('Peee yew! Someone forgot their pit stick this morning') and, Willa noticed, a tiny bit edgier. ('No wonder they skipped over all these bits in the books. Writing about doing the same chores day after day would not have made these bestsellers.')

Willa bit her tongue. That would change. Later today, if everything went well. But on the off chance it didn't, she was sworn to silence.

Finn joined them, holding out a plate piled high with steaming scones and a pot of raspberry jam.

Gabe demurred. Willa took one then stepped back as her fellow travellers greedily fell upon the rest of the pile.

'Wow!' Jules pointed at her half-eaten scone. 'These are amazing! How does Orla get them so light?'

'They're actually from Balcraigie Bakehouse,' Finn explained. 'Orla's mate from school runs it now. Mhairi Pringle.'

Willa took a bite of her untouched scone. Then another. And another. It was amazing. Fluffy. Light. Buttery. If there was a heaven, these should be the clouds. 'They're incredible.'

'Aye. Her bread's brilliant too,' Finn said, lavishing his own scone with a huge dollop of jam. 'She uses the same oven the bakehouse had installed when it was built away back in the nineteenth century.'

After enjoying the few remaining mouthfuls, a thought came to her. 'Gabe?' she asked as innocently as she could.

'Mmm?'

'If you had to give tips to one of your clients who was, say, trying to rehabilitate their image with a community who might be predisposed to find them . . . standoffish . . . What would you advise?'

Finn pointedly poured the remains of the jam on to his scone.

Gabe stared at his plate while he considered the question. 'Depends.'

'On what?'

He glanced across at Finn who instantly looked away, then caught Willa's eyes. 'Why they'd had the rift in the first place.'

'Oh, well . . . a misunderstanding. This is totally hypothetical, of course.'

'Of course.' Gabe gave her a sure-it-is nod.

Finn carried the platter round the group again, but Willa could tell he was still listening.

'So, if this hypothetical person had been the unfortunate victim of say . . . poor branding . . . people thought they were one thing when, really, they were something else altogether . . . what would you say their best line of combatting the ill will would be?'

'Behave the way they wanted people to see them. Even if they weren't feeling it yet. Project the image and the energy of the type of person you want them to respond to.' Gabe licked some jam off his fingers then finished his coffee. 'No matter how broad-minded people like to think they are, we're wired to be responsive to threats. If you normally wander round in a cloud of thunder . . .' Again, his eyes drifted to Finn.

Willa cut in, 'Like you did the first time we met?'

Gabe laughed. 'Yes. Until you plied me with Rocky Mountain Bear Fuckers, I was a bit of an ass.'

She pressed her hands to her heart with a squishy *awww*. 'Don't worry. You made up for it.'

There had been extenuating circumstances. Same for Finn.

'And I made up for it by . . .' Gabe beckoned for her to repeat the lesson he'd just taught her.

'Behaving the way you wanted to be perceived.'

Again, Val's note came to her. *Sometimes you have to step away from the person you think you are, to become the person you want to be.*

'Thanks, *muchacho*.' She rose and gave his cheek a kiss. 'Right, then, Finlay.' She turned round, nearly knocking Finn over with her skirts. 'You ready to head into the roaring metropolis that is downtown Balcraigie?'

◆　◆　◆

'Very subtle, Willa.' Finn jammed the key into his jeep.

'Thank you.' She beamed at him angelically. 'I thought so.'

He scowled. 'I know how to behave nicely.'

'Obviously. I am bearing witness to it.' She clicked her seatbelt in place nanoseconds before Finn pressed his steel-toed boot to the accelerator. After a few minutes of terse silence she said, 'I just thought as Gabe does this for a living – rebrands people – a few last-minute tips wouldn't go astray.'

'I know.' He huffed out a sigh then admitted, 'I guess I'm a bit nervous. Orla's the one who usually goes into town and does this kind of thing.'

'Why didn't you ask her to come?'

She knew why but thought Finn could do with the reminder.

'Because there's no future for me here if I keep pushing people away.'

'Very good, Finn. That was very Dr Phil of you.' She gave him a sunshiny grin. 'Now then. Let me see your most charming smile.'

He shot her a rictus-like grin.

It was going to be a long day.

◆ ◆ ◆

'Finn.' Willa nudged him. 'You have to go *into* the shop to make a transaction.'

'I know. Don't rush me, lass.'

They both stared at the glass-paned door, its name written in swirly gold letters just like it had been since the store had opened in 1843 according to the little plaque to the left of it.

She gave him a few moments, but . . . nothing.

'Dude. It's a ribbon store.'

'Aye,' he snapped back. 'I know what type of shop it is. And I'll thank you to remember it's actually called a haberdashery establishment.'

An elderly couple passing by overheard the exchange and tsked.

Willa sniggered. For some reason she was finding this fun. Loads better than convincing the latest Coachella stars into a pre-performance interview. This version of Finn in a grump was delightful. It was like being with the Grinch as he fought his deeply ingrained habits in order to embody new ones that allowed him to be happy.

They'd started at the bakery on the premise that, as the owner was Orla's long-term school friend and they'd just scoffed down a massive pile of her scones, it would be easy. It hadn't gone quite as smoothly as anticipated. Instead of adopting the happy-to-help-a-mate tone Finn had been hoping for, Mhairi, who ran the place, went full on so-you're-the-asshole-who's-been-treating-his-stepsister-like-shite-all-these-years. To the point Willa, who had decided to stand outside and peep in on the whole thing through the window, had heard every word.

Rant finished, Willa expected Finn to nod, thank her for her feedback and walk out.

But he'd surprised her. Stuck to his guns. He'd taken Mhairi's criticisms on the chin, agreed that he could've done more on the farm and, using Jules's new project as bait, convinced her to come out to Balcraigie to take a look at the castle's old oven and bring along a few loaves of bread as well. Day old, but still. He'd walked out with a smile on his face and a little kick to his step. It had been fun to be a part of it.

Before she had a chance to come up with some more words of encouragement, Finn had sucked in a big breath, grabbed the brass doorknob, and pulled her inside with him as he offered hearty greetings over the tinkling of the entry bell.

'Well,' said the proprietress, a Mrs-Claus-type figure dressed in a long tartan skirt and an immaculate white top. 'If it isn't young Finlay Jamieson.'

'Good morning, Mrs Donaldson.' Finn nodded his head. 'Are you well today?'

'Oh, aye. Not much changed since the last time you were in.'

His face clouded briefly as the memory of whatever it was she'd referred to hit. Whatever it was, it wasn't good.

'Apologies for that, Mrs Donaldson. I wasn't myself then.'

'Oh, I wasn't chastising you, lad. How could you've been on top form what with laying your father to rest and all.'

Willa sent him a look and, perhaps because he hadn't expected the kindness of Mrs Donaldson's response, he explained to Willa, 'I came with my mum before Dad's funeral and might have knocked all the button jars off the counter.' He pointed at five huge jars filled with a mismatch of buttons.

Mrs Donaldson explained. 'Folk bring in their spares and when someone's putting together a new outfit, we try to help with these.' She looked at Finn and said, 'It took some time to pick them all up, didn't it? Two days, was it? Three? Anyway, back in town for the tattie holidays, are you? Taking some time off from the bright lights of Inverness and slumming it with the country folk?'

Willa hid a smirk. From what Finn had told her, Inverness was about as rock and roll as the Yukon.

Finn nodded. 'I thought Orla and Dougie might need a hand what with . . .' He cleared his throat. '. . . things being tricky at the farm.'

Mrs Donaldson gave him a savvy look. 'I'm sure they appreciate that help, Finlay. And that of your – is this your girlfriend?'

Willa looked at Finn. This should be interesting.

'She's, ah . . . she's my – *mo nighean donn*.' He gave a solid nod as if he'd decided to commit to the whole *Outlander* thing.

Mrs Donaldson unleashed a full bright smile. 'Ah, well. That's lovely to hear. Many congratulations to you, Finlay and . . .'

'Willa.' Willa reached forward and the women shook hands.

'Very good, very good.' Mrs Donaldson wiped her hands as if that was the gossip part of their session finished, freeing them to move on to other, more pressing topics. 'So! What brings you to Donaldson Haberdashery today?'

Chapter Thirty

A few hours later, Willa stood back so Finn could have a preview of her efforts. Swags of heather, courtesy of the local forager, hung from the exposed beams, and kerosene lamps (borrowed from a local auction house) warmed the darker corners the fading sunlight didn't reach. The old breakfast table had been scrubbed until it glowed like honey. He'd never seen the potting shed look this inviting. More than that, it looked Jacobean. 'There's no need for the collywobbles, Willa. They're going to love it.'

Her forehead crinkled. 'Collywobbles?'

'Nerves.'

She bit down on her full bottom lip and shook her head. She didn't believe him. He almost laughed at the role reversal. She'd been his maypole throughout the morning's 'amends trip' as he'd named it. She'd been there for him, a kind, generous cheerleader as he'd rehabilitated his image to the community.

It was his turn to do the same for her.

He held out his hands and looked around. 'I feel like I'm in the show.'

'Really? How can you? I mean . . . No offence, but we're not the superfans.' She pointed out to the courtyard where the other guests were gathering. 'I really want them to love this and Orla's set such a high standard.'

'Orla thinks it's genius.'

His stepsister had actually cried when he and Willa told her about the *Outlander*-centric activities they'd either planned or had agreed to take over when Orla admitted to having been over-ambitious with her promises in the brochure.

Willa gave the thick piece of cloth they'd picked up in town a swipe with her hand, fretting at its edges as she asked, 'Orla knows we're using orange soda instead of pee for the tweed-dyeing, right?'

'Aye. And she's given me buckets of fresh water so everyone can wash their hands and all. It'll be fine, Willa.'

'But what if it isn't? What if they're all, "That tweed doesn't exist in *Outlander*. That tweed's from the future. You're a sham!"' She looked up at him, little creases of strain fanning out from her dark eyes. Her cheeks were flushed with activity and nerves, tendrils of hair escaping her wayward, messy bun. She looked beautiful. A stress bucket, but beautiful.

He shook away the thought and put on his 'Jamie' accent. 'Dinnae worry, Sassenach.'

'Oh my god! If you're trying to prove to me you're the best source of feedback on whether or not I got this right, you have just fallen at the first hurdle.'

He tried again. 'Dinnae worry, lass.' He took her by the shoulders and turned her round as one of the women from the Balcraigie Women's Institute illuminated a string of artificial candles that even he wouldn't have known were fakes.

'Oh.' She pressed her hands to her collarbones and did a little *squeee!* 'It looks amazing.'

It did as well. Under the extended eaves of the low-ceilinged potting shed, the setting was a near exact replica of the show's. Four women of various ages were arranging the huge skein of tweed she and Finn had bargained out of the nearby woollen mill's seconds bin. At one end sat a big wooden bucket filled with warm, yellow liquid. He'd been assured by the WI grannies that a bit of Irn-Bru wouldn't hurt the cloth at all.

When they called the group in from the stables yard, everyone's eyes lit up in recognition of the scene before them. The women at the table, all dressed in yesteryear frocks, began pouring out liquid on to the table as the oldest of them, a beautiful dried-apple-faced woman, began singing in a voice as pure as a young girl's.

Willa was, of course, first in, plunging her hands into the soppy fabric and sloshing it about with verve. Jules, ChiChi, Jennifer, Fenella and Rosa were right behind her. The fairy lights played off Willa's hair like starlight and even though she didn't have the remotest clue what the women were singing, she joined in on choruses, eyes sparkling with delight as the local women beamed in pleasure at her enthusiasm.

To everyone's surprise, Jennifer knew most of the songs. ('YouTube,' she explained.) Finn faded into the background as they rolled up their sleeves, paying no mind to the fizzy orange liquid splashing on their arms and faces. Their 'husbands', as expected, begged off the wool-dyeing, saying they were going to take advantage of the early night to head down to the pub. Jeff and Dougie joined them, while Lachlan and Gabe 'nipped off for a wee nocturnal road trip'. Finn could've gone to the pub too. The lads were always trying to get him down there when they caught wind he was at Balcraigie. Usually he said no, he was knackered. But it was really the wagging tongues that got to him. Gossip about why he was there, if this was the time he was finally going to claim ownership of Balcraigie or, as others speculated, sell it. But this time he said no because he was one hundred per cent enjoying being exactly where he was.

Listening to the women, watching them turn hard, physical work into something beautiful, touched something dormant in him. A vital spark. He closed his eyes and let the sounds take over until he finally pinned down the elusive sensation he'd been feeling. He felt Scottish. Organically so. It wasn't about politics or the kilt grazing his knees or the scent of the nation's popular soft drink. It was the blood running through his veins. The songs in the air. The earth beneath his feet. The ground he'd learnt to crawl, then walk, upon.

Though he understood only a fraction of the Gaelic songs the women pulled out of their memories one after the other like endless spools of thread, he felt the history in them. The longing. The relationship to the land that provided them with sustenance and shelter.

He thought of his mum and the position she must have been in when his father died. A heartbroken widow with a bewildered, angry son living in a caravan, whose dreams of crafting the 'family seat' from the ruins of another had been destroyed. He'd been furious with her for not following through on his father's plans. They had some money, she'd said, but not enough. Without his dad there, and his income, restoring the castle would be impossible. Then she'd married Duncan who'd taken the money earmarked for the castle and built the modern, pebble-dashed atrocity that, admittedly, had kept them all much warmer and drier than the caravan ever had, and life had moved on. Or, more accurately, changed course. Though they never spoke of it, his mum, like himself, had never set foot in the castle again. Not with Orla. Not with Duncan. No one.

He'd not been there once until a few mornings back when he'd chased Willa in after she'd crashed into his life like Dorothy in Oz.

He'd barely thought twice about it, following her in. And once they'd left, he hadn't given it a second thought. But now, the moment struck him as significant. He'd done exactly what his father had done when he'd bought his new bride a castle without a roof. He'd followed his gut. Or, to shift the instinctive urge to another organ, his heart.

He allowed himself to be absorbed in the moment. Swept away by the songs of the past swirling round him. The atmosphere was thick with history and emotion, making it impossible not to think long and hard about how to move forward. His gut – his heart – everything was telling him not to let the farm go. Was finding a way to do up Balcraigie a fool's errand? A desperate attempt at exorcising old ghosts? Or would it be honouring his father's love for his mother without undermining the graft Duncan, Orla and Dougie had poured into the place in his stead?

It felt Shakespearean.

A complex mix of family, history, death and passion so knotted up in itself it was impossible to discern one end of the tale from the other. He looked down at his kilt pin. Though the kilt itself was modern, the pin was one of the only Jamieson heirlooms he possessed. Shaped like a tiny sword, it had been fashioned to look like a Celtic knot – a loosely woven tie that had no start or finish. It represented eternity. Never-ending loyalty, faith, friendship . . . love.

He traced his finger along the pin, then looked up, his eyes catching with Willa's.

He mouthed, 'You having fun?'

Her soft smile stretched into a happy grin. 'The best,' she mouthed back, before, once again, raising her voice to join the others in a reprise of an ancient-sounding choral refrain: *hì rì rì hù lò, mo nigh'n donn hò gù.*

As he listened to the women sing, he let his eyes drift from them to the heather thatch on the cutting-shed roof and beyond to where he could just make out the crenellated outline of the castle walls standing proud of the farm buildings. It was an amazing structure. It had once housed great rooms for both the laird and his lady. A dining hall with enormous fireplaces at either end. Private chambers for the castle's caretaker, and, of course, extended family and staff. Secret passageways. An underground passage from the cellars to the loch. At least two very inventive wee wee shoppes.

Filled with love, laughter and joy, Balcraigie Castle would be a thing of wonder.

He knew what he wanted. The end game. He'd known it all along. He'd simply had no idea how to get there.

Now, he allowed himself a sliver of belief. A flicker of hope that it might just be within reach.

One of the grannies beckoned to him to join them at the wool-waulking table. Her face was as wrinkled as her eyes were bright. 'C'mon, laddie! Get yourself over here. We're all on our way to being fair puckled.'

He smiled at the auld Scots word meaning knackered.

'This'll no' end well if we don't get some extra muscle into it,' she chided.

As he walked towards them, he felt the music physically surround him. Songs of love lost and found lifting and rising up and above the shed where they worked out to the sprawling landscape that stretched off into the North Sea beyond them. He squeezed himself in amongst the women, across the table from Willa. It felt strange and perfect all at once. Being here. Gathering strength from the eyes of a woman who'd helped open his much wider. Flanked by women whose ancestors had sung through the creation of countless reams of cloth that still hung in cupboards round the land. For the first time in over a decade he felt he was exactly where he was meant to be. At home.

A weird sound hummed through the atmosphere. Weird because it was the theme song from *Jaws*. He scanned the table, seeing if anyone else heard it, when he saw Willa dipping into her bodice, pulling out her phone, looking at it, grimacing, then climbing out from her spot on the bench, apologising to everyone and, if he wasn't mistaken, actively avoiding eye contact with him.

A few hours later, some of the guests were singing folk songs from their own countries (or, in Fenella's case, Kylie), round the campfire. Finn had yet to catch up with Willa and ask her if everything was okay. He wasn't sure whether she was avoiding him, but each time he looked for her, she veered off and joined in someone else's conversation. Right now she was talking with ChiChi and Alastair about light pollution in Los Angeles ('we literally do not see stars unless they're on a red carpet'). It was bittersweet hearing her talk about her life there because, stupidly, he could only picture her here. Or maybe it was the only place he wanted to picture her.

Though Orla was obviously the heart of this project, Willa's efforts today had made her part of it too, and now, with the fire crackling and Rosa's beautiful voice swirling round them, the place felt properly atmospheric. As if anyone stepping through the stone passageway and into the courtyard might genuinely think they had stepped back in time.

All of which was a moot point if the spare parts for the harvester didn't arrive on Monday. Two more nail-biting days to wonder if they'd get the potato crop in. It was their biggest chunk of income of the year, and the only way to keep the bank happy.

He'd accounted for repair time, harvest time and then, two weeks from now, the end game when the weather window for getting the crop closed. At that point, the driech Scottish weather took over and consumed the Highlands until spring.

If the parts didn't arrive, Finn had assured Orla he'd sell a portion of his soul to the agricultural college in order to use their harvesters overnight, at a breathtaking cost, but . . . the harvest would come in.

It wasn't the best of plans, but, strangely, Finn was feeling optimistic. As Willa kept reminding him, 'bending like the willow' was the only way to survive with your sanity intact. As if the thought had conjured her, she appeared by his side.

'Hey,' she said.

'Hey, yourself. Everything okay?'

'A few of us are going up to the doocat to stargaze,' she said instead of answering his question. 'Interested?'

Chapter Thirty-One

'So, when we're looking up at the sky,' ChiChi was saying, 'we're looking back in time.'

'Look, Mum.' Jules pointed up to the heavens. 'That's you before you married Dad.'

'Jules . . .'

'ChiChi, can I borrow your pointer thingy? I want to show Mum what she looks like when she's happy.'

'All you need is to look at my face, love. I'm here with you. What more could a mother want.'

'A divorce?'

'Shush. We're interrupting ChiChi's astrology talk.'

'Astronomy.'

'If anyone wants, I brought my tarot deck. I can do readings later.'

'Hush.'

'And what we're seeing here . . .' ChiChi whirled her laser pointer round a yellowish glow '. . . is a star that is dying.'

'Which star are we—? Oh! The one with the laser on it. How sad.'

'Outer space. It's the fucking dog's bollocks.'

'And if you follow the bright star, the yellowish one?'

'Sirius?'

'Well done, Alastair. You've been improving.'

'I didn't realise there were so many named after Harry Potter characters.'

'I think it's the other way round, actually.'

'Pay attention! ChiChi's trying to— Ooo! Blair, you minx. That tickles.'

'If you follow it a bit to the right . . .'

'Orion's belt!'

'Sexy Orion and his big, long sword.'

'Amazing isn't it, Jeff? That we can live five thousand miles away and see the exact same sky.'

'We see ours through some god-awful pollution, truth be told. Nothing like LA, though. No offence, Willa.'

She reached out and met Jeff's apology fist bump. 'None taken.'

'Come down to Oz and you can see a whole different sky. Trevor! You're hogging the bloody rug, mate. Shift your arse.'

'I can't believe your laser reaches all the way up to the heavens, ChiChi.'

Willa shivered. It was beautiful up here. But it was also freaking cold. Time to head back to her hayloft and start making phone calls. Bryony had sparked off Victoria Beckham divorce rumours when she'd called her publicist and asked which 'hot date' David would be bringing to fashion week. This, when she'd been specifically asked to hunt down David *Duchovny's* latest girlfriend. Little bit different.

Just as she was about to get up and make her excuses, Finn, who'd been keeping a wary eye on her ever since she'd received her latest deluge of texts from Bryony, fetched a blanket for her. He'd been such a hero today, really wearing his heart on his sleeve in front of the villagers, it didn't seem fair to blow him off. Especially now that he was kneeling down behind her to wrap the blanket around her shoulders. It was proper romantic-hero behaviour and she had to admit . . . she liked it.

God, he smelt good. All warm hay and marshmallow. He stayed there, kneeling behind her, looking up at the sky, as ChiChi worked her way round the constellations. Willa shivered again. In a move she didn't see coming, Finn edged himself closer so that he could serve as a sort of warm-blooded back support.

'Is this okay?'

It was more than okay. Which made it a problem. She was going to have to leave. Soon. Bryony was making too many fuck-ups and still somehow managing to come out smelling of roses. It was only a matter of time before one of them blew up in some-body's face and Willa needed to make sure it wasn't hers.

When she shivered again, Finn overruled her lack of an answer. He sat down and budged up close until his chest met her back and his thighs flanked hers. He made a show of tucking the blanket tight round her but then left his hands where they were. On her thighs.

It felt like a proper boyfriend-girlfriend moment.

'You know how the stars are twinkling?' Finn's voice rumbled against her back. Her body, taken with the warm timbre of it, snuggled in closer. So much for the this-is-all-perfectly-fine-and-sensible-considering-it's-freezing vibe she was trying to emit.

'It's called stellar scintillation.'

'I like that,' she whispered back.

'I like you.'

Willa stiffened. She liked him too. A lot. She also knew saying something like that was big for Finn.

'That's sweet.'

The instant the words were out she regretted them. Her mouth was an idiot! Why had it spoken before she'd had a chance to properly think of the right response? She'd just given him the verbal equivalent of a puppy pat on the head.

They'd not discussed their feelings. Past, present or, more pressingly, future. Whispering his feelings for her, here, amongst the rest of the stargazing Jacobeans was . . . was . . . Her heart skipped a beat as it came to her. It was something Jamie would've said to Claire to make her feel safe. Cared for.

I like you.

She needed to say something else. Something better.

I think I'm falling in love with you.

Definitely *not* what she needed to say. Just because she'd been instantly smitten with his photograph didn't mean it was true in real life. Sure, he gave her butterflies. Yes, her reproductive system threw frequent glitter parties in his presence. But there was that tiny little thing called reality waiting to slip a huge wedge between them. He lived here. She lived in LA. He wanted to be a farmer. She wanted to – well, she wanted to interview film stars, obviously. Be one of the growing team of exec producers on TiTs. That had been her trajectory the day she'd left LA. Five days in a corset with the most attractive, kind, generous human she'd ever laid eyes on hadn't changed that.

Had it?

She gave his hands a squeeze because words were failing her. To her relief, he gave them a slight squeeze back, but then, to her horror, he whispered something about needing to check on the cows and slipped away into the darkness, the cold instantly skidding down her spine.

Idiot! If no one was around she'd be pounding her fists against her head. *Idiot! Idiot! Idiot!*

Why hadn't she told Finn she liked him too? He'd been so amazing today. And yesterday. All of the days. Even though everything about this whole immersive experience was epically outside his wheelhouse, he was here. Trying, helping, occasionally poking fun at Willa, but mostly he was being a hero. He listened. He offered advice. Good advice. He let her hold piglets and taught her how to stick straw up a calf's nose if it wasn't breathing when it was born. And she'd just pooped on everything she'd encouraged him to be: open, vulnerable, honest. No wonder he'd walked away.

'Of course,' ChiChi switched off her laser, 'many of these stars have already died. What we're seeing now is actually hundreds of light years' worth of history. And one day, all of it will – poof! Disappear. As if it had never existed at all.'

Chapter Thirty-Two

Finn had gone straight to the barn this morning, asking Orla to let Willa know he'd be there when she finished her breakfast.

He wanted to get his head straight before they talked. Before the questions inevitably arose about last night.

He did like her. He fancied her too. But it wasn't like they were going to start dating or anything. She was going to be here for another week, then head back to her shiny, sparkly star-studded life.

''lo.'

He looked up and saw Duncan. He gave him a nod, which was returned.

'Will this do?'

Finn examined the piece of plywood Duncan was propping against the barn wall. It had a wee door cut into the centre and hinges had been pre-drilled on to the edges. Duncan had also painted some flowers on the exterior wall, which was very un-Duncan like. Maybe one of Orla's kids had done it?

Duncan saw where his gaze had snagged and said, 'Your wee girl insisted. Said she wanted to cheer you up.'

His heart tried to squish through his ribcage, taking what little dignity remained with it.

The *that's sweet* moment last night had been a proper kick in the teeth. Not because she'd been rude. Or dismissive. She'd squeezed his hands, not catapulted out of his weird I'm-trying-to-keep-you-warm embrace. It was more . . .

I like you.

What was he? Twelve?

He felt stupid for even going there. No one in their right mind would want to have a holiday romance, let alone a proper relationship, with a guy mired in debt, at odds with his stepfamily, who picked ultra-awkward times and places to confess his affections. Especially when she would have to move eight thousand miles away from home to live here if – and it was a big if – he managed to save Balcraigie.

He gave the plywood the thumbs-up. 'That's perfect, Duncan. The piglets will love it. Thanks.'

They gathered the tools they needed to put the creche together, then set to work, barely a word passing between them. That was normal. The pair of them had a long history of silence to lean back on. What was different was the atmosphere. It lacked the usual tension.

'Aye, lad. That's right. Drill it in on the wall, there.'

Duncan was holding the plywood against the corner of the stall. The space behind it would offer a safe, warm area for the piglets to nap and rest away from their mum who was prone to rolling on her wee bairns.

'I like the nameplate, Dunc.'

Duncan's eyes flicked to his, then moved across to the hand-hewn wooden nameplate, already attached to the plywood. It had been sanded, polished and carved with care. It read, 'Bonnie'.

Duncan said nothing in response. Standard practice.

In the early days he'd tried engaging with his new stepson, but Finn had been so angry he'd put up a forcefield of resentment and point blank refused to let Duncan in. No matter how often his mother had explained that Duncan would never replace Finn's father, had said the love they shared was more . . . 'an understanding' . . . Finn knew, with Duncan in their lives, the plans he, his mother and father had made would never see the light of day.

He'd not played truant, or vandalised things or neglected his chores. But he'd glowed with hostility. Burnt with anger fuelled by an incandescent rage that Balcraigie's deterioration stood as a daily reminder that big dreams founded on love didn't come true.

But now that he worked with kids himself – mostly teenagers who'd been kicked out of traditional school because maths and literature and sitting still at a desk all day wasn't their forte – he saw that, in his own way, Duncan had never once stopped trying. He'd provided for Finn. Cared for his mother. Put food on their table. Kept the farm running by the skin of his teeth, even after Finn's mum had died, so that one day, if he chose, it could be Finn's for the taking. In other words: he'd been there. Like a father.

This from a man who'd most likely known from the off that he might never win Finn's affections. A man who knew he was his wife's second choice. Someone she'd turned to after her heart had been broken and who had never, fully, returned his affections.

Duncan had loved Finn's mother and him as if they were blood, knowing the love he received in return would never match it.

Finn's heart cracked open, finally allowing his stepfather the access he deserved.

Because wordsmithery was obviously his gift, he tipped his drill towards the nameplate and said, 'Did you pick the name because she's a bonnie lassie, Dunc?'

Duncan nodded. 'Aye. Another screw should do the trick.'

Old Finn would've bridled. Would've silently narked that *he was trying to make conversation here*, mate. *The least you could do is play along.*

They would've finished the task in angry silence, then collected their tools and headed off in different directions.

He pressed on the drill until the screw head was flush with the ply, then they both stood back so they could admire their handiwork. It looked nice.

'The littl'uns will enjoy that,' Finn said, possibly a bit too heartily. 'No fear of getting crushed.' He glanced over at Duncan who, as ever, absorbed the comment silently before responding.

You looked after me with the same care, he silently willed Duncan to hear. *I'm grateful.*

'Aye,' Duncan eventually agreed after running a scraggy bit of sandpaper along the doorframe the piglets would run through. 'Well.' He took off his flat cap, gave what remained of his hair a swipe through with his work-stained fingers then put it back on. 'Your mother would've wanted it painted like this, of course. Made pretty. I wouldnae thought of that on my own if Willa hadn't intervened, so . . .'

Finn gave his own head a finger scrub, desperate to come up with a compliment specific to Duncan. 'You're a mean hand with the jigsaw.'

What the actual fuck?

A lightning strike would be welcome about now.

They looked at one another, gazes cautious. Finn was suddenly desperate to finish this. Put an end to their decades of wary circling.

'I'm sorry I've been an arse,' he finally said.

'There's some more paint up in the shed.' Duncan lifted his chin in the direction of the tool store. 'Nice shade of heather.'

Finn continued, 'And I think Orla's plans for the castle, to get tourists who want to volunteer to help clear and restore it, is a good one.'

'Brushes should be up there as well,' Duncan said.

'I was thinking of maybe going part-time at the college. Putting some more hours in here. If you're happy with that.' He hadn't really. The idea had just come to him. But now that he'd said it, he knew it was the right call. He wanted to be part of Balcraigie's future. More than that, he wanted Duncan to know he'd earn his way back into the fold the same way Duncan had. By being here.

Duncan frowned, nodded, pulled his cap off again, scratched his head, then popped the tweed flat cap back on to his balding bonnet. 'It's no bother, son. No bother.'

It was the first time in twenty years that Duncan had called him son.

They stood there and stared at their handiwork, then, after a quick handshake, touched the brims of their flat caps and went about the rest of their chores. It wasn't until later that Finn realised he'd had a smile on his face all day long, and that Duncan, whenever their paths crossed, had been whistling.

Chapter Thirty-Three

'Fuck me, your bloke is hot.' Fenella patted the seat beside her. 'C'mon, doll. You might as well join us as we perv on your boyf.'

Willa sat down next to Fenella on the stretch of log benches where she, Jules, Jennifer, ChiChi and Rosa had taken up posts to watch Finn chop wood for that evening's fire. Jennifer was heating up some of Orla's 'famous Scottish fajitas' in a skillet hung over the open fire, explaining that Orla looked 'a little under the weather' when she'd come out with the ingredients.

Whack! Whack! Whack!

Oh look! A fresh pile of firewood.

He was hot.

And sweaty and muscly and also really cross with her from the looks of things.

Whack! Whack! Whack!

He glanced over. Their eyes caught and cinched, and although there weren't actual murderous laser beams coming out of his eyes, she felt their heat. As if he was trying to sear his disappointment right into her skull. Branded. The McIdiot Who Failed at Flirting.

It was a misunderstanding, Finn! I do like you. I just can't fall in love with you.

He looked away.

They hadn't talked for almost two days now. She'd tried to find him a couple of times, if only to ask after the harvester update, but their paths never crossed. Tactically, no doubt.

Soooo sweet.

Who even *was* she?

'Are you two shagging or what?' Fenella stage-whispered.

'No! God, no.'

'Are you sure?'

'I think I'd know.'

'What are you waiting for, girl? Get in there.' Fenella began to do a very disconcerting bouncy, thrusting thing with her hips.

Willa panic-laughed, trying to make her stop. 'He doesn't feel that way about me.'

Fenella belly-laughed, then pointed at Finn, who quickly turned away. 'He can't stop looking over here now that you're with us. Face it, buttercup, when that man looks at you, he's definitely picturing you naked.'

Willa pressed her hands to the bench to get up.

'Cool your jets.' Fenella ran her finger along her lower lip then, after a beat asked, 'Do you mind if I have a go?'

'Fen!' ChiChi chided, briskly standing up and patting out her skirts. 'You've got someone at home desperate to have you back in his arms.'

Fenella bristled. 'I told you about my fiancé in confidence.'

The group fell silent. Fenella had never mentioned having a partner, let alone a fiancé.

Finn abruptly lobbed his axe into the stump he'd been chopping wood on and headed over to the outdoor tap for a drink of water, then disappeared around the corner.

'But . . .' ChiChi looked completely bewildered.

'I've got cold feet, alright?' Fenella threw her hands wide, accidentally whacking Willa in the face. She didn't notice. 'Shoot me.

I don't know if I want to marry him. How can I when every week for years I see this guy on telly and read about him in the books. A guy who's so incredibly perfect. So unbelievably patient and loving, even if his wife is being a right royal pain in the arse.'

'He did beat her once,' Jules pointed out. 'Like, full-on whipping.'

Fenella waved her hand as if one eighteenth-century flogging was dismissible. 'They had sex after.'

'Oh, love,' Rosa cut in kindly. 'Jamie's a unicorn. As much as we adore him, he's a fiction.'

'I want what he and Claire have,' Fenella insisted.

'No one has that.' Rosa looked round the group for support and received a couple of nods.

'He's the perfection we all seek. There are examples of Jamie-like figures in most mythologies—' ChiChi began.

Fenella cut her off, pointing an accusatory finger at Rosa. 'You do. You and Jeff are exactly like Claire and Jamie—'

Rosa held up her hand. 'Jeff and I met later in life, after we'd both had some pretty awful experiences with love. We'd learnt by then that "they" weren't kidding when they said love demands compromise. And it's still not perfect. Far from it. Honey, ten years we've been together and this is the first time I've been able to pick the destination. It's about prioritising. Would you rather have someone who knows how to open a dishwasher and put the dirty plates in? Or have a man whose smile lights up every time he sees you?'

'Dishwasher skills *and* the one-hundred-watt smile would be nice,' Jennifer joked. Sort of.

Rosa tried to take one of Fenella's hands, but Fenella wasn't having any of it. 'Jamie's different, he—'

'Jamie's a fantasy, Fenella.' Jules overrode her. 'He's like McDonald's French fries or Nando's when you've had too much to drink. You can't get enough. He's MSG for women. A gorgeously rugged ultra-rogue who saves vulnerable people from peril. Of course you love him! He put his life on the line for Claire, like, a gazillion times. He rescues her over and over, whether or not she deserves it, loves giving her orgasms, and then, once he's done that, stays up hours chatting, laughing at Claire's impetuous, modern-thinking ways.' Jules's voice grew serious. 'Tell me, honestly, how many men do you know who would withstand a near-death flogging and then make sweet, tender, selfless love to his wife after she'd been the one to put him in that position in the first place?'

No one said anything.

Jules crossed her arms, satisfied her point had been made. 'Believing that someone like him is real is not good for your mental health.'

'If he's so toxic or triggery or whatever, why are you even here?' Fenella snapped back. 'To rub it in? Show us all your witchcraft? Prove lesbians had it right all along?'

Jennifer started to say something but Fenella thundered on. 'And, anyway, what's wrong with wanting someone to love you that much?' Her eyes blazed with defiance as she bashed her hand against her chest. 'I deserve it. We all do. And I don't know if I have that with my bloke back home so, sensible or not, I've left my fiancé and flown to the other side of the world to see if there are real Jamies.' She threw them all a despairing look. 'I deserve someone more evolved than your average Aussie plonker, right?'

They said, 'Right,' or 'Definitely,' and from Jennifer a very solid, 'Absolutely nothing less, love. Nothing less.'

Fenella, usually so strong and fiery, wilted. 'The choices are limited in the whoop-whoop, people. Too bloody limited.'

The atmosphere shifted from fraught to compassionate.

'Riley's not a plonker,' ChiChi said into the silence.

Fenella bucked back to look at her. 'And how exactly would you know this?'

ChiChi frowned, her dark cheeks colouring. 'I . . . He – he's been writing to me. He found me on the fanfic site. Ever since we got here he's been sending texts and emails. He's worried about you.'

As Fenella's eyes rapid-blinked out some sort of what-the-actual-fuck Morse code to ChiChi, Gabe pulled up a stump and plonked himself down next to Willa with a cheery, *'Hola, chicas. Que pasa?'*

'We were perving on Willa's boyfriend and wondering whether she's lying about not having shagged him yet,' Fenella ground out.

Jules aimed her boot toe towards Fenella. 'But now we're trying to figure out why Fenella's left her fiancé back in Oz to spend two weeks with Trevor.'

Fenella screamed a hair-raising *urrrghh* as she punched her hands to the heavens with a 'Bloody Trevor!' following in their wake.

Rosa got up and headed to the fire. 'And I'm going to help Jennifer make Orla's famous Scottish fajitas.'

'Famous?' Gabe asked.

'She makes them for an annual supper with the amateur dramatics society,' Jennifer called across from the fire. 'She said for authenticity, we're using bannocks instead of tortillas.'

Rosa opened her mouth, then decided against commenting.

'Just to be clear, I am not sleeping with Finn,' Willa said.

'He's not her type,' Gabe said, tugging off one of his boots and tipping out some tiny stones.

'That's not true!' Willa protested. 'He's very much my type. His eyes, for example—' She stopped mid-flow and, too late, tried to affect an air of casual indifference. 'Why do you think he isn't my type?'

Gabe looked confused. 'He's – umm – Scottish.'

Howls of protest filled the air. Enough for Gabe to lean in and whisper, 'I've heard you two at night, *bendita.* I'm covering for you.'

Willa flushed. Gabe had heard *Outlander* sex at night. Claire's moans and groans. Jamie's grunts and sighs. Not hers and Finn's.

'So, why are you two here? For real?' Fenella asked, holding a 'talk to the hand' palm up in front of a visibly upset ChiChi.

Gabe looked to Willa. She shrugged. *Go ahead.*

'My sister died. She loved us both and wanted us to find something.'

'What?' Jules asked, truly interested. 'Are you both Scottish?'

Gabe gave her a *look at me, this towering example of manhood is obviously pure Latino* face then said, 'She sent me here to let me know our family didn't hate me for being gay.'

Jules threw her hands up in a preach gesture, then gave her mum a cuddle.

'The whole Lachlan reunion was . . .' He scratched at his throat. 'It was to remind me how good it felt to be in love.'

'And are you two, like, hooking up?' Fenella's voice was more hopeful than anything. Grateful not to be the only one with a screwed-up love life.

Gabe shrugged. 'I don't know. His life's here, mine is . . . mine is . . .' His eyes moved to Willa's. She got it. His used to be set in stone and now maybe that he wasn't hiding from the world, perhaps it'd be different. Perhaps he'd be different.

'So, why'd she send you, Willa?'

Too many eyes turned to her. She thought of the unopened letter sitting in her room. The one that would be her last ever interaction with Valentina. She made a *duh* face and said, 'Scotland superfan!'

It wasn't entirely a lie. She did like it here. Felt weirdly at home for a place she'd never been to before. Or maybe that was just Balcraigie and the people who made it home. She knew them in the way she knew her own home community. Hard working, honest people who wanted to put some good back into the world.

Which did raise the thorny question: why was she more at home with this version of her family than her own?

Luckily, her comment evoked an impassioned 'Thank you,' from Rosa, who aimed a pointed 'See?' at a newly arrived Jeff. 'I'm not the only one who thinks Texas is not the best stand-in for the mother country.'

Jeff took umbrage, and an impassioned debate on the state of LARPing in America ensued.

◆ ◆ ◆

Later, after Scottish fajitas and a fair amount of acrimonious conversation made it clear they'd reached the point in their immersive experience where they were getting on one another's nerves, Willa heaved the basket of dirty plates and cutlery on to her hip, headed out of the courtyard and up the path towards the house. It was a longer walk than she'd anticipated and made her appreciate, yet again, just how hard Orla worked. And with a smile throughout.

When she got to the house, no one answered her knock, so she walked round the back where she found the kitchen door open. She took a step inside.

It looked like a hurricane had hit it. The huge trays of lasagne they'd eaten like wolves the night before were stacked in sloppy piles of dishwashing soap and burnt-on cheese. Trug buckets full of potatoes sat, unpeeled, on the floor. Huge slabs of salmon stuck out of another trug, the pink flesh obscured by frost suggesting they'd just been taken out of a chest freezer. There were heaped baskets of dirty and clean laundry. It was difficult to discern which was which. There were multiple drying racks covered in children's clothes. Sheets draped on doorframes. On the centre of the round, wooden kitchen table were stacks of paperwork, half-opened mail, an embarrassment of envelopes with bold, red lettering on them, some very serious-looking documents that bore the stamp of an impressive-looking bank, a couple of geriatric laptops, a calculator, an abacus, and a five-litre paint tin filled to overflowing with stub ends of candles. Sitting in a room just beyond the kitchen – the dining room from the looks of the long rectangular table and the formal, high-backed chairs, sat Orla, Dougie, Duncan and Finn. They were completely silent and wore a collective look of shock.

'Hey, guys.' She waved, openly freaked out at their tableau. 'Everything okay?'

Duncan looked at and then through her.

Dougie dropped his head into his hands.

Big, fat tears began skidding down Orla's cheeks, down her chin and into the knitted shoulder and neck wrap Jennifer had given her that morning with a detailed explanation as to how she'd done it in the MacKenzie clan colours. She wasn't bothering to wipe them away.

'Harvester,' Finn managed, his blue-grey eyes wide with disbelief. 'We won't be able to fix the harvester. And the college can't lend us theirs.' The look he gave her spoke volumes. They'd run out of options. He got up, walked straight past her, and went outside. A few moments later she heard the *whack, whack, whack* of his axe cleaving logs into firewood.

Chapter Thirty-Four

Text Messages: Your Message Mailbox is full. Please delete some messages.

Voicemail: Willa. Jenkins. You have . . . one hundred . . . and . . . twelve . . . voice . . . messages. To listen to your . . . messages . . .

Email: You have 137 unread emails.

Chapter Thirty-Five

O, happy days! Bryony, it turned out, had forgotten to tell everyone she was off for a girls' trip to Hawaii with her mother on the same weekend all of the sweeps-week specials were meant to be filmed.

Rather than firing her (children of senior level executives did not get fired), the production team, in their wisdom, had decided their only option was to turn to Willa to fix it.

The slew of messages ran something like this:

Willa, where's the [fill in the blank with whatever thing they couldn't find that was exactly where it always was]?

Willa, do you know if/when the interview's going to start/end/happen/be cancelled?

Willa, could you resend all of the information you've already sent because trawling through the emails to find it would be hard?

PR dogsbodies, PR VPs, marketing managers, freelance promotions teams, studios, streaming channels, Indies, YouTubers, TikTok glitterati and, of course, actual celebrities. Countless fame-seekers pleading for a bite of precious airtime, sweet-talking you while it mattered, blanking you when it didn't.

That was Hollywood.

She picked some straw out of her corset.

And this was Scotland.

Was this the moment she bailed and went back to LA?

When she weighed up what Finn and his family were going through versus what the highly paid TiTs production team had decided was their best course of action (turn to the one person who was legitimately on vacation), she knew where she wanted to put her skills to use.

When she finally came out of her hayloft, all eyes rose to her. She forced on a smile.

'Everything alright?' Jennifer asked, knitting needles clacking away. The rest of the group was still hanging around the firepit, the acrimony from lunchtime still simmering. Everyone was quietly nursing mugs of tea or darning a hem or readjusting their kilt straps (Jeff had both grown and shrunk over the course of the week). Gabe and Lachlan were stacking Finn's pile of abandoned firewood into something that deserved to be admired for its beauty, but all she could manage was a paltry thumbs-up.

Normally by this time of day, they would've been heading back out for their afternoon chores. But the Scots – Errol, Trevor, Kirk, Alastair and now Blair – were nowhere to be seen. They'd been called to the house to hear the news, no doubt. Or, more worryingly, gone off to find work elsewhere.

Nerves churned round Willa's stomach like the contents of a cement mixer as she relived the moment when she'd found Finn and his family. With no ability to bring in the harvest, there was no point in carrying on this mad charade any longer. Orla wasn't up to it, physically or emotionally. They couldn't afford it. And soon the bank would come calling. Not to mention the fact the rosy hue of 'immersive Jacobean style labour' had lost its rosy hue.

But somewhere between the house, her barrage of messages from TiTs and rejoining this strangely beautiful collection of mismatched superfans – a group of strangers all seeking the same thing:

a moment of purity in their complicated lives – she'd come up with an idea.

This was your classic make-or-break movie moment. The risk Michael J. Fox took when he pressed his foot on the gas pedal and raced, head on, towards the town hall. Dorothy's decision to follow the yellow brick road. Bambi's mother's decision to go into the clearing. Life-altering decisions that could elevate or destroy.

'Willa?' Jennifer asked again, putting her knitting down in her lap. 'Is everything okay?'

Her normal, go-to work answer was *Absolutely!* Then she'd shove whatever it was that had been bothering her down to the bottom of her things-that-mattered pile and get on with improving someone else's life. The only time when she hadn't felt the need to lie was with Valentina.

And that's when it hit her. This was why she was here. She didn't need to read Val's letter to know what was in it. The one person who had always believed in Willa, even – no, *especially* – when she hadn't believed in herself, had been Valentina Ortiz: dental hygienist to the stars.

Val would have loved her plan.

More than that, she would've championed it and thrown herself in feet first. Now it was Willa's turn to wear the mantle so ably worn by her best friend, a woman who had taught her all the very best things there were to know about loyalty, love and sacrifice.

So when Jennifer asked her for a third time if everything was alright, she turned to her and said, 'No.'

A dam's worth of pent-up regrets broke through her taped-up heart and poured through her. This was *her* make-or-break moment. It wasn't fiction. There was no guaranteed happily ever after. It was all terrifyingly real. But she wanted to do it anyway. She looked Jennifer in the eye and said, 'It's the opposite, actually. Everything's awful.'

She waited until the entire group gathered round before she explained. And when she did, she told them everything. About the farm's precarious financial position. About the castle's history (both old and new). About how Orla and her family had been doing their best to caretake Balcraigie Farm while Finn decided what he wanted to do about his inheritance.

She knew it was a risk, this level of honesty. It exposed Orla and her duplicity. It shone a light on Finn and his lack of decision making. Herself for not saying anything earlier.

She didn't paint the picture in terms of deceit. Life wasn't that black and white. This was family. It was complicated. There were feelings involved. History. And, if, according to Lachlan's Guide to the Scottish Emotional Spectrum, the Gaelic people had only been offered the world's tiniest emotional toolbox to work with, it was little wonder it had taken an actual, life-changing crisis to bring them to this point. One where, if they were agreed, they could bring all their energies together and put some good into the world.

Though it was yet another beautiful, sunny, crisp autumnal day, Willa's skin felt clammy. Her nerves grew as the group's collective silence deepened while she spoke.

They were within their rights to turn on Orla and Finn, demand their money back, report them to whoever you reported fraudulent immersive Jacobean experiences in the Highlands.

The simple truth was that Orla had charged them a lot of money for the privilege of doing farm chores.

Their anger, if that's what they were feeling – it was hard to tell because they were all staring at her gape-mouthed – would be justified. And, as such, there were a number of ways this could go.

They might shout, scream, then remember that Orla was actually a kick-ass cook and that they'd all, up until this moment, had a really good time even though their personal hygiene had gone to pot.

They could sue for emotional distress. Physical injury. Fraud.

Maybe they'd pack their bags, call a taxi, and head to Edinburgh and take a real tour.

They could expose everything on Twitter.

Maybe they'd blame Willa. After all, she'd known the situation pretty much from the start. Part of her hoped they'd channel their hurt on her. Go ballistic the way her exec producers did when she informed them a celeb had decided against baring their darkest, most intimate selves to the American public at 8/7 Central.

She could take it. For Finn. For not watching boxsets with Val. For wishing she'd been born into a different family.

All of these things were possibilities.

But the truth was, she knew deep down, that each and every one of these people – these epic, big-hearted, kind, generous super-fans – believed this had been about as close to a perfect experience as you could get. It lacked the whole raping, pillaging and sword-fighting element, sure, but . . . they all had jobs to return to, long lives yet to live. Orla had largely delivered what the brochure had promised. A Jamie (or Claire). Jacobean fayre. Jacobean clothes. And an authentic understanding of how the Highlanders went about their day-to-day lives.

Stripped of the amenities of modern-day life, they'd all come to enjoy the ice-cold showers, the searing heat on one side of their body at the fire circle, the satisfaction of a hard day's work. The porridge! The porridge just kept getting better and better. Not to mention the meat pies and the festy cocks – delicious oatmeal pancakes, which were the Scots comfort food version of cheese on toast.

Willa made that point and many more. From the moment they'd landed, Finn and Orla had done their level best to provide an authentic Jacobean experience. Exactly what the brochure had advertised. It hadn't mentioned filming sites or meeting the celebs or any of tchotchkes the other tours had on offer.

They'd asked one simple thing of their visitors: to take a step into yesteryear.

And what could be more olden days than getting to midwife cows and unearth walled gardens and build stone walls for livestock on the shores of a bonnie loch?

No one said a word.

So she carried on advocating for them, knowing that the more she talked, the more she was setting herself up for some serious backlash. If not from these lovely people here, their hosts: Finn and Orla.

But that was just the way the shortbread was going to crumble today.

She'd do her best to take the brunt of it. Years of working at TiTs – being the most convenient person to scream at, to blame, to hold accountable for things that had never been within her control let alone her fault – had made being the object of someone's wrath commonplace.

What did scare her was Finn's reaction to her decision to tell everyone the truth.

He liked her. She liked him too. Had from the moment she'd laid eyes on him in that stupid, flimsy brochure with those perfectly beautiful blue-grey eyes of his looking thoughtfully off into the middle distance. Back then he'd been a fiction. Not a living, breathing, complicated, intelligent, thoughtful, insightful man. He was real. Losing the connection that had grown between them over this last week wasn't something she was willing to do. Not yet, anyway. Not until she'd done her level best to prove to him that when she'd said 'sweet', she'd meant like honey. Natural, golden perfection. The type of man she'd never imagined herself with because he came with a life she'd convinced herself she didn't want. But now, like the way his dad had changed chores into Farm Delights, the life she thought she'd wanted may have been there all along, it just needed a little spin. Like a kaleidoscope. The same colours seen by the same mirrors, but with just the right change in perspective.

'This was the first time I got to pick our experience.' Rosa looked as if she was going to hyperventilate. 'Are you saying that . . . that it's over?'

The question broke the dam.

What had happened to their money? How long had Willa known this? Was she complicit in it? Could they get a refund? They'd got actual blisters from working here – did Orla and her so-called 'team' know this? Did they appreciate how hard everyone had worked to save the money to get here only to be conned? There were people they could call. People who would know people who could get them out of this. Had anyone noticed if the place was ABTA certified?

Jennifer didn't seem to be able to absorb any of it. She sat, her knitting on her lap, looking as if she'd just been told her cat had died. 'I haven't finished Duncan's scarf. I promised him . . .'

ChiChi wrapped her arms around herself and said to no one in particular, '*Outlander* has brought me to my happy place so many times. So many times.'

The reminder of why they'd all come here stopped everyone short. Talk turned to Jamie and Claire and what they did when things didn't go the way they'd planned.

Jules shifted gears from angry dragon to fired-up unicorn. 'Blair and I did *not* get blisters and calluses and cuts and bruises to see some nameless, faceless, corporate fucker slap a foreclosure notice on this place.' She kicked the log bench, howled in pain, then punched her fist into the air. 'This place is *not* going down. Not on my watch!'

Fenella rose from the bench. 'Willa, are you saying that the lads – our fake hubsters – are going to be out of jobs for real?'

'That's up to us,' Willa said. 'I don't think Finn and Orla can see the wood for the trees right now.'

A chorus of 'What do you mean?'s shot across the fire circle.

'I mean,' Willa said, her idea gaining traction, 'that if you're willing to try something a bit outside of the box . . . we might be able to help them.'

The suggestion hovered in the air as everyone considered what they wanted to do. There were two choices. They could take a risk that what Willa was suggesting might work, or pack their bags and walk away.

After an excruciatingly taut silence, Jeff broke it.

'I'm willing.' He pulled Rosa in close to him. 'This is the trip of a lifetime for us and, I know I'm speaking for Rosa here, but we want it to end on a high. If we can be a part of saving this place, we want to play our roles.'

Rosa beamed up at him and mouthed, 'My hero.'

'I'm in,' Gabe said, his eyes latching on to Willa's. 'I've got resources. Let's make use of them.'

ChiChi said she knew she wasn't very practical, but she was willing to put her hands to anything she couldn't break.

Jennifer stabbed her knitting needles into her basket and pronounced herself a woman of action.

Jules cheered and shouted, 'I fucking love you, Mother!'

They all threw around enthusiastic high fives and fist bumps and Jeff, the largest of all of them, pulled everyone into a massive group hug. They all stank. Their clothes were filthy. Their smiles cut through it all.

When they eventually untangled themselves, all eyes, once again, turned to Willa.

'Right, then, chook.' Fenella gave her a little salute. 'You've got your army, now run us through what it was you wanted us to do.'

Chapter Thirty-Six

Willa's plan was out there, but . . .

The alternative was eating Finn alive.

When she'd come to him and told him her idea, he'd been dubious. What had made him agree to come out here to the stable's courtyard was the spark in her eye. The one that flared bright when she spoke about Balcraigie and how much being part of their immersive experience had meant to her. How much being with him had meant to her.

So, here he was, sitting with a group of people he'd planned on turning away from his home, only to discover they were all willing to give everything they had to help him keep it.

When they'd got there, everyone looked nervous. Finn and his family. All the guests. Even the lads – Errol, Trevor and Alastair – men who Finn had rarely seen crack so much as a sweat during a fistfight down the pub. They were quiet and restless. Fidgety.

Finn was still trying to wrap his head round the proposal. He used Willa's trick of repeating what he'd just heard back to her. 'So, what you're saying is, you want me to announce to the world that we're broke and that we need their help.'

'Not the *world*.' Willa shook her head. 'Just the superfans.'

He scratched his short nails into his scalp as if the accompanying pain might summon a voice – his father's, his mother's, anyone with a solid, pragmatic Scots approach – to tell him that saying yes would be akin to pleading guilty to murders he hadn't committed.

He looked across and caught Duncan's eye. He was the most practical of all of them. The first to announce he thought someone was a barmstick for dreaming dreams beyond their station. Surely, he'd say no to this.

And yet, against the odds, Duncan gave him one of those nods that in Duncan-speak translated as, *Go ahead, lad. It's a risk worth taking.*

The plan was simple. Clear. Ask superfans to help them harvest the potatoes by hand. If no one showed up, they would be back where they were today – on the brink of bankruptcy – but at least then they knew they would have tried.

And that was what made the difference, wasn't it? Trying. Giving a desperate situation a last blast of passion instead of shaking your head and saying, 'No chance.'

He'd walked away from Balcraigie once. He didn't want to do it again.

Willa was literally shaking with nerves, her dark eyes almost as black as her irises.

He turned to his stepsister and asked, 'Are you happy with this? Giving it a go?'

His heart ached for Orla. Tear-streaked, red-cheeked, visibly exhausted from the hard work and emotional strain – and yet, against the odds, she was smiling. 'It's not like much else could go wrong, could it?'

Oh, there was a lot that could go wrong. No one could come. The rain could come early. There wouldn't be a market for traditionally harvested heritage tatties.

And yet, despite this, a thousand other bleak outcomes begging to be considered, not to mention the endless list of health-and-safety concerns he could rattle off with barely a thought . . .

'Aye,' he finally said. 'I think it'll work.'

The collective roar of approval was deafening.

He scanned the group. They were charged with infectious enthusiasm for the challenge rather than cowed by it. Young, old, fit, not so fit. They were mostly city folk. An academic. A hippy baker. An entertainment reporter who knew how to call in cows ten acres away.

They were all so different, but at this moment they had one crucial passion in common: they all wanted to save Balcraigie.

And he had Willa Jenkins to thank for this. The girl behind the curtain.

He never in his wildest dreams would've come up with her idea – to ask fans to literally dig in to save the farm from penury. But that's what they were hoping to do. Open their arms to the world and say what few Scots were willing to do in private let alone in public. We need help.

◆ ◆ ◆

A few hours later, Finn was fully convinced that Willa could not only run an army, but that the world would be a nicer place for it. She knew how to break down complex situations into simple action plans without belittling anyone or their questions. She assigned the right person to the right job as naturally as he knew when a calf would be born. And she did it all with that low-key, good-humoured charm of hers.

After Orla had retrieved all the mobiles and iPads and laptops from the gun safe, everyone set to work in earnest.

So far, Gabe and Lachlan had set up a crowd-funding site. Gabe had also offered to reach out to his many, many 'strategic communication' contacts.

When Finn had asked what those were, Willa had translated: spin doctors.

Jeff, who turned out to be quite the Twitter geek, had whipped up some 'assets': banners and memes featuring the logo: *Any Time's a Good Time for Hot Tattie* embossed over a picture of a shirtless, kilt-wearing Lachlan doing the yoga tree pose as he took a bite out of a hot, buttery, baked potato.

Blair had directed a hilarious set of TikTok videos featuring the lads in their kilts frolicking in the tattie fields, then fading to a scene of Jennifer sipping a glass of champagne in her claw-footed bath, covered up to her décolletage in beautiful, creamy potatoes.

ChiChi drew a pencil sketch of Balcraigie Castle that took Finn's breath away. It was an outline of the castle, the loch, the sprawl of fields and the Highlands beyond. There were silhouettes of a man in a kilt and a woman in Jacobean dress standing in the gateway to the castle. It was detailed, suggestively atmospheric, and everything he'd known Balcraigie to be: pure magic.

At one point a couple of the lads jogged up and asked him where the tractor keys were.

They were in his pocket.

When he'd found out about the potato harvester parts not coming in and the college not being able to loan theirs, his brain had short-circuited. All he'd wanted was his mum and dad. He knew he couldn't have either of them, but he did have the land they'd bought when they'd dreamt of a future together. The three of them. The last thing he wanted was to say goodbye to it, to them, or their dreams, so he'd decided he was going to drive the old tractor, the one his dad had bought at auction for thirty quid twenty-five years back, around the farm. Do a victory lap. Then call the auction house he'd spoken to in Inverness so that they could start selling everything that wasn't nailed down. Then he'd load up the girls and head to Kirkcudbright. The decision had broken his heart, but he'd made it and that had been that, right up until Willa had raced up to him as he'd been walking to the barn.

Breathless, she'd panted out her plan. It was so utterly harebrained it actually seemed possible. He'd gone all *gawp, gawp, gawp* to the point she'd thought he hated it.

'The cows,' he'd finally managed.

As if she'd known all along that selling the herd had been the one thing that would break him, she leant in, gave him a soft kiss and whispered, 'If you can hang on for one more week, you might not have to sell them.' In that moment she had felt more like a real spouse than a fake one. A woman who had vowed to the heavens and everyone who knew her that she would have his back no matter how bad things got.

If there was even a sliver of a chance they could save all of this – his family's heritage – he had to do it. And doing it with Willa by his side was even better.

After some fact gathering and a dividing up of 'territories' – Finn, Duncan and Dougie were assigned to spearheading the hands-on farming elements, while Willa focused on 'producing' the event. Poor Orla was still suffering from a bit of shellshock, but, with the aid of some of Jules's calming herbal tea and a kitchen takeover by Jennifer who had been restoring order as if she'd been born to it, she was feeling better.

'Right,' Willa said to the group when they'd all gathered together for some fresh boiled potatoes and salmon grilled on a salt-water soaked plank. 'Let's inventory our assets before we hit the green light on social media, okay?'

Everyone was sitting to attention on the smattering of logs around the firepit. They looked battle ready. Jeff had even smeared some blue paint on his cheeks.

'I'm free to do whatever.' Fenella gave a raunchy shimmy. 'Make me your tattie beeyatch, people!'

'The bread oven's ready,' Jules said. 'Mhairi from the local bakery came over and gave it the thumbs-up. Blair's seeing if she can get the local young farmers' group over to help me knead.'

'I've made about twenty "Claire" shawls,' Jennifer said. 'Over the week,' she clarified. 'Not just today.'

ChiChi raised her hand. 'Errol's trying to get the old potato harvester working.'

Fenella held her phone up. 'Trevor's just texted and he's getting an olde worlde harvester from some guy down the village, the little love bug.'

All their heads swivelled towards Fenella.

'Aw, c'mon. Don't be like that. You lot have judged the little kilted tyke too harshly.' She cackled, unable to hold her serious expression. 'I've been giving him love advice and he's already hooked up with a couple of girls on Tinder courtesy of *moi* tweaking his profile. He'll do anything for me now, the adorable numpty.'

Gabe stood up and brushed some invisible dirt off his immaculate kilt. 'Walled garden's clear and the stretch down to the loch. It'd be safe for small campfires if people wanted to camp there.'

Finn tipped his head towards Jeff and Rosa. 'And you two? I'm embarrassed to admit I don't know what you've been getting on with this past week.'

'We've sorted out the great hall.'

All heads snapped to the pair.

'What?'

'The great hall. You know . . . enough room for a village?'

Willa gave her head a shake. 'When you say "sorted out", what do you mean?'

'Well . . . it's still not got a roof, but we've got the big fireplace up and running. The floor's a combo of stone and compact earth so . . . that's not technically finished either, but if we hang up the solar-powered fairy lights in there, it should be pretty cool.'

It sounded better than cool. The environment they'd created – a welcoming one – sounded exactly the way his father had envisioned it.

Willa nodded, absorbed and added each item to the long list she'd been writing.

The hum of excitement was growing. A focused euphoria that, if people responded to the idea, could actually work.

'And where will they all go?' ChiChi asked.

'The people or the potatoes?'

'Potatoes. We already discussed the people.'

Dougie stood up and talked them through how a traditional harvest worked. The potatoes would be unearthed by the old-fashioned harvesters. People would follow them, pick up the potatoes, put them in trugs, transfer them into huge crates at the end of the rows, then stack them in an open-sided barn for the wholesalers to come and take away to specialist drying sheds. 'It's not the type of work for people who like to stay neat and tidy.'

'They'll only come and collect if we have a certain amount, though,' Finn cautioned.

'Which is . . . ?' Willa prompted.

Finn named a tonnage that took all their breaths away.

It was a big ask. This felt like a Mission: Impossible. Minus Tom Cruise to fix everything. Right now they only had a dozen or so pairs of hands and, if Trevor came up trumps, an old, limping, geriatric harvester on its way. But his dad's idea of buying his mum a castle had been out there too and he'd done it.

Willa faltered for a nanosecond as she registered the tonnage of tatties they'd need, then, smile ever bright, regrouped as if she met this sort of challenge on a daily basis.

He remembered her telling him about an interview suite they'd had to prepare to a celeb's specific specs. They'd wanted it decorated entirely in white except for a ten-litre fishbowl which need to be full to the brim with pink jelly babies.

He smiled, picturing her listening to the demands of the massive star, nodding and taking down notes just as she was now. Not judging. Breathing in and out as her mind whirled at lightning-fast speed, trying to figure out how to make someone else's dreams come true.

An awful thought came to him.

Was she doing this as penance? An apology for not caring for him as much as he cared for her?

He hoped not.

Over the past week, he'd convinced himself that Willa loved Balcraigie as much as he did. Had stupidly let himself imagine a future with her in it. Yes, she was helping. But that's what Willa did. She helped people. And then she would go back to her life in LA.

The threat of her absence knocked him off balance.

It took a big leap of faith to believe that fans of a time-travelling nurse and her Jacobite Scottish husband would save the farm. And yet . . . he was willing to take it, because of Willa. She was the missing link – the homing beacon he'd needed – to make his way back here to the place his father had imagined him starting a family of his own. A future.

For years Balcraigie had felt like a sentence to Finn. A weighty burden to bear. But this past week, seeing the place through Willa's eyes, had torn the scales away. It wasn't a burden. It was a privilege.

He set himself a task: to devote the same amount of energy she was pouring into the farm, to show her that maybe, just maybe, she belonged here with him and not Los Angeles.

Independent of his feelings for her, he'd watched her blossom since she'd arrived. She'd morphed from a lippy, defensively observant woman, well within her rights to tell him where to shove it when he'd elbowed into the handfasting ceremony to 'save' Dougie the trouble, into someone who laughed easily, offered suggestions without apology, and made his heart skip a beat when she appeared.

He cursed himself for even thinking about turning everyone away that first day. And not with a charming, *Och, away, we've had a wee bit of a Gaelic drama down the farm and I'm afraid you're no' welcome here, lads and lassies. Away you go. Back to yer fantasy lands and tellies.*

He regretted how dismissive he'd been of them. They weren't dreamers. They were realists. People who'd literally got down in the muck and worked hard with no fancy soaps or spa treatments or fluffy bathrobes in sight. Especially Willa. She'd come on this trip not having a solitary clue why she was here apart from the fact her best friend had asked her to go. That had taken courage. And he wanted her to know just how much he admired her for it.

But first, they had to get these ruddy tatties out of the ground.

'Right,' Willa was saying, pointing her pen at Orla. 'If we don't hit the mark for the wholesalers, we're going to go local. Do you have farm shops round here?'

'Aye, there are a few, but they've already got suppli—'

Willa tutted. 'Remember . . .' She lowered her voice so that it was sultry, alluring. 'These aren't just any potatoes.' She kicked into American cheerleader mode. 'These are specially hand-harvested potatoes that reunite older generations with new ones. These are Balcraigie Heirloom Tatties.'

There was a collective frown and then, just as quickly, a group cheer. Then everyone followed instructions on how to plug identical messages into their phones – Twitter, Instagram, Facebook, TikTok, and anything else they had loaded.

'Right, people.' Willa threw a bright grin at Finn. Her eyes were shining and her face glowed with excitement. She hovered her thumb above her phone and everyone followed suit. 'Who's ready to potato harvest the shit out of this place?'

'We are!' they roared, thumbs descending to press 'Send'.

After they'd all done it and agreed pressing your phone with your thumb wasn't as satisfying as, say, setting off the bells at the New York Stock Exchange, Jennifer asked, 'Now what?'

Everyone turned to Willa.

She shrugged and grinned. 'We wait.'

Chapter Thirty-Seven

Although Willa had spent half the night sorting things out for TiTs, she was awake before dawn, already buzzing for the day to come. There'd been a fair amount of activity on the socials and the Kilts&Tatties hashtag that Jennifer had suggested was trending.

She just might have used her work email to reach out to local television stations and the production company who filmed *Outlander* here in Scotland. It was rare for her to get this excited, or to use her job as a means of getting her foot in the door, but this was a project she believed in. It wasn't about box-office figures or raising someone's status from Netflix Romcommer to Silver Screen Powerhouse. This was about real life. Orla and Duncan's and Dougie's. The lads who worked here. People who would have to find jobs and places to live if they failed. And, of course, it was about Finn.

She heard a soft knock on the door that could only be his because her corset was undone and who else showed up when there was a huge chance she'd flash someone.

Time, not modesty, was of the essence. Pressing the corset to her chest, she opened the door with a hurried twirl and said, 'Lace me and up and talk to me,' as if she said that sort of thing all the time.

'Errr . . .' He was silent for a couple of throat-pounding heart-beats, then, after shifting her hair from her back across and over her shoulder, he did as he was told, his fingers occasionally brushing against her bare skin as he tugged the ribbons into place.

Each delicate touch was a featherlight flint stone against her skin, unleashing hot sparks into her blood stream. She felt, rather than heard, him breathe her in, the same way she inhaled his warm-hay-and-fresh-cut-wood scent whenever she thought he wasn't noticing.

Her thoughts swept back to that perfect kiss they'd shared when they'd promised to be true to one another. To honour and respect each other's wishes. And how, when he'd pulled back, his eyes had been dark with something she hadn't allowed herself to fully acknowledge. Desire. She'd felt it then and she felt it now.

When a low moan threatened to roll up and out of her throat, she knew it was her responsibility to stop this before it went any further.

Falling for Finn at this juncture wouldn't be any different to the countless film stars who succumbed to a film-set romance. Passion born of a fiction and really good catering. A hunger for one another that would only prove soluble when they re-entered the real world. Feelings – so intense when it had just been the two of them trying to create something magical together, something beautiful – unable to withstand the rigors of real life. That's where they were now. Fighting the big fight. Together. But he knew it was temporary. And he wasn't the kind of guy to hook up with the American tourist just because he could. He'd do it because he cared for her. And the truth was she didn't trust her feelings when it came to him. Being with Finn tugged at a part of her she actively hid from people in LA. The side that knew and liked hanging out with cows. The part that loved family-style meals where everyone ate what they were given without giving a diatribe on their latest holistic-eating routine. The side she regularly told her family she didn't have in the way they did. They were wired differently, she'd said. Wanted different things from life. So she liked going through a day knowing her white jeans would stay white. Was that so bad?

But when she was with Finn, all the things she'd convinced herself she wanted in life got muddled. And today, of all days, she didn't have time for cloudy thinking.

'Finn?'

'Yeah?'

'Why are you here?'

'I . . . ehmm – I—'

His fingertips brushed over that tender, vulnerable spot at the base of her neck. A hot shiver of approval swept down her spine.

'Sorry.'

'No.' She pulled back and away from him. 'It's just, you know, busy day ahead.'

He nodded, parked his hands on his hips, eyes searching for some invisible thing on the floor. He looked like a sexy Scottish cowboy. She wanted to jump him so much she ached.

When he looked back up at her his expression was resigned. 'I guess you'll be looking forward to getting back to LA and your real life.'

She barked a laugh. 'You're kidding, right?'

'No. You're working on your vacation.'

'This?' She pointed at the courtyard beyond the door. 'This does not feel like work. Being at work feels like work.'

He spun his finger round indicating he would finish her corset.

'I don't follow what you're saying.' Tug. Tug.

She dug her heels into the ground, trying to stay balanced, her brain fuzzing periodically as his fingers made contact with her skin.

What was she saying? She wanted him to see how flimsy her professional life felt in contrast to what he was fighting for. 'You spent half the night fixing tractors and preparing them to harvest dozens of hectares of potatoes that will feed people and your family. I spent half the night talking someone through a Top Ten Tchotchkes for the Alpha Generation segment.'

'I understood about two of the words you just said.'

'Exactly.'

Finn tied the knot at the small of her back, then ran his thumbs up along the criss-crossed ribbons before coming to rest on her shoulders. Her body was on fire. 'There you are, lass. All done.'

They stood, silent for a moment. She could feel his breath upon her neck. His height. His strength. The intensity of his curiosity about her. It was like living through a rewind of the Jamie and Claire wedding night when Jamie, the virginal groom, painstakingly slowly, undressed his new bride, wanting to ensure that everything he did made her feel beautiful, desired, and most of all, cared for. Safe.

Her breath caught in her throat. This was Finn's version of preparing her for his world, for the life he lived, and asking her to tell him just how much of herself she was willing to give to him.

She wanted to tell him that she believed in him. In everything he was doing. And that even though her plan was to leave, it didn't diminish the power of what he was doing for Balcraigie or, indeed, the time they were spending together. And then it hit her. She wanted him to ask her to stay.

The handful of centimetres between their bodies felt electric. Charged with an energy that lay taut, coiled between them as if their proximity to one another created another life force.

More than anything she wanted to lean into his touch and tell him she was falling for him. Instead she blurted, 'What I do is made of glitter. Stardust. It's inconsequential.'

'According to Gabe, what you do is highly commoditable.'

'You grow food, Finlay. That's highly commoditable.'

'You make entertainment. People pay for entertainment. Food? Not so much.'

'Why are you devaluing what you do?' When he said nothing she pressed, 'If we can get the worlds of entertainment and farming to collide this week? It'll start a new trend. Like . . .' She sought something he could relate to. 'A week-long *Field of Dreams* experience. With kilts.'

'That was corn.'

She flicked her hand. 'Whatever.'

'What if no one comes?'

Ah.

Her heart dropped.

There it was. The real reason he was here. He'd sought her out to get reassurance, not to play sexy, sexy with her corset ribbons and convince her to stay.

She realigned her features and flicked her thumb in the direction of the main drive where they'd asked people to gather. 'You haven't been out there yet?'

He shook his head. 'Nah.' He did the cap-and-head-scratch thing. 'Too embarrassed.'

'Embarrassed? Why?' Embarrassed was the last thing he should feel. She ached to pull him to her. Soothe away the worry lines on his forehead. But she was Kevin Costner in this scenario. She'd built a dream. Now it was time to prove to Finn that he was right to have put his faith in her.

'I might've done something,' he said.

'What?'

He reached into his pocket and tugged out his phone, thumbed through a couple of pages until he hit an app. He pressed play and turned it round.

She glanced up at him, confused. 'What is this?'

'Just . . . watch it.'

It was Finn. And pictures of her he must've taken when she hadn't been watching. There were some of the others as well, but mostly they were of her. Willa beaming with cow poo on her face. Willa singing off key during the wool waulking. Willa proving it was possible to toast and eat three marshmallows at once. And over the images of the LARPers and the farm, was Finn's beautiful voice explaining what had happened in his life, how he thought he'd messed it up. How he was hoping he could fix it. How he knew he couldn't do it alone and he knew being a man who had a castle wasn't exactly the world's worst problem, but that really, the true heart of Balcraigie was the farm, and they were going to lose it. 'And all of this, asking you folk for your time, your energy, is the dream child of someone who comes from an entirely different world to mine. She's brought colour back into our lives. And, no matter what happens, I will always be grateful to Willa Jenkins for everything she's done for me and my family.'

He'd put it on YouTube. And Twitter. And Instagram. Everything he could think of. Thousands of people had watched it. Judging by the number of retweets and the number of likes, thousands more would.

It was the biggest show of gratitude anyone had ever done for her.

Instead of kissing him, which was what she really wanted to do, she took one of his hands in hers and did a weird sort of victory punch thing, as if she was a boxing coach who'd known her outsider could beat the odds. 'Let's go mega-potato!'

And with that, she swished past him, flung open the door and headed to the main entrance, praying he was following because otherwise the big, dramatic reveal she was hoping for would have been for nothing.

◆ ◆ ◆

'Oh my god,' said Finn when he caught up with her.

Willa nodded in silent agreement. Even she, a girl who always hoped for the best, hadn't expected this.

Orla, Fenella, Jennifer, Jules, ChiChi, Rosa and Jeff – everyone she'd come to think of as a friend over these past few days – ran past her, squeezing her shoulder, telling her what a good job she'd done, all flying to action stations while she stood there like a Jacobite wax figure.

She'd been to big events before. Huge. Stadiums filled with seventy-thousand fans all cheering for one tiny singer. Festivals that sprawled across the desert to the horizon. She'd even been to an event in Austria celebrating a long-dead Mozart that drew three *million* superfans.

There weren't three million people here. Not even close. But somehow this felt bigger. More authentic. Because it wasn't about getting hammered, or high, or cultured, or even about getting a glimpse of a person who had enriched your life because of their music/movie/good looks. It was about helping someone. Someone who'd torn their heart out of their chest, put it on their sleeve, then put that sleeve out there for the whole world to see.

Dougie was standing outside the main entrance directing an endless stream of camper vans, hippy mobiles and a surprising number of horse and carts into a nearby field to park up. Duncan was directing a handful of tractors with old-fashioned harvester attachments towards the fields that abutted the loch.

Willa knew they'd put this out to the universe. That they had literally asked people to do this. To come to Balcraigie, roll up their shirtsleeves, and get down and dirty. But she was astonished at just how loudly the universe had answered their plea for help.

Everyone was wearing at least one thing that gave a sound nod to Scottish clothing over the ages. Great kilts, modern 'working man' kilts, tartan 'trouse', ghillie tops with a cord of leather lacing at the neck. Stoplight-red tam o' shanters with shaggy clumps of bright orange hair (real and synthetic) warming the wearer's ears. Knee pads with the saltire or favourite football clubs emblazoned on them.

These people were bursting with passion for Scotland. They were also here to work.

The men carried pitchforks and shovels and buckets and – holy shit – one man had brought an entire trailer full of hessian potato sacks with . . . was that . . . the silhouette ChiChi had done of the castle emblazoned on its side. He must've worked through the night to get that done.

The women were equally impressive. There was, of course, a preponderance of 'Claire' costumes. Plaid, earth-toned skirts and bodices, huge pinafores, petticoats, knitted shawls and wraps. Some women had refashioned potato sacks into on-trend garments. A few wore steampunk outfits, but, hey, pairs of hands were pairs of hands, right?

Even the children flying out of the cars, off the carts, and arriving on foot were dressed in yesteryear potato-picking garb. If Willa hadn't felt transported a week ago when she'd arrived here at Balcraigie, she did now.

Many folk had baskets hanging from their arms or balanced on their hips. The covered ones were presumably filled with the provisions they'd asked people to bring to feed themselves as there was no way, if more than five people had shown up, Orla would have been able to feed them all. It was an all-hands-on-deck scenario and right now there were hundreds of pairs of hands all heading out to the fields, attached to people who, judging by the hubbub, thought this was the best fun *ever*. They were laughing, singing, introducing themselves to one another. Valentina would have been beside herself.

Sometimes you have to step away from who you think you are, to become the person you want to be.

This was who she wanted to be. A person who organised events that really mattered. Made an impact at grassroots level. Or, in this case, tuber level. She wanted to be someone who created gatherings that made a difference for years to come. Generations even.

She fished around in the deep skirt pockets Jennifer had added to her dress and pulled out her phone.

She thumbed past the email notifications, deleted a few texts that began with the words 'Bryony was meant to' or 'Martina suggested I check in with you', then clicked on the Balcraigie crowd-funding page.

Her heart flew into her throat.

People were contributing. Adding five pounds here. Two dollars there. Euros. Yen. Renminbis. It all added up. It was mind-blowing, really. It had been less than twelve hours since she'd put Balcraigie's future into the hands of the fates and they had answered . . . in spades.

She clicked on to her Twitter feed and instantly went light-headed.

Ben Affleck had retweeted her post. *This Canadian reporter knows her stuff! If she says the potatoes are to die for? Get in there, peeps!*

And it wasn't just Ben. All sorts of famous *Outlander* superfans hadn't just crept out of the woodwork, they'd leapt out, social media guns blazing: Lin-Manuel Miranda, William Shatner, Michelle

Obama. Even the series' actors had retweeted multiple posts and pledged their support.

#KeepingItRealScotsStyle

#TattieHolsAreTheNewBlack

#SaveBalcraigieLikeAJacobite

And on and on it went.

The rest of the morning was lost in a blur of activity.

The day was bright, but the wind had a bite to it.

Half an hour's worth of picking turned many of the pickers' fingers white with cold. Duncan got a few volunteers to help him build three big bonfires around the periphery of the fields. Before they set them ablaze, they dug pits and charged them with a few buckets of the freshly unearthed potatoes.

Orla was helping shop owners from down the village set up pop-up stands along the loch edge for those who hadn't brought enough food or wanted to try some local fare.

Trevor used the tractor to drag a couple of the logs from the barnyard over for people to rest on. There were so many people that even if groups of them were resting, warming themselves by the fire or accepting one of Jennifer's rapidly increasing knitting circle scarves, it meant there were still scores of people following the tractors, baskets steadily filling up with farm-fresh potatoes.

'Willa?' Dougie appeared by her side and nodded towards the drive. 'I think you might need to see to this.' He turned her around.

A television satellite truck was lumbering past the stables.

Fuuuuuuuuuuuuck.

This had just become, very, very real.

Her world colliding with . . . what was this? Her new one? Her temporary one? She and Finn hadn't really tackled that part of their conversation this morning. Whatever it was, part of her heart lived here now.

She scanned the area, desperate to find Finn. He should be the face and voice of this whole thing, not her. She couldn't see him anywhere.

She asked Dougie to send the truck down to the loch's edge – she'd meet them there – then ran towards the fields where a dozen geriatric tractors were churning up hundreds upon thousands of potatoes, for the men, women and children following steadily in their wake, collecting them just as their forefathers (or someone's forefathers) had for centuries. By hand.

They were chatting, singing, making the best of a back-breaking task with the shared joy of one another's company.

A pure, crystal-clear voice rang out and above all of the pickers. The singer, a tall woman with short shock-white hair, had on a hessian dress, Doc Martens, plaid gardening gloves and a blue sequin-covered tam o' shanter. Her voice was familiar and otherworldly all at once. She was singing a Eurythmics song Willa's mom used to sing to her dad when she was doing dishes and wanted him to come and help dry. 'Right by Your Side'. Not in the regular way – fast paced and in need of a techno beat back-up. A cappella. Beautifully cadenced. And utterly unforgettable.

Willa put her hand above her eyes and stared at the woman. Hard.

Her breath abandoned her when she realised who it was. There, in the field, with dirt on her face and her hands full of potatoes, was Annie Lennox. Picking tatties along with the commoners. No one seemed particularly fussed that one of the top singers on the entire planet was serenading them as they worked. In LA there would've been mammoth security guards holding off a massive throng of autograph seekers and then the whole thing would have to be shut down when the potatoes began to be trampled on or a tractor ran over a child or any number of other horrible things that could happen during a publicity stunt gone wrong.

But not here. Because it wasn't a stunt. Or for show. Everyone was respecting the unspoken message voicelessly whispered through the throngs of people pouring down to the fields literally preparing to dig in: we're here to work. Everything else is gravy.

Her attention was snagged by the news crew who pulled up to the side of the field. It was a standard team. A producer (easily identified by the multiple phones and attempts to micromanage everyone). A very well-groomed twenty-something man dressed in a kilt – the talent, probably. A camerawoman and a sound man (both of whom were also wearing kilts).

She ran across to them. 'Hey! Hi. Can I help you?'

'Aye, lass.' The producer made a scoffing noise and in an entirely non-subtle aside said to the crew, 'Didn't I tell you an American would be the first at the gate?'

Before Willa could ask him what the hell that meant, he continued in an even thicker Scots accent, 'Can you point us in the direction of whoever's properly in charge of this wee affair? We're here from the BBC.' He shook his head in disbelief as he looked out at the scores of people already filling their baskets with freshly unearthed potatoes. 'I have to tell you. I didnae expect this. A few bampots in kilts, mebbe—'

'Oi!' cut in the camerawoman. 'First of all, are you saying this wee lassie here can't be in charge because she's a woman? Or because she's American?' She held up her hand. 'Don't answer that. It'll instantly be offensive no matter what you say. And as for the bampots – I'll have you know my mither is among them.'

Willa grinned. This woman was awesome. If she had half of her chutzpah when she spoke to Martina, she'd probably be exec producer by now.

'Your mither?' The producer fuzzed his lips. 'Next you'll be telling me she did this as a wee one to keep food on the table.'

'Aye, she did as well, you snotty old so and so,' the camera-woman shot back. 'She was poor and needing money.' Her voice rang with pride as she continued, 'She used to ride out on the buses during the tattie hols. Earn her ten pound and all. Right up through the eighties. And for the record, the pickers aren't bampots. They're called howkers.'

'Eh,' he said. 'Well.' He gave his head a scratch, finally having the grace to realise he'd been a presumptive asshole. 'I didnae ken.'

'Well' – she gave him a short, sharp nod, then popped her camera on to her shoulder – 'you ken noo.'

'Hey!' Finn jogged up to Willa. Her heart grew wings and began flapping around her ribcage.

He'd changed. He was kitted out in his workman's kilt, ghillie and his weather-battered wax jacket. His flat cap was tipped back, exposing those thick, shiny tufts of straw-coloured hair. His blue eyes were bright, lit from within. This was a man in his element. It was the happiest she'd ever seen him.

She jogged towards him, meeting him a few metres away from the crew.

'Everything alright, Willa?' He glanced at the TV crew. 'Do you want me tae give these jokers the boot?'

She grinned. 'I think using them to your advantage might a wiser use of your time. Maybe tell them what you're doing here?'

He flicked his thumb over his shoulder to where people were still pouring into the fields, taking up places behind slow-moving tractors now backloaded with enormous crates. 'I don't think it's much of a secret any more.'

'No, but . . .' She held up her phone and showed him the con-stantly changing numbers on the Crowdfunder page.

He gave her a double take. Then took her phone. Rather than jump for joy, which would have been the normal reaction – the movie reaction, anyway – he went pale.

'Finn? Are you okay?'

'Aye. Yes.'

He definitely wasn't.

'Finn. You've practically got the funding for a brand new harvester if you want it. One or two more days . . .'

'Yeah,' he said in tone more suited to a terminal diagnosis. 'I know.'

Willa ducked her head so she could catch his gaze, desperately trying to divine what she was missing here when all of the sudden it hit her. 'You like it this way, don't you?'

He nodded, his shoulders relaxing as if she'd just released a great tension. 'My dad would've loved this.' They turned and looked out to the fields, the people, the chatter, the songs, the celebrities (Andy Murray had shown up with his wife, and his mother Judy had almost instantly turned the picking competitive. Tickets to Wimbledon were on offer. And a pair of Andy's old rackets. She even got them to perform a stadium-wave every twenty minutes, standing up row by row with their hands in the air, so that no one got lower back ache. It was beyond awesome).

'Well.' Willa held out her hands. 'On the basis that I have never in my life heard more people describe something as "pure dead brilliant" there's no reason why you can't keep it like this.'

He squinted at her. 'How d'you mean?'

'Run with the immersive farm experience. Instead of buying the harvester which would exclude people, use the Crowdfunder money to buy restoration materials for the farm and castle. Or set up apprenticeships to revive dying arts. Hire some proper craftsmen. Thatchers. Stonemasons. Blacksmiths. I bet there's loads of old people who'd love to make sure skills they learnt as children are passed on to new generations. Do whatever you want! Hold an annual retreat for architecture students and name it after your father!'

297

Finn grinned. 'My dad would have adored that.'

She beamed back at him. 'You could put up some of those yurts everyone's in love with for people to stay in until rooms in the castle are restored.' She swung her arms around. 'There are *countless* things you could do. All you have to do is imagine them.'

Finn laughed. 'I think you're forgetting not everyone has your imagination, Willa.'

'You can dream up whatever you want to, Finlay Jamieson. You just haven't given yourself the chance to believe in yourself as much as I do.'

Finn swallowed, his energy concentrating around just the two of them. 'Is that what all this is? Your belief in me?'

The question hovered between them . . . a boomerang that didn't know whether it had been a rhetorical question or if Finn truly sought an answer.

She wanted to answer. She really did. But telling him what was in her heart would make saying goodbye impossible.

'We should get you over to the television crew, yeah? See what comes up in the interview?'

'What are you afraid of, Willa?' he asked, catching her arm as she turned to go.

She stared at him, begging him to see that she cared for him, that she might even love him, but that she wasn't brave enough to change her life course. Not yet. Not in the throes of all this endorphin-inducing magic. She knew first-hand how wrong this sort of thing could go. What went up, always came down.

'We've got to go,' she said, tugging her hand free. When he didn't move, she beckoned for him to join her as the BBC producer gave her an irritated *time's a-ticking* tap on his watch. He called out to them. 'Is it you two then who'll be doing the interview?'

Finn said, 'This is a family farm. If this is going to go on the telly, I'd like to do it with my family.'

It shouldn't have, but the comment hit her like a slap. Obviously, she wasn't family, and Finn was absolutely right to want to do the interview with his, but . . .

Wow. So this was what happened when you didn't tell a man you loved him when you had the chance. He reminded you of the person you were when you first came to him: an outsider.

These past few days, sharing their problems, helping with the solutions, she'd felt like she *was* part of Finn's family. Mucking in, doing chores, laughing, crying, stressing, soothing. All the things she'd wanted to share with her own family and hadn't managed to. All the things she'd shared with Valentina's family and couldn't any more.

Finn, distracted now as the sound guy fed a microphone wire up his ghillie, pointed at his eyes then out to the crowd. 'You wouldn't mind, would you, Willa? Having a quick run round to find them?'

It was a simple request. A *sensible* request. And yet, as she pasted a smile onto her face and bobbed out some *yes, of course she would help* nods, she felt her heart break clean in two. This was Finn drawing a line between them.

He'd asked her if she'd believed in him. The unspoken part of his question, of course, was *Do you believe in me enough to stand by my side?* And she'd refused to answer.

If he'd been a film star asking her if she loved the film she would have instantly said yes. Lied straight to his face if necessary. But when Finn, a man who deserved every single fibre of her belief, had asked her to tell him where she stood – by his side or elsewhere – she'd let him down. Just like she'd let Valentina down when all her friend had wanted was to have someone she loved and trusted by her side while she confronted the most terrifying future a person could face. *She'd* chosen the coward's route. Not Val. Not Finn. So, yeah. She deserved this. Deserved her supporting role as Little Miss Reliable because it was only the people who truly risked their hearts who could reap the rewards.

'Willa?' Finn prompted when she hadn't yet moved. 'Are you okay to find them?'

'Absolutely,' she said, desperately trying to keep her smile bright. 'Always here to help.'

Chapter Thirty-Eight

By the fourth day of the harvest, Finn was riding such a high he was convinced he was wearing a jetpack. He wasn't used to being this happy. A crash seemed inevitable, but paradoxically impossible. He glanced up at the sky. It was bright blue now, but he could see dark, ominous grey clouds gathering away up on the hills to the north.

Though the stream of fans had remained steady, the work was hard, so folk tended to do a day or so, then headed off with a complimentary sack of potatoes in thanks. Those who weren't keen to howk for tatties, bought them.

Before Finn had even got hold of the wholesaler, the freshly picked potatoes had started flying out of the huge bins and into the cars of well-wishers who wanted a bite of Balcraigie. The honesty jar – a huge old stoneware pot his father had unearthed decades back – had to be emptied several times a day.

It had begun with a kilo here or there, but now people were buying the huge jute bags the howkers filled up at the edges of the fields, saying they liked the idea of having a few months' worth of quality food. Farm shops wanted them. A greengrocer's in Glasgow. A chain in Edinburgh. Orla's children were running a roadside stand that kept selling out. If it kept going like this, they wouldn't need the wholesaler. He felt like Rumpelstiltskin spinning gold from straw, only his gold was potato-coloured.

And at the heart of it all was Willa.

He'd been, and continued to be, floored by her work ethic. After he'd done that BBC interview, some sort of switch had flicked in her and she'd gone into what she kept telling him was her 'production mode'.

He knew they valued her back home at her work and now that he was seeing her in action, he wasn't surprised. She'd booked countless interviews for him and the family – even Orla's kids had had their ten minutes of fame. She ensured the TV crews who randomly pulled up without an appointment didn't interfere with the picking. The whole point of this, she regularly reminded them, was to get the harvest in. The celebs who showed up were asked to only do interviews if they had a memory about the Scotland they'd grown up in or could sing a song their grandmother might have sung to them, recite a poem their grandfather had loved. Mike Myers flew in to do a stint of picking, then, with some of the potatoes that had been damaged, convinced Orla to help him make a cauldron of mash – both of them pretending they were in *Shrek* the entire time. It had been hilarious. And, of course, encouraged by Willa, Mike made a show of reminding everyone about the hard work that went into not only the harvesting of the potatoes, but of farming in general. 'There's nothing magical about food production,' Mike had said in his interview. 'But seeing something like this, here at Balcraigie, people helping other people in times of need, it's hard to believe otherwise. Pure Scottish magic.'

And she didn't only organise things for the telly. She kept the volunteers happy. Somehow, word got out that she was trying to set up a mini Highland Games and even more people came out of the woodwork, so that every afternoon, as the day began to set in, there was tea and shortbread or tablet, and caber tossing or axe throwing or a musket shooting display. She'd even got a couple of guys who worked at the museum over at Culloden to bring a couple of the cannons over and shoot them into the water. It was impressive stuff. Yesterday, a gentleman had pulled up in a van filled with falconry birds and owls. He'd been on his way to a Living History Fayre down in England and pulled a detour when he'd heard about the 'Tattie Fest' on the radio.

Willa had suggested to Finn that he reach out to his students, still on their hols, to see if they wanted a go at working for Jules, who had set up a Rumbledethump Chain Gang – a kitchen squad devoted to making the handheld potato and cabbage pies his grand-mother had made for his mother. A few of the kids had responded and they were loving it. Jules was the perfect type of taskmaster. Using that cheeky smile of hers, she demanded brutal consistency and had them slavishly eating out of her hand.

Jennifer had convinced a nearby knitting shop to ask customers to come along and set up their spinning wheels and aged looms in the castle's great hall. The gentle *thwick-thwack* of their work providing a rhythmic beat for the dozen or so pairs of hands always at work in the kitchen kneading bread for the crowdie sandwiches they provided for the howkers.

She'd even reached out to her show, Topline in Tinseltown, who'd sent a freelance crew from Glasgow to film a daily feature of what was happening here. They never interfered with the work, dis-creetly asking dirt-covered celebrities who'd just spent a few hours picking to host short segments highlighting the various elements of what they were trying to do here at Balcraigie. Traditional, organic farming with rare-breed animals and, hopefully, a sensitive resto-ration of a castle that was once home to generations of Highlanders before it had fallen to ruin.

Scores of Scots who'd worked on *Outlander* showed up. Extras. Costumiers. Stuntmen and women. Sword and knife fighting specialists. And not one of them was there to show off. They were there to show up. Lend an hour or three – whatever they had spare – to help a Scottish family in need.

Finn felt proud of his country in a way he'd never experienced before. As if the genetics that ran through them all had homing beacons, warning calls that went out when a fellow countryman was in need.

This morning he'd rung the agricultural college and given his notice. They weren't surprised. They were when he asked if he could host apprentices at Balcraigie – take in the odd student who had a difficult home life who might benefit from a bit of one-to-one tutoring. Duncan had been the one to suggest that.

Balcraigie was alive in a way that far surpassed his father's dreams.

'Hey.' Willa appeared beside him at what had become his regular post – the large arched gateway that led to the tattie fields.

'Hey.' He smiled at her and leant in to pick some dried potato leaves out of her hair, but really, he just wanted to get close to her. He didn't know if it was the workload, or all the people constantly buzzing round the place, but something had shifted between them over the past few days, and he didn't know what. She was still as friendly and smiley as ever, but when their eyes met there was something missing that had definitely been there before. Maybe he'd been too pushy. Trying to get her to tell him how she felt about him instead of growing a pair and saying what was constantly on his mind. He was falling in love with her. When she turned, he caught her scent and tried to memorise it. She smelt like a peach that had been rolled in honey and toasted cardamom. Don't ask him how he knew. He just did.

He wished they could stay here and talk. Really talk. He'd tried a couple of times, but whenever he'd attempted to 'pull a Jamie' as Fenella had taken to calling the deep and meaningful chats he and 'Claire' had, Willa brightly reminded him how much work they had to do, then went out and immersed herself in yet another project.

'You alright?' he finally asked. 'I feel like we've barely seen one another.'

'We have,' she countered.

'Not really, though.' Not the way they had a few days' back when the two of them sat in the pig pens and talked and laughed and shared things with one another knowing whatever they said, they'd be heard without judgement.

'Finn.' She frowned at him. 'The rain is coming tomorrow. Deadlines are deadlines.'

'Aye, but—' He floundered. The weather wasn't the only thing that was closing in. Her flight was on Saturday. Three short days away. And the last thing he wanted was for Willa to get on that plane.

Without waiting for him to finish his thought, she began reeling off a list of things that were happening in advance of the ceilidh Fenella and ChiChi were organising. The band was already here. Volunteers were hanging up yet more fairy lights round the castle courtyard. A local distillery wondered if it was all right to send over a barrel of whisky. A beef farmer who specialised in Highland cows was offering a massive spit roast. 'But he needs to know, like, now, because of timing, yeah? Finn? Hell-loooo? Earth to Finlay Jamieson?'

He heard her. Nodded. Answered her questions. But through it all, all he could think was, *Stay*. It ran on a loop in his head. *Staystaystaystay with me*. It was a huge ask. Expecting someone to upend her life, leave behind her friends, her family, her country.

But more than anything that's what he wanted.

Was it something he'd be willing to do for her?

His gut twisted as if someone had literally reached in and wrenched it tight.

No. He wouldn't. He couldn't. This was home.

Would it feel that way once she was gone?

He watched her lips as she floated someone's plan to offer deep-fried Mars bars instead of cranachan as pudding. He didn't care. He cared about her. He wanted to kiss her. Find out if she really did taste of cardamom and peach. He wanted to make her scream with pleasure. Feel her hands grab his hair in her fists. Clutch his hips with her thighs. Scratch her nails down his back and moan his name while she did it.

But even as his heart expanded with the acknowledgement that he was in love with Willa, it contracted with the recognition that somewhere between the first blade of the potato harvester hitting the ground and right now . . . something about her had changed.

She'd *glowed* last week. Her cheeks had literally pinked up with pleasure when they'd tended to a newborn calf or a fleet of piglets had stampeded across her feet or Orla appeared with something new to eat that she'd never heard of. She'd loved saying all the Scots words he'd taught her. Cackled like a hyena when she couldn't mimic his accent. Grew shy when she noticed his gaze resting upon her.

That was the real Willa. This one? The one with clipboards and checklists and an ability to answer every question but the ones he was asking her, was only a fraction of the woman he knew she could be and it bugged him. How could she want to return to a life that didn't make her feel alive?

'Right!' Willa gave her clipboard a rat-a-tat-tat with her pen. 'That covers that. I'll see you at the ceilidh tonight?' Before he could say anything, she turned and disappeared into the crowd.

The ceilidh was everything a proper Scottish knees-up was meant to be. Booze, food, laughing, singing, traditional country dancing, the whole nine yards.

And Willa, who'd been on her phone most of the night, appeared to be the only one who wasn't enjoying it.

'Come on.' Finn was practically begging now. 'Dance with me.'

Willa pursed her lips and shook her head. 'You go ahead. You're the one who should be leading all the dances.' Her eyes brightened for a second, the way they did when an idea struck. 'You should lead this with Orla. The laird and his lady.'

'Willa,' Finn pleaded, taking her wrist and pressing it to his. 'C'mon. You're my lady.'

'Your fictional lady.'

'Aye, but—'

'Aye but nothing.' She tugged her wrist away from his hand and pointed towards the dancefloor. 'Go on. Lead this dance with Orla.'

He reached out to her again. Their eyes caught and latched. She pressed her lips together until they thinned, widening again as she swallowed down whatever it was she wasn't telling him.

He didn't know what the hell was going on, but enough was enough. He couldn't leave things like this.

'We're a team, Willa. At least I thought we were. But I'm getting the feeling you're ghosting me to my face.'

'We were never together, Finn. It was all play-acting.'

He swore under his breath. 'No,' he countered. 'It wasn't. I'm not talking about the handfasting or anything like that. The costumes. I'm talking about you and me and the connection we built. The vision we created for this place. *Together.*' He waved his hand round the great hall. 'All of this wasn't pretending. This was *you*, Willa. I saw the effort you put into getting us here. You cannae tell me you did all of this because you're good at pretending.'

She gave him a one shouldered shrug. 'It's what I do. Create illusions.'

'What about any of this is fake?' When she didn't answer, he put his hands on her shoulders, forcing her to look at him. 'Tell me this meant nothing to you. That you'll find it easy to walk away.'

She stared at him. Hard. As if he were some simpering, whiny, unappreciative arsehole who'd just sucked a year's worth of life out of her.

'You said it yourself, Finn. I'm useful. I'm handy to have around. But I'm not family. I'm staff.' She gave him a little pat on the shoulder. 'Don't worry. With all your TV spots, I'm sure a nice, young Scottish lassie out there will present herself to you, ready and willing to fill my shoes.'

There was some truth in her words. He'd had more girls hit on him in the last few days than he'd had in his entire life. But she was wrong about everything else.

'I don't want them. I want *you*, Willa.' God it felt good to be honest. 'I don't care if you ever look at a clipboard again. I want *you*. Please consider staying. Not for the chores. Not for the To Do Lists. For me.'

She'd changed him. Forever. And he wanted her to be a part of the world she'd helped create.

'Please, Willa. You don't have to answer now, but tell me you'll consider staying.'

'I have a job.'

'I just quit mine. You could quit yours.' He took her hands in his. 'What do you say? You and me figuring out what to do with the rest of our lives together.'

She stared at him as if he'd suggested she donate one of her kidneys to a serial killer. 'Finn.' She looked away and then back at him. 'I've been offered a promotion. I'm going back to LA tomorrow.'

'But you hate it there.'

'It's a promotion, Finn.' Her voice sounded empty, as if she'd poured all her emotions into the loch and left them there. 'It's what I've always wanted.'

He swore again.

'No. It isn't. You told me yourself it was a soulless job. Why would you go back to that when you know could be happy here?'

'That's just it, Finn.' She took a pointed step away from him. 'I don't know that. I'm a stranger here. This has been quite the holiday – but the last thing it has been is real. What is real is the job offer. The one I have accepted.'

He could see that arguing with her was pointless. Nor would it be fair to beg her to stay. She was right. The weather had been amazing. The guests had been a good fit. These past few days had been . . . beyond description. Perhaps in a few days he too would think it had all just been a dream.

The music, which had been rollicking along suddenly ground to a halt. There was a commotion at the far end of the hall where Dougie had cobbled together a small stage out of yet more pallets.

A piper climbed on to the stage and Fenella bellowed, 'Take it off!'

Finn looked round for Willa but she'd taken the brief to distraction to disappear into the crowd.

If he was in a bad mood, he wanted time on his own, so he made the call to stay put, praying it wasn't the wrong one.

The piper gave a kick that produced a bit of leg. The women whooped. A few of the men took this as their cue to head back to the bar to recharge their glasses. Lachlan made a show of covering Gabe's eyes. The piper took centre stage and played a surprisingly good version of 'Highland Cathedral' by the Red Hot Chilli Peppers. He finished to rapturous applause. A group of men in kilts came up on the stage. None of them looked familiar. The piper began again, this time accompanied by the ceilidh musicians. The song was strangely familiar and, through Fenella's now steady cry to 'take it off', Finn finally recognised the song. 'It's Raining Men'. And that's when he figured out what the guys were doing onstage. Stripping.

Okay. He was down with people enjoying themselves, but this wasn't his bag. Anyway, he needed some fresh air. A chance away from all of the hullabaloo to figure out what the hell he wanted. Minutes ago he'd seen everything clearly. He wanted Willa. Balcraigie. Job done. But maybe she was right. He'd got too caught up in things. Forgotten it had begun as a con he alone had wanted to stop. He huffed out a mirthless laugh. Well, that showed him.

As he strode towards the loch, an ominous rumble of thunder sounded from the hills. A few moments later, a flash of lightning lit up the sky.

The rain would come soon.

They hadn't got the full crop in, but they'd done a fair job of it. The Crowdfunding site – tweaked to say profits would now be going to the sympathetic restoration of Balcraigie and a scholarship fund for training in traditional crafts – would allow them to get in seed potatoes for next year's crop.

Without stone walls between him and the Highland winds, the cold easily worked its way past the fabric of his shirt into his shoulders, his chest. He'd left his wax jacket back in the courtyard, but didn't bother hunching against it. A few lashings of wind and rain wouldn't kill him. Especially if he held it up against the pain of his heart being pulverised by the slow-dawning realisation that Willa was actually leaving.

It hurt. Bone deep. Organ-clenching pain. If there'd been a moon out tonight, he'd be howling at it.

He opted for second best.

There weren't real standing stones on the farm, but one of the set builders from *Outlander* had brought along some dummy versions and set them up on a small knoll a short distance from the loch. Cleverly painted polystyrene slabs weighted down by internal sandbags.

Loads of folk had been posing for photos by them, and last night Jules had led some sort of firelit Wiccan ritual in advance of All Soul's Night which wasn't too far off now. One poor woman had eaten some 'wild' mushrooms that turned out to be a bit too wild for her digestive tract and had ended up in A&E. She was fine now and, mercifully, the only real casualty over the week.

Unless you counted whatever was coming to an end between him and Willa.

He forced himself to stop the pity party. Regroup. Instead of being all *O! Woe is me*, he needed to pull up his bootstraps and get on with his life. He'd been living in a holding pattern for years now and he'd be damned if he did it again.

He braced himself against the weather and headed up to the fake stones.

Someone had beaten him to it. He recognised her silhouette instantly.

Willa.

Her hands were pressed to the largest of the stones, her head bowed as if in prayer. She was clicking her heels together and, if he wasn't mistaken, chanting, 'There's no place like home,' on repeat.

When she heard him approach, she threw him a sharp look. Instead of screaming at him to back the fuck off and give her space like she was well within her rights to do, she gave one of those sweet, self-deprecating laughs of hers and said, 'You caught me.'

'Was it working?'

She dropped her hands from the stone, her features only slightly visible courtesy of a strip of moon. '*The Wizard of Oz* and *Outlander* matrix doesn't appear to be working tonight.'

'Were you hoping to open your eyes and find yourself in LA?'

'Something like that.'

It wasn't a yes. And it wasn't a no.

A rumble of thunder vibrated low and dangerous through the air.

She tugged her shawl closer round her shoulders.

He wished he had a candle. Or a torch. Something, anything, so that he could read whatever it was in her eyes that she wasn't telling him.

A huge crack of lightning flared across the sky.

That worked.

Unfortunately . . . he hadn't liked what he'd seen. There was a coldness in her expression – or maybe it was more of an absence of the warmth he'd been so certain about a few days ago.

She turned to go.

He reached out and grabbed her hand.

She pulled it loose with a growled, 'Don't *do* that. This isn't the olden days when you can just grab what you want and have it.'

He held his hands up. 'I'm sorry. Willa, I just— For what it's worth . . . I think you make a fine match to Balcraigie.' *And to me.*

She laughed but it wasn't a tinkly, happy sound. 'Yup. Sounds about right. Like I said, I'm always useful to have around. But you don't offer a paycheque at the end of the week, so . . . sorry, bud. My skills are going elsewhere.'

'Hey, now. You know I didn't mean it like that.'

'Do I? Because there wasn't much room for interpretation in your word choice, Finlay. I'm handy. You got what you wanted. Now if you don't mind, I'm getting wet, and I'd like to go.'

The rain had started and he hadn't even noticed.

'Willa—'

'Finlay—' She mimicked his plaintive tone, and tied it off with a sneer that seemed so unnatural, so unlike her, he wondered if there was yet another version of her he'd not yet met. 'Look,' she

312

began, the rain coming down more heavily now – tiny, excruciatingly painful daggers punctuating each word coming out of her mouth. 'I've got a new job to go back to. A promotion that I have literally worked for years to get. This is your world, Finn. The land, the cows, the castle. All of this is literally yours. My world? It's made of the same stuff as this.' She punched the standing stone with surprising force and her fist shot straight through to the other side. 'Illusion. Facades. Nothing is real. You breathe pure Scottish air. The air I breathe at home? Helium. Anything you don't pin down just blows away in the breeze, never to be seen again. So if I don't go back and accept this promotion, they'll find someone else and that person won't have earned it.' She stopped, looked away and then, more gently said, 'You need someone who wants to be here permanently, Finn. Put down roots. That's not me.'

She tipped her head up to the sky and though the catches in her voice had sounded like she was crying, it was impossible to tell because the rain was so heavy. When she looked back at him again, he knew on a cellular level that her mind was made up. That there was no point in fighting. This was a battle he'd lost before he'd even begun to fight and the wounds it inflicted felt fatal.

'Goodbye, Finlay Jamieson. For what it's worth, you're a great fake husband. I hope whoever wins you in the end deserves the real deal.' Then she turned and ran away.

Chapter Thirty-Nine

'You know, Willa, I've been having a wee think.' Orla yanked the Land Rover off the main motorway towards Glasgow airport, finally – mercifully – breaking the weighted silence hovering between them. Willa braced herself. Whatever Orla was going to say, she deserved it. Skulking out before dawn, not saying goodbye to anyone apart from Gabe, but even that goodbye had been in a hastily written note. She'd behaved poorly. Was behaving poorly. So if Orla was going to give her what for . . . she was ready for it.

After a super-awkward throat clearing Orla said, 'You'll have to forgive me. I'm not really good at this sort of thing – feelings and suchlike, but . . .'

Oh god. Here it comes.

'I wanted to thank you for everything you've done.'

Willa's heart caved in on itself. Fluffy folds of buttercream icing when she'd been expecting daggers.

'The far-um . . .' Orla's voice cracked. 'Balcraigie,' she tried again, stopped, swept her hand over her mouth, then began patting her chest as if trying to physically tamp down a swell of rising emotion. 'You saved our home, Willa. Our family. There's no thanking someone properly for that, short of handing over the keys, but that would sort of defeat the purpose, what with you heading back to Los Angeles, and us Scots are a frugal folk—' She chanced a sly grin, which, when their eyes met, became a shared, friendly smile. In the warmth that followed, Orla continued, 'We consider you family now.'

Willa's heart reverberated like a kettle drum in the midst of an orchestral climax.

'So, you're welcome here. Whenever you want.' Orla gave Willa a pointed look that made it clear she hadn't been blind to Things. 'You alone understood what I was trying to do with the immersive experience.'

'Oh, I—' Willa spluttered.

'No. No,' Orla reprimanded. 'You managed to do what my husband never has. To peek into my brain, take the muddle of ideas and lift them to a level I never could have imagined. For that alone I will be eternally grateful. I mean . . .' The Land Rover veered into another lane as Orla looked over, her grin arcing into a gleeful banana smile. '. . . *the* Annie Lennox picked tatties at Balcraigie! It doesn't get much better than that, does it? Actually—' she interrupted herself and continued more soberly, 'it does. You gave me my brother. Finn's always been . . . complicated. Just out of reach. Whatever you said or did flicked a switch in him. He's *present* with me now. Really engaged.' She swept away a tear. 'Deary me. Sorry, sorry. Overtired, probably. But honestly, Willa, I cannae thank you enough.'

A pumpkin-sized lump of emotion jammed in Willa's throat – the pressure so intense her nervous system began to short circuit. And then a civil war broke out between the two halves of her brain.

Right Brain: Willa? Did Finn really meant to exclude you from 'the family' thing?

Left Brain: He so did. Why else would he have sent you off to find them without having swept you into a deep and meaningful embrace, pulling back to tenderly tuck a stray tendril of hair behind your ear before mouthing, *I love you, ma wee Yankee doodle lassie.*

Right Brain: Errr . . . because he is a male mortal not hand-crafted for television. And also? You're the one running away. He loves you. You love him. But you're a scaredy cat because if it goes wrong, it'll hurt every bit as much as much as losing Val does, and you don't think you can handle the heartache. So you've chosen cowardice over a happily ever after. Nice one.

Left Brain: Shut up! That wasn't it at all!

Right brain: No, you shut up!

Left Brain: You're not the boss of me! Anyway, I'm not running away, I'm *returning*. I'm not panicked. I'm adulting. Working girls who've devoted a decade of their life to climbing to the top do that. Follow through. Accept promotions. Become card-carrying members of the cult of celebrity. Sensible people, like *moi*, acknowledge simple truths even if they're ugly: loving Valentina with every fibre of my being didn't stop the cancer and loving Finn doesn't alter the fact that my life is in LA and his is here. Being together is impossible. The dream stops now.

Right Brain: What? I'm not saying anything. It's a good point.

Orla tippity-tapped her fingers along the top of the steering wheel. 'It's an amazing thing.'

'What?'

'Making someone's dreams come true. I mean, did you see everyone's faces? It was dead brilliant. And those Highland strippers! Ha. I've never seen the like. I'll be getting those laddies back, you can count on that.'

Willa's barely taped together heart cracked open, her body flooding with all the feelings she had only just stuffed back into her *let's proceed sensibly* cupboard. She managed a vague, 'Mmm,' in response.

Orla drove in happy reflection, then suddenly hit her forehead with the heel of her hand. Streaks of red crept up her neck as she shot Willa an embarrassed smile. 'Sorry. I must sound a right numpty. You see events like that every day in your real life, don't you? Properly, I mean. Big stars, huge movie studios. What we did at Balcraigie was . . .'

Perfection.

'. . . amateur hour.' She sucked her teeth. 'Saying that, it surprised me how much I loved having folk about. The guests, I mean. You learnt ever so much from them. Do you think it might be worth doing other immersive experiences? Like . . . a ladies-only Queen of Scots thing – minus the beheading, of course. And the prison term. Maybe a Norman castle construction team would be better? Ach.' She scrubbed the notions away with her hand. 'I'm not creative like you are. I'm sure we'll muddle through. And, anyway, thanks to you we've not got to panic any more, so that's enough of me blethering on like an idiot.' She patted the steering wheel as if the matter was finished. 'Here you are. International departures. Off you pop to find a trolley. I'll fetch your bag, and here's a wee packet of that millionaire's shortbread you like.'

Willa accepted the small parcel wrapped in brown paper and tied with twine, trying to find the right words to say how incredible her experience had been. Not only as a Jacobean farm labourer, but as part of something so challenging, so nourishing it had made her come alive again in a way she'd thought entirely impossible after Valentina had died.

'Shortbread,' she managed. 'So good.'

'It's the least I can do for you, Willa. The very least.'

And then, because time was precious, especially to someone like Orla, Willa was on her own again, waiting for the boarding call for the City of Angels.

Chapter Forty

'Look who's heeeeeeeere! It's LA's Little Miss Superstar!'

A few whoops greeted her as she walked into the hospitality suite. Charlie Foster instantly roused the usual motley crew of reporters and producers into a standing ovation as he dubbed her 'the Siren of Sweeps Week'.

'Chef wants you to know she's joined a Waste Not Want Not programme that donates food to a nearby shelter,' said the room's hospitality manager before he was crowded out by Willa's peers.

'Have you seen Bryony since The Great Expenses Swindle?' asked a reporter from Cincinnatti. 'I heard she bought seven muu-muus at the Royal Hawaiian on Aubrey's card!'

'I never liked her. Team Willa all the way!'

'Don't you mean, Madame Exec Producer?' Charlie corrected. 'Why are you here anyway? Don't you have any plebs to send along?'

'We're still down for that lunch, right, woman?' Priya asked.

'Hey, Willa! Check out my human bagpipes. Bowm bowm dee bowm deeee bowm deeee—'

'I didn't think you had it in you, girl.' Charlie plopped himself down beside her after Willa and Priya had managed to put a tentative date in the calendar. 'Crushing the competition like that.'

'What? You mean *Entertainment Tonight*?'

'And *Access*, and *E!*, and anyone else trying to kill it in this game. You go, girl! I always knew you had it in you.'

She pulled a face. 'You literally just said you didn't think I had it in me.'

'Did I?' He laughed. 'You know I'm your biggest fan, right?' Charlie booped her on the nose as if she were an adorable puppy. 'I want to be you when I grow up.'

'Yeah, right.' They clinked iced tea glasses and, she had to admit, the praise felt like arriving at an oasis after a long, painful journey through the desert. TiTs had smashed it in sweeps week. For the first time ever, she'd been sent a gift basket piled high with all sorts of ridiculous chocolates and speciality snacks and wine she definitely wouldn't have been able to afford on her old salary. Her latest pay packet had come with a bump. And, of course, there was the new job title. They hadn't found anyone to replace her yet, so she was doing her old job and the new one, but it wasn't like she'd expected everything to change. Sure, the hours were longer and the stress levels exponentially higher, but it wasn't as if she was working in the coal mines.

She gave her hair a sassy flick and sat back as the usual inane how-was-such-and-such-a-celeb-today chitchat got underway. As nice as it felt to be lauded by the pack she'd once felt sidelined by . . . she wasn't feeling it. She wasn't feeling any of it. She'd been home less than a week, but from the moment she'd landed . . . it felt wrong. And lonely. How could she be surrounded by all the people she'd physically ached to be friends with and still feel lonely?

'Hey, Pendleton!'

Willa looked to the doorway where Matt Damon stood proud of a team of senior publicity VPs. He flashed his brighter-than-bright smile. 'Good work in the Highlands.' He put on a Scottish accent. 'Art imitating life. I love it, lassie.'

She offered him a feeble smile and they had a mini finger pistol shoot out. Everyone laughed and applauded and when he was whisked away, the studio staff huddled round her to ask if Matt had flown out to pick potatoes too.

This was the sort of attention she had craved for years. Being the alpha producer who could snap her fingers and things would actually happen. Magical things. Like Matt Damon knowing exactly who she was.

But Matt Damon didn't know who she was. Not really. And what had happened in Balcraigie wasn't even close to art imitating life. It was life imitating art and then getting a kick in the gut as a blunt reminder that life was still life when the credits rolled.

And that's when she finally *knew*. Actually, genuinely, right down to her marrow understood why Valentina had sent her to Scotland.

She, Willa Jenkins, was the biggest superfan of all.

Her entire life she'd been a Hollywood devotee. The hopes, the dreams, the endless fantasies. They'd been the things that had kept her head above water when she feared she would drown in a life that didn't sing to her. Not Val. She was a woman who'd actively engaged with her life. Shook it up when it needed a change. Fixed it when it was broken. Squeezed everything she'd ever wanted out of it and then some. And in her spare time she enjoyed a few wistful what ifs in front of the television.

Willa had gone miles beyond that. She'd worshipped at the altar of showbiz. The lights, the cameras, the action. Moved away from the community where her family had built their lives. Disassociated herself from them to the point that, much like Gabe, they may as well be estranged. She hadn't told them she'd been in Scotland. Or about her promotion. Or about Finn.

She'd become the type of person she liked to mock. Like Charlie. A person who bought the buzz, hook line and sinker. A slave to the actors who seemed to shapeshift extraordinary fictions into reality. She'd believed that if she'd been closer to it – to them – she too could live a different life to the one she'd felt predestined to live back home.

But the truth was, as a TiTs producer – a job she'd thought was the apex of living the dream – she would only ever be an observer.

She'd thought she'd finally won her version of an Oscar, but actually? It felt like the booby prize.

These past two weeks she'd *lived*. There were the piglets, the cows, the potatoes and so much more. She'd got blisters and bruises and reeked more than she ever had in her life. She'd dyed traditional fabric with soda pop. She'd made friends. Good ones.

She'd been a bride.

A fake one, granted, but from the second her hand had been bound to Finn's – their heartbeats pulsing against one another's through their radial arteries – the time they'd shared together had felt more real than anything else she'd ever experienced.

And she'd seen *The Matrix* at Imax.

She closed her eyes tight and thought of the moment she'd pressed her hands to the standing stones at Balcraigie. She'd never felt more torn in her life. She'd been offered a new role. More pay. More respect. Her own team.

But something about it hadn't felt right. As if this – the power and perceived prestige – wasn't actually hers to take.

Or, more to the point, not what she'd wanted after all.

So she'd pressed her hands to those stupid fake stones and begged for a sign. Pleaded with them to transport her to the place she was meant to be. And when she'd opened her eyes, the very first thing she'd seen was Finn.

And what had she done?

Run away.

Her right brain had completely nailed that one.

She'd run away from the sign the universe had sent her.

Finlay Jamieson was her home. Him and his sister, and her family and the animals and the sheer joy they'd manifested trying to make their real-life dreams come true by realising other people's fantasies.

And what had she done? Told him to suck it.

Her heart dropped like a stone, fissures forming low in her gut. How could she have been so stupid? She needed to go back. Clear the air at least. Or maybe, if she wasn't too late, start a new future?

'Hey, Willa? You okay there?' Tiny Baby Publicist touched her shoulder. 'Dwayne is ready for you.'

'Who?'

The publicist winced. 'Dwayne "The Rock" Johnson? The film's co-star?'

'Ah ha ha ha!' Willa stood and gave her hair a ridiculously showy flick. 'I was, like, totes kidding.' She cupped her hands and fake shouted, 'I'm so ready to rummmmmmbllllllllllle!'

When she got into the room her heart was pounding. She'd never interviewed The Rock before and normally she would have been all *Woot-woot! Getting me a new story for the cocktail party circuit!* Today he was a blockade she needed to barge through in order to get on with the rest of her life.

'Willa, hieee.' The room publicist ushered her in. 'So good to see you. WillaDwayne, DwayneWilla.'

'We don't need an introduction,' he boomed, launching himself from his chair and squishing her hand in his. 'I know this girl. She saved a castle!'

'No, you don't, and no, I didn't.'

Holy shit. Had she just back-chatted The Rock?

She extracted her hand from his and sat down in her director's chair with a pointed look at her wristwatch. Tick-tock. She had things to do. 'Shall we?'

'Apologies.' He clapped his hand on his boulder of a chest. 'It's your story to tell, not mine.'

She gave a little damn-straight-it-is huff.

Dwayne went all okay-gurl wide-eyed on her, but his voice was kind, gentle even, when he said, 'The floor is yours.'

The publicity team stood to attention, fractionally leaning in, prepared to pounce. One more snappy comment and The Rock would use whatever secret signal he had to wrap things up and her ten-minute slot would magically be reduced to two. Not that it had ever happened to her before, but she knew plenty of producers who'd fallen foul of the Inappropriate Question Guillotine. Interviews could be stopped for countless reasons. Shaking hands with someone who famously didn't like being touched. Cracking a joke about something they would've had no idea the star didn't find funny. Intimating the film may not be the best thing in the whole entire universe when put on a par with world peace.

'It was a farm,' she corrected, waiting for a finger flick or a wink or a foot tap. Nothing. 'Run by an amazing family. The MacKenzies and the Jamiesons.' She told him everything. About the cows and the pigs and the crumbling ruin that was, yes, a castle, but not the main point of the place. It was the people who lived there who mattered. People who worked until they were exhausted. Folk who got down in the dirt and crawled under broken tractors and had the blood squeezed out of their arms by a pregnant cow and any number of other things she'd seen or done over the past two weeks, missing each and every one of them the more she talked.

When she finished, Dwayne propped his epic chin on one of his fists and fixed her in a studied gaze. 'Are you alright?'

He was genuinely asking. So she gave him a real answer.

'No.'

'Anything I can do to help?'

Short of driving her to the airport, no, not really.

The room timer gave her an exaggerated reminder that she had two minutes.

'What's the scariest thing you've ever done?' Willa asked Dwayne 'The Rock' Johnson.

He hooted and ran a massive hand over his shiny bald head. He wove his fingers together and jabbed his index fingers under his chin. 'Everything I do is scary, Willa Jenkins. Life is scary.'

'Even yours?' She found that hard to believe.

'Yeah. Even mine.' He held out his arm. 'Pinch it.'

She did.

'Human. Just like you. When I get cut? I bleed. When I get dumped? My heart aches. When I let myself down by not being the man I know I could be, I drag around a boulder of shame until I fix it. When you're sitting in the glare of all this' – he spread his arms to indicate the multiple cameras and lighting fixtures – 'it's not always easy. But sometimes, even though it scares the hell out of me, I have to step outside the person I think I am to become the one I want to be.'

He smiled. His teeth were immaculate.

Holy shit.

She knew there were a lot of really good teeth on display here in Hollywood, but . . .

'What?' Dwayne asked, his hand quickly covering his mouth. 'Have I got spinach stuck in there?'

She shook her head. 'Did you ever go to a dental hygienist called Valentina Ortiz?'

He flinched as if the words had physically hurt him.

The timer flicked her the wrap-it-up signal. Willa didn't have a solitary quote they could use in tonight's programme. For the first time ever, she didn't care.

'Yes, I did.' The Rock swept his hand across his mouth, then pressed it to his heart. 'Val was an amazing woman. Wise. We used to brainstorm some of my sayings. When she found out she was sick? She gave me permission to use her lines for interviews just like this one.'

'That one you just said. That was one of hers.'

'Yes, it was.' He frowned. 'Wait a minute. You're Willaford Jenkins, aren't you?'

She nodded, that too familiar prick of tears stinging at the back of her throat.

'Dude,' said Dwayne. 'She loved you like blood.'

She nodded again, swiping at tears that refused to go unspilt. Then she hiccough-laughed through some more.

'How do you do it?' she asked after she'd blown her nose into a tissue he made the make-up guy give her. 'The scary stuff?'

The timer drew her finger across her neck. Willa gave her a little out-of-my-control shrug. She wasn't about to stop The Rock in the middle of a life-coaching session.

'Tear open your chest, allow yourself to be vulnerable. Know you'll probably get hurt, but also know you'll never once have to ask yourself, *I wonder what would've happened if . . .*'

'That question never has a good answer, does it?'

'Nope. It's usually *I guess I'll never know* because if you're asking yourself that question, chances are high you've never tried anything that scared you.' He clapped his meaty paws together and gave them a rub. 'Life's for living, Willaford Jenkins.'

'Amen to that, Dwayne "The Rock" Johnson.' They high fived, grinned at one another and then Willa unclipped her lapel mic. 'I've got to go.'

'I know you do,' he said, as if he'd been waiting for this moment – the one when a person who made their living by interviewing famous people realises she wasn't actually living – to finally arrive.

'C'mere!' He rose and opened his arms wide once the sound tech helped her untangle herself from the wires. 'Good luck,' he whispered when he'd pulled her into a bone-crushing hug. 'And enjoy the terror of knowing you're doing the right thing.'

She went back to the hospitality suite, asked Charlie to do the rest of her interviews, grabbed her tote – the one that still had her unopened letter from her dead best friend in it – and left.

If saying goodbye to her best friend had been the hardest thing Willa had ever done, saying the same to Finlay had come a very close second.

No, he wasn't dying. Yes, she could live without him. But the truth of the matter was, she didn't want to.

She loved him. She might even love him as much as she loved Val. The jury was still out on that one, but it was impossible to ignore the fact that when she was with him she felt alive in a way she never had here in LA or at home in Oregon.

After careering through traffic for half an hour, she clomped up the stairs to her apartment and did what she should've done two weeks ago. Reached into her tote and pulled out Valentina's letter.

Hola, Chica!

So. Knowing you the way I do (and yes, since I'm up here in heaven for eternity, everything gets to be in the present tense) . . . I am guessing you didn't open my letter until you got back.

If I'm wrong . . . everything still holds true, but I doubt I'm wrong. (Such a curse being right all of the *time!* LOL.) Anyway, I wanted you to know what I hope you've known in your heart already. That to me, you are family. Always were, always will be. The best friend a girl could have ever hoped to find in a town of four million people. Diego and the girls are probably back in Austin, so you better go down there and get them to take you out for barbecue when you can, okay? Also, tell him to stop moping and go find love again. Cliché, I know, but he and the girls deserve more than a life full of moping even though the best *mamacita* in the world isn't on earth any more. Someone (almost) as fab can fill a pair of equally kick-ass shoes.

Muchas gracias for being with Gabe when I Ghost-of-Christmas-Past-ed him. He was always there for me as a kid, and it means so much that he had family with him in Scotland. Did it go well? If they have the best gay wedding in the world, please make a speech and tell everyone it was totally because of me. If I royally fucked up (and I don't believe this is a possibility because dead people are always perfect), pretend I had no idea Lachlan was going to show up. Freak occurrence.

I hope you don't hate me forever for the full-immersion experience. Tossing you into the *Outlander* deep end wasn't really the goal. Throwing you a life ring to get you out of Tinselhell was. You're worth so much more than you think you are, *guapita*. You have the biggest heart of anyone I have ever met. The kindest soul. You are made of generosity. Go home. Tell your family you love them. Then pursue *your real* dreams. You've helped enough people reach theirs. It's your turn, *mija*. Your moment to shine bright.

I can and will wait a loooong time for you to join me up here at the Guac and Talk Margarita Party in the sky because the good things in (after)life are totally worth waiting for. Now go on, *bonita*. Shake some boom-boom into your booty and get living for you!

Love you always, *muchos besos*, Vx

PS – Didn't you just LOVE Lawful Falafels! 1-800-FOR-EVER!!!!

◆ ◆ ◆

Willa didn't need to hear the pilot's announcement to know this particular group of travellers was headed to Pendleton, Oregon. Like the mismatched group of superfans finding 'their people' in Glasgow airport, there was a certain aesthetic attached to the Eastern Oregonian. A preponderance of Carhartt. Lots of clothing with Native-American-inspired patterns. Jeans with dirt ground into the fibres. Thrift-store chic.

It was one of the poorest states in the country, but somehow the graft that came with poverty was never what shone through to Willa whenever she returned home. The smiles were. The natural lean into kindness. The instinct to help a neighbour when turning a blind eye would be the easier option.

'Being nice is free,' her mother always used to say. 'Being mean comes with a price.'

Willa headed to baggage claim as that and countless more cross-stitch-worthy sayings crept out of her mental woodwork.

A smile makes a good impression, but a frown cuts deep.

If you're true to yourself, you'll always be honest with others.

She laughed when, as she heaved her enormous tote off the luggage carousel, a marine stepped in and popped it on to a wheelie cart for her.

'Thank you for your service.' She gave him a little salute.

The guy touched the rim of his hat. 'Thank you for the honour of serving.'

And that's what it boiled down to. Finding the role that suited you best. A position in life that felt like an honour.

'Willa?' Her mom jogged through the sliding doors of the arrivals hall. 'Sorry I'm late, honey. Things got a bit hairy at school with a couple of the kids.'

She looked so worried. So concerned that she'd let Willa down, but the truth was, no matter what, her mom had always been there.

She thought of Finn and how he and his mother had left so many things unsaid and how he was using actions – quitting his job, devoting himself to Balcraigie, making peace with his stepfamily – to try to compensate for a wound that would probably never fully heal.

'It's okay, Mom. You're here now.' She pulled her into a hug and by her mother's initial stiffness, knew she hadn't been expecting it. But when her mom's arms finally wrapped around her, squeezing her tight, she knew Dwayne 'The Rock' Johnson had been right. Ripping yourself open and making yourself vulnerable was the scariest form of bravery out there. But when that openness was returned, it only made you stronger.

She spent a week at home in the end. The longest she'd stayed in years without breaking out in hives. Knowing the years of separation meant they wouldn't become overnight BFFs, they began the healing process by handing out teeny tiny olive branches that grew in strength as the days sped by.

She volunteered down at the school to help her mom. Went skinny dipping in the river with some old debate club friends who now ran a local co-op. She ate at her favourite cafe where you could get the world's best blueberry pancakes from 6 a.m. then come back at night to eat peanuts and drink beer until two. She bought a canary yellow wheelbarrow from the hardware store when her dad complained there was nothing to put the leaves in. (It looked like Finn's favourite wheelbarrow and it was nice to think of him each time she charged it with a mountain of leaves.) She stepped up and into the all-county bowling tournament after her sister-in-law broke a finger playing ice hockey. She helped unload the moving van (1-800-WEMOVEU) that contained the startlingly meagre number of belongings a team of ex-convicts packed at her LA apartment. She and her brothers stacked them in a shed behind the auto shop with a proviso that they could donate everything to Goodwill if she wasn't back in a year.

She went to the drive-in. Ate way too much cheese. Bought a pair of second-hand shit-kickers that looked brand new after a two-hour polish (during which she watched *Outlander*).

When she grew misty-eyed over the Rainbow Cafe's tuna melt, she realised what she was really doing. She was saying goodbye. No. Not that. It was more . . . until we meet again. Taking a snapshot tour of a place she'd never believed she'd miss for more than a New York second. But this time she saw her family's community through a different lens. She would miss it. The people and places that were ingrained in her like her own family's DNA.

DNA she willed to be strong enough to get her on a plane and fly several thousand miles to tell a man she'd only just met that she loved him.

◆　◆　◆

Willa's nerves properly kicked in when the captain announced it was time to disembark from the plane.

After a very awkward out-loud conversation with herself about what The Rock would do, she forced herself to unbuckle her seat-belt and walk down the aisle towards the exit.

She'd decided not to tell Finn she was coming. He hadn't reached out to her. Nor had anyone from his family. Spying on their socials had seemed wrong, so for all she knew, he'd taken up with one of the scores of women who'd been batting their eyelashes at him at the ceilidh. Not that she could blame him. She had cut and run when things had got just a tiny bit tough. Not even that. Things had been golden. So good she couldn't get herself to believe any of it was meant to include her. Not exactly the trait a man yearns for in a life partner.

Well, if everything went to pot, there had been a 'Help Wanted' sign up at the Rainbow Cafe so she could always go back, rent a double wide, become a waitress and eat tuna melts until she exploded. Heartache came in many forms.

As she walked out of the plane, she was surprised to see that, instead of going down the usual tunnel-type affair international travellers navigated to get to customs, they were disembarking through a glassed-off area just on the other side of the waiting area where travellers were already gathering for the return flight to Portland.

There were enough men in Mighty Duck sweatshirts and women with salt-and-pepper-hair to indicate the plane was mostly full of Americans returning home.

There was also a guy in a flat cap. Little twist of straw blond hair sticking out in tufts. Shoulders that looked as if they'd have no problem having a girl like Willa flipped over one of them to keep her safe from a herd of black and white striped cows.

And then, as if he'd heard her thinking about him, Finn looked up and straight into her eyes.

Chapter Forty-One

Finn had never moved through a crowd of people so fast in his life.

'Willa!' he shouted through the glass.

'Finn!' she shouted back.

They laughed. Mouthed *what the* . . . at each other. Laughed again. Pressed their hands against the glass, playing a weird game of mime. Then, suddenly, Finn became painfully aware that Willa was heading one direction while he was holding a boarding pass to head to another.

She looked beautiful. She wasn't wearing Jacobean gear. Surprise, surprise. She had on a huge duffel coat with a fluffy lining round the hood that tickled the edges of her face. God he'd missed that face.

Desperation swept through him. 'I've got feelings!' he shouted through the glass. 'Lots of them!'

Well done, Shakespeare.

Willa beamed. Matching dimples appeared deep in her cheeks. He scrubbed his fingers against the glass, desperate to pull her close to him.

'That's great!' she shouted back. 'McFeelings are good.'

'That's the thing,' he yelled back. 'I don't think they're Scottish!'

She pulled a face. 'How do you know?'

'They feel foreign.' It was true. He'd thought he was fairly familiar with the full gamut of human emotions, but this moment – being so close to Willa and a thousand miles away – was confirmation that he didn't have a clue.

'Can you identify them?' she asked.

'I feel . . .' He bounced up and down on his heels to try to get the right word to come to him. '. . . joyful. Something well beyond a feeling of general happiness, you know?'

Poet laureate stuff here. A born Cyrano.

'And that's not Scottish?' She looked perplexed.

'No. We're a dour and bleak people. Just like the landscape.'

He vaguely heard a mutter of dissent from behind him but was too busy stumbling through the worst wooing scene of his life, so he ignored it.

'Finn.' Willa shook her head at him. 'It's ridiculously beautiful where you live.'

'Aye. It is that,' he said, but also no. It was having her there with him that made it beautiful. Without her, the sun didn't shine as bright. The moon looked sad. The stars barely managed to twinkle. It had begun raining the day she left and hadn't stopped since.

Conversation at a standstill, Willa stepped in closer to the glass as more passengers strode past, intent on getting through to customs and on with their lives.

They held their hands to the thick, bullet-proof glass and stared at one another, their expressions shifting from shocked to elated to disbelieving that they had found one another here of all places, in the land of in-between.

'Are you—' they both said at the same time.

'Why didn't you—' they began again.

'You go.' A third attempt also gone wrong-ended in a stalemate.

Finn ended it by pretending to zip his lips shut and pointing at her.

'I'm worried. With all of these foreign feelings crashing around inside of you – do you think we should call for help?'

He laughed and pointed at a nearby defibrillator. 'We can use that.'

She knocked on the glass, then said, 'I think this means they're going to have to use it.'

He turned around and saw a semi-circle of people had gathered behind him, openly listening to their conversation, which, to be fair, was being shouted at top volume.

They waved. His cheeks grew hot. This day was not going at all according to plan. And yet . . . what day ever really did?

Maybe this was what life with Willa was going to be like. Regularly finding himself on brand new emotional frontiers. Trying things he would've previously scoffed at. Scottish males weren't exactly equipped for public displays of emotion except at football matches and yet . . . here he was, baring his soul in public because when she had gone, he'd felt broken.

'You went away,' he said.

She nodded. 'I did.'

'I hated it.'

'You did?'

'Very, very much.'

She scrunched her fingers against the glass as if trying to weave hers between his. 'Say that again.'

He smiled and gave extra attention to the Rs as he repeated himself. 'I don't know what I did wrong, but I thought I was doing the right thing by giving you space instead of running you down and pinning you to Balcraigie like I wanted to. It wasnae my place to tell you where you belonged. But then, not having you here felt like dying inside so I thought I'd fly over and do some sort of grand-gesture thing in the vain hope that you'd decide our wee, poorly lit nook of Scotland was more alluring than the bright lights of Hollywood.'

'You didn't do anything wrong,' Willa said softly. 'I should've stayed. Listened. Told you how I really felt.'

The lead weight he'd been carrying round in his chest lifted, finally allowing a fraction of hope to pump through his veins.

'What were you going to do?' she asked. 'When you got to LA?'

'The grand gesture?'

'Yes. The grand gesture.'

'Ach, no. It was ridiculous.'

'Grand gestures are meant to be ridiculous.'

He looked over his shoulder. The crowd had grown. Should he just go for it?

'Go on then.' She glanced behind her. The flight crew were disembarking now. 'I've got to decide whether or not to go through immigration or figure out a way to smash through this glass wall.'

'But . . .' Finn threw another look back at his fellow passengers. 'I'd planned to do it in LA where that sort of thing is more normal.'

She feigned shock. 'Finlay Jamieson. Are you going to deny me my grand gesture just because it's in the wrong country?'

'No. But . . . give me a moment, alright?' He turned his back to her, gave the crowd behind him a quick nod, then pressed 'Play'.

Chapter Forty-Two

Willa had never wanted to climb up and over a glass wall more than she did at this moment. If there hadn't been actual airport police, she just might have.

Finn had pulled off a miracle.

The crowd she'd thought had just been curious fellow passengers had shape-shifted into a flash mob of kilted and tartan-clothed travellers doing the world's most awkward dad dance to 'I'm Gonna Be (500 Miles)'.

When she wasn't laughing she was crying, but mostly she was doing both right up until she began slapping her hands against the glass screaming, 'Let me in!' Finally, an airport official took pity on her and escorted her through the security barriers so that a sweaty, red-faced Finn could pick her up in his arms and kiss her.

Every particle in her body was vibrating with happiness. This was where she belonged. In his arms. Her lips pressed to his. Smelling his sweet hay and tangy pine scent. This wonderful, brave man loved her. Not sensible her. Or helpful her. Or the Willa who'd interviewed countless famous people. He loved this version. The messy, complicated, emotionally bruised woman who'd rocked up to his farm a handful of weeks ago intent on being miserable. Or, if not miserable, proactively belligerent.

She'd been completely wrong about him having a teensy tiny emotional toolbox. It was huge. But he'd only allowed himself access to the top tray, not realising you could open it up and that a thousand new layers of possibility were waiting for him to use.

The long car ride home wasn't silent for a moment. They talked about everything. Hopes, dreams, their families. Willa's family because, as Finn pointed out, she'd never spoken about them much. She was honest. Said she wasn't particularly close to them, but she could see things improving as time went by.

'What? Now that you're several thousand miles away?' He was smiling, but she could hear the concern in his voice. Family was important to him. And it was one of the reasons she loved him. It was important to her too, and seeing him break free of his own self-imposed family-history shackles had been an inspiration to her to do the same.

'There are planes that go to Oregon all the time,' she said. 'I have a hunch my parents will want to meet this stranger from a strange land who's captured their daughter's heart.'

'And your brothers? I won't have to fist fight them or anything, will I?'

She grinned and while shaking her head no said, 'Only a little.'

'Eh, well. That's fine, then.'

Later, when they pulled up to the farm, a brand new set of feelings surfaced.

Finn must've seen her mood shift because he turned to her and apologetically flicked his thumb towards the drizzle outside. 'I'm afraid the days of bagpipes and tatties in the courtyard are over for the season.'

It was freezing. And wet and muddy and cold, but because she was young and in love with someone who had stepped so far away from his comfort zone to win her heart, she didn't care. She pressed her hand against her chest as if taking a solemn pledge. 'I am prepared to alter my wardrobe to suit the task.'

Finn barked a laugh and pointed at the muddy barnyard. 'I wouldnae be getting anything beyond a set of waterproof breeks.'

'Breeks?'

'Like trouse, but less stylish.'

'Trouse?'

'And so it begins.' Finn put on a grave, sonorous voice. 'Two young lovers divided by the same language.'

'Ha ha,' she intoned through a stupidly happy grin. 'We could always give up talking and stay in bed until spring? Two birds, one stone?'

He pulled her in for a long, slow kiss. 'That would be absolutely brilliant if there weren't cows to feed and pigs to muck out and—'

'Farm Delights!'

'Aye. Farm Delights.'

He stroked the backs of his fingers against her cheek. 'You might hate it, you know. It's not an easy life.'

'And you think interviewing the likes of Kim Kardashian is?'

He gave a wry nod. 'Good point. I'll take a breech calf any day of the week.'

They stopped by the house where Orla and Dougie went through a hilarious panoply of facial expressions, plying the pair of them with food and drink until it became clear that they were itching to be alone. Orla nodded at the door. 'I guess you two'll be away to the shepherd's hut, then?'

Willa looked at Finn. 'Shepherd's hut?'

'It's where I stay when I'm here. Where we'll stay until—'

'Until?'

'Until we decide what we want to do next.'

What she wanted most was tear his clothes off and have deeply orgasmic sex. But the shepherd's hut was so completely gorgeous – beautifully carved wood, a sumptuously inviting bed, a tiny yesteryear kitchen, a wood stove crackling away in the corner, antler coat racks, a massive Highland cow rug – she gave it her full attention for about ninety seconds and then began to ravage her Scottish beau.

Later, warm and naked and feeling that delicious tingly half-awake half-asleep feeling, she ran her fingers along his chest and asked, 'How did you do that? Get all of those people to learn the dance?'

'Ah!' He tapped the side of his nose. 'I have been learning my way around this magical thing called social media. I put out a message saying I was going to be on the flight and what I had in mind for Los Angeles. I had people DM me. If they were into it, I sent them a video of me and Trevor doing the choreography.'

She propped herself up on her elbow and beamed at him. 'Finlay Jamieson, will wonders never cease?'

The corners of his mouth tweaked into that lovely, warm smile of his. 'I think you'll find this thirty-something dog is quite capable of learning some new tricks.'

She smiled, gave his cheek a kiss and then, serious, said, 'You're not the only one who'll have to learn new tricks. I dare say my pitchforking technique could do with a bit of improvement.'

'Don't you worry about that now, lass. There'll always be plenty of poop to scoop.'

She swept her hand across her forehead with a 'Phew.'

He pulled her in closer, nuzzling into the nook between her jaw and neck.

'I can help,' she said, wanting to make it clear she wasn't here to freeload. 'Do stuff.'

Finn pulled back, then scooched himself up higher on the bank of pillows. 'I know. But I don't just love you because you're useful.'

'But I have to be! What if you discover things about me you don't like?'

He snorted. 'Willa, will you stop with the dour Scots act? There is no couple on earth who adores every single thing about one another. Besides' – he traced his index finger along her shoulder and down her arm – 'if we were perfect, we'd never have make-up sex.'

'I don't know. You've not met me when I'm pre-menstrual.'

'Uh-oh!' He pulled a comedy terror face. 'Do you turn beastly?'

'Worse. Tearful. I will be unreasonable and emotional and demand to watch inspirational sports dramas, and by sports dramas I mean cheerleader films that all have the same plot but a different soundtrack. And then I'll want to practise cartwheels and handstands and eat my body weight in chocolate.'

He twisted his mouth to the side, taking the scenario she'd painted on board. 'Aye, well. When you put it that way, perhaps we are looking at a deal-breaker.'

She sat up. 'What? You'd dump me because—'

Finn was laughing. 'Noooo. After all, you're going to have to put up with me when I become groom-zilla.'

She did a double take. Was this . . . Was he proposing? I mean, she was down with it, but they had only known one another for two weeks.

She cocked a hand to her ear. 'Beg pardon?'

'You heard me,' Finn said. 'Jules read my tea leaves before she left and it looks like I'm going to make a very fretful future husband.'

'Finn.' She poked him in the chest with her finger. 'I think I might've missed something.'

'Eh?'

Oh, well now this was awkward. 'The proposal?'

'Oh!' He pretended to be shocked. 'So you want to be asked if you'd like to be my wedded bride, do you?'

'Uhhh . . . Scottish man? Haggis lover!'

'Just because you're Scottish doesn't automatically mean you love offal.' He was properly laughing now.

'You're being awful.' She was laughing too, but also a tiny bit panicked that she was completely misreading the situation.

She closed her eyes and pressed the heels of her hands to them, willing her brain to regroup and separate fact from the land of hopes and dreams.

When she opened them, Finn was flicking open a small box. She gasped as her eyes focused in on the ring. It was propped upon a whorl of evergreen velvet and was, quite simply, the most stunning piece of jewellery she'd ever seen. Tiny little trinity knots adorned the three bands of the ring that was inlaid with small but perfect emeralds.

When she failed to locate the power of speech to express just how bone-achingly happy she felt, Finn got panicky. 'They had all sorts. Ones with standing stones and ones with trees of life and solitaires and then there were all of the different colours of gold—'

She silenced him with a kiss. 'It's perfect,' she eventually whispered against his lips. 'But . . .'

'No buts . . .' he whispered back. 'You've already survived a fake marriage to me. And if it's easier to think of this as a promise ring, let's do that. If it works, we'll start finding out today. If it doesn't . . . at least we'll know we tried. That's better than wondering "what if", isn't it?'

She smiled and gave an invisible wink to The Rock, wherever he was.

Agreeing to marry at any point in a relationship was a risk. After one breathtaking night or fifteen years of gradually getting to know everything there was about one another. The former could last forever, the latter could end the next day. Things changed. *People* changed. But losing Valentina, Willa's BFF and family all rolled into one for eight precious years, had taught her one very important lesson: life was too short to waste time with guessing games. It hurt. And there would be tears. And some days she probably wouldn't like Finn very much, just as there would likely be days he wouldn't be her greatest fan. But there would also be days like this one where it didn't matter how awful the weather was because with him the world was made of sunshine.

Life had put her and Finn in one another's paths. She didn't know if she believed in destiny or fate or even the tarot card the Ancient Chinese Man had given her all those weeks ago back on Venice Beach. The star. A card indicating she was on the brink of leaving behind a dark, confusing time in her life and, if she was willing, about to step into a period of hope and faith. A moment in time when it would be truly possible to believe that dreams could really come true.

She laughed, looking out of the small window to the sky above where she knew Valentina was giving a triumphant fist pump. *Gracias, mija*, she silently thanked her friend. *For everything.*

'C'mon now, lassie!' Finn was pleading, hands in prayer position. 'Please tell me what is happening in your brain!'

She grinned a happy, toothy smile. 'Isn't it hilarious that I thought all of my dreams would come true in Hollywood and that pretty much the opposite was true?'

'Is this your version of a *yes, please, Finlay, even though you're not a movie star and smell like the back end of a goat, I'd like to marry you and love you until the end of time?*'

'Goat?' she protested. 'Cow, more like.'

They laughed and when their smiles grew soft and dreamy, she said, 'Will you take a plain old *yes, please?*'

Finn looked her straight in the eye and in a tone one might think was more fitting for a rebuke he said, 'There's nothing plain about you, Willaford Jenkins. Not a single, solitary thing. I love you and if you'll let me, I will do my very best to spend the rest of my life showing you just how special I think you are.'

At last, she let what was happening sink in. This man, this beautiful kind man, who had unzipped something in her that felt wild and courageous and still a bit unfamiliar to her, was hers to explore life with. Her partner. Her future.

She finally allowed herself to reach out and touch the ring. It was beautiful. He explained how the delicate knots symbolised interconnection with a loved one as well as the seamless flow from one life event to another. She'd never seen life like that until now. How everything you experienced mattered. The ups, the downs, the tartan. And she couldn't wait to see what happened next.

Finn slid the ring on to her finger, then lowered his mouth to the back of her hand to give it a soft kiss.

When he looked up at her she told him she loved him. His blue eyes lit up as if she'd ignited actual flames in them. Or perhaps it was a reflection of what she felt burning bright in her heart. A hunger for the future they would share. And a heartfelt desire to begin it now.

'Can we just circle back to something you said earlier?' she asked.

'Aye.'

'Next time we go out there,' she flicked her thumb towards the stables, 'there won't be bagpipes?'

He shook his head. 'I'm afraid from here on out there won't be bagpipes until you're walking down the aisle to me. Or corsets. Or haylofts or pinafores made out of tattie sacks, for that matter.'

'What will there be?'

'Whatever we want, lass. The future is ours for the making.'

Chapter Forty-Three

Two Years Later

'Lights . . .'

Willa's eyelashes fluttered against Finn's hand as he removed it.

'Camera . . .'

He put his hands on her shoulders and slowly spun her round so that she was facing the stairwell she had been forbidden from climbing for the past year.

'And action.'

The dozen or so guests who had gathered at the bottom of the swirling spiral stairwell whooped as Finn scooped Willa up, tipped her over his shoulder as he climbed, one hand tucked under her bum, the other holding on to the guide rope that led up to the top.

'I cannae see!' he shouted. 'The woman's got on one too many petticoats!'

'Not for long if you're gonna prove yourself a worthy husband!' came a voice from below them.

'Trevor?' Willa asked her new spouse's back.

'Trevor,' came Finn's dry response.

In an impressive move straight out of 1-800-ROMANCE, Finn shifted her round in his arms and carried her over the threshold into the room they would occupy as the official caretakers of Balcraigie Castle.

'That was McSexy.' She popped a kiss on to his cheek.

'You've not seen anything yet, McWifey. Hold thy horses . . .' He set her down so that her back was to him, then slipped his arms around her waist. 'Behold . . . the Laird and Lady's Suite.'

She'd not been permitted even a tiny glimpse of this upstairs suite – the only room with a proper roof on it – while they'd been renovating. A restriction that had nearly driven her wild with anticipation. But now that she was here in the arms of her shiny new husband, she realised it hadn't been the room she'd been waiting for at all. It had always and only ever been him.

'C'mon,' he encouraged when she kept looking up and over her shoulder to moon at him. 'Say something appreciative.'

'You look McFabulous.' He did as well. He was knee-weakeningly perfect in his formal kilt. He'd chosen the muted purple, green and red Mackintosh tartan, his mother's. And a kilt pin from his father's clan that included three tiny little sailing ships that felt like a nod to his overseas wife. He also wore a thistle buttonhole with a twist of ribbon in Duncan's family tartan. 'Mmmm.' She nuzzled into him. 'You're McEdible. McYummy.'

'Not about me, woman. The room!'

'How can I appreciate a room when my husband is—'

He cupped her head between his hands and turned it so that she was forced to look at it.

Ohhhhh. She could appreciate a room. She could appreciate a room a lot.

The castle was still a massive work in progress. Though it felt like they'd achieved some heroic milestones two years ago during that first immersive Jacobean experience, all of their work had proved to be the first of countless steps yet to come.

Today, there were a handful rooms that were mostly finished – the kitchen, elements of the great hall and a wee snug where guests could gather for private whisky tastings. But it turned out the price of a potato harvester was just a drop in the bucket compared to what it took to renovate a building that had stood open to the elements for over a hundred years.

Castles were expensive. Luckily, they'd learnt early on that the finished product wasn't so much the goal as the experiences they shared with the specialist craftspeople, as well as the scores of volunteers who'd joined them for the various immersive experiences Orla was now running as a proper business.

Here, in the only room that would be just for them, the ceilings were high, as was frequently the case in Scotland. They'd kept the far walls clean of paint, preferring instead to enjoy the gorgeous grey solid stone that was used throughout the castle. Behind the indulgently large four-poster bed, a sprawl of wallpaper covered with purple, white and green speckles made it look as if the bedroom was in the centre of a field full of heather in bloom. There was a fireplace big enough to stand in. A cosy little bed for their new puppy, Skye. A claw-footed tub that looked so inviting that if there hadn't been a hundred plus guests outside – including her entire family who'd flown over a week earlier for their own immersive holiday – she would've suggested a bubble bath. Immediately.

But they were all here. Everyone who'd played a role in bringing the two of them together. Everyone except her bestie. Willa had decided Val was best symbolised by the Star tarot card and, as such, was tucked in the clutch bag Jennifer had embroidered for her. The bag was a deep midnight blue silk covered in brilliant gold-thread bees and the card was a reminder that change was a choice.

A peek out of the window showed that everyone was beginning to file into the great hall, where Orla and Jules had prepared the wedding breakfast: vegetarian haggis rolls, deep-fried haggis bon bons, wild Scottish salmon smoked right here on the shores of Balcraigie and countless more platters celebrating local cuisine. Rosa and Jeff had flown in on the proviso that Willa and Finn wouldn't mind if, after the wedding ceremony, they renewed their vows again. Willa was convinced they were handfasting addicts.

Diego and the girls were here, as were Lachlan and Gabe. The two of them had been living between Palm Springs and Scotland and were shortly off to a Highlands photo shoot for Lachlan's new *Rogue Yoga* book, the eagerly anticipated follow-up to *Desert Yoga*. ChiChi and Alastair were fresh back from a holiday in Nigeria. Fenella and Trevor could be heard bickering about whether or not a kilt was meant to fasten on the left or the right if you were a woman. Fenella's husband, the 'Aussie plonker' turned out to be a shy and utterly love-struck accountant.

'It's incredible,' she finally said, breaking through Finn's stream of increasingly worried commentary about how actually, really, if she looked very closely there wasn't a solitary element of the room that was finished yet.

'It's a work in progress,' she said. 'Just like us.'

'Is that how you see us?' He feigned offence. 'I was under the impression we were absolutely perfect.'

'No!' she protested. 'Well . . . yes, but . . .'

'Willa?' Finn put on his stern face. 'Now is not the time to inform me that you'd have been better off opening a tuna melt cafe in Pendleton.'

She sniggered. 'A town that size couldn't handle two tuna melt joints.'

Finn pulled her close to him. 'So what are we then, if we're not perfect?'

'In love,' she finally settled on.

'Is that it?' he asked.

She pulled back, aghast. 'Isn't that everything?'

'Aye.' He nodded, a quiet smile playing on his lips. 'It is, darlin'. Now that I know what it actually feels like, it most certainly is.' He tipped his head to her uplifted one and gave her a soft kiss. As if on cue, the warm, predatory notes of a bagpipe about to launch into song sang out. 'Right, then, missus. What do you say we go on out there and show them how a ceilidh's really supposed to be?'

She put her hand in his and, running down the stairs to begin the rest of their lives with the people they held most dear, they did just that.

Later, when the high of being a newlywed kept her up long after the guests had gone to bed and Finn had fallen asleep with a soft dopey smile on his face, Willa snuck back down to the great hall – a room that had, in its several hundred years of existence seen countless formative events like today's wedding. She went over to the fire, took a stick out of the massive wicker basket and stuck a marshmallow on it, because that's what newlyweds who lived in partially finished castles in Scotland did after their wedding. She toasted it, burnt the roof of her mouth on its brown-sugar exterior, then popped the stick into the embers, a sacrifice to the gods of fluffy, nice things. Much like the kitchen fireplace, the great hall's massive stone fireplace was huge. Large enough to fit a family of five in. She knew because she'd forced Orla and her growing brood to be photographed in there countless times since she'd returned. Along the internal stone walls they'd hung mementos from the past they'd unearthed as the renovations trundled ever onwards. A belt buckle. A spur. A sgian-dubh bearing the interlocked Luckenbooth hearts and crown, symbolising affection, loyalty and love.

She hovered her hand above the engraved words and symbols carved into the stone by one of the guests who'd come along to a specialised stonemasonry week. As ever, she grew glassy-eyed as her fingers worked their way along the letters.

TUI NUMQUAM OBLIVISCAR, VALENTINA

She didn't even bother to swallow back the tears. Today had been utterly perfect. All the people they loved had been here to support them as they publicly declared their love for one another. They'd even shouted their *I Do*s up to the heavens expressly for Valentina to hear, but now, here, alone in this quiet space, she could admit it wasn't enough. It would never be enough. She would always be missed and, as such, Finn had long ago suggested they find a way for her to be with them. So here she was, engraved into their hearth. Their home. The place where she had led Willa when she was most lost in the world. Her very best friend. The person who'd taught her that the impossible was, in fact, entirely possible if only you held out your hand to the terror of loss and let it guide you out of the darkness and into the light.

THE McENDING

ORLA'S READY BY TEATIME MILLIONAIRE'S SHORTBREAD

The Shortbread

Ingredients

250g mix of crushed shortbread and ginger biscuits (you could try Graham Crackers and Nilla Wafers if you're American and can't get hold of the former. Use GF if needed.)

55g melted butter

Method

Smash everything together (or whizz, if you prefer) until a fine-ish crumb. Mix with melted butter and press into a buttered or parchment paper lined 8″ x 8″ or 9″ x 9″ pan. Chill for 20 minutes.

NB: If you're out of biscuits or don't feel like smashing someone else's into bits or crushing them in a food processor – so cathartic! – you can easily make your own shortbread. It's all-purpose flour (240g), caster sugar (120g), butter (230g) and a pinch of salt all whizzed together until crumbly. Press into a buttered or parchment-paper-lined 8″ x 8″ or 9″ x 9″ pan, bake at 350F/170C for 30–35 minutes until golden. Cool completely.

The Caramel

Ingredients

150g butter

150 g soft dark brown sugar (but whatever you have that is darker than white will work if you are out of dark)

1 x 400g tin of condensed milk (the big one, not the half-sized one – don't open another can if yours is 395-397g)

Method

Heat butter and sugar in a non-stick pan on low-ish heat until melted. Add condensed milk and, if you're feeling a bit sassy, a good pinch of ground ginger. Turn up heat and stir continuously as you bring to a rapid boil. Cook until sauce has thickened – should be about a minute or two. Remove from heat and pour the beautiful caramel over your baked biscuit base. Cool, then pop in the refrigerator until set.

The Chocolate Topping

Ingredients

200g dark chocolate (or whatever favourite flavour chocolate you like, or the melted-down remains of your Easter chocolate if that's all your cupboards have to spare)

Method

Melt chocolate, pour over caramel. Chill until set.

To divide into slices, if you are going to share, dip knife in hot water, dry on towel, slice.

ENJOY!

AUTHOR'S NOTE AND ACKNOWLEDGEMENTS

This is probably the most autobiographical – without being at all autobiographical – book I have ever written. I was an entertainment news producer in Los Angeles and absolutely loved it. Film and television have always been magical worlds to me and getting to interview the people who created the shows and movies I adored was a dream come true. Until it wasn't. And please believe me when I say this is not a slight to my job. I simply found myself wanting to do the things I was observing as much as I enjoyed watching them. This peaked when I was filming a series on trainee RSPCA inspectors in the UK. Whatever they learnt, I learnt too. And I itched to do more. At the same time I met and fell in love with a Scotsman who was looking for a 'wee place' out in the country. Instead, we found a small, neglected farm that landed me at the bottom of a very steep learning curve. I can now proudly announce I have had my arm inside the back end of a cow and, after some hair-raising moments rearranging his limbs, produced a live calf. We've also had pigs and bees and chickens and, for a fleeting period, an injured crow (he flew away all healed). When my former employers heard about my new line of work, they said I should write my autobiography. Instead, I came up with this. The research was great fun. I got to read and watch the *Outlander* series (it was six TV series and a gazillion books deep by the time I got to it). Thanks to my amazing friend and *Outlander* superfan Karin Bain, who gave me the heads up on a last-minute book signing in London where I nearly died of delight when Diana Gabaldon not only signed my book, but liked my dinosaur pinafore dress (she is a dinosaur fan), and then, later, featured me in her monthly newsletter (I am the grinning idiot in the dinosaur pinafore). The fans were pure joy. They are a passionate group of readers and fans of the series. One even showed up in a redcoat outfit (a tri-cornered hat tip to you, m'lady). As part of my research, I also went on a two-day Jacobean history tour with the incredible Diane and Andrew Nicholson who offer *Outlander: The Past Lives Experience* tour. We went to castles and Culloden and touched standing stones and ate cream tea at Culloden House. Their passion for Scottish history and Scotland is top notch. It was an extraordinary experience. Who knew I could wander round the Highlands with a couple dressed in Jacobite clothing and think absolutely nothing of it.

Despite having been to Scotland many times to pick raspberries for some epically delicious jam, I have yet to participate in a huge potato harvest. Most are (if not all) mechanised nowadays. But into the 1980s, Scottish tatties were harvested by hand, by school children. To any farmers who read this and despair at my limited grasp of harvesting, please forgive me. The mistakes are, obviously, my own. I didnae ken!

There are no direct flights from Portland to Glasgow. That is pure fiction (a girl can dream!).

And now to the thanks. First to my editor, *muchas gracias* to Victoria Pepe for loving this book when it was just a twinkly elevator pitch in my eye. Gratitude as well for championing it (and me) when the odd attack of writer's doubt crept in. You are a joy to work with. My heartfelt thanks to Salma Begum. You're an aurora borealis of editorial guidance and this book wouldn't be what it is today without you. Thanks as well to the entire editorial team at Lake Union Publishing. Melissa Hyder, Swati Gamble, Victoria Oundjian, Nicole Wagner et al, you are a wonderous lot with magnifying glass skills at spotting errors I completely missed. I am your humble servant. Thanks as well to Nicole Wager and the PR and marketing folk who are an amazing bunch.

To Cressy McLaughlin, whose emails full of cheerleading and encouragement were the wind beneath my wings during some choppy weather. To Michelle Kem, for reading a very rough and ready draft. It was akin to offering you a barn dance but handing you a pitchfork and saying, 'You don't mind a wee bit of tidying beforehand, do you?' To Annie, Chantal, Michelle and Pam, for reading and reminding me which Scottish and British lingo translates on the far side of the pond. To my wonderful sister-in-law Kymberley, for her ideas and brainstorming powers. Particularly the kilt-wearing housekeepers. They didn't make this cut, but can I just say . . . Adelaide, you must be one magical city. To Debbie Macomber, whose support is an undimmable 100-watt bulb. A big bouncy castle's worth of thanks to Al, Ruth, Janet, Kate, Jeev and Immi. You are powerhouses of encouragement and support. To my sister, Michelle, whose encouraging emails regularly remind me that super brainy scientists need escapism as much as anyone else. To all of the fans whose passion made this idea possible. I've met some of you in real life and have zero doubt you would answer a cry for help from a Scotsman in need.

Heart-pumping thanks to my own Scotlander, the initial inspiration for it all. You may not have come from farming stock, but you didn't let that stand in the way of believing we could do it. You are McSexy in (and out) of a kilt and recalling that first time you said, 'Och, away, don't be daft, woman,' still gives me butterflies. When you said six-thirrrrrrrrty about five seconds later I knew I was done for. (The fact that you're kind, honourable and drive a tractor like a primo ballerino also helps). Thank you for taking my hand and leading me into a whole new world. Thanks to our Belted Galloway cows and to the hounds, Skye and Harris, who accompanied me on every single plot walk. You are all McMarvellous and I love you. But most of all, thank you to Scotland, the foundation of so much inspiration, beauty and splendour. You are an incredible land and, in the words of Dolly Parton, I will always love you.

ABOUT THE AUTHOR

Sheila McClure lives in the English countryside with her Scottish husband, their dogs, Harris and Skye, and a small herd of delightfully striped Belted Galloway cattle. Prior to rural life in the UK, she was a camerawoman and news producer for Associated Press Television. As she's originally from Seattle, she began her working life as a barista. She has also written books as Annie O'Neil and Daisy Tate. She will never refuse a quality dill pickle.

Follow the Author on Amazon

If you enjoyed this book, follow Sheila McClure on Amazon to be notified when the author releases a new book!
To do this, please follow these instructions:

Desktop:

1) Search for the author's name on Amazon or in the Amazon App.
2) Click on the author's name to arrive on their Amazon page.
3) Click the 'Follow' button.

Mobile and Tablet:

1) Search for the author's name on Amazon or in the Amazon App.
2) Click on one of the author's books.
3) Click on the author's name to arrive on their Amazon page.
4) Click the 'Follow' button.

Kindle eReader and Kindle App:

If you enjoyed this book on a Kindle eReader or in the Kindle App, you will find the author 'Follow' button after the last page.